"JAMES BOND, EAT YOUR HEART OUT. . .

a partial list of the UKDs (Unusual Killing Devices): a flashlight, a shoe, a chess piece, a dinner plate, a soft-boiled egg, and a prostitute's breast . . . Mancuso and Borgneff . . . entertain, page after page . . . an action-packed adventure."

Best Sellers

THE SLEEPING SPY

"FAST-PACED EXCITEMENT ALL THE WAY."
Cosmopolitan

"GOOD OLD-FASHIONED FUN."
St. Louis Post-Dispatch

HERBERT BURKHOLZ AND CLIFFORD IRVING "can turn out some of the finest hi-tech espionage suspense since James Bond tried to keep the world safe for democracy . . . a pair of engaging rogues and a novel with considerable excitement, delightfully sudden twists of plot and an assortment of bad guys that would bring a sly smile to James Bond's late creator."

Pittsburgh Press

Also by Herbert Burkholz and Clifford Irving
Published by Ballantine Books:

THE DEATH FREAK

THE SLEEPING SPY

**Herbert Burkholz
and
Clifford Irving**

BALLANTINE BOOKS • NEW YORK

Library of Congress Catalog Card Number: 81-69140

ISBN 0-345-31465-4

This edition published by arrangement with Atheneum

Printed in Canada

First Ballantine Books Edition: July 1984

For BERNIE *and* ADELE FELDMAN
  who have raised patience from a virtue to a fine art

And—with gratitude and affection—to CLEO CROUCH

Contents

I

Operation Gunfire

Chapter 1 _____

O n those spring mornings in the last days of the war the fog came early to the valley of the Elbe, settling down in darkness before sunrise, blanketing the torn and rutted fields, and masking the armies encamped on either side of the river. Those armies, the U.S. First on the western shore and the First Ukrainian on the eastern, were at rest. The meeting of these American and Russian forces had effectively cut Germany in two. The war would go on for a few days more. Hitler would die in his bunker in Berlin, overtures for peace would be made and accepted, but the soldiers encamped on the banks of the Elbe knew that for practical purposes the war was won, and on both sides of the river the Russians and the Americans rested gratefully.

Late that night, on the eastern side of the river, four officers of the Russian secret service, the NKVD, sat in an abandoned barn around a rough-hewn wooden table poring over a litter of photographs and handwritten notes. Three men and a woman, they worked with controlled haste, examining the photos carefully and stacking them in piles. They worked by the light of two kerosene lamps, which gave off a glow that barely reached the nearest wall of the barn. Just within the reach of that glow another officer, a young lieutenant, lazed against a pile of straw reading a book, removed from the activity at the table.

The only other person in the barn was Major Konstantin Grigorian, commanding officer of the Third Battalion, 173rd Regiment of Guards, who had been ordered to cooperate with the NKVD in these, the closing phases of *Operation Gunfire*. Gri-

gorian had been a soldier in the Red Army all of his adult life
and so was no stranger to those moments when the political
needs of the Communist Party took precedence over the orderli-
ness of military procedure, but never before in his career had he
been called upon, in the name of political necessity, to execute
the type of orders he now held in his hand. Those orders, in effect, instructed him to place himself and his entire unit under
the temporary command of Captain Andrei Petrovich of the
NKVD, the Ministry of State Security.

Grigorian shifted uncomfortably in his seat. The barn was
cold and damp, and it stank of horses and piss-soaked straw.
His eyes flicked down to the orders in his hand, then back to
the four people working at the table. The orders identified
them all as officers of the NKVD, with Petrovich in charge, a
tall, broad, and ham-fisted man with an air of heavy authority.
Across the table sat Boris Radichek, also a captain, but apparently cast from a finer mold than his leader, with a slim, oval
face and inquiring eyes. Next to Radichek sat the woman. Her
papers identified her as Lieutenant Anya Ignatiev, and Grigorian studied her covertly. Women in the Red Army were no
novelty, but rarely was one seen this close to the front. Of
course, she wasn't really army, and he decided that this
NKVD baby would be able to take care of herself no matter
where she landed, notwithstanding a lush body that bordered
on the opulent, and lazy violet eyes. He shifted his gaze away
from those eyes to inspect the man sitting next to her. Pavel
Kolodny, lieutenant. Yes, he knew the type well. Pale, intense, and with the determined lines of a fanatic stamped
about his lips and eyes. From Grigorian's knowledge of
NKVD operations this Kolodny would be the one to do the
dirty work whenever it was required. And enjoy doing it, too.

These four officers working at the table fell into a pattern that
Grigorian could understand; they were all familiar types to
him, but the young lieutenant lounging against the straw baffled
him completely. He had about himself an air of elitism that the
major had seen before only in fighter pilots, ski troops, and
commandos, a mannered superiority that was the mark of a specialist. Grigorian had to wonder what that specialty might be,

and he decided that, whatever it was, it had to be something very special indeed judging by the way the young man held himself aloof, separating himself from his superiors like a treasured pet, a well-trained greyhound about to be put into play. A very young greyhound, the major noted. Eighteen years old, nineteen at the most, but that prideful bearing and the steady, knowing eyes belied the years.

The activities of the officers at the table fascinated Grigorian, even though he had no conception of the nature of their work. He watched carefully as Andrei Petrovich gathered together the photographs before him and arranged them in neat piles. All the photos were of American soldiers in units camped directly across the river, all of them taken within the past few days by cameramen and correspondents from *Pravda, izvestia,* and *Trud.* The journalists circulated freely within the American lines, trading vodka for whiskey and caviar for K-rations as they interviewed the young GIs and snapped their pictures in an aura of Allied fraternity. Now Petrovich collated those same glossy prints, referring from time to time to the handwritten notes on the table and marking the backs of the photos with quick jottings. The others at the table did the same, working at an even, rapid pace.

They had been working that way for over an hour when Petrovich raised his massive head and said, "Time is short. I want your final lists in the next few minutes."

The elegant Radichek gracefully smothered a yawn and said, "Mine is ready now." The other two only nodded and kept on working. Minutes later the woman handed in her paper, much like a student completing an examination, and shortly after that Kolodny did the same. Petrovich scanned the lists, compared them with his own, and then set to work to make a composite of them all. When he was finished he showed the others the result.

Pvt. Paul R. Benski (1/plt) ....New York, N.Y.
Pfc. Alan P. Cohen (3/plt) ....Jacksonville, Fla.
Pvt. Jose N. Salazar (1/plt) ....San Juan, Puerto Rico
Pvt. James W. Emerson (2/plt) ......Point Balboa, Calif.

Pvt. Lionel A. Gooding (1/plt) ....Chicago, Ill.
Pfc. William X. Cooney (3/plt ....Boston, Mass.

"Photographs, please," said Petrovich. Radichek handed him six pictures keyed to the names on the list. The captain laid them out on the table.

"Very well," he said, "we now commence phase two of *Operation Gunfire*. As you all know, the *Gunfire* plan calls for a candidate who is eighteen or nineteen years old, is of average build, and has no distinguishing scars or marks. Most important, he must have no close living relatives." Petrovich sat back and waggled a finger at the list. "The last point is imperative to *Operation Gunfire*. The candidate must be not only an orphan in the technical sense, he must also be truly alone in the world. According to the information gathered by our newspaper people, these six Americans qualify on all counts. I now invite comment on the candidates."

Radichek said quietly, "You can eliminate Salazar at once. His native language would be Spanish."

Petrovich nodded and drew a line through the name.

Anya Ignatiev lit a cigarette and screwed up her eyes against the rising smoke. "There are geographical factors," she said. "The *Gunfire* plan reasons that residents of large cities in the United States are more easily identifiable than others since the urban centers tend to keep more extensive and accurate records than do other parts of the country. On that basis, Benski, Gooding, and Cooney should be eliminated."

"Accepted," said Petrovich. "That leaves Emerson and Cohen. Comments?"

"Eliminate Cohen," Kolodny said promptly. "We don't need a *zhid* in this operation."

"The American won't exactly be involved in the operation," Radichek pointed out.

Kolodny shrugged. "Still, a Jew . . . it's bad luck, you know?"

"There is also the matter of circumcision," murmured Anya Ignatiev.

Kolodny grinned. "Trust you to think of that."

"Enough," said Petrovich impatiently. "Emerson is the one." He checked his wrist for the time. "Let me point out that he belongs to the second platoon of Baker Company, which is due to patrol this side of the river at dawn. That gives us less than five hours, so let's move along. Yuri, get up here."

Again Major Grigorian was intrigued by the way that the young lieutenant, Yuri Volanov, rose lazily from the straw, stretched, and then ambled over to the table. He picked up the photograph that Petrovich thrust at him and studied it carefully. Finished, he casually flicked it back across the table.

"Not much of a resemblance," he said, "but close enough."

Petrovich nodded. "He doesn't have to be your twin, you know." He consulted his notes again. "This Emerson comes from someplace in California. Will that present a problem to you?"

Volanov shook his head. "None at all. As the Comrade Captain knows, I am adept in all accents of American English. There is no geographical location that would trouble me. I am familiar with every state in the Union."

Petrovich regarded the young man with admiration. Volanov's self-confidence was inspiring, considering that this was his first trip beyond the borders of the Soviet Union. But it was understandable, for he was a graduate of Gaczyna, the massive NKVD training school southeast of Kuibyshev.

From the day that Yuri Volanov had entered the gates of Gaczyna at the age of fifteen he had been totally immersed in the American way of life. During the ensuing years he lived in exact duplications of American cities and towns, speaking English only with native-born Americans hired for the job. He drank milk shakes and ate hamburgers at drugstore counters. He drove a 1937 Ford to school every day, and if he exceeded the speed limit he was bawled out by an American-style traffic cop. He listened to American music, saw American films, and paid for his purchases in dollars. He learned to root for the Brooklyn Dodgers in the summer and Notre Dame in the fall. He also learned to change his shirt and socks daily, to wear sunglasses in July, to stand with his hands in his pockets, and to chew gum naturally. He studied American history, geography, and literature, and took intensive courses in the various regional accents of the country. After three years at Gaczyna Yuri Volanov knew more about America than did most Americans. All this, and a dedicated Communist, ideologically pure. Petrovich regarded him with justifiable pride, then turned back to the business at hand.

"Major Grigorian," he said and motioned for that officer to come forward.

Grigorian stepped off three paces and stood at rigid attention. Although Petrovich wore only a captain's insignia, as NKVD he outranked Red Army officers up to the rank of colonel.

"Report readiness," said Petrovich.

Grigorian said in a monotone, "Third Battalion reports two companies told off for special assignment and armed with captured German equipment, mostly Schmeisser submachine guns."

"*Nu kharasho* . . . very good." Petrovich handed him the photograph. "This is the subject in question. Repeat your orders."

Grigorian glanced briefly at the picture, then returned his eyes frontward. "My troops are presently deployed in concealment at the point in the river where the American patrols have permission to land. Once the Americans are safely ashore they will be surrounded and immobilized. I anticipate no difficulty with this phase of the operation. The Amis will protest, but they will not fire on soldiers of the Red Army. I will then separate the subject, this James Emerson, from the others and bring him here for interrogation."

"And then?" Petrovich asked, waiting.

Grigorian hesitated, then said stiffly, "The other Americans will be shot and killed. Two of the Schmeissers and various other pieces of German equipment will be left at the scene to indicate that the work was done by Nazi guerrillas."

Petrovich drummed on the table with his fingers. "No slipups, Grigorian, no mistakes, and no excuses. If you leave even one of those Yanks other than James Emerson alive on that shore, I will personally put a bullet between your eyes."

Grigorian saluted, turned correctly, and stomped out, his footsteps echoing in the empty barn. Petrovich leaned back in his chair and looked around at the others. "So, it commences," he said. "For better or worse, we are committed. Anya, do you think you could make us some tea?"

In the absolute darkness just before dawn, Anya Ignatiev and Yuri Volanov strolled aimlessly around the yard in back of the abandoned barn, his arm around her waist, her head against his shoulder. They both breathed deeply as they walked, relishing the fresh air. Damp and heavy with mist, it was still a refreshing change from the close, horse-laden atmosphere of the barn. They walked silently, clinging to each other. They had been lovers for a month, ever since Yuri had joined the unit, and they both were aware, without dramatics, that after this night they would never be lovers again.

"Excited?" she asked.

"What a question." His hand slipped from her waist to her buttock and stroked it softly. "You know how you always excite me. All I have to do is touch you."

Anya laughed softly. Her hand reached for his, held it, but did not move it away. "Idiot," she murmured. "That's not what I meant. I was talking about *Gunfire.*"

"There is nothing to be excited about," he said sternly. "After all, this is what I've been trained for."

Anya smiled at the gruffness in his voice, her smile hidden by the darkness. There were times when she forgot how very young he was, only eighteen, and how very much he needed to appear both manly and mature. At twenty-four she felt centuries older than this brilliant and earnest boy, more like an older sister than a lover. She knew what was waiting for him in the next several hours, and in that moment she wanted nothing more than to hold his head to her breast and comfort him. Unable to do that, she did the next best thing, turning to him, pressing herself close, and kissing him warmly and firmly.

"There," she said. "That's what *I've* been trained for."

He responded to her kiss, then drew away slightly. "Do you really mean that?"

"Mean what?"

"What you just said." His voice was low and tight. "Were you really trained to make love to me?"

She was silent for a moment, debating whether to be angry or to laugh. In truth, she was not sure about the answer to his question. She knew how good she was as an intelligence officer, knew that she performed a valuable function within the unit, but she had often wondered if she would have received the assignment if she had not been a young and attractive woman. No one had ever ordered her to make love to Yuri Volanov, no one had ever had to, but everyone had made it quite clear that nothing was too good for the main character in *Operation Gunfire*.

She sighed and said, "I was just thinking how I forget sometimes how young you are. Only a very young and very foolish boy would say something like that. When you grow older you'll know that a woman is always in training for love."

It was Yuri's turn to be silent. Finally, he said, "I'm sorry. You're quite right. It was a foolish thing to say."

"Yes."

"I misunderstood what you meant."

"Yes."

"It's the night," he said, excusing himself. "It's a long night, and when the dawn comes . . . everything changes. Not that I'm nervous, or excited, as you said. It's just that there is so much to do, so much to remember."

"You will do what you have to do, and you will do it well," she assured him. "Everyone knows it. You're the best we have."

"Yes." He said it without pride, simply stating a fact. "I should be. I've been training for years. Sometimes it feels as if I've been training all my life."

"Then you know how I feel. About training."

"Yes." He looked to the sky. There was still no light in the east. "Do you think we have time?"

She smiled. "For training?"

"For practicing what you've been trained for."

As an answer she took his hand and led him across the yard to the back of the barn and in through a door that hung loose on its hinges. They worked their way silently in the darkness, avoiding a rusty plow, the vicious edges of a spreader, and a pile of ancient harness. From the front of the barn came the murmur of voices and the faint glow of the kerosene lamps. They slipped into an abandoned stall that was half-filled with hay, and once inside they fell upon each other eagerly. They made love to each other fully clothed, unable to wait, driving intensely; and when they were finished Anya had her wish, holding his head against her breast, soothing and easing with soft words. They stayed that way for quite some time, half asleep and half awake, listening for the sounds in the night that would signal the dawn. The sounds came at last in a far-off rumble and the coughing bark of Schmeissers from down near the river. Yuri stirred and moved away from her.

"That's it," he said.

"Come back." Anya reached for him. "Rest with me. We have time until they bring him here."

There was silence in the barn. There was the hissing of the lamps, the burble of the samovar, and the crackle of straw underfoot, but still there was silence. Andrei Petrovich sat at the long trestle table. Opposite him sat a young American soldier slouched in his seat. His chin was on his chest, his eyes were vacant, and his arms dangled loosely. The other four NKVD officers stood with Major Grigorian in the shadows, waiting. Petrovich broke the silence, drinking tea from a glass, sucking it up noisily.

"Emerson," he said. He reached across the table and touched the boy's shoulder. There was no reaction. The young face stayed pale and vacant. "Emerson?"

"It will take time," said Grigorian, stepping out of the shadows and speaking in Russian. "He's upset, of course, at being separated from his unit. He doesn't understand. He heard some shots, quite a few shots, and he's worried that something may have happened to his friends. His *buddies*, as he put it. We've tried to reassure him, but . . ."

Petrovich slammed the thick glass tumbler on the table. "All right, Comrade Major, your job here is done. You will report at

once to Division. State only that you have discovered the remains of nineteen American soldiers, apparently ambushed by
the Fascists. They will instruct you to collect the bodies for
shipment to the Americans across the river. You will do so.
That's all for the moment. I will have further orders for you
later.''

When Grigorian had left, Petrovich turned again to the
American soldier. The boy looked incredibly young, his imma-
ture face covered with light fuzz and blemishes. His cheeks
were desperately drawn and pale, sucked in like saucers. Without warning, he began to cry. The tears ran silently out of his
eyes and streamed over his cheeks and chin. Petrovich grimaced, but he made an encouraging noise and pushed a glass of
tea and a pack of *papirosi* cigarettes across the table.

"Easy, boy, drink the tea," he said. "It will help. Drink the
tea and smoke a cigarette, and then we will talk."

Emerson stared blankly ahead. It was as if he had not heard a
word. Yuri Volanov approached the table and looked inquiringly at the captain. Petrovich nodded. Volanov squatted down
next to Emerson and began to speak softly in clear, accent-free
American.

"Hey, Jim," he said. "Look, fella, drink the tea like the
man says and then we'll have us a little talk, OK? Just you and
me, nobody else. Your buddies are OK now—take my word for
it. Hey, cheer up, will ya? The war's almost over and we'll all
be going back home soon. Sound good? Hey, what's the matter? Don't you want to go home?"

Yuri paused. Emerson sat still, silent, unfocused. The tears
continued to flow.

"Tell me about home," Yuri said, his soft voice urging.
"You're from California, right? What's it like there, Jim?
Come on, tell me about it."

He went on that way, pushing, compelling, his voice a velvet
web of persuasion, but without results. Emerson sat as still as a
weeping statue.

"This can't go on," Petrovich growled. "We don't have the
time."

"Comrade Captain?" Anya Ignatiev stood close to Petrovich, bent over, and spoke softly into his ear. He looked up at her sharply and murmured a question. She nodded firmly and said something more.

"Try it," he said. "It can do no harm."

Anya came around the table and crouched down in front of Emerson. She looked up for a moment, her eyes on Yuri's face, the fraction of a question dangling between them. Yuri's eyes were cold and hard. He looked away. Anya smiled and leaned forward until her face was close to the American's. She called his name softly.

"Jimmy," she said, her lips only inches from his. "Is that what they call you? What do the girls call you, Jimmy?"

She waited for an answer, and when none came she leaned forward the few inches and kissed him full on the lips. The boy reacted as if he had been poked with a hot wire. His head snapped back, twisting away, and his arms came up protectively.

"Hey, cut that out," he said in a whining, nasal voice.

"What's the matter?" she asked, a taunting lilt in her voice. "Didn't you like it?"

"I don't get it," he muttered. "Where's my unit?"

"I'll bet you liked it a lot."

He was silent for a beat, his eyes staring into hers, then he said reluctantly, "It was OK, I guess. It's just that you surprised me, sneaking up that way."

"You're right," Anya said gravely. "It wasn't fair, sneaking up. This time I won't sneak. This time you do it."

"You mean it?" His lips twisted and his hands gripped the arms of the chair.

"Of course I do. Go ahead."

He drew back and looked around. "No. This is crazy."

"But I thought you liked it. And we're friends. We're Russians. You're a Yank. We're all friends. I want to show you how friendly we really are."

"Not with them watching," he said quietly.

"Of course. That was stupid of me." She straightened up and put her hand over his. She pulled lightly and he came up out of the chair. "Come . . . we'll go where they can't watch."

She took a lantern and led him back to the enclosed, hay-filled stall that she had just shared with Yuri Volanov. She coaxed him inside gently, hung the lantern on a peg, and closed the door.

"Go ahead," she said, turning to face him. "You do it this time. The rest of them have gone to find your unit. We've got plenty of time. Let's not waste it."

He put his arms around her and kissed her. She let him do it until they both were out of breath. Then she stepped back and began to remove her clothing. She undressed quickly, not making a game of it, partly because she knew that time was going quickly and partly because she was embarrassed by her coarse and bulky army-issue underwear. With her clothing gone, she turned to face him again. He had not moved. He was staring at her body, entranced again. His gaze was so openly and innocently lustful that she realized that this was probably the first time he had ever seen a totally nude woman.

"Have you had many girls?" she asked, although sure of the answer.

He shook his head, and his eyes slipped away from hers.

"Ni bispakoityes, ni vazhna," she murmured. "Don't worry, it doesn't matter."

She took his hands and brought them to her breasts. He squeezed convulsively, hurting her, but she had not expected finesse. She reached for him, felt him, and found him hard and ready. She snapped open the buckle of his belt and pulled him down to the straw. He entered her quickly and climaxed at once. She sighed, rolled out from under him, and went to work with her hands and lips until he was ready again. The second time she retained control with a slow and thrusting motion that kept him going to full completion. She even managed a tiny spark of pleasure of her own. Then she lay next to him, the sweat drying on their bodies, their fingers lightly twined. His breathing was firm and steady. He was still shocked, but he was functioning again.

"How do you feel now?" she asked.

"I'm OK."

"Just OK?"

"I feel good, very good." His face was pressed against her shoulder and his voice was muffled.

"No more tears?"

He shook his head, but a tremor ran through his body, then another, and he began to quiver wildly. She held him close to her until the tremors passed.

"Jimmy, you're safe now," she said quietly. "No one is going to harm you."

"Where's my unit?" he asked, not quite as anxiously as before.

"You'll be with them soon. Don't worry. And soon you'll all be going home."

His voice was unsure. "Do you really think so? That the war will be over soon?"

"Yes. And then home to Point Balboa."

"Do you know Point Balboa?" He moved out from under her arm and sat up. Looking down at her, his eyes were bright and he was smiling. For a moment she thought that he wanted her again, then she realized that he wanted only to talk. "You ever been to the States?"

"No, never. But I'd love to go. What is it like?"

"Where I live, it's up in northern California, close to the Oregon border. You ever heard of Eureka?"

"No, but I'd like to hear."

"Well, Eureka's the nearest city, about twenty-five miles down the coast. They've got three movie houses there and trolley cars and the department store. Eureka's OK, I guess, but I wouldn't want to live there. Too many people bumping into you all the time and rushing around like they was going to a fire or something."

"Not like Point Balboa?"

"Hell, no. Nobody hurries in Point Balboa if they can help it. My dad used to say that the town is a backwater. My dad used to say that the town's in a rut, and a rut's just a grave with the ends knocked out. But there's nothing wrong with Point Balboa. Good hunting, good fishing, most of the time. Good people."

"Tell me more."

And he told her. He told her about growing up in Point Balboa as the son of God-fearing, churchgoing people, and how fine the life was before they died, and how very different it was afterwards. He told her about the car crash that took them both only a year before, and the sudden shock of knowing that he was alone in the world, so truly alone that the Army seemed like a home and a haven. He told her about that, and he told her about the hardware store on Arbor Street where he worked after school, and the three-speed bike that he bought with the money he earned; and about Mrs. Kupferman, who baked the best loganberry pies in town and would always give you a piece if you asked nice, and her husband, Jake, who was close to being the town drunk except that nobody dared to say it out loud. He told her about playing end for Humboldt High; about Chub Portman, who was his best friend and who went into the Navy and got killed off Guadalcanal; about a girl called Betty, who would never give him a date, and another girl, called Pauline, who let him put his hand between her legs once in the back seat of her father's Plymouth, but that was all she ever let him do. He told her about the football game on Thanksgiving Day and the big parade on the Fourth of July, which was his own very special day, birthday and holiday combined, because he was a Yankee Doodle Dandy, born on the Fourth, and when he was a kid he truly believed that the whole town turned out on that day just to celebrate with him.

"Wonderful," Anya whispered.

He told her about the Point Balboa Methodist Church, and the new minister nobody liked, and the cake sales and the Friday Night Suppers and the Christian Fellowship meetings before Bible class on Sunday mornings; about the whales that you could sometimes see cruising offshore, and the tidewater pools below the rocks of the point where the crabs were good, and the old men who surf cast for bass from the beach every day at sundown; about the brother he never had and desperately wanted, about the baby sister who died when he was four, and what it was like to grow up as an only child. He told her all he knew. He gave her the collected impressions of eighteen years of small-town living, the accumulated baggage of his short life.

He opened up the bags and displayed it all before her, a pathetic return for the gift she had given, and he was over an hour in the telling of it all. Twice during that time, newly confident, he casually mounted her and exploded within her, then rested for a while and talked some more. He told her all he knew, which wasn't very much, but which was more than enough for the purpose at hand.

Yuri Volanov, sitting on the other side of the wooden wall, listened intently, his chin cupped in his hand. He made no written notes; he had no need of them, for another of the skills learned at Gaczyna was the ability to memorize verbatim and to retain that memory indefinitely. He listened carefully, clearing his brain to note and file it all away, moving from his spot only when he heard the thrashing sounds of sex. The first time it happened his face turned pale and he bit his lip. The second time he moved to the front of the barn to drink tea with the others. Petrovich raised an eyebrow when he saw him leave his post.

"They're at it again," Yuri explained, his face set in hard lines.

"How does it go?" asked Radichek.

"I'm getting all I need." He cupped his tea in his hands, and the lines in his face eased. "Point Balboa, California. It sounds like a pleasant place."

"It's the one place you'll never see," Radichek said sternly. "You understand that, don't you?"

"I understand very well." He took another sip of his tea and went back to listen again.

It was fully light, and Kolodny had extinguished the sputtering lanterns when Yuri decided that he had heard enough. He stood, knocked lightly on the door to the stall, and said, "All right, Anya, that's it."

He went back to join the others at the table. Minutes later Anya came out of the stall, buttoning her blouse and brushing straw from her uniform skirt. Behind her, Emerson stood uncomfortably, blinking his eyes and grinning sheepishly. Anya looked at Yuri, her face weary and pale; he looked away from her. She nodded, as if confirming some inner thought, and strode directly to where Petrovich stood.

"Comrade Captain," she said formally. "Permission to make a request?"

Petrovich looked at her curiously. "Go ahead."

"I request that the next step in the operation be done quickly. Efficiently."

"Of course. We are not barbarians. Yuri?"

He nodded to young Yuri Volanov, who drew a pistol from his belt holster and shot young James Emerson through the left temple. Emerson was dead when he hit the floor. His blood ran into the straw. Kolodny and Radichek at once began to strip the corpse of its clothing. They had trouble with the trousers, pulling and jerking at the belt and cuffs.

"Anya, you got these off once before," Kolodny called. "Come show us how."

She stared down at him, a look of disgust on her face, then turned and walked away to stand in the open doorway, looking out at the barnyard. Kolodny smiled mockingly at her back.

Yuri Volanov disrobed quickly, folding each item of his uniform into a neat square and placing it on the table. Equally quickly, he dressed himself in Emerson's uniform, examining each piece of clothing before putting it on. Within minutes he was dressed in the combat fatigues of an American Army private, with Emerson's dog tags around his neck and Emerson's wallet resting in his pocket. The American's clothing pinched at him in several places, but not enough to call for comment. Only the boots were truly uncomfortable; they were a full size too small. He presented himself to Petrovich.

"Are you ready, Yuri Aleksandrovich?" asked the captain.

"Yes, sir."

"I will not insult you by asking if you have any last questions. You are too well trained for that. I will only wish you the best of fortune." He pressed Yuri's hand warmly, then nodded to Kolodny, who picked up the pistol Yuri had left on the table.

"Careful of the bone," muttered Petrovich.

Kolodny looked at him with a trace of reproach, then turned and shot Yuri through the upper left arm. The young lieutenant staggered but did not fall. His face screwed up with pain. Kolodny shot him again through the meaty portion of the right thigh. Now Yuri fell to the floor and lay there moaning. Kolodny put away the pistol and reached for a standard-issue Red Army rifle propped against the table. Petrovich put out a restraining hand.

"Let me have that," he said. "You enjoy this too much."

He took the rifle, bent over the twisted figure of Yuri Volanov, and carefully, almost tenderly, used the butt to break the young officer's right cheekbone and jaw.

"Quickly now," he said. "You two, the body. Anya, get over here and get to work."

Radichek and Kolodny dragged Emerson's body out into the barnyard, covered it with piles of brushwood, and then doused it liberally from a jerrican of gasoline. Kolodny stood back, tossed a match, and a tower of flame shot up. The two men backed off from the sudden heat and watched as skin and flesh blackened, bubbled, and broke away.

While they were tending the fire, Anya tended to Yuri. His arm and his thigh she simply cleansed and bandaged, giving the gunshot wounds the same basic attention that a Russian field medic would have given them. His face and head she bandaged more thoroughly, winding swaths of white gauze around and around. Yuri watched her silently as she worked, his eyes filled with pain.

When she was finished, she looked at him for a moment, then said, "I'm sorry about the sex, Yuri. It was part of the job. Please remember that, always. It was part of the job."

With great difficulty, Yuri dragged out the words. "It was what you were trained for."

Anya stood up and reported to Petrovich, "Finished over here."

"Finished," Radichek reported, coming in from the barnyard.

"Very well." Petrovich picked up the field telephone and rang through to the headquarters of the Third Battalion. "Grigorian? Petrovich here. These are your final instructions. You will order an immediate reconnaissance of this area. In the barn you will find the sole survivor of the American platoon that was ambushed earlier by the Fascists. He is badly wounded. You will at once notify Division and arrange for the transfer of the wounded man to an American field hospital on the other side of the river. That is all.''

He replaced the phone and to the others said, ''Move out. Everything into the truck.''

He knelt over the still figure of Yuri Volanov and put a gentle hand on his shoulder. ''*Dasvidanya*, Private Emerson,'' he said. ''You had a short war but a good one.''

Beneath the bandages the lips managed a painful grin, and a cracked and muffled voice replied, ''You bet your ass, buster. I'm headin' back to the good old U.S.A.''

Chapter 2

From the Class Bulletin 1980

The Class of 1950, New York University, on the occasion of its Thirtieth Annual Reunion, is pleased to name as its Man of the Year, The Honorable James Walter Emerson, Assistant Secretary of Defense for Air.

JAMES (JIMBO) EMERSON
Hallowbrook Farm, Princess Falls, Va.; clubs: University (NY), NYAC, Burning Tree (Wash.), Bohemian; AB (NYU 1950), LLB (NYU Law 1952); m. Janet Sykes 1955; d. Katherine 1958.

I wish first to thank the trustees of the Alumni Association of New York University, Washington Square College, and the officers of the Class of 1950 for this singular honor. I am, after all, nothing more than a practicing attorney who, three years ago, answered the call of his country to serve in the Department of Defense. If this qualifies me for honors, then so be it. I humbly accept the designation, and in response to the Committee's invitation, I am pleased to set forth on these pages some of the highlights of my life.

I suppose that like anyone else who saw military service in World War II, the Army was my first memorable experience. Not that I saw all that much service, since I started off my military career as a private in the 273rd Regiment of the 69th Infantry Division and ended it holding the same exalted rank. I spent most of 1945 and part of the following year in various Army

21

hospitals recovering from wounds received during the final days of the war against Nazi Germany, and in 1946 I was finally discharged and began my four years at New York University.

I know that nowadays it's fashionable to sneer at the kind of life that NYU has to offer its students outside the classroom . . . no football team, no campus, things like that. But for a small-town boy like myself, a hick from Point Balboa, California, being on my own at the age of twenty and attending college in New York City certainly was a heady experience. There was the excitement of living in Greenwich Village, the parties, the girls, and getting together with the gang at places like Ed Winston's, and Rocky's on Washington Place. I wonder how many people today remember standing at the bar in Rocky's with me that afternoon in October 1947, listening to the World Series on the radio, when Cookie Lavagetto hit the pinch-hit double to spoil Bill Bevens' no-hitter. Some of those people still owe me money from that game.

But it wasn't all peaches and cream. Being on your own at twenty generally means being broke, and I was no exception. Of course, there was the GI Bill, but that didn't go very far, and during my four years at NYU and two years more at law school I worked six nights a week at Gimbels department store, being what was euphemistically called, in those days, a resident engineer. I was, in fact, a glorified janitor, and the work was hard and boring, but I managed.

Actually, I managed very nicely, and at this point I want to make it clear that I am in no way complaining about the manner in which I had to put myself through college. I was brought up with a belief in certain virtues that are considered somewhat unfashionable these days, and one of those beliefs is the bedrock conviction that any man, and particularly any American, can attain whatever goal he has set for himself in life, so long as he works hard enough, and with enough dedication, to achieve it. This simple fact, which is our nation's most precious asset, is what distinguishes our society from that of the totalitarian East and godless Communism, and I am proud that my own experiences as a young man were representative of the American way of life.

So much for college days, and the grind of law school. Next came my admission to the New York Bar in 1953, and hard upon the heels of that, the day I went to work for the distinguished law firm of Swan and O'Mara at 75 Maiden Lane. Edwin Swan, senior partner of the firm, was like a father to me, and no other single person (with one exception to be mentioned later on) influenced my life as much as he did.

When I use the phrase "like a father to me," I do not use it lightly. My own father, along with my mother, died tragically when I was seventeen years of age, and from that time until the day that I met Mr. Swan I was without the older man that every young man needs to admire and to emulate. Edwin Swan provided that function in my life. He was, and still is, a tall, soft-spoken man of distinguished appearance, high intelligence, and impeccable character. The very first day that I met him I resolved to model myself on this man in every way. From observing him daily, I learned about the clothing with which a civilized man garbs himself. From dining with him, I learned that the preparation of food can be raised to the level of a fine art. As the years went by he encouraged my interests in baroque music, nineteenth-century American literature, and postimpressionist painting. He inculcated in me the habits of a lifetime, and when, in 1968, he left private practice to become Deputy Director of the Central Intelligence Agency he set one final example for me, one which I was proud to follow when my turn came to be called to public service.

But all that came later. Back in 1953 I doubt that Mr. Swan took any particular notice of me. Just as I had been a glorified janitor at Gimbels, at Swan and O'Mara I was nothing more than a glorified law clerk, one of a dozen, who ran errands, looked up citations, researched decisions, and in general did all the scut work that enables the legal mills to grind, no matter how slowly. It was, in fact, a first-rate education in the day-to-day workings of the law, and as such was an invaluable experience.

It was in 1954 that Edwin Swan indicated that he was not entirely unaware of my existence. In fact, he made it clear that he had had his eye on me for some time, and in the fall of that year I was plucked from the ranks of the lowly, given a tiny office of my own, and put to work preparing corporate documents for some of our largest clients. Of course, in keeping with tradition, I wasn't paid any more than I had been before, but I knew that my mentor thought well of me, and that I had a future with the firm.

Now for that exception I mentioned earlier, and she certainly is an exceptional woman. Any of my classmates who have had the privilege of meeting Mrs. Emerson will need no description of her, and for you others, I will only say that she is beautiful, witty, and intelligent, and I say this after twenty-five years of marriage. It was just about the time that I began to move up the ladder at Swan and O'Mara that I first met Rusty (her name is Janet, but no one calls her that), and a very proper meeting it was, too. Nowadays, I guess if you asked every man you know how he met his wife, about half would say through a mutual friend, and the other half would say, "Well, I was standing at this bar and in walked . . ." I'll bet on it. But it was nothing like that with Rusty and me. We met, of all places, at a church supper. Just imagine it! Shades of the eighteen nineties. There I was, munching away on my fried chicken and trying to figure out how the heck a man can be expected to eat potato chips with a knife and fork, when I looked up and there she was. I guess she didn't have the same kind of reservations about those chips that I did, because she picked one up with her fingers, very ladylike, of course, and popped it into her mouth. Then, to my amazement, she picked up another one, reached across the table, and popped it into mine. And smiled at me. And gentlemen, right at that moment my fate was sealed, so I guess there are some fringe benefits, after all, to being a Methodist.

As the saying goes, I chased her until she caught me. It was love at first sight, all right, but please remember that I was making the munificent salary of $110 per week at Swan and O'Mara, not very much even for 1954, and another one of those old-fashioned virtues that I was brought up to believe in is that a man doesn't marry until he is financially able to support a wife.

Rusty and I kept company for most of 1954 and well into the next year, and I suppose we'd be keeping company still if she hadn't sat me down one night and said, "Jimbo, it's time to fish or cut bait." (Rusty can be a very determined lady when the mood is on her.) Rusty pulled out the old pencil and paper and started making like a CPA, showing me how we could manage easily on our two salaries, and, as I said before, the lady can be very determined. It was no contest; she had her way with me, and we were married a month later in the very same church where we had met. Three years later our daughter, Ginger, was born, and my happiness was complete.

After that, events occurred, but they were nothing more than the orderly process of a man's life and career. I went up the ladder in the firm, and in 1968 I was offered a full partnership, an offer which I regretfully declined. That was the year Edwin Swan left the firm to enter public service as Deputy Director of the Central Intelligence Agency, and without him at the helm I could see no purpose in remaining there myself. I therefore resolved to open my own offices, something I did later that year at 2 Wall Street. The firm, which eventually became Emerson, Jacobs and Blake, prospered from the start, and in the natural course of events honors and obligations came my way. Finally, three years ago, came the call from our President, to come to Washington to serve as Assistant Secretary of Defense for Air. This call I answered willingly, despite some personal sacrifice. I have just used the words "honors and obligations," and I should like to make it clear that while I consider this service to my country to be both an honor and an obligation, the emphasis is on the latter, not the former. Yes, surely it's an honor to serve one's country, but according to the old-fashioned verities that I mentioned before, the ones I learned first at my father's knee, and later from Edwin Swan, the primary obligation that goes with citizenship is an uncomplaining service to the community, which in the largest possible sense means service to one's country.

Old-fashioned yes, indeed, but you have to remember that I'm an old-fashioned fellow, a Yankee Doodle Dandy born on the Fourth of July, and it comes naturally to me. Not that I think that the happy coincidence of my birthday gives me a monopoly on the patriotic impulse, but I do believe that citizenship in a country such as ours is a two-way proposition, like double-entry bookkeeping. An American citizen is the most privileged person on the face of this earth. He is the recipient of advantages which, in the natural order of things, should belong to all men but which, in this century at least, are particularly his. These privileges have to be paid for. All of us know that there's no such thing as a free lunch, and the manner in which we pay for the privilege of being Americans includes a dedicated service to the state. That's not much of a price to pay, is it? I don't think so. I think that being an American is the best deal on earth.

These words of James Emerson, printed in an obscure commemorative album, should have slipped gracefully into oblivion, but no sparrow is too small for its fall not to be noted by the intelligence services of the Soviet Union. Within a week after their publication, the words had been absorbed into the information-gathering network of the KGB, had been translated, taped, fed into a computer; and eventually were distributed to all interested parties within the organization.

One of those interested parties was Colonel Andrei Petrovich, who read the words of James Emerson with a broad smile on his face, silently congratulating the Assistant Secretary of Defense for Air on his guile, his duplicity, and his command of American patriotic rhetoric.

What Petrovich did not realize was that James Emerson meant every word of it.

II

Operation Homefire

Chapter 3 _____

James Emerson opened his eyes and was at once awake. This was something he was always able to do, no matter how late he had gone to bed the night before, no matter how many brandies he had taken after dinner, no matter how weary his body might be. It was a habit he had developed early in life, and it had served him well.

On this morning, the day before his fifty-third birthday, he awoke minutes after six and was at once aware of the sunlight that filtered into his bedroom through closed curtains, of the song of a cardinal piping over the Virginia countryside, of the pungent smell of freshly cut grass, of the regular breathing of his wife asleep beside him, and of a faintly metallic taste in his mouth which he correctly attributed to the sauce *marchand du vin* that had accompanied his chateaubriand the night before.

The people in this town will eat anything, he thought, remembering the restaurant and the meal. I'll never understand Washington, and I'll never understand people who cook with wine that they wouldn't dream of drinking.

Half an hour later, shaved, showered, and with a dark suit of conservative cut draped over his lean body, he stood over the bed looking down at his sleeping wife. Her copper-colored hair, the reason she was universally called Rusty, was spread in a rich wave over her pillow, and as he watched a tendril fell across her face and she stirred in her sleep. Carefully, delicately, he brushed the lock of hair aside. It was his custom every morning to say good-bye for the day to her this way, standing over her silently. They had been married for over twenty-five years, and he truly believed that she was as lovely now as the day he had met her. The outlines of her body showed clearly through the light covering, and he felt a flush of warmth and a rush of temptation rise up within him. In other, younger days he would have succumbed to the temptation by waking her gently to lead her up and down the hills and valleys of desire that were so much a part of the topography of their marriage. But not now. Not that desire had lessened all that much with the years, but because he lived a life of rigid schedules and competing priorities. It was part of his job; he accepted it as such, and he pushed away temptation as he bent to kiss her cheek.

Downstairs in the neat and modern kitchen, which he secretly thought to be a touch too neat and too modern, he drank a glass of unsweetened grapefruit juice and turned on the automatic coffee-maker. While he was waiting for the coffee he flicked on the FM radio and lowered the volume as the strains of Copland's *Appalachian Spring* swelled through the room. He spun the dial. He had nothing against Copland; enjoyed him, in fact, despite his personal preference for the clean astringencies of the baroque period, but with the Fourth of July coming up he knew that he could expect a surfeit of American composers on the local stations. It was that way every year, as if an annual homage could atone for the neglect that the nation otherwise heaped on its native musicians. Sure enough, the next station had Piston's *Incredible Flutist*. He smiled and let it play, resigned to the absurdity.

When the coffee was ready he cut two thin slices from a loaf of dark bread, two thick slices from the butt end of a Smithfield ham, and took himself to the kitchen table to consume his simple breakfast. It was the one meal he preferred to eat alone. Rusty always slept late; their daughter, Ginger, no longer lived with them; and Ellen, the one servant they still employed, did not arrive until midmorning. Thus, his lonely breakfast had become something of a ritual, a transfer time between his private persona and his public image. These were some of the few moments of the day when he was left completely alone with time for contemplation, and he had come to cherish the minutes.

Sipping his coffee, he consulted his pocket diary and reviewed his appointments for the day. He had a fairly light schedule for a change. Nine thirty with the Secretary for a progress report on the B2B bomber, Senator Ferguson at eleven for the umpteenth round of a continuing battle over a missile contract, lunch with the Brazilian Attaché for Air, staff meetings in the afternoon, and then, with luck, a quick getaway in anticipation of the Fourth of July weekend and his birthday tomorrow.

Perhaps there'll even be time to have a drink with Swan before I head home, he thought happily. It would be nice to have a birthday drink with him.

Fifty-three, not the happiest of birthdays; not a round number, so it's nothing more than age without honor. The thought of his age bounced around his brain like a sad little marble in a pinball machine, and on the heels of the thought came the reminder that he actually had been fifty-three for over six months. The Fourth of July belonged to James Emerson . . . Yuri Volanov's birthday was late in November . . . but he had been Emerson, and only Emerson, for so long now that the November date was all but forgotten, along with everything else that his youth had represented. In fact, the Fourth of July, and the birthday that came with it, was one of the few times during the year when he was forced to remember who he really was.

I know who I am, he thought with a sudden surge of irritation. I'm James Emerson, husband, father, and the Assistant Secretary of Defense for Air. That's me, and tomorrow's my birthday, and if nothing else I'll get to see my daughter for a change. She's never missed a birthday of mine yet, and she's not going to start now, even if it means coming down from New York. It also means that we'll be blessed with the presence of Mr. Eddie Angelotti, but I can put up with a lot more than that if it means seeing Ginger.

Warmed by the thought of his daughter's visit, he finished his coffee, and ten minutes later, at exactly seven thirty, he came out of his house and into the sweetness of a summer morning in Virginia. His car and driver, both from the Pentagon pool, stood waiting at the top of the driveway, but he paused for a moment in front of his door to breathe in the odors of grass and magnolia, to soak in a touch of the pale sunshine, and to revel in the sight of the land, the rolling lawn that was more like a manicured meadow stretching down to the road and the whitewashed split-rail fences there that marked the limits of his property. Five full acres of Virginia's best. The sight of this land, his land, was always a source of pleasure to him, although at times he could surprise himself with his passion for owner-ship.

You're turning into a goddamn squire of the manse, he told himself. Well, why not? I worked hard for this land. I earned every square foot of it.

As he stepped into the black Lincoln limousine, he nodded to the driver who stood holding the door. "Good morning, Mi-chael," he said. "Well, they did it again."

"That they did, sir," said the driver, closing the door, and then when he was seated behind the wheel and they were rolling down the driveway, he added, "The Orioles have got more ways of losing a ball game than any other team in baseball."

"I take it that you would have bunted?"

"In the ninth, sir? Yes, indeed, sure I would. One out, men on first and second, down by two in the ninth, the book says bunt. Get those two men into scoring position."

"The book also says that you play to tie at home and to win on the road."

"Yes, sir, I know that, but I still would have bunted. But not Mr. Weaver, oh no. Mr. Weaver has him hit away into the prettiest double play you ever saw, and there goes the ball game."

"Yes . . . ." Emerson sighed. "There it went. But it was Weaver's decision to make, not yours or mine. That's some consolation."

"Indeed it is, sir. I wouldn't have his job for the world."

"Nor mine, for that matter, I imagine."

"Definitely not yours, sir. Especially not yours. I'm a re-sponsible man, I am, but I wouldn't want that kind of responsi-bility weighing on my shoulders. All those airplanes and rockets and missiles whirling around up there. No, thank you, not me. No offense intended, but I'd rather have Earl Weaver's job than yours any day."

"Frankly, Michael, so would I. In fact, I'd rather enjoy it. In my next life, I might try."

The two men laughed quietly. The driver, about to say something more, thought better of it and shifted in his seat to concentrate on the driving. The moment of intimacy between master and man, the common interest in sports that was the great leveler in a supposedly classless society, had lasted just long enough. In the rear seat the passenger also recognized this limitation and settled back for the forty-five-minute drive to the Pentagon. For a moment he glanced out at the familiar landscape flowing by, the gently rolling hills and fields that he loved, and then he turned his attention to what lay beside him on the rear seat. As every morning, there was a copy of the *Washington Post*, one of the *New York Times*, and on top of them both a thin leather dispatch case containing the overnights received by his office and ferried out by Michael to be read during the drive to work.

He unlocked the case with a tiny key on his chain and began to pore through the flimsy sheets methodically. Most of the overnights were routine, and only one file caught his attention, the one marked *Operation Homefire*. The flimsy was a transcript of an intercept monitored by Military Intelligence, an exchange between the Czech Ministry of Security and its opposite number in East Germany. The intercept was, on the surface, innocuous, being nothing more than a high-level discussion of impending military maneuvers within the Warsaw Pact nations. Only the passing reference to *Homefire* took it out of the ordinary. Emerson's eyes sought out the passage.

> . . . *consideration should be given to the postponement of exercises until the completion of* Operation Homefire *because of the potential propaganda value of the latter. The Elders predict a far more favorable political climate following its completion and so suggest that* . . .

Emerson frowned. *The Elders* was only a catch phrase used by the East European agencies when referring to the big brothers in Moscow. What bothered him was the ambiguity of the reference. It was no different from any of the others he had seen. *Homefire* was a name, a rumor, and nothing more. For the past three weeks that name had appeared on the intercepts of communications between various East European agencies and missions: the Czechs to the Poles, the Hungarians to the Bulgarians, the Bulgarians to the Czechs. In all cases *Operation Homefire* was referred to by name, and little else. It was almost as if the satellite nations had been promised a triumph by Moscow but had not been told what the prize would be. His own Military Intelligence had been able to adduce only that a major Soviet propaganda operation was in the making, a nonmilitary, noneconomic ploy soon to be mounted against the West. More than that they could not say, and so the guessing game continued.

He put aside the *Homefire* file and went on paging through the flimsies. Fifteen minutes saw him at the bottom of the pile with nothing left in the case but a plain sealed envelope with his name written on the front. He tore the envelope open and began to read, scanning the handwritten lines quickly.

> . . . *including this in the pouch because you said you were in a hurry for it, but I'd just as soon you shredded it after reading, so I'm writing it by hand with no copies. I have the feeling that some Senate committee of the future might not cotton to the idea of Military Intelligence running a review on your prospective son-in-law, not that I see any harm in it, being always willing to help out a buddy. Well, pal, here it is, and I don't think you're going to like it. I sure as hell wouldn't if it were my daughter who was involved.*
>
> *Your question to me was: what does this guy Eddie Angelotti do for a living? The answer: nothing at all. Let's hit the basics first. As you know, he and Ginger are living together in a studio apartment at 203 East Eleventh Street in New York . . . not the greatest of neighborhoods, but not the worst, either. You know what he looks like, and he seems to be in good shape for a little fellow*

in his late thirties. Jogs every morning, plays pick-up basketball at the Y, and spends a lot of time working on his Overlander camper. That, apparently, is all he does, except keep house with your daughter.

He has a Social Security card.

He has a New York State driver's license.

He has New York plates on the Overlander.

He banks at Citibank, savings and checking; combined current balance is about twelve grand.

And that, old buddy, is it. Nothing more. That's the bag.

You've been around long enough to grasp what I mean. It isn't enough. It isn't half enough. It isn't a tenth enough. Nobody in this day and age gets to be thirty-eight years old without putting his hoofmark on something more than a Social Security card and a couple of Motor Vehicle forms.

A little less than a year ago Mr. Edward Angelotti appears out of nowhere, rents an apartment, buys an expensive camper, and takes out a New York State driver's license. Before that, nada. Before that, Mr. Edward Angelotti never paid a gas or electric bill, never had a telephone, never registered with any governmental agency including Selective Service, never was a member of the armed forces, and never paid a penny's worth of income tax. Impossible? No—a fact. And just to make it a touch more complicated, let's go back to his bank account. Where does the money come from? Monthly deposits from a blind account in the Bahamas. The Swiss Bank in Nassau. Double protection. Neat.

So there it is. You didn't ask me to draw any conclusions, but one thing is clear. Edward Angelotti isn't the type that you want playing footsie with your daughter. I know, she's a big girl now. They're all big boys and girls now, but they're our own, and all we've got.

Let's have lunch soon. I'm sure you'll understand if I don't sign this.

* * *

Emerson read the last few lines of the note over again, nodding in silent agreement. He was not very surprised by what he had just read, since it only confirmed what he and Rusty had already concluded. When your loving and well-loved daughter moves to New York City to study design at the age of twenty-two, you hold your breath and wait for the casualty reports to come in, hoping that reality won't be half as bad as what your imagination conjures up in the middle of the night. Reality, unfortunately, has an imagination of its own.

The trouble is, I like Eddie, he thought. By every standard that I have I should despise him, but I don't. Either he's a lazy bastard who refuses to work for a living, or he's some kind of a con man with enough money stashed away to live for a while. He's taken my only daughter in what we used to call Unholy Wedlock, a girl brought up with every advantage, and has her living in a cheap flat on the Lower East Side. He reads *Playboy* for intellectual stimulation, relaxes to the music of Mantovani, and his palate aspires to nothing more sublime than a good linguine with clam sauce. He is, in short, everything I'm not, and whatever happened to the idea that girls look for men who resemble their fathers? Not this time, that's for sure.

But for all of that, I like Eddie. He's aloof, evasive, sometimes downright surly, and half the time I have the feeling that he's laughing at me; but he's sharp and witty, and he has a kind of strength that I can't put my finger on. It's buried in the man, but not too far from the surface, and that must be what Ginger sees.

He sighed as he slipped the handwritten pages into his pocket. The sigh was louder than he had intended, for Michael shifted on the front seat and their eyes met in the rear-vision mirror.

"Something wrong?" the driver asked.

"Nothing I can do anything about. How are your children these days?"

"All of them fine, thank you, and the grandchildren, too. Is that what the sighing was all about? The daughter in New York?"

"I don't understand her, Michael. I don't understand any of them."

A knowing nod came from the driver. "Well, you're not the first man to say those words, and you won't be the last. Will she be coming down tomorrow for your birthday?"

"Oh, sure, she wouldn't miss that."

"That's OK, then. So long as the family sticks together, that's the important thing."

Emerson nodded in doubtful agreement, wondering exactly how much of Mr. Eddie Angelotti he wanted adhering to his family. He pushed aside the dispatch case and glanced out the window. Even at this early hour the traffic was heavy on the Shirley Memorial Highway coming into Washington, not bumper-to-bumper yet, but a steady flow that would reach a peak shortly. Following his unchanging morning routine, he opened the *New York Times*, turned to the business section, and quickly searched out four stocks that he was backing with a hard-nosed optimism. He groaned. Who didn't, these days? After that he read the front page, the sports section, the lead editorial, and the bridge column, and then, with a tiny silver pencil, he rapidly filled in the crossword puzzle.

A glance out the window told him that they were still ten minutes away from the office. He reached for the copy of the *Washington Post* and turned to the lost-and-found section in the back of the paper. This, too, was a part of his never-changing routine. All of his adult life, without exception, he had read the lost-and-found column of the local paper wherever he lived. In New York it had been the *Times*. Now, in Washington, it was the column in the *Post* that he read dutifully every morning. Drawing easily on his cigar, he folded the paper over and ran his eyes down the listings.

   . . . .FOUND, silver bracelet in the lounge of. . .
   . . . .LOST, lady's handbag, Sheraton Hotel on. . .
   . . . .LOST, gold cuff link with initials EMB. . .
   . . . .LOST, black male corgi, answers to King. . .
   . . . .FOUND, miniature poodle, no collar. . .

He stopped. He shifted his eyes up one space. He read
again.

. . . .LOST, black male corgi, answers to King. Vicin-
ity of Senate Office Building. Prompt and ample reward.
Call 676-1848, all hours.

His eyes bulged out, his face turned pale, and he started to
double over as if hit by a strong right hand to the stomach. Still
staring at the paper, he felt the welling up of nausea within him
and tasted bile in the back of his throat. He dropped the paper
and clenched his teeth. He closed his eyes a moment, fighting
for control over the spasms. The control would not come. He
rapped wildly on the back of the front seat. Michael, working his way through the heavy traffic, spared him a quick
glance.

"Pull over," Emerson managed to say, even with his teeth
clamped tight.

"What? What?"

"Pull over, damn it."

Michael took another quick look at his passenger's face and
twisted the wheel sharply, cutting across two lanes of traffic
with a screech of tires that drew a response of protesting horns
and shouted curses. The Lincoln bumped over the low curbing,
scraping metal on stone, rolled up onto the verge, and came to a
stop. Michael twisted around in his seat.

"Better do it outside, sir."

It all came up, the bread, the ham, the juice, the coffee, and
everything else as he knelt on the grass, retching horribly, tears
streaming from his eyes. A solicitous Michael stood over him,
as much to shield his embarrassment from the passing cars as to
offer any aid. When it was all over he rocked back on his heels,
breathing deeply, then struggled to his feet, a hand on Michael's arm. He breathed deeply once more, caught the full
force of the highway's collection of noxious fumes, and
thought that he would be sick again. But there was nothing left
to lose. After a moment he found a handkerchief, wiped his
lips, then his entire face, and clambered back into the car.

"Will we be going on?" asked Michael. "Or should I take you home?"

"No, go on," he said in a weary voice. "It's nothing. I'm all right now."

"It didn't look like nothing to me."

"Really, I'm all right. Just a sudden spasm."

"Something you ate, then?"

"Probably. Yes, probably something I ate."

He closed his eyes, sat back in the seat, and tried to breathe evenly as Michael worked the car off the verge and into traffic again. He tried to clear his mind of panic, but he could not. The words from the paper repeated themselves in a silent scream, over and over: *Black male corgi, answers to King, black male, Senate Office, prompt reward, call 676-1848 all hours.*

It can't be, he thought. Not after all these years. It can't be.

But it was. He opened his eyes again and stared at the lost-and-found section. He was still staring at the paper when the Lincoln pulled into Pentagon Parking Lot D and eased into his reserved space.

His stomach was calmer now, but his brain still churned the words over and over, *black male corgi, black male,* as he entered the building, crossed the rotunda, and rode up to the third floor. Once in his office, it took him no more than half an hour to clear his calendar, deputize for all his appointments, and advise his principal aides that he was going home with an upset stomach. Half an hour later he had crossed the Potomac and made his way to a public telephone booth on C Street. His face was covered with a film of perspiration, and his fingers shook as he fumbled in his pocket for coins. He breathed deeply several times, then dropped the money in the slot and dialed the number listed in the newspaper. Someone answered on the third ring.

"House of Joy, good morning." It was a woman's voice, light but businesslike.

"Good morning. I'm calling about the ad in the paper, the one about the dog."

"I see." He sensed a change of tone in the voice. "Would you say that again, please?"

His stomach went into spasm, and he thought: Oh my God, I screwed it up. What do they expect after thirty-five years? He ran over the phrasing in his mind and tried it again. "Good morning. I'm calling about the ad in *today's* paper, the one about the *lost* dog."

"Very good." The voice returned to normal. "Have you found my dog?"

"No, but I think I know where it is."

"How wonderful. Will you help me to find it?"

"I'll be glad to. I'm a dog lover myself."

With the last of the barely remembered recognition phrases complete, he slumped back in the booth. There was something disturbingly familiar about the voice. He knew that he was perspiring heavily, and he reached for a handkerchief to dab at his face. As he mopped his cheeks he heard the voice give him an address on Thirtieth Street near the Whitehurst Freeway.

"Can you be here in thirty minutes?" she asked.

"Yes." Again, there was an eerie sense of familiarity.

"Good. Please ask for me personally. Joy Mackenzie."

"Joy Mackenzie," he repeated. "The House of Joy."

"That's right." This time there was a hint of laughter in the voice that rang a faraway bell. "You won't have any trouble finding it. It's a sex shop."

He hung up and sat without moving. He went over the conversation in his mind, searching for a connection. There was none. He went over it again, this time laboriously translating the phrases into Russian. He nodded. Looking down at his right hand, he saw that his fingers were shaking. His left hand was no better. He made a conscious effort, but he could not stop the shaking. He knew now, without a doubt, that the voice on the phone had been that of Anya Ignatiev.

"I tell you frankly, I don't think that I could do it," said Andrei Petrovich. "All those years?"

"You make too much of it," said Radichek. "With all respect, to be a sleeper is a job just like any other job in this delightful profession of ours. Nothing more, nothing less."

"*Ya ni saglasyen svami.*" Petrovich slapped the desk with

the palm of his hand for emphasis. "I could not agree with you less. Being a sleeper is the most difficult assignment there is in what you choose to call our delightful profession. It's the loneliest job in the world. Don't you agree, Pavel?"

Kolodny shrugged. He sat slouched in a wicker chair, his shining boots perched on top of a small wooden table. "Some people can do it, others can't. Volanov was a natural; he was born for the job."

Time had not treated the three KGB officers equally well. Andrei Petrovich, now just over sixty and a full colonel, still was tall and burly with fists like hams and a heavy air of authority. Promotion had come less rapidly to Radichek; he was still a major, but his slim, oval face was unlined, and at times his eyes danced with the cynical amusement of his younger days. Kolodny, however, had changed radically. Once high-strung and wiry, he had grown into a corpulent balloon with tiny eyes set deep in folds of flesh, sausagelike fingers, and layers of fat that quivered whenever he moved.

"No one is born to do such a job," insisted Petrovich. "That kind of life is contrary to all of man's natural instincts."

He moved away from his desk to stand in front of the window. From there he could see across the stretch of meadows, now thick with grass, that sloped down to the town of Zhukovka. Tiny wildflowers dotted the lea, and above the village the clouds were dainty puffballs on parade. The sight, as always, was as refreshing to him as a glass of cold *kvass* on this hot July afternoon. Only twenty-five miles southwest of Moscow, the village was perched high on a bluff overlooking the gently flowing Moskva River. He turned back to look at his two old comrades. Since that night on the Elbe River years before, they had managed to keep in touch with each other, and with Anya Ignatiev. This had not always been easy. They had served at different times in different units, and on different projects, and their careers had proceeded unevenly. Now, for the first time in years, they were gathered together to witness the culmination of the project they had begun so long ago: the activation of the sleeping spy, Yuri Volanov.

In the parlance of their trade, a sleeper was an agent who had been introduced into a target territory for an unspecified purpose in the future. A sleeper was a gamble, a wild card to be played when and if an opportunity presented itself; and, as the name implied, a sleeper was expected to remain in place for long periods of time—half a lifetime if necessary—before becoming operational. During that sleeping period the agent was forbidden to engage in intelligence or espionage activities of any kind. He was forbidden to associate with the political left or do anything else that might lead to a questioning of his loyalties. As a sleeper his only instructions were to become a thriving part of the target society, to achieve a position of eminence in a chosen field, and at times to hold himself ready for the trigger message that would make him operational. For ten, twenty, thirty years or more it was his duty to live out his pretense severed from the sights and sounds of the motherland. Most of what made a man's lot in life bearable was denied to him: the comforting murmur of the language of his youth, the familiar foods of home, the rough and the smooth of his native climate, and the companionship of comrades. Only the most dedicated and ideologically sound agents could be used for such an assignment, for, as Petrovich knew, every sleeper lived only for the day when he could come home again.

"What a life," he said, looking out the window once more. Never was the feeling of *rodina*, of the motherland, so strong within him as when he looked out over the fields and forests of Zhukovka. "Imagine living out a lifetime without all of this. Without sniffing a Russian flower, or breathing Russian air, or feeling the earth of Mother Russia crumble beneath your fingers. Just imagine it."

"I can imagine it very easily," said Kolodny, who was a Ukrainian. He wheezed heavily at his own humor. "I imagine it every time I go home to Odessa."

Petrovich frowned, then shook his head in mock despair. Within the group he made some allowances for the familiarity of old comrades. "Then try to imagine a life without *shashliki* or *bitochki*. A life without sturgeon, or halvah, or any of the other delicacies that you stuff yourself with. Like that jellied fish that they make where you come from."

"Do without *zalivnaya riba?*" said Kolodny with a shudder that set him to jiggling. He raised a pudgy hand. "I surrender, Comrade Colonel. You have convinced me."

"With all respect," said Radichek softly. "All covert agents operate under such conditions. All of us here have done it at one time or another. With a sleeper, the difference is only one of time."

"*Only* one of time? But Boris Ivanovich, that's the whole point. That man has been out there for thirty-five years without a word from us, never knowing when he would be activated."

"That is the standard procedure," Radichek pointed out.

"But thirty-five years?"

"Thirty-five good years," said Kolodny, laughing. "And little Yuri has done well for himself. How much money does an American commissar make at his level?"

"Not a fortune, not to them," said Radichek. "But he was a successful lawyer for years, and he made good investments. He's comfortable, very comfortable indeed. A big house, a good wife, a fine daughter. No, I can't feel sorry for Yuri. He's made himself into the typical American success story."

"Which was exactly what he was supposed to do," said Petrovich. From the bottom drawer of his desk he took a bottle of purple Georgian wine and three glasses. He filled them and passed them around.

"He is like a flower in full bloom," said Radichek. "A long time blooming."

"And ready to be plucked." Kolodny raised his glass. "Well, here's to our Yuri."

"And to an absent comrade," Radichek added. "To Anya Ignatiev."

"And to the operation," said Petrovich. "Most important of all, to *Homefire.*"

They drank.

Chapter 4

On this same morning before the American Day of Independence, the man who called himself Eddie Angelotti was engaged in the ancient and dangerous game of trying to awaken a sleeping woman without having his head handed to him. Eddie wiggled cautiously, then wiggled again, moving himself slowly across the oversized bed that occupied most of one wall of the studio apartment. On the other side of the bed, Ginger Emerson slept soundly, her auburn hair, a shade or two darker than her mother's, a beckoning beacon on the pillow slip. She slept on her side with her back to him, covers thrown off in the night, and the sight of that back sloping down to well-turned buttocks and thighs was as much a beacon as her flaming hair. He wiggled again, gained six inches, and stopped. She did not move, and he wiggled again. The object of the exercise was to tuck himself next to her, spoon-fashion, without waking her, thereby finding a resting place between her thighs for the usual early-morning-just-woke-up-with-it-how-the-hell-did-it-get-so-big erection that was presently causing him a moderate amount of discomfort. One of two things would then happen. She would either come swimming up lazily from slumber, a complacent carp bent on bending the pole; or she would come up like a flash, a furious shark striking out at whatever had dragged her up from the comfortable depths. The result was never predictable, and the uncertainty gave piquancy to each morning's fishing expedition.

On this particular morning the patience of the angler was rewarded. Moving in close, tucking himself in, casting his bait, so to speak, upon the waters, he was rewarded first by a gentle

44

tug, then a definite connection as flesh responded, followed by a long and languorous murmur that signaled the catch swimming up in lazy circles to break the surface with a sigh as Ginger awoke and rolled over, pressing herself close to him.

"Got me," she said, her eyes still closed. "You did it again."

"It's all in the touch. Takes years to learn."

"Mmmm. The advantages of an older man. One of these days you're going to catch a whale with that thing, and then what will you do?"

"Run like hell, I guess."

"Better not." She nuzzled his shoulder. "Some brave fisherman you are."

"Nobody's brave at seven in the morning."

"I like that. It sounds like something from Hemingway." Her eyes popped open. "Is it really seven?"

"More like seven thirty."

"God, I've got a nine o'clock class." She sat up suddenly and started to swing her legs over the edge of the bed. He caught her at the hips before she could complete the motion. He flipped her over on her back and rolled on top of her. She squealed in protest. "Hey, whatever happened to foreplay?"

"You've got an early class."

"Look, be a nice guy and throw me back. I'm just a little fish."

"Plenty big enough for me."

"Really, I'll grow up and taste better later."

"You taste just fine," he said, tasting her. "After all, a fish in the net is worth two in the . . . what?"

"Bush," she sighed, surrendering happily.

Afterwards, she preempted the tiny shower while he lay on his back and studied the ceiling, cuddling his contentment. You are one lucky son of a bitch, he told himself. He had always thought of himself as being lucky. Indeed, in his occupation . . . his former occupation, he reminded himself . . . luck had always been a necessary factor for success, a basic ingredient, not an added bonus. He had once been considered the best in his field, and he was honest enough to admit that luck had played its part. And now he was lucky again with a different kind of luck. The girl was a prize, the kind of treasure he had won and lost in the past, the kind he had thought he would never have again. He knew exactly how lucky he was to have her, and he meant to keep her.

Even if it means driving down to Washington for the old man's birthday, he thought, sighing inwardly at the predictable pattern that he knew the visit would follow. Five hours driving down there in the camper, get there just in time for a big dinner with too much rich food and fancy wine, and then the old man beats me two games out of three in backgammon while the mother tries to pump Ginger about what's going on up here. Happy birthday, Jimbo; open up the presents, ooh and aah, have a nightcap, and then everybody up to bed, Ginger in her old room like a teenage kid and me in the guest room with dragons on guard outside just like they have no idea we've been living together for six months.

Still, he knew it was worth it as he watched her standing in front of the mirror smoothing her skirt. She ran a comb through her hair, then reached for her handbag and the large portfolio of sketches on the table. He jumped out of bed and wrapped himself in his robe.

"No breakfast?" he asked.

"No time, thanks to you." She put up her face to be kissed. "I'll get a container of coffee on the way."

"Hell of a way to start the day."

"It was a lovely way to start the day, much better than breakfast." They walked together to the door, and he helped her to undo the two cylinder locks, the deadbolt, and the Fox Police Bar jammed into a plate in the floor. With the door open, she kissed him again and said lightly, "Got any plans for today?"

"Plans?"

"You know. What are you doing today?"

"The same thing I do every day," he said in an even tone. "Nothing. A little jogging, that's all. Maybe buy some books. Why?"

"Just asking." Her voice was still light. "I don't know how you do it."

"What?"

"Nothing."

"It's easy. I'll show you the trick sometime."

"No thanks," she said, shaking her head. There was no frown on her face, but there might have been one in her voice. "I don't think I'd be very good at it."

"You could learn. Like I said, it's easy."

"Not for me. It's a knack you have to be born with."

"Ginger, get off it. All the way off. I'm not your father, and I'm not the kind of guy you grew up with. I never will be."

"I'm not trying to . . ."

"Sure you are, and this isn't the first time. Just remember, I don't have any fucking work ethic jammed up my ass. Where I come from a work ethic was something my father brought home in an envelope and gave to my mother to pay the rent."

"I know that, darling."

"Where you come from," he said, "they don't have pay envelopes stuffed with dollar bills and nickels and dimes. They have government checks and bank accounts, and people work hard because that's the Christian thing to do. Work ethic, shit. In my old neighborhood the people would laugh themselves silly if a guy worked when he didn't have to. He'd be a freak, a *pazzo*. Do I look like a *pazzo?*"

"Eddie, I don't even know what a *pazzo* is," she said quietly.

"Exactly. So don't say you know how it is, because you don't. The way it is, right now I'm doing nothing. Maybe someday I'll do something again, but not now. So get off it."

"All right, I'm off it," she said, and this time she was.

"Until the next time."

"There won't be any next time. I'm sorry."

"You always are," he said, but she looked so desolate that he gave her a smile to take the edge of it away. "Go ahead, get going; you'll be late."

When she was gone he closed and bolted the door, standing still and staring at it for a moment. Doing nothing, he thought. Almost a year now of doing nothing, and she thinks I enjoy it.

Christ, if she knew what I used to do she'd want me to keep on doing nothing for the rest of my life. Nothing at all.

And then, as it had every once in a while for the past year, the sadness came. It was a gentle sadness now, toned down by the months he had lived with it. And first the sadness had been raging and raw, an active grief which had come close to tearing him apart. But meeting Ginger had changed all that, for the sadness was nothing he could share with her, ever, and so he had buried it far from her sight. Perhaps being buried had muted the grief, but now whenever he was alone he was able to live with it, to bring it out of hiding on occasion and let it shape his mood. And there was still a sadness. He still grieved for the loss of the two people who once had been closest to him.

Loss? He allowed himself a mental chuckle` at the euphemism. You didn't *lose* them, Eddie. You lose car keys and a ball game. You lose time and you lose your way. But you don't lose people. You don't just lose the woman you love and the man who was your closest friend. You kill them, Eddie, you don't lose them. You killed Vasily, and you let Chalice kill herself. You lost a lot last year, but you didn't lose those people; you killed them.

It was a measure of his sadness that he did not stop to think that at the same time the two of them had also been trying to kill him. The sadness was still too strong for logic.

Still brooding, he checked out the refrigerator for something to eat. There was a container of milk, a carton of eggs, half a pizza covered with desiccated anchovies, a shelf full of beer, and two bags of fudge, one light and one dark, that he kept in the fridge because of the roaches. He poured a glass of milk and took it to the table with two pieces of fudge. A cockroach scurried away at his approach.

"Bloody roaches," he muttered. His hatred of the insects had been branded into him in childhood. "I've got a quarter of a million in the bank in Geneva, the same in the Bahamas, the house in Mexico, and I still have to live in a goddamn cockroach factory."

The sight of the cockroach forced thoughts of Mexico to his mind. The Mexican decision was one that he had faced daily for months, ever since he had met Ginger, and every day he postponed making the decision just one more time. The thought of the house in Atotonilco—the cool patios, the flowers, and the fountains—tugged at him. Mexico was security, Mexico was safety, Mexico was anonymity. That was where he belonged, he knew, not putting his ass on the line every time he walked the streets of New York.

I've gotten away with it so far, he thought. But how much longer? I keep this up and I have to get hit. All it takes is one slob from the old days, standing in a saloon when I walk in, and he thinks, *Hey, that's Eddie Mancuso! Where's the telephone, who's got a dime?* And I'm dead. Shit, I've got to get out of here, and Mexico is the only place to go.

That was his daily argument, and the rebuttal came back in its usual form.

You split for Mexico and you lose the girl. She'd never go with you, and even if she would, how do you explain it? How do you tell her the danger you're in? How do you tell her about Vasily and Chalice? How do you tell her about being on the run? You tell her that, or any part of it, and you lose her, anyway. So how do you win?

As always, the argument refused to be resolved. It was Mexico or the girl, as simple as that, and he was not prepared to walk away from her. Then, as always, the argument entered its third—and final—stage.

I'll just cool it for a while, he thought, slipping gratefully into the familiar compromise. Maybe after a while the heat will ease up. Maybe after a while I'll be able to tell her about things. Maybe after a while we'll be able to head down to Mexico together. Maybe.

He knew that he was kidding himself, that he would never tell her because the people who wanted his ass were not the kind who would ease up after a while. They were bureaucrats, gray and faceless and well accustomed to waiting.

Thoughts of Mexico still in his mind, he finished his breakfast and dressed for his morning run. As he dressed, he checked each item of clothing carefully before putting it on. There were running shoes and socks, a support, a sweat shirt, and a pair of shorts, all brand-name items bought in local shops, but he had spent many hours working on them in his makeshift lab in the camper. The work had been a foolish pandering to his pride, but after a year of enforced idleness, asking him not to use his hands that way would have been like asking an out-of-work musician to throw away his fiddle.

He put on the support first. The metal cup of the jock was made of a high-intensity aluminum that could withstand the blow of a sledgehammer.

He pulled on his running shorts. The rear pocket could be torn away, squeezed, and thrown to explode like a hand grenade.

He slipped on the sweat shirt. The left cuff contained a whiplike length of serrated steel that could cut to the bone.

He sat down to pull on his socks and his running shoes. The right shoe was quite ordinary. The toe cap of the left shoe contained an explosive device which, when the heel was stamped sharply, would fire a charge heavy enough to take off someone's leg ten feet away.

He stood up and looked at himself in the mirror. He didn't much like what he saw. He saw a man who now called himself Eddie Angelotti, a man who looked like an average New Yorker ready to go for a run but who was, in fact, a jogging arsenal of death and destruction. He also saw a man called Eddie Mancuso, who, until a year ago, had been recognized by the intelligence agencies of the world as the most inventive and prolific creator of the sophisticated weaponry known in the trade as UKDs, Unusual Killing Devices. And, in the end, he saw a man whose ass was up for grabs, whose body was wanted dead or alive by every major American intelligence organization. There was, he knew, an Open Warrant out on him. He had seen such things before, and knew what his own must look like.

FOR EYES OF:	*Closed list only*
SUBJECT:	*Edward Mancuso*
AGE:	*39*
LAST KNOWN ADDRESS:	*410 E. 82 St. New York, N.Y.*

DESCRIPTION: *Height: 5'8". Weight: 145–150 lbs.*
                                Eyes: Brown. Hair: Black. Skin: Olive. Distinguishing marks: Puckered scar right forearm; transverse furrow left thigh

WARRANT: *Clandestine apprehension or total extraction required*

EXPENSE AUTHORIZATION $50,000

BACKGROUND: Until recently Mancuso was a specialist in the manufacture of Unusual Killing Devices (UKDs) and was under continuous contract to the Agency for twenty years. During those years he was considered the leading expert in this field, his reputation being rivaled only by that of Soviet scientist Vasily Borgneff of the KGB (Ref. #U/7924). While employed by the Agency, Mancuso supplied UKDs to the Special Operations Section IV, Technical Services Division (TSD), then known intra-Agency as the Colonial Squad, now defunct. He is noted primarily for his development of the Mancuso Effect (quick-release neurotoxin heart-attack simulator) and the Mancuso antidote (tablet size and compress inhaler both). He has also been responsible for many other UKDs. Principal but partial list follows:

Mancuso barium chromate and boron fuse.

"Little Devil" blowback silencer for various types of pistols (self-destruct model).

Model R-84 anaphylactic-shock cartridge.

Mancuso felt-tip pen. Flair or Bic model containing tiger-snake venom.

Model R-24 miniature detonators.

Mancuso Blow-off Wheel Remover (for all model U.S. cars manufactured after 1967).

Mancuso's association with the Agency was terminated when he conspired with Soviet agent Vasily Borgneff (see above) to eliminate the entire Colonial Squad and its KGB counterpart, the Zhukovka O Group. The apparent motivation on the part of both Mancuso and Borgneff was a desire for nonprejudicial retirement from active service (nongrantable), but in Mancuso's case the most recent series-J psychoprofiles also indicate a deep-seated revulsion against any further involvement with death-dealing devices.

The Mancuso-Borgneff coup, which was almost entirely successful, resulted in the total elimination of the Colonial Squad, including its commanding officer, Colonel Frederick W. Parker, and his wife, Catherine (Chalice) Parker, known to have been Mancuso's mistress. The attempt fell short of total success only because of a falling-out between Mancuso and Borgneff. Mancuso then disappeared and has not been seen since.

SUMMARY: Mancuso may be described as being street-wise rather than well educated, with an intuitive rather than an empirical mind. Naturally brilliant in his own and closely related fields, he is indifferent to most others, a weakness which allows for various avenues of approach. Despite this, and despite his apparent distaste for his former specialty, he is certain to have maintained his expertise in the field.

He should be considered highly dangerous. Approach only with extreme caution.

While James Emerson was consulting the lost-and-found column, and Eddie Mancuso was fishing between Ginger's legs, and the KGB, time zones away, was toasting itself with Georgian wine, the Director of the Central Intelligence Agency, Harvey Christianson, was presiding over the weekly breakfast meeting of his deputy directors in the seventh-floor executive offices at Langley, Virginia. Sitting at the end of a long boardroom table that was dotted with coffee cups and the crusts of half-eaten pastries, Christianson buried a sigh as he listened to the babble of voices around him discussing the Soviet operation known only by its code name, *Homefire*.

Like other DCIs in the past, Christianson was a political appointee without any previous training or experience in intelligence work. The qualifications that had secured him his job were a hard-edged mind, an inquiring nature, a highly successful career as a manufacturer of electronic software, and an unshakable loyalty to the President and the party he represented. After three years in the job, he was sadly aware of how little these qualifications counted in the day-to-day operations of the Agency, and, equally sadly, he was aware of how much he was forced to depend on the opinions of his senior staff and deputy directors.

Homefire was a case in point. Christianson had more input on the subject than anyone else in Washington. Every intercepted reference to the operation crossed his desk, as did every analysis made by the evaluation teams and every prediction hypothesized as to the nature of the beast. But with all that information available to him, Christianson still had no more idea of what *Homefire* represented than did the lowliest clerk in Langley.

His deputies seemed equally bewildered, and the suggestions they just had offered had run the gamut of possibilities from the idiotic to the spine-chilling. The DD1, in charge of Operations, had suggested that it was the code name for a projected test of nuclear weapons in outer space. The DD2, in charge of Intelligence, was sure that it signaled a Communist coup d'etat in Egypt. The DD3, in charge of Science and Technology, was equally certain that a Soviet invasion of Yugoslavia was imminent; while the DD4, in charge of Support, had opted for a secret rapprochement between Moscow and Peking. Only Edwin Swan, the DD5, had not yet offered an opinion.

Christianson looked down the table at the impeccably dressed gentleman whose face was lined with age and whose patrician bearing and calculated disdain had been known to shrivel the ego of the most hardened bureaucrats. Edwin Swan held the position of DD5, or Deputy in charge of the Fifth Directorate; but his title was, in itself, misleading, for the organizational table of the Agency provided for only the four directorates represented by the other men at the meeting. The Fifth Directorate did not appear on the table, and, administratively, it could be said not to exist at all, since its funds were drawn from an unaccounted General Reserve. The Fifth Directorate was Edwin Swan's personal domain. Concerning itself with the entire spectrum of activities within the CIA as well as all other intelligence organizations, the Fifth was, in effect, an

Agency within and without the Agency and, as such, had been
a source of concern to every DCI under whom Swan had
served. Some of these Directors had accepted the situation with
resignation; others had fought to have the Fifth abolished, but
of these latter not one had ever come close to succeeding. In
Washington shorthand, Edwin Swan knew where the bodies
were buried, and he could not be touched. There was simply
too much political power and explosive information concentrated in the Fifth, and for years all of it had been under the control of Edwin Swan and his three associates in the directorate,
who were known collectively as the Gang of Four.

Edwin Swan, Gerard Krause, Peter Andriakis, and Joseph
Wolfe . . . labeling these men after the Chinese Gang of Four
had been the kind of joke that bureaucrats thrive on, but no one
within the Agency truly thought that there was anything humor-
ous about them. Like their Chinese namesakes, the members of
the American Gang of Four were looked upon with fear and respect, but with no affection at all. The four men were extraordinarily close. They shared the same political ideology, the same
contempt for the post-Watergate restrictions that the Congress
and the nation had placed upon the Agency. All of them were
products of those freewheeling days when the Agency had been
a power and a law unto itself, and all of them lived for the day
when that power would be returned to them.

At least I was able to break up that clique, thought Christianson, his eyes still on Swan.

One of his first moves after taking office had been to disman-
tle the Gang of Four. Peter Andriakis had been transferred out
of the Fifth Directorate to an obscure station in Corfu, where he
was now involved in the relatively unimportant work of running agents in Albania. Joseph Wolfe had been pried loose
from his Langley desk and returned to his previous station in
Barcelona, a distinct demotion. Gerard Krause virtually had
been put on the shelf with a transfer to Brissago on the Swiss-
Italian border, where he occupied himself with vetting police
reports on Milan's Red Brigade terrorists.

Only Swan had proved to be untouchable, retaining control
of his Fifth Directorate and all the powers that went with it. He

was the one man in Washington whom Christianson both feared and despised, and without realizing it he frowned as he saw that Swan was finally about to speak.

"I am an intuitive person," said Swan. His voice was mild, but it commanded immediate attention. The others at the table stopped their murmurings, and coffee cups clinked into saucers. "I admit it openly, I rely on my intuition. Some of you may see that as a sign of weakness, but I don't. In this world that we live in we operate so often in gray areas, without guidelines, that we are forced to depend on such things. In twenty years my intuition has rarely failed me."

Christianson nodded understandingly. "We all get those gut feelings sometimes."

Swan wrinkled his nose in distaste. It was not a phrase he would have chosen. He had little liking or respect for the Director, but there were conventions to be followed, and so he only murmured, "Yes, no doubt we do."

"And what does your intuition tell you?"

Swan stirred himself and said, "*Homefire* is like the three blind men with the elephant. The first one grasps the elephant's tail and thinks that he's caught a reptile. The second one bumps against a leg and deduces that he's walked into a tree. The third one feels the trunk and concludes that he's holding an accordion. The three men put their heads together and decide, on the basis of the evidence, that they've stumbled into an Italian wedding being held in a forest full of snakes. That's the way we are with our current enigma, gentlemen. Blind men playing with an elephant."

The DD1 sipped his coffee and asked archly, "And which part of the elephant have you gotten hold of?"

"No part at all. I'm trying to avoid the analogy, not conform to it. I've given our elephant a great deal of thought." Swan's tone of voice indicated that he engaged in thought the way other men engaged in prayer. "And I'm afraid that I can't agree with any of you. I don't see a breakthrough in weaponry, I don't see a deal with the Chinese, and I certainly can't give any weight to the Egyptian or the Yugoslav theory. Because, gentlemen, all of those possibilities have a purpose in and of themselves.

Think a moment. Our intercepts have told us that whatever the nature of *Homefire* as an operation, its principal effect—the one that the boys in the Kremlin are most interested in—will be in the field of pure propaganda. Isn't that so?''

The others nodded.

''Then,'' said Swan, ''isn't it possible that propaganda may be *Homefire*'s actual purpose . . . and not merely a significant result? Its purpose—'' he hesitated—''and, indeed, its nature.''

Swan sat back in his seat as the other four deputies looked at each other doubtfully. Christianson tapped the table lightly with a pencil. ''Propaganda,'' he said. ''Not military, not technical, not political. You're excluding those options?''

''I am.''

The DD2 asked, ''And you base this on your intuition?''

''My intuition, my experience, and one other factor. We live in a world of information where the battle is for the minds of men. Not for their weapons or their wealth, but for their minds and their loyalties. The one sure thing that we know about *Homefire* is that it is an operation on a grand scale, and in today's world the grand coup is the propaganda triumph, something that will sway the minds of millions of men.''

''And what form do you see this coup taking?'' asked the DD4.

Swan shrugged and made it an elegant gesture. ''I have no idea. Some massive form of disinformation, I suspect, some great lie magnified even more greatly through the lenses of the communications media.'' He leaned forward in his seat and spat out the next words. ''Something that will make us look like a pack of fools, no doubt, while we sit here dithering about coups in Cairo and similar nonsense.''

Voices rose in protest, particularly that of the DD2 who had been the author of the Egyptian option, and Christianson tapped his pencil again. ''Edwin, those are strong words when all you have is an intuition. But if you do feel that way about it, perhaps you wouldn't mind running up a position paper for us. Just the essentials of your theory and a suggested course of action.''

''A position paper.'' Swan's voice was cold. ''That's just

what we need, one more position paper on *Operation Home-fire*.''

''You prefer not to?''

''Oh no, I'll do it, all right. I've had a great deal of experience in preparing position papers for the occupant of this office, whoever he is at the time.''

''Thank you, Edwin.'' The Director once again buried a sigh, this time of relief. He looked at the clock on the wall. ''I think we can pass on to the Brazilian question now.''

Forty-five minutes later Swan entered his own office, also on the coveted seventh floor, and ordered his principal aide to set up a telephone conference call on the pry-proof network with his three colleagues in the so-called Gang of Four, a phrase he loathed. Once Andriakis was on the phone in Corfu, Wolfe in Barcelona, and Krause in Brissago, Swan filled them in on the essentials of the meeting he had just left. This was something he did regularly. The Gang of Four might be disbanded for the moment, but Swan made sure that his three associates, rusticating as they were in the boondocks, were kept current with Agency affairs. When he was finished, he asked them for their thoughts on *Homefire*.

Andriakis answered first. ''You're probably right,'' he said, ''you usually are. But don't count on any bright ideas from me. The trouble is, I'm too far away from the sources of information. I know that you try to keep us up to date, but it's not the same as being back at Langley. Sorry, Edwin, but I'm turning into a Greek yokel.''

''Gerard?''

''I'm in the same position as Peter, not enough input. All I do here is sit on my duff and rubber-stamp reports.''

''No ideas?''

''None.''

''Joseph?''

Known as the Chessmaster, Joseph Wolfe had the most incisive mind of the four, but he, too, refused to offer an opinion. ''The propaganda theory makes sense, but as to what form it will take . . .'' The others could almost hear his shrug over the telephone. ''I'm accustomed to solving problems laid out on a board. I can't play a game where I don't know the value of the pieces.''

There was silence on the line as Swan mentally damned Harvey Christianson for having condemned three of the finest minds in the Agency to virtual exile. At that moment he hated with equal passion Christianson for his mindless vendetta against the Fifth and all the reformers, liberals, and bleeding hearts in Congress who had cut off the Agency's legs at the knees.

Controlling his fury, he said, ''I understand, Joseph. I know it can't be easy for you, being stuck where you are. One of these days you three will be back here with me at Langley, I promise you that.''

Krause broke in. ''Does that mean that you're working on something? Something to do with *Homefire?*''

''It's possible. Solving that little puzzle might give me just the kind of leverage I need to make some changes around here. But it's too early to say. I'll be in touch with you all soon.''

With the conference call completed, Swan cleared his desk and descended to the parking lot where his car was waiting. His driver asked, ''Back to the Coolidge?''

''No, the Fun House first,'' said Swan, for this was his day to visit with Vasily Borgneff. The meeting was routine, a monthly visit that Swan had been making ever since the Russian had recovered from his wound and had been moved from the hospital in Bethesda to the safety of the Fun House. There he had been kept in storage, seven months now, while Swan debated what to do with him. The decision was not an easy one to make. Borgneff was a man whom all the world thought dead, including the Agency outside of the Fifth Directorate, including his own KGB bosses, and including Eddie Mancuso, the man who thought he had killed him.

We should have let him die, thought Swan. The dead are never a problem, but what do you do with the resurrected?

As his driver worked his way out of the downtown Washington traffic and onto Interstate 95, Swan opened the case on the seat beside him and took out the Borgneff file. He went through the pages carefully, at times making notes in the margins with a neat, almost fussy hand.

SUBJECT: *Vasily Borgneff*
REFERENCE: *U/7924*
POB: *USSR*
AGE: *47*
CLASSIFICATION: *Equivalent of US category ARM-I*

BACKGROUND SUMMARY: Borgneff was, for over twenty years, a contract employee of the Fourth Division of the Second Directorate of the KGB involved in the creation, invention, refinement, and manufacture of Unusual Killing Devices . . . UKDs. [Truly murderous stuff, Swan noted.] During this period of time he was considered to be one of the leading experts in the field, second only in reputation to the American Eddie Mancuso. [My opinion: just as good.] In fact, the careers of Borgneff and Mancuso followed parallel tracks that converged when both men decided to seek early retirement from their respective agencies, a request certain to be denied because of the highly sensitive nature of their work. They thereupon joined forces in a brilliantly planned operation designed to eliminate their immediate superiors, an action which, because of the cell-like structure of their organizations [since abandoned, at least by us], would have effectively freed them from both service and retribution.

OPERATIONAL SUMMARY: That these plans succeeded as well as they did is a tribute to the genius and determination of both Borgneff and Mancuso. The operation, in fact, would have been totally effective had there not been a falling out between the two men [over that bitch, Chalice Parker!] that eventually came to violence and resulted in Borgneff's being blinded in one eye and left for dead in a field near Williamsburg, Virginia [and with the Parker woman dead on the sands at Virginia Beach].

It was at this point that Mancuso disappeared from sight, and since then all attempts to locate him have been unsuccessful. He is now under open warrant.

Borgneff then passed into Agency hands and, after three

months of recovery and rehabilitation, has since been held in preventive detention pending disposition of his case. Repeated requests for information about Borgneff have been received through unofficial channels from the Second Directorate of the KGB. These requests have been ignored. [They'd just love to get their hands on him. They'd have his guts for garters.]

ACTION STATUS: On permanent hold pending decision by the Deputy Director, Five.

Swan closed the folder as his car swung up the exit ramp of the Interstate just below Woodbridge and crossed above the highway to follow the garishly painted red, white, and blue signs that advertised and pointed the way to the All-American Amusement Park, a recreational area that covered over one hundred acres of Virginia countryside. As the car pulled into the parking lot, he was pleased to note that even at this early hour the tourists were out in droves. All-American Amusements was one of the more profitable enterprises of the Fifth Directorate, and although its primary purpose was concealed, the fact that the cover operation made money as well was always a source of contentment to him.

Getting out of the car, he ignored the signs that invited the visitor to sample the wonders of the Jungle Safari, the Authentic Frontier Stampede and Rodeo, the Parachute Tower, and the South Seas Aquarium and made directly for the Fun House, a large and rambling structure with the façade of a decaying Scottish castle. He followed a group of tourists in, paying his way, and steadied himself to negotiate the Rolling Barrel entrance. Once through it, he bypassed the ride through the Tunnel of Love and strode confidently down the Ghostly Corridor impervious to the recorded moans, the rattling of chains, and the slamming of doors. He brushed by disembodied heads and hands that popped out at him and entered the Mirror Maze, composed of hundreds of sections of warped and twisted glass. Counting his steps and staring at the floor so as not to be confused by the reflected images, he made a sharp right turn through an apparently solid wall and then another turn that took him out of the traffic flow entirely. The last turn brought him face to face with a large, uniformed guard.

"Morning, Mr. Swan," said the guard, touching the peak of his cap with a forefinger and standing aside to let him pass.

"Good morning, Stein," said Swan, brushing by. A left turn brought him out of the maze and into the storage room of the Wax Museum, filled with statuary groupings that depicted some of the more celebrated slayings in the annals of history and crime. Lizzie Borden was there with her ax, Jack the Ripper in the act of disemboweling a London prostitute, the two little Princes about to be smothered in the Tower of London, and John Dillinger cut down by FBI tommyguns while the Lady in Red looked on, horrified . . . all of it set in glistening wax. At the end of the room two more guards, un-uniformed this time, passed him through a steel door that opened into a long, dank hallway. At the end of the hallway was still another door, this one with a speaker set beside it. Swan stood in front of the door without moving.

A voice from the speaker said, "Statement, please."

"This is the Deputy Director Five," said Swan, and repeated the phrase. He said it slowly and clearly so that the computerized impression-reader on the other side of the door would have no difficulty in identifying his voice pattern. After a moment the door slid open.

He stepped into a small anteroom where two portal guards greeted him. On the far side of the room was an antiquated freight elevator. On one side of the elevator was the door to a stairway. On the other side was the mouth of a curved aluminum chute, a relic of earlier days in the Fun House. In other earlier days, when he was younger, Swan had occasionally delighted in using the chute to slide to the floor below, just as the younger men on the staff did now. But nowadays he used the elevator, and moments later he was thirty feet below ground level under the Fun House in the depths of a bastion that served a multitude of functions for the Fifth Directorate.

One of those functions was the supervision of storage operations, the unofficial confinement of opposition agents being held for future use. It was, essentially, a tiresome and thankless job, particularly in the case of Vasily Borgneff, who was an active and tireless complainer. On this particular morning he was in top form.

"I hardly expect to be treated according to the rules of the Geneva Convention," he told Swan, "but may I ask if I am being used in some form of medical experiment?"

"Certainly not. Whatever gave you that bizarre idea?"

"The so-called food I've been getting. It occurred to me that your people might be trying to determine how long a civilized man can manage to exist on pig swill."

"I'm sorry that you don't like the food, but we do the best we can," said Swan. "I'd hardly call it swill."

"You would if you had to eat it."

Swan made a note in a small black book. "I'll have it looked into. Any other complaints?"

"Yes, these cretins of yours who guard me. Not one of them plays chess, and half of them move their lips when they read. Really, Swan, where do you recruit such people?"

"They weren't chosen for their intellects," Swan admitted. "I'm afraid you'll just have to put up with them. Any other complaints?"

"Does a mushroom complain in the cellar?" Borgneff's voice was high and angry. "I haven't seen the sun in seven months. I'm going out of my mind with boredom."

"I thought you seemed a trifle grumpy today."

"At least you could let me upstairs to play in the Fun House."

"You're not supposed to know about that," Swan said reprovingly. "Aren't you getting your sunlamp treatments?"

"Sunlamps just make me feel more like a mushroom."

The room was large and comfortable, with an oversupply of sofas and chairs and thick cushions. The walls were bare but clean, and the blank eye of a television set stared out of the corner. Borgneff paced nervously from one side of the room to the other, his hands clasped behind his back. He was a hawklike man, tall and stooped. His face was long, the features drawn fine, and he wore a black patch where his left eye once had been.

Swan sat in one of the overstuffed chairs, his legs crossed casually, an untouched cup of coffee steaming on the table beside him. "Boredom is concomitant to captivity," he noted. "Better bored than dead, no?"

"Not necessarily." Borgneff turned on him with a savage look. "Swan, I respect you the way one respects a worthy opponent. So I mean no disrespect when I point out that you are an elderly and proper gentleman, and therefore you probably don't know what it's like to be without a woman for seven months. Or if you ever did, you've forgotten."

"I can assure you that there is nothing wrong with my memory."

"Seven months! I'm not even counting the three months in the hospital. I'll give you those. I admit it, I couldn't have used a woman then under any circumstances. But seven months more? Really, Swan, for a man of my temperament this is impossible."

"Temperament," Swan murmured, amused by the word. "You should have said something sooner. I'm sure I'll be able to arrange something."

"You'll arrange nothing," Borgneff exploded. He took three quick steps and stood over Swan, almost threateningly. Behind a door, an unseen guard stirred and then subsided. "Do you think I want one of your tame birdbrains, all tits and ass? Someone to drain me dry and keep me happy?"

"We have some excellent connections," Swan said stiffly.

"I don't want a connection, I want a woman. I want to sit across a table from her and toast her eyes with wine. I want to share a meal with her, and music, and starlight. I want to trade dreams with her."

"Nothing more?"

"Of course. Then I want to fuck her to exhaustion. But only then, not before."

"You're not talking about a woman," Swan pointed out. "You're talking about freedom."

Borgneff ran his fingers through his hair nervously. "Yes,

I suppose I am." He sat down abruptly, leaning forward. "Look, Swan, please talk to me frankly. What sort of a future do I have? Will I ever get out of here?"

Swan put a finger along the side of his nose. "You are rather a problem for us, you know. We don't know quite *what* to do with you. We could trade you back to your own people, of course, but . . ."

"I would die very painfully," Borgneff said simply.

"No doubt you would. But as I was saying, there is no one that your people have whom we want right now. A few dissidents, one or two Jews, but no one important. The other alternative would be to put you to work for us."

Borgneff sat up, alerted. "You mean you haven't replaced Eddie?"

"No one could replace Eddie Mancuso. Except you, of course. But the truth of it is, we've more or less gone out of the death-and-destruction business. Changing times, you know. We're quite a respectable outfit now."

Borgneff grinned knowingly. "The Agency itself, perhaps, but not the Fifth Directorate."

Swan's hand described a languid acknowledgment. "Oh, we still have our moments. Individual jobs, one-time extractions. But nothing of a volume that would warrant your creative talents. No, I'm afraid we'd have nothing for you at all."

"So I sit here until I rot," Borgneff said bitterly.

Swan shrugged. "I certainly don't want it that way. Perhaps someone will come up with an idea that will make you useful to us. Unless that happens . . ." He shrugged again.

"I thought you might get around to that." Borgneff nodded slowly. "You'd sanction me? Just like that?"

Swan looked hurt. "My dear Borgneff, you know how it is. We spent a great deal of money to keep you alive, but the cost of your upkeep is staggering. All these men, and the supplies. We have to answer to auditors, you know. Changing times, as I said before. It's a whole new world out there."

Borgneff was silent for a long moment, his eyes fixed on a

point above Swan's head. Then he said slowly, "What if I could give you Mancuso?"

"What makes you think that we want him?"

"You want him, all right. Just like my people want me."

"Perhaps we do, but this sounds like desperation. You have no more idea of where Eddie is than we do, and we've had an intensive search going for almost a year."

"Any leads?"

"Nothing," Swan admitted.

Mexico, thought Borgneff. If he's not in the States, he's in Mexico. He has to be. He's probably down there right now in that house that's half mine, sitting in the garden and drinking margaritas. No one knows about that house but Eddie and me. "I'm not surprised," he said casually. "You won't find him, not the way you're going about it."

"And you could?"

"You have to remember that no one knows Eddie the way I do." Borgneff stood up and started to pace again. "There was a time when we were like brothers. Closer than brothers. I know what his reactions are, his instincts. I know what trail he takes in the jungle. Yes, I could find him for you. Given the time and the support, I could find him."

"It's a thought. It's something to consider." Swan looked at his watch and stood up. "It's nothing I could agree to on the spot, but I'll think about it. Right now I have to get back to town."

"When can you give me an answer? Next visit?"

"Perhaps sooner than that." He smiled, a bleak attempt at cordiality. "And now I really must be going."

"You'll do something about the food?"

Swan tapped the notebook in his breast pocket. "As I promised."

"Please don't forget. Frozen fish fingers lose their charm after a while."

"Frozen fish . . . ?"

"And canned chili."

"Good God!"

"And something called toaster waffles."

"Borgneff, I had no idea." Swan was truly shocked. "I'll take care of it at once."

Chapter 5

Anya Ignatiev rose from her chair as Emerson came through the door. She came around the desk with a smile on her lips and her arms extended. She stood off from him, examining him with her head cocked over to one side.

Finally she said, "Of course, I've seen your pictures in the papers, but I had to be sure. You're still my Yuri, no mistake about that. And now you're supposed to tell me that I haven't changed a bit. It would be a lovely lie, and you really should say it."

"Actually, you look much as I remember you."

Emerson chose his words carefully, a compound of truth and gallantry. Obviously, this woman bore only a fleeting resemblance to the girl who had been his lover so many years ago in the valley of the Elbe River, but, given her age as he knew it to be, she was still remarkably well kept and attractive. The lazy violet eyes still shone, the full lips pouted, and the contours of the opulent body were only slightly softened by the years.

She must be in her late fifties, he thought, and she looks about forty.

As if reading his thoughts, Anya laughed delightedly. "America helps keep Joy Mackenzie looking young. The health spas, the cosmetics, things like that, you know?"

Emerson neither knew nor cared, but he kept his voice neutral. "How long have you been Joy Mackenzie?"

"Long enough, long enough," she said vaguely, looking around the room. "I guess you might say that this place helps to keep me young as well."

It was, Emerson decided, one hell of a setting for a clandestine meeting. The back room of the House of Joy was filled with stacks of pornographic magazines and books, cartons of video cassettes, cardboard display panels touting the joys of hand-held vibrators, rubber and plastic dildoes, tubes of creams and balms, jars of hormone energizers, vials of musk-ox oil, and leather devices the uses of which he could only guess at. Outside, in the front room, the same merchandise was offered to a steady stream of customers, along with ten booths featuring X-rated loop films and a glassed-in enclosure that framed the antics of three girls dancing in topless, bottomless, absolutely nothingness.

Anya had followed the movements of his eyes, and she laughed. "It's a touch on the flamboyant side, of course, and very *nikulturni,* but it makes an effective cover. Totally secure, too." She still watched him closely and finally nodded with some touch of apparent sympathy. "This must be something like a dream to you," she said.

"That's too mild a word." A fist clenched in his stomach, and he fought down a spasm. "That notice in the paper. It was like being hit over the head with a club."

"Did you think we had forgotten about you?"

I was sure as hell hoping you had, he thought bitterly, but he kept his voice bright and enthusiastic. "No, I never lost faith. Remember, I was trained to expect a long wait."

"Even thirty-five years?"

He forced himself to nod soberly. "Even that."

She beamed her approval. "Exactly as we expected. I want you to know that none of us ever doubted that, Yuri."

"If you please, I prefer the name James Emerson."

She looked at him questioningly. "James Emerson died thirty-five years ago."

"And the name has been mine ever since. I'm accustomed to it."

"I can understand that. But to me you will always be Yuri, the boy who meant so much to me."

"That boy is dead, Anya. He died the same day that Emerson did.'' He willed himself to appear eager. ''Enough of the past; tell me about the future.''

''It's a very bright future, Colonel Volanov.''

''I really do prefer . . .'' He stopped. ''Did you say Colonel?''

''I am instructed to inform you that on December tenth of last year you were promoted colonel.''

Emerson remembered that it was the custom of the secret service to issue periodic, but secret, promotions to agents on long-term field assignment, but it was strange to realize that through all the years he had been progressing in rank.

''First, I have several procedural points to cover,'' said Anya. ''I am instructed to inform you that your accrued salary for the various ranks held while on service in the field, together with hazard pay for external service, plus adjustments to conform to the Uniform Pay Code of 1957 . . .''

''For God's sake, Anya.''

''. . . have been deposited regularly in the Vneshtorgbank at Serpukhovsky Val Eight in Moscow. Do you wish to know the current balance?''

He shook his head. ''I don't believe any of this. I don't even know what a ruble is worth.''

Anya went on relentlessly. ''I am further instructed to inform you that on the first of January 1971, you were named a Hero of the Soviet Union. The award was made secretly, and the citation was recorded in your file. Congratulations, Colonel.''

Emerson only nodded as he tried to get a grip on a whirling reality.

''I regret that I must now inform you of the death of your parents,'' said Anya, the mood of her voice changing to suit the situation.

''When?''

''Your father in 1968, your mother three years later. Both of natural causes.''

''I see.'' The news did not move him. Years ago he had assumed the probable dates of their deaths and had made his private farewells to them then. ''Go on.''

"I also regret to inform you of the death of your brother, Anatoli Ivanovich. An industrial accident six years ago."

He tried to summon up an image, but all he could remember was a pale-haired child playing with a battered wooden wheel, dragging it around through the garden dirt.

"Anya, this is all meaningless to me, all this family crap, the medals and promotions. What do you want?"

"Nothing much," she said lightly. "I have one further item. I am instructed to convey to you the fraternal greetings of Colonel Andrei Petrovich, Major Boris Radichek, and Captain Pavel Kolodny."

"Thank you," he said absently. "Please convey my greetings in return."

"That won't be necessary." There was mischief in her eyes. "You'll be able to greet them yourself very shortly."

He did not trust himself to speak. He nodded for her to continue.

"Yuri, you should see your face," she said delightedly. "You've guessed, haven't you?"

He managed to say, "I'm not much good at guessing games. What is it that you're trying to say?"

"I'm trying to give you some very good news. I'm trying to tell you that you've been ordered home."

"Home?"

"Home. To the Soviet Union."

"You can't be serious."

"Those are your orders, to return to the Soviet Union. Sometime next week you will be smuggled aboard a Polish freighter in New York Harbor. The ship will leave the next morning for Gdansk. From there you will be flown to Moscow, and let me tell you that I envy you very much."

"Envy? Yes, of course." Moscow, he thought dully. A two-room apartment and a drafty *dacha* near Zhukovka. Cocktails with Kim Philby and all those other dreary traitors. He forced himself to be calm. "Let me understand this. You're activating me after all these years just to send me back to Russia?"

"You sound disappointed."

"No, no, not at all," he assured her, at the same time

conjuring up visions of black bread and herring, lumpy shoes and ill-fitting suits. "It's just that I expected something different."

"An espionage assignment?"

He shrugged. "After all, that was what I was trained for. I don't mean to question orders, Anya, but . . ."

"You don't have to be so respectful," she said, laughing. "First of all, we're old lovers; and second of all, you're now my superior officer."

No more Baltimore Orioles, he thought. Say good-bye to the Washington Redskins. He realized how frivolous it seemed, on the surface, but what were the roots of patriotism if not the love of childhood's foods and home teams? Pulling himself together, he said, "In that case I'll speak freely. This just doesn't make any sense. Why send me back to Moscow when I could be so much more valuable here?"

"I can assure you that there are reasons, excellent reasons." She leaned forward excitedly. "Look, Yuri, I admire what you're saying. You're willing to pass up a chance to go home, and that's wonderful, admirable. It's the kind of devotion that makes our service what it is."

"It's only common sense," he interjected.

"From your point of view, yes, but you don't see the whole picture, and I can't tell you everything I know. But take my word for it. Moscow is where you belong right now. And Moscow is where you are going."

And may God have mercy on my soul, he thought. He squared his shoulders and arranged his features carefully, hoping for a noble expression. "I am, of course, prepared to do my duty. If my orders are to return, then that's what I shall do. But I must tell you, Anya, as an old friend, that I cannot see the slightest sense in it. What earthly good will it do for Yuri Volanov to go back to Moscow after all these years?"

"None."

"I beg your pardon?"

"It would have no value at all. That's just the point you're missing. Yuri Volanov isn't going back to Moscow."

He stared at her narrowly, uncomprehending.

"James Emerson is going to Moscow," she said. "The Assistant Secretary of Defense for Air is about to defect to the Soviet Union." She smiled triumphantly. "Now is it clear to you?"

Suddenly it was all very clear, indeed.

"Aside from the shock you must feel about me," said Emerson bitterly, "you must realize that it's the answer to *Operation Homefire*. It has to be. I'm it. Don't you agree?"

"I daresay you're right," said Edwin Swan. "Everything seems to point that way. James, for God's sake, sit down and compose yourself. You're making me nervous with your pacing."

The DD5 sat back in his chair and drew on his pipe. A longtime widower, he had no need for an elaborate establishment, and so he kept himself tidily in a modest suite at the old and respectable Coolidge Hotel. The sitting room of the suite had been tailored over the years to his personality: large, overstuffed chairs; Edwardian prints; a silver tea service on the sideboard; and over it all an aura of genteel mustiness that defined the atmosphere.

"Have you had your lunch?" Swan asked. "The kitchen could do something quickly."

"Couldn't possibly." Emerson waved aside the thought of food. "A small cognac might help."

"On the sideboard, as you know."

Emerson splashed some cognac into a glass and forced himself to sip slowly, striving to emulate the older man's casual air. He had just poured out to his friend the secret he had preserved for thirty-five years. He had held back nothing; he had told it all, going back as far as his Leningrad childhood, the NKVD school at Gaczyna, the massacre at the River Elbe, the subsequent years of deception, the awakening message in this morning's paper, and the meeting at the House of Joy. He had opened the bag and spilled it all out on the table in an orgy of confession—omitting only one thing.

"And then, after Anya Ignatiev had finished with him in the

barn, and I knew the essential details about Point Balboa, the boy was shot and killed."

"Twenty Americans all told," Swan murmured.

"Yes. Twenty."

What difference then if he, the new James Emerson, né Yuri Volanov, had pulled the trigger to dispatch his namesake? Twenty American soldiers had died that awful spring day on the Elbe. He was as responsible for the deaths of the other nineteen as he was for the boy born in Point Balboa. It had been an act of war—an undeclared war, then, but nonetheless real. That's how he had thought of it, if at all; since then he had not thought of it at all, until now. He had been visited by no nightmares or daytime demons. The accumulation of the years, all thirty-five of them, had washed over him as the waters of Lethe and allowed him to forget.

Until now . . .

Throughout the recital Swan had done nothing more than ask an occasional question. He had shown no anger, only a kind of resigned acceptance. It was almost as if he were listening to the confession of some embezzlement or a sexual aberration.

"You're taking this too well," said Emerson, setting down his cognac. "I expected a different reaction."

"Outrage? Moral indignation?"

"Yes. Surely this can't be all that common an experience for you."

"Not this particular experience . . . no, not at all. After all, how many old and trusted friends am I likely to have who are serving officers in the KGB?"

" 'Old and trusted friends,' " Emerson repeated, with a grimace. "So, among other things, you feel personally betrayed."

"Let's not bother with words like that." Swan waved smoke away from his eyes. "Over the years I've had the sad experience of viewing every kink and quirk of the human condition in this job. I've dealt with every sort of man and woman that the good Lord created, and some, no doubt, who managed to escape His attention entirely. Once you've done that, you tend to grow tolerant of other people's weaknesses."

"A saintly attitude. It does you credit. You always were a saintly sort of man."

"Don't crowd me, James. I'm not showing everything I feel."

"Ah, so you *are* outraged. That's much more human. And better," he admitted, "for me."

"No. Outraged is not correct. Disgusted is more the word."

"Because of the twenty men," Emerson muttered.

"That was wartime. You didn't kill them. No . . . I'm disgusted because you didn't come to me years ago with this."

Emerson shook his head. "That's easy to say now. You see, there was always a chance that they'd leave me alone."

"There was never any chance of that, and you were a fool to think that there could be." Swan's lips were drawn in a thin line. Then the line eased, and he sighed. He tapped his teeth with the stem of his pipe. "What puzzles me is why you ran right out and made that damn telephone call. What was the hurry?"

Emerson looked surprised. "It never occurred to me not to."

"Training?"

A slow nod. "It sounds odd, but yes. Even after all these years. My teachers at Gaczyna were quite thorough." He closed his eyes and recited, "*Awakening procedure requires that the field agent respond to the request for a* treff *by calling the designated telephone number without delay.*" He opened his eyes and repeated, "Without delay."

"I see." The pipe stem went tap, tap, tap. "And so you went trotting off to your *treff* like a good little boy, ready to give the Russkies whatever they wanted."

"I gave them nothing, Edwin. That's my point. That's why I feel justified in coming to you."

"You get no points from me for that. They didn't ask you for any hard information."

"Not in that sense, no. It would have been simpler if they had. My decision would have been more apparent to everyone, including you. But you're right—I came to you after the fact." He tried to smile. "There's a consolation, of course. If I'd come to you before I knew what they wanted, you wouldn't know I was the key to *Homefire*."

Swan nodded, conceding the point, his calm demeanor masking an inner joy that his estimate of the forthcoming coup had been so accurate. "Amazing," he murmured. "The defection of a high-level American official to the Soviet Union. The first time ever! An American Kim Philby! I remember," he mused, "how the Brits suffered over that one. Wouldn't the world laugh now—at *us*. It would have been a magnificent stroke if Moscow could have pulled it off." More sharply, he said to Emerson, "How was it left between you and the Ignatiev woman?"

"Another *treff* on Monday to make arrangements for my . . . departure. I gave her my assurances of complete cooperation. I was very convincing."

"And then you came straight to Uncle Edwin. Why?"

Emerson sat up straight in his chair. "That should be obvious. I'm an American. This is my country. I have no intention of going to Moscow. I almost laughed in her face when she said she was sending me home. What the hell does she know about my home? I *am* home."

"Yes, of course you are," Swan said softly. "Would you care for some tea?"

"No, I couldn't."

"It's no bother, you know. I'd simply call down for it."

"Edwin, my stomach is so jumpy today that I can't handle anything. I mean, can you imagine me living in the Soviet Union? Living in a tiny apartment, eating black bread and herring? It's laughable, just the thought of it."

"Our Russian friends dine very well at a certain level," Swan observed. "And you're a Hero of the Soviet Union. I should think they'd let you skip the herring."

"You know exactly what I mean. It's not my way of life."

"Quite. Am I to take it, then, that you decline to return to the Soviet Union for reasons of culinary preference?"

"For God's sake," Emerson growled, "stop trying to make a joke of it. Can't you see how I feel?" He got up from his chair and paced across the room, turned at the window and paced back with his head sunk low and his hands clasped behind his back.

"I didn't have the good fortune to be born in this country," he said slowly, "and so I was never exposed in my childhood to the myths and the half-truths that children are taught about America the Beautiful. Instead, I came here as a young man trained in the ways of the country by the NKVD. In many ways they trained me well. They taught me to talk, act, think, and dress American. But in other ways their teaching was faulty. They taught me that the drive to open the American West was a perfect example of Yankee imperialism, but they never told me about the pioneer spirit that made it possible. They taught me all about the oppressed minorities, but they never told me about the immigrant parents who slaved in sweatshops so that their children could be doctors and judges. They taught me about the corruption of the American system of government—the bribes and the payoffs, the political deals—but they never told me that that system, as corrupt and as inefficient as it can be at times, is still the safest and sanest way for men to govern themselves. They taught me nothing about the essence of this country. I had to find that out myself, I had to rediscover America, and as I did I came to know her as no other person possibly could. No native-born American certainly, not even an immigrant searching for streets paved with gold, could ever . . ."

He stopped and looked around helplessly.

"Say love," Swan said softly. "It's quite an acceptable word."

Emerson nodded. "Thank you. Yes, love. No one else could ever love this country the way I do, because no one ever came to it the way I did. Determined to destroy it. And now, thirty-five years later, I am determined never to leave it. And I won't. You're quite right, Edwin; it isn't just the herring and the black bread. I may be a serving officer in the KGB, but for the last thirty years I've been just as good an American as you, no matter how I started out."

"Yes, of course. No one doubts that." Swan took a snowy

handkerchief from his breast pocket and blew his nose. He took his eyeglasses off, stared at them against the light, then began to polish them vigorously. "Sit down, James, please."

Emerson seated himself and said with composure, "Which is why I've come to you."

Swan replaced his glasses and stared at him intently. "This really isn't my pigeon, you know. You really should have gone to the FBI."

"One hears certain things," Emerson said vaguely. "You apparently have a rather unusual latitude within the Agency."

"God bless the Washington rumor industry. I suppose you mean that Gang of Four nonsense that people are always talking about."

"I've heard the phrase used," Emerson admitted.

"There's not much to it."

Emerson shrugged. "It really doesn't matter," he said. "I didn't want to go to a stranger. I came to you because in all this world—and I don't mean only Washington—you are the man I most trust and respect. I need your help. If you can't give that to me, then I need your advice."

"I'm flattered."

"Wouldn't dream of taking my business elsewhere," said Emerson, trying to smile. "Perhaps I will have that tea, after all."

Swan unfolded himself from the chair with an old man's economy of motion and went to the telephone table. He spoke softly into the instrument, then came back and settled himself in again. "You realize that you're in a devil of a mess, don't you?"

Emerson made a steeple of his fingers, lacing them together and staring at Swan over the tip of the spire. "I'm a sleeper, Edwin, not a spy. Since the war I've done nothing illegal except for the manner in which I came into this country. But you're right—it's a hell of a mess."

"I didn't mean with us so much. I meant with your own people."

"I prefer not to think of them as *mine*."

"As you wish. However . . ." He was interrupted by a knock

on the door. "Yes, come in." The door opened, and a liveried waiter wheeled in a table set for tea. "Just leave it, Bernard, we'll help ourselves."

When the waiter was gone, he said, "James, would you mind pouring? These hands of mine . . ." His voice trailed off into an embarrassed silence; then he spoke again. "I'm sure I don't have to tell you about the long arm of the KGB. They want a high-level American defector, someone they can parade before the cameras of the world as living proof of the desirability of the Soviet system. They want you back in Moscow badly. It's my belief they'll stop at nothing to get you there. Do you understand?"

"Yes, I do. That's one of the reasons I came to you. Lovely tea. Is it Cloud Mist?"

"Dragon Well. They keep it for me here. What did you have in mind, James?"

"Immunity, plus a new name, new papers, plastic surgery if necessary, relocation, the whole package. Your people have done it before."

"Not as often as you might think. And what do we get in exchange for all this?"

"Edwin, I've already given you the connection with Anya Ignatiev. Anything else I know is thirty-five years out of date. I'm not an active agent—I'm a sleeper. What you're really getting is a successful conclusion to *Homefire*. Isn't that enough?"

"It's considerable," Swan conceded.

"Does this mean that you'll deal with me?"

Swan thought for a moment. "Yes," he said. "I'll deal. I'll get you out of your mess."

Setting down his cup, Emerson let out a deep breath. "I never doubted that you'd help, but I must admit that I'm relieved. I came to the one man I can trust. You've given me a good birthday present."

Swan's pale eyes glittered behind the heavy glasses. "You realize, of course, that you'll have to tell Rusty."

"Tell her what?"

Swan looked surprised. "About yourself, of course. Everything you've just told me."

"Edwin, she knows. She's known for years."

Swan's face went blank with amazement. "You *told* her?"

"Many years ago, just after we were married." Emerson wiggled uncomfortably in his seat and looked away. "You know how it is with Rusty and me. We have a good marriage; we trust each other. I had to tell her. I couldn't have lived with it otherwise."

"And so you broke your cover and told your wife! Good Lord, James . . . what a rotten spy you would have made! What was her reaction?"

"What you'd expect. She felt betrayed, deceived. It was a bad time for us both, but after a while she learned to live with it. Just as I did."

"And she's kept the secret all these years," Swan marveled.

"That's right."

"Amazing. All these years, that remarkable woman I've admired so much . . . all along she knew that you . . ." He broke off, shaking his head.

Emerson said anxiously, "There won't be any trouble for her, will there? I mean, I'm assuming that whatever you do for me you'll be doing for her as well."

"No, no trouble." Swan thought for a moment. "No, I can assure you of that. Wherever you go, Rusty will go with you. That's a promise."

"We only have until Monday. Can you work that quickly?"

"Just barely. We have the holiday weekend to contend with, but we'll manage." Swan rose, an indication that it was time to leave. "I'll be in touch with you within twenty-four hours. Right now, I want you to go home and stay home. Don't leave the house under any circumstances. You understand?"

"Perfectly."

"Twenty-four hours. You'll hear from me by tomorrow evening. Until then, your job is to stay calm and leave things to me."

"I will. I'm placing myself in your hands, Edwin."

Emerson rose. It was not the custom of the two men to shake

hands, but they did so now, firmly. At the door Emerson hesitated, then turned.

"Edwin, I have one thing more to say to you. We've known each other many years. I flatter myself that we have always been far more than business associates, and in the past twenty years a good deal more than close friends. I've treated you in many respects like a father . . . so I understand a bit of how you must feel right now. What I'm trying to say . . ."

"There's no need for that," Swan managed to interrupt. "Sons are born to disappoint their fathers. You lived by your lights, and in the end you acted honorably. There's something to be proud of in that."

"Thank you." Emerson's voice was husky. "I've never done anything to harm my country. You know that, don't you?"

"I do," Swan assured him. "And the country is in your debt for what you are doing now. Think about it that way, if you can."

"I will. And I thank you for saying it." Emerson blinked his eyes rapidly, then shook his head. "I'll wait to hear from you."

Swan closed the door behind him. He went back to the tea table and poured what was left in the pot into his cup. The tea was cold. He grimaced and set it aside, then picked up the scrambler telephone, a duplicate of the one in his office, and made arrangements for a conference call with Wolfe, Andriakis, and Krause. Once all three were on the line, he gave them a precise report of his conversation with Emerson.

When he was finished, Andriakis whistled softly and said, "Christ, what a beautiful scheme."

"If it had worked," Krause pointed out.

Wolfe simply said, "Congratulations, Edwin."

"It's too early for that," said Swan. "Let's examine the ramifications. First of all, it's clear that the man cannot be allowed to return to Moscow. That leaves us several alternatives. The first is to let him hang. Not literally, but turn him over to the FBI and let him stand trial."

"Impossible," said Wolfe. "That would be almost as bad as letting them get away with it. The Assistant Secretary of Defense is a Soviet agent . . . can you imagine what the media would make out of that? We'd be doing the Russians' work for them."

The other two made noises of agreement.

"The next alternative," Swan continued, satisfied, "is to give Emerson what he wants. Asylum and a new identity. Any comments?"

This time it was Andriakis who responded, his voice low and thoughtful. "Those change-of-identity deals look good on paper, but you can't hide a man from the KGB forever. I mean, he's not a small-time hood. We'd be spending the rest of our lives keeping Emerson's cover for him. It's not worth it."

"I agree with you, " said Swan. "He was naive to think that we'd do it. But that's the point. He *is* naive. Which leaves the final alternative."

"We're wasting time," said Krause.

Swan's voice was reproving. "I'm trying to do this in an orderly fashion. Let's examine the possibilities."

"They've already been examined," said Wolfe. "With due respect, Edwin, Gerard is right; we're wasting time. We can't let the man go back to Moscow, we can't put him on trial, and we can't let him loose. The man has to be sanctioned."

"You'll never get approval from Christianson," Andriakis warned. "We're supposed to be out of that business."

"That's Edwin's department. He can handle it."

Swan sighed. "Yes, it would have to be kept within the Fifth. I could present it to Christianson . . . afterwards. A fait accompli. An accident, of course, or something like that." He hesitated, then said, "Do I hear any comments?"

There was silence on the line.

Swan said, "Under the circumstances, I'd like to hear your actual approval or disapproval of this project. Joseph?"

"Extraction," said Wolfe.

"Gerard?"

"Extraction," echoed Krause.

"Peter?"

"Just make sure it looks good," Andriakis said.

"Very well," said Swan. "I'll report to you all when the extraction has been concluded."

He hung up the telephone and sat staring for quite a while at the door through which Emerson had passed, and only then did he realize that he had not wished his old friend a happy birthday.

"Happy birthday," he muttered to himself. "Happy birthday, you fool."

After Emerson had left the back room of the House of Joy, Anya Ignatiev sat silently at her desk, the only sound the percussive beat of the disco music from the dance enclosure in the front room. She lit a cigarette, screwing up her eyes against the smoke, leaned back in her swivel chair, and stared at the ceiling. She seemed to be waiting for something. When nothing happened, she glanced at a door in the corner of the room and said impatiently, "Sasha, come in here, for God's sake."

The door opened, and a slim, blond man with pale gray eyes came into the room. In his mid-thirties, his peaked eyebrows and elfin features made him look much younger, and his lemon-colored slacks and tank top showed off a smooth musculature. He walked gracefully, almost gliding in quick, pointed steps. He did not prance and he did not swish, but he very obviously did not prance or swish.

"Well, what do you think of him?" Anya asked.

"Absolutely yummy, Mummy." Sasha smiled at her mockingly. "He must have been a knockout back in the Dark Ages when he did you."

"Don't talk that way." Anya said it automatically, as if she had said the words many times before. "He's still a very handsome man."

"Handsome? Come on, Mother darling, you were wetting your panties just sitting there talking to him. I could see you on the screen trying to push out those remarkably preserved tits."

He moved behind her and put his hands on her shoulders. "You could strain your back that way, you know. Want me to give you a rub?"

"Fool!" She twisted around and knocked his hands away. "Isn't he a remarkable man, to have done what he did? Thirty-five years!"

Sasha lowered his eyes in mock humility. "Yes, you're right. He's a remarkable man. He's a father to be proud of."

"Sweetheart, I never said that." Anya looked at him reproachfully. "I only said that he *might* be your father."

"Either him, or the real Emerson."

She managed to look prettily confused and even to blush slightly. "It could have been either."

"So you've told me." He smiled at her thinly. "I suppose that makes me unique. The man with two fathers. At least, I assume it was only two. For all I know, you were balling half the Red Army in those days."

"Sashinka, I'm warning you—"

"Well, Mother, you must admit that you did have one hell of a war. Other people got medals and ribbons, but all you got out of it was the crabs. And me."

Anya looked at her son thoughtfully. There were times when she regretted having told him about the two men named James Emerson. When he was a child she had let him believe that his father had died a soldier's death in the Great Patriotic War, but as he grew older the urge to tell him the truth grew obsessive. When he was a grown man, and himself a contract agent for the KGB, she had finally felt him old enough to know.

She shook her head sadly. "I didn't have to tell you, but I did. Give me credit for that much."

"Bullshit, sweetie, you were just trying to show me how liberated you were back in the days when the nice girls kept their legs crossed."

"Sasha!"

He pulled himself up to a position of stiff attention and saluted several times rapidly. "Yes, Mother. Yes, Comrade Major."

He let his body sag into a lounging position, resting one hip against her desk. Anya shrugged helplessly and laughed.

"You're impossible," she said. "Stop clowning, and tell me what you think of our Mr. Emerson."

"*Your* Mr. Emerson," he said pointedly. "Personally, I wouldn't touch him with a ten-foot pole. That is, if I had a ten-foot pole, which I don't." He suddenly dropped the bantering tone and looked down at his fingernails, studying them carefully. "I suppose you'll want the usual surveillance on him? Four-man teams around the clock?"

"What on earth for?"

"In case he decides against an ocean voyage, obviously."

"That's absurd," she said, shocked. "You're talking about Yuri Volanov. A loyal, dedicated officer!"

"Is that who he is? Listen, *babushka,* you're thinking with your uterus instead of your brain. . . ."

"Don't call me that." Her voice was sharp. "Go get yourself married and have some children, and then you call me a grandmother."

Sasha was studying his fingernails again, buffing them listlessly against his knee. "All right, Mother dear, no *babushka* for you yet, but I don't agree with you about dear old Daddy. Maybe you're right—maybe he's really a loyal, dedicated officer. But I'd keep an eye on him just the same."

No matter what else she thought of her son, Anya respected his native shrewdness. Curiosity conquered irritation. "Why?" she asked.

"Because I have the disgusting habit of thinking that everyone else is as naughty as I am." He raised his arms over his head, clasped his hands together, and stretched like a lithe, muscular cat. "If I got the orders that he got today, I'd think twice about going back. He's got a good life here. Of course, he owes us for it, but nobody likes to pay thirty-five years' worth of back rent all at once. I'd watch him, sweet Momma. I'd watch him carefully."

"You're right, you can be quite disgusting." Anya tapped a pencil thoughtfully against her teeth. "You hate him very much, don't you?"

Sasha looked down at his mother, his face impassive, and decided that there was a lot about hate that he could tell her. Like growing up hating an unknown father because he was dead, and then later on hating him because he was alive. Like the hundreds of times he had killed the man in his dreams, gleefully smashing him, and the other hundreds of times in those very same dreams when he had curled himself contentedly in his father's arms.

Instead, he gave her his brightest smile and said gaily, "Sweetie, do it your own way. I couldn't care less—thank God, I'm just a contract agent. But if that man doesn't make it to the boat on time, it's your cute little tushy that's on the line, not mine."

Anya said slowly, "Full surveillance? Around the clock?"

"If you're going to do it at all . . ." Sasha flipped his hands palms up and shrugged.

She nodded in sudden decision. "I don't agree with you, but we won't take any chances. Do you have the men for it?"

"I'll have to borrow some embassy people."

"Do it, then. Handle it personally."

"That's my sweet old momma; that's playing it smart. I'll get right on it." He slid off the desk and started for the door. He opened it to a blast of disco music from the front room where the nude girls danced ceaselessly. Anya stopped him before he could leave.

"Sasha . . . one of the dancers, that girl Rosita. She has some bad bruises on her belly and back."

Sasha met her gaze. "The little bitch was holding out on the tips. You know I can't allow that."

"Yes, my darling, I know, but the men won't pay to see girls with banged-up bodies. Can't you do your disciplining more carefully?"

"I do what I have to do."

"No, you do what you want to do. In this town, getting a

girl to beat up is a very simple matter. Don't damage our dancers.''

Their eyes locked in a contest of wills. He would have kept it up longer, but he felt the first twinges of a headache and he looked away. He went out of the room, and as he carefully closed the door behind him he thought he heard his mother chuckle softly.

Chapter 6 _____

"You're a fool," said Rusty.

Emerson shook his head. "No doubt I am, about many things, but not about this."

"A fool," she repeated. "The first sign of trouble and you went running to Edwin Swan. Before you even told me about it."

He reached out a hand to soothe her. "What else could I have done?"

She pulled her hand away. "You could have waited until you got home. We could have talked it over."

"There's nothing to talk about. I'm not going back, and if I don't go back I need protection. That means Swan."

Rusty shook her head, unconvinced. "You've burned your bridges. You have no option left. You should have waited."

"You don't know these people the way I do." He leaned forward intently. "I had no options; I guess I never had any."

They sat across the dining room table from each other, the untouched plates of a cold dinner in front of them. They had left off the lights, as if their words needed darkness for safety, and only candles glowed. The house was still, and beyond the house were only the night sounds of small animals, the harsh crash of cans as a coon went foraging, the far-off glissando of a whippoorwill's call. Rusty shivered at the sound of the bird.

"He'll turn you in," she said bitterly. "I know he will. They'll lock you up in some place like Leavenworth. You'll be there the rest of your life, Jim."

"There comes a time when you have to trust someone, and I

do trust Edwin . . . In twenty-four hours we'll know how we stand. That's what he promised."

"I wish I could believe it. All these years, I was sure it would never happen. I was sure they'd forgotten all about you." She said it wistfully, the bitterness gone. She raised her glass, sipped some wine, and stared into the rosy reflection in the crystal. "But they didn't forget . . . did they? They let you sleep—and now—I suppose they'll see you as a monster."

"I find it hard to believe," he said quietly, "that they didn't foresee the outcome. Rusty . . . they took a teenage kid, admittedly a trained atheist and a Communist, but still a teenage kid. They told him, 'Go be a good American. That's your job. Be an American, do as the Americans do, learn to think as the Americans think. Educate yourself, make money, go to school, go to church, pull yourself up by your bootstraps. Enjoy the good life.' Well, I did it. I did exactly what they told me to do. I learned to enjoy the good life, and I learned *why* it's a good life. Not a perfect one, but a better one than anywhere else. I became a good American . . . and I intend to stay one. It's hardly a crime, is it?"

"Not to you. But to them? You'll still seem like a monster."

"The Frankenstein of the KGB," he said lightly. He waited, but she was silent. He heard her breathing change, and he knew that she was crying. He reached for her hand again. "Please don't."

"I won't, not for long." She dabbed at her eyes. "It just hit me all at once. This is all finished, isn't it? The house, your career, our family life . . . everything you and I have worked for. Everything!"

"Yes, I'm afraid so. No matter what else happens, that part of it is finished. But not you and I, Rusty. Please stop crying."

"I have," she said, and her voice was clear. "Where will we go if Edwin keeps his promise? Have you any idea?"

"There hasn't been much time to think." He smiled at her sadly. "There's one thought. It may be a crazy idea, but . . . how does Point Balboa sound? I've never been there, it was the one place I couldn't go. I've always wondered what it would be like. I could go there now, with a new name and a new face.

I've never forgotten how he made it sound so pleasant. A backwater, but a sunny one.''

He heard the shot again, over the span of thirty-five years felt the grip of the pistol and saw the boy fall heavily to the earth.

I don't want to think about that.

"It might work," she said and leaned over to kiss him.

Later, after she had cleared the table, she walked through the darkened rooms of the house looking for her husband. She had no doubt where she would find him. On the south side of the building, overlooking the back lawn that descended in levels to the creek, was a second sitting room that opened onto a veranda. It was a cool and quiet room, built as a summer haven, and she found him there as she had known she would. The room was dark, the only lights the small pools projected upward from under the paintings that hung on the walls. There were three such lights. One illuminated a Braque still life of fruits and a plate in graceful juxtaposition. Another shone on a series of Picasso sketches from the *Toro y Toreros* collection, quick, angular representations of horses, lances, and men. The third bathed a small Matisse of pure and vivid colors that jumped joyously from the wall.

Rusty paused in the doorway. In the darkness she could just make out where her husband was sitting, reclined in a chair so placed that he could see all three without moving his head. There were other paintings in the house, but these were the three he loved most, and she realized sadly that he was saying good-bye to them. She came into the room stepping softly, trying not to disturb, but the swish of her skirt alerted him, and he looked up.

"Shade your eyes," he said. "I'll turn on the light."

"Don't, it's nicer this way."

"I thought I was the romantic in the family." He clicked a switch, and the lamp on the table beside him went on. He clicked another, and the illumination faded from the paintings. Rusty sank gracefully to the carpeted floor beside the chair, resting against his leg.

"We're going to have to tell Ginger," she said.

"Yes. Tomorrow, as soon as she gets here."

"It won't be much of a birthday for you."

"She has to be told. I just wish she were coming alone." He reached into his jacket pocket and took out the memorandum from Military Intelligence. He handed it to her. "I think you'd better read this."

Rusty took the papers, read the first few lines, and looked up. "But this is about Ginger. From Military Intelligence?"

"Just a little back scratching. Somebody owed me a favor." He saw the stern disapproval on her face and said quickly, "Look, we've both been worried about this guy, Angelotti. This was the quickest way to get some input."

"A very ugly way. Spying on your daughter."

He set his face grimly. "If it is, it's the only spying I've ever done."

She nodded at that, then read the pages carefully. When she was finished she stacked the sheets, squared them, and handed them back. Her fingers brushed the back of his hand.

"Not a very pretty picture," she said.

"No, it isn't." He went searching for a cigarette in a sandalwood box on the table. He rarely used cigarettes, but he lit this one hungrily. "I like Eddie, you know I do, but . . ."

"You scarcely know him. You've only met him twice."

"That's usually enough for me. I like him, but after that . . . ?" He flicked the report with his finger.

"I know. It makes him seem like some middle-aged hoodlum, or a con man."

"Not that bad, I hope. I can't see Ginger getting mixed up with someone like that, can you?"

"Why ask me?" she said with a touch of asperity. "My God, these games that you fathers play with your daughters. Look, I'm a woman, and I know what women do. She wouldn't be the first young girl to fall for a flashy guy with a big roll of money."

"Just like you did?"

She laughed. "Oh yes. The flashy one! Holes in your shoes and your nose in a law book."

"Was it that bad?"

"Who paid for the movies every Saturday night?"

"But I paid for dinner," he said.

"The Imperial Jade Gardens. One order of egg rolls for two and the chow mein special. A dollar twenty-five."

"Plus tip."

She nodded dreamily. "A quarter for the waiter. That was a big tip for the Imperial Jade Gardens. Why was it that everybody tipped Chinese waiters less in those days? Were we all such terrible racists?"

"The conventional wisdom was that the Chinese were happy to work for a handful of rice and a place to sleep. So people tipped them with nickels and dimes."

"But not you. You had to leave a quarter."

"I told you. Diamond Jim Emerson."

They laughed quietly together. Then Rusty said, "It doesn't seem fair. She doesn't know anything about things like that. Counting up pennies for Saturday night."

"Seventy-nine cents for the cheapest sherry. Had to have seventy-nine cents in the old jelly jar by Friday night."

"Baking muffins on Sunday. A dozen muffins every Sunday morning."

"Good muffins, too. When was the last time you made muffins?"

She sighed and shook her head. "It doesn't pay to bake anymore. Now you open a box and squeeze a bag. Instant muffins."

"Instant happiness."

"Instant love. That poor kid. There are so many things that she doesn't know about."

"Well, why should she? I worked damn hard to make sure that she'd never have to count pennies."

She looked up at him, and then slowly around the room. "And now you're going to lose it all. We'll be living the rest of our lives on the run."

"It may not be that bad."

"It will be. It will be that bad, and worse." She leaned

back against his legs. "Jimbo, I really wish you hadn't told Swan."

"You let me worry about Edwin. You concentrate on handling your daughter and her boyfriend tomorrow."

"I know how I'd *like* to handle her," said Rusty, suddenly grim. "But she's too old for that."

"Take it easy on her, will you? It's going to be enough of a shock when we tell her about me."

Rusty said in a tight, fierce voice, "You've done absolutely nothing to be ashamed of. You're the finest, truest man who ever lived. You're a wonderful husband and a devoted father, and if that young woman says just one word . . ."

"All right, all right." He pressed his palm softly to her lips. "I also leap buildings at a single bound."

She kissed his palm and brushed her cheek against his hand. She pulled his arm around her shoulder. "Turn the lights back down. I want to look at the Matisse again."

"It's a terrible way to look at paintings."

"I know, but I like it that way."

He clicked the switches. The room grew dark and the small lights glowed. They sat quietly, without moving, his arm around her shoulder, her arm around his knees. Down the meadow the whippoorwill sang again, but this time Rusty did not shiver, and when the coon went banging in the cans she did not stir.

"Point Balboa," she said. "It's beginning to sound like a wonderful idea. Do you think Swan could arrange it for us?"

"I don't see why not. I'll ask him when he calls tomorrow." He was silent for a moment, then said, "I want you to know that up until now, no matter what else happens, it's been the best that a man could ask for."

"The best for me, too." She nodded in the darkness. "And it isn't over. It isn't even close to being over."

"Even if it is."

He started to say more and then stopped himself. After that they sat silently in the darkness for what seemed like a very long time listening to the bird song and the sound of the foraging coon, and when the animal noises were finally stilled, they turned out the lights and went up to bed. It was just after midnight, the Fourth of July, and somewhere a star shell burst and flared.

Chapter 7 _____

T he intruders came just before dusk on the Fourth of July, driving through the tiny town of Princess Falls with its one main street decked out for the holiday in bunting and banners, the street alive and the sparklers and pinwheels already blazing bravely. They drove the length of the street, in and out of town in minutes, the black Camaro cruising slowly and the two men in the front seat slouched and staring straight ahead. Once out of town, they took the road that would lead them out to the Emerson house, but less than a mile down that road the driver checked a penciled map that was taped to the dashboard, slowed for a turn, and made it onto a rutted stretch of dirt track that bordered the edge of a field of corn. The track ran straight and true for more than a mile before it began to curve to the west in a broad arc that would pass by the rear of the Emerson property. The car bounced and bucked on the ugly road, and the driver cursed as he wrestled the wheel.

"How much more to go?" asked the second intruder, the one in the passenger seat.

"We should be close."

The driver checked the map again, then peered down the road in the waning light. Off to the right the land sloped up to a gentle ridge, and just above the ridge line he could see the dormer windows and the white-painted shingles of the second story of the Emerson house. He cut the engine and let the car roll up on a grassy verge and under the spread of a set of trees. He sat back and lit a cigarette.

"Close enough," he said. "Now we wait."

"It's almost eight," the other pointed out.

"I want it dark, real dark."

The driver's name was Georgie Silk, a name not his own but one he had taken because he felt that it suited his image. He thought of himself as being smooth as silk, a top-line operator adept in a wide range of firearms and sharp instruments, who did his work with a minimum of fuss and a maximum of efficiency. In another age he would have chosen to be known as Silky or Slick, but in a time when men of his occupation could shuffle and deal identity cards like a riverboat gambler flashing aces, he preferred the more formal, if temporary, surname of Silk. He was comfortable with the name. It suited his style of life, his style of work, and anybody who killed for a living knew it well.

In fact, Georgie Silk knew that he was kidding himself and had been for some time. He simply wasn't all that good. Back in the days, just a few years before, when the Agency had operated a truly professional and sophisticated extraction squad, Georgie had been very definitely second string, a junior-varsity killer used only for routine assignments, and then only when top men were unavailable. The Freedom of Information Act had changed all that. In the general disintegration of the extraction squad that followed the public disclosures of Agency activities, the best men moved out and men like Georgie moved up. Now he drew the bonus-money hits that made the work so much sweeter. The promotion changed only his pay scale, not his ability. He was still unquestionably second rate, a capable but unimaginative operator.

"We do this one strictly by the numbers," he said as they waited. "Nothing fancy. First we push in, and then we immobilize them."

"Immobilize?" said Pico.

Georgie shook his head. "Tie them up, shmuck. Then we go through the house and boost a few top pieces. Some jewelry, maybe a painting, something like that. Anything to make it look good. Then we whack 'em."

"Why don't we whack 'em first? Makes it easier."

Georgie looked at him pityingly. "Because you don't do it that way. It isn't professional."

"I don't get it. You whack 'em first, or you whack 'em later, what's the difference?"

"You ever work a job like this before?" Georgie's voice was generous, but patronizing. "It's supposed to look like a regular break-in, a couple of guys out boosting a house, but the people are home and they get whacked. Sort of accidental, almost. So you gotta do it like it was real. Couple of guys break into a place and the people are home, what do they do? Do they whack 'em out right away? Shit, no. They tie 'em up while they figure out what to do. I mean, they're no hit men, they're a couple of boosters. So they go through the house and they take what they want, and then they figure, son of a bitch, we gotta waste these people because they seen us and everything. That's when they whack 'em, you see? Not before. And we do it the same way. You gotta do it like it was real. That's the right way, the professional way, understand?"

"Yeah, yeah." Pico, who had been listening carefully, nodded his understanding. He was new to the work, eager to learn, and he considered himself lucky to be working a job with Georgie Silk. Georgie was top line, the real goods, the straight jack, and he knew he could learn from him. Pico, unfortunately, was too young ever to have worked with a truly top-line operator. A city dweller who has never eaten a farm-fresh egg thinks that the cold-storage product that he buys at the supermarket is the real thing. Pico didn't know much about eggs, and he knew less about first-class work.

"Professional," he said admiringly. "Yeah, I get what you mean. Very professional."

"We give it ten more minutes and then we move," said Georgie. Having delivered his lecture, he sat back contented.

He would have been less contented and pleased with himself if he had known that the black Camaro had been under surveillance ever since leaving Princess Falls. One of Sasha Ignatiev's watchers had checked out the car on the edge of town; a second, posted near the cornfield turn, had reported it there; and a third, in the fields to the rear of the Emerson property, had it under observation now. All three watchers reported the presence of the car to Sasha, who was in position at the front of the house. He spoke softly into the radio link connecting the watchers.

"Nikolai, what do you think of them?"

Nikolai, the embassy man posted behind the house, answered slowly, "It could be nothing. Maybe neighbors."

"Possibly, but it's an odd place to park. Keep me informed."

"What do I do if they start for the house?"

"Notify me."

"I don't stop them?"

Sasha cursed softly under his breath. This was the worst part of using embassy people. They were generally clumsy and unused to fieldwork, but they had to be treated with deference. Keeping a mild tone, he said, "Sweetie pie, you're thinking again. Please don't. If those people make a move, you just call me up on the dingaling and then follow discreetly."

"Discreetly?"

"On tiptoe, darling. Like a little elf."

He clicked off and reached into the glove compartment for a bottle of aspirin. The sharp edge of a headache cut him just above his left ear. The pain came as an old, unwelcome friend. It was the kind of headache he had lived with, on and off, for years, and he was not surprised by its onset. The old friend often came to visit at times like these. He swallowed two aspirins dry and kept his eyes on the front of the house. His car was parked in a deserted lane concealed from the road by a high hedge grown wild and thorny. He could see the front of the house through a gap in the hedge, the Georgian façade gleaming whitely in the fading sunset.

That house would go up like a torch, he thought. It would burn like a dream.

In his mind's eye he saw the flicker of orange in a lower window, the ball of oily smoke as the flames burst free and climbed the walls in jagged streaks to the roof, the walls split open now in gaping wounds of cherry red as the inferno roared inside and raced from room to room destroying, blasting, burning; and then he was out of the car and into the house beating his way through the smoke and flames toward the sound of his father's voice calling for help; seeking, finding, saving, holding him safely and leading him out of the fiery hell, gasping for air as they reached the lawn and pitched forward to lie on the grass all covered with sweat and soot and gratitude.

He shook his head sharply and reached again for the aspirin. He took two more tablets, this time swallowing them with difficulty, and resumed his watch on the front of the house.

Inside the house the three members of the Emerson family occupied the second sitting room overlooking the back lawn. Emerson paced nervously, Rusty sat tense and coiled in an easy chair, and Ginger reclined on a wicker couch, listening. Eddie had been asked to twiddle his thumbs elsewhere for an hour or two.

"They're going to give me a hard time about you, sweetie," Ginger had told him. "I can smell it a mile away."

"What's the big deal?" Eddie asked. "You're grown up, aren't you?"

"You know it, and I know it, but they've still got to be convinced. I'm their only daughter. You're the big bad wolf from the big city."

"Give me a deck of cards so I can play solitaire." Eddie sighed. "If you can survive it, I suppose I can."

But Ginger had been wrong. They hadn't asked her questions and they hadn't lectured her. Her father had done all the talking. He had told her that for the past thirty-five years—and of course that included all of her life—he had been a serving officer in the KGB and, before that, its predecessor, the NKVD. He had not been born in Point Balboa, California, but in a suburb of Moscow in the Russian Soviet Socialist Republic.

"I know it's not a joke," Ginger said quietly when James Emerson had finished his confession. "No one could make up such a story as a joke . . . least of all you, Daddy. But—it's—it *is* a little hard for me to swallow all in one gulp . . ."

"I understand," her father said.

Ginger turned to her mother. "Did you know?"

"Yes," Rusty said.

"Always?"

"Not too long after we were married, he told me. It wasn't easy. I learned to live with it."

"Well. Well, well, well." Ginger began to chuckle, then laugh, and finally there were tears that blurred her eyes even through the laughter. "Sorry," she managed. "It's just a little hard for me to swallow . . . oh, I said that, didn't I? It's just . . . well, it isn't every day a girl finds out she's half Russian. And that her father's a Russian spy." She hugged herself, as though she were cold.

"No," Emerson said. "I'm not a Soviet spy—that's what I've been trying to tell you. I'm meant to be one, I was trained to be one, and I've just been ordered to act as one—to defect to the Soviet Union as part of a massive propaganda coup. But I'm not going to do it, Ginger. That's the point. And I've never in my entire life, since I came to this country at the age of nineteen, acted against the interest of the United States. I've never been contacted before this by the NKVD or the KGB or any Soviet citizen or Soviet agent. Do you understand? I was living a lie, but it became the truth. I'm an American, Ginger. My loyalty is here. I'm not going back there. And," he finished, his voice trembling a bit now, too, "I need your help and your loyalty to do what I have to do—for my own sake, for your mother's sake, for your sake, and for the sake of this country."

"Wow," Ginger said.

Rusty tapped her fingers impatiently. "Is that all you can say?"

Emerson said softly, "Take it easy, Rusty. Maybe *wow* says it all."

"I don't think so," Rusty shot back. "It's not exactly a bedtime story you've told her, and we need her help. We certainly need something a little more explicit than *wow*." She turned on Ginger. "Would you mind?"

Ginger's eyes met Rusty's and held them. In a quiet, precise voice, she said, "Mother, I'd be infinitely grateful if you wouldn't adopt that tone of voice with me, as if I'd spilled ink on the carpet and you wanted to know if I were *really* contrite. You two have just dropped an absolute shit storm into my life, and I'm trying with great difficulty to keep from screaming, crying, and climbing up the wall. Snapping at me doesn't improve the situation.'' She turned to her father. "I can tell you one thing, Daddy. For better or for worse, this makes you the most fascinating man I know. You now lead the parade.''

Emerson smiled thinly. "I don't care whether you find me fascinating or not. I care that you believe what I've told you and that you don't turn your back on me.''

"You're my father," Ginger said. "I love you no matter what you've done. And I respect what you've told me about what you intend to do.'' Her voice shook again. "I'd bust out crying now if I said any more, and I don't want to do that. Just tell me this—what happens now?''

"Edwin Swan is going to make arrangements for your mother and me to drop out of sight. For a long, long while.''

"And me?''

"I don't know yet. We certainly won't be in contact for a time. Edwin will arrange all that. Whatever happens, you can't breathe a word of what I've told you. Not to anybody.''

"I understand.''

"We'll talk again," he said. "Meanwhile, you'd better go rescue Eddie. Assure him that we haven't bitten your head off because you brought him down here for my birthday. Under the circumstances, I'd rather he wasn't here . . . but what's done is done. We'll make the best of it.''

They watched her go out through the screen doors, across the veranda, and down the successive levels of the back lawn toward the stand of trees near the creek where Eddie had parked the Overlander camper. The last rays of the late-afternoon sun slanted through the trees and marked the grass with golden ovals, and from somewhere to the west the recurring crackle of exploding fireworks built and diminished like the roar of surf on the shore.

"Odd," said Emerson. "I thought she'd be more angry. I thought she'd feel in some sense betrayed.''

"But she wasn't.''

"Not really. She wasn't even frightened. She was shocked, of course, but then she got over it. I got the feeling, by the time she left us, that she'd accepted everything as the normal course of events.''

"I suppose," Rusty said, "there's tribute to be paid to television and those James Bond movies . . . and even Vietnam, and Watergate. In our time the unthinkable has become quite ordinary.''

James Emerson sighed. He went outside to look at the fieldstone barbecue pit set in the turf near the edge of the lawn. He checked the glowing of the oak-chip embers, the rows of shell steaks neatly arranged, and the ears of corn wrapped in aluminum foil; then he came back inside to wander aimlessly around the room. He stopped in front of a table piled high with his birthday gifts: a stack of shirts and a new Omega from Rusty, who always insisted that he had everything; a hand-tooled alligator wallet from Ginger, who had been giving him wallets ever since she was old enough to go shopping; and a fifteen-inch astronomical globe from Eddie, who, in this area at least, seemed to have more good sense than the others combined. He spun the globe idly, feeling very unbirthdaylike, and for the second time in two days reminded himself that it really wasn't his birthday at all.

"Is she going to tell him?" he asked.

"Eddie? Of course." Rusty's eyes were still on her daughter as she strode across the lowest level of the lawn toward the camper.

"Why do you say of course? She promised that she wouldn't. She won't break her word.''

Rusty sniffed. "If you're so sure of that, then why bother asking me?''

Excluded by request from the family conference, Eddie spent the late-afternoon hours playing with his toys. His toys were poisons and explosives, firing mechanisms and delayed-action fuses, charges and propellants, and all the other esoterica that once had been his stock in trade. The toy closet itself had been built into a recess in the forward wall of the camper. Only exhaustive scrutiny would have revealed the sliding door that locked with a fingertip-pressure combination, and no one had ever looked that closely, not even Ginger. The closet was a laboratory in miniature, the breakable vials and flasks, the carboys of acids and venoms, all craftily stored in padded niches. The space above was a storage area for metal equipment and the disassembled components of various firearms; and above that a shelf pulled out to form a work area large enough to accommodate a microscope, a Bunsen burner, a small vise, and an electric drill that could double as a makeshift lathe. The laboratory itself was makeshift, nothing like the elaborate facilities that had been his pride in the days when he worked for the Agency. It wasn't even on a level with the Jerry-built lab that he had shared with Vasily in Mexico. It was basic equipment, nothing more, but it was all that he had to work with these days, and whenever he could he played with his toys to keep his fingers nimble and his brain awake. Since it was the Fourth of July, his fingers worked idly with a mixture of sulphur, charcoal, niter, and gunpowder to form a Roman candle that he would never use.

They're giving her hell over there on account of me, he thought as he worked, and there's nothing I can do to help her. There are so many things I can't explain to her. Simple things, like why did we have to drive down here, why didn't we fly? How do I tell her about the rotating stakeouts at the airports and the bus terminals, and when you're laying low like me you drive whenever you can? How can I tell her anything? How can I tell her about the crazy business I used to be in? I could never talk about that, not to anybody until I met Vasily, and he was different. He was in the business himself, so we could talk. But even then, we never talked about it plainly. We always talked around it. You have to do it that way. You don't say, "Whoeee, this here little gadget'll take that sucker out quicker'n hell could singe a feather . . . goddamn, his head's gonna hit concrete before his feet stop moving." No, you look very dignified and professional, and you say, "Now, if it's done right, the introduction of the substance into the bloodstream of the target should result in immediate local edema, followed by neural inflammation, followed by cardiac arrest within five minutes." That's the way you do it. Nobody wants to talk about death; it's built into us not to, and I guess that people like me are no exceptions.

He finished off the Roman candle he was working on, looked at it critically, and set it aside.

A good piece of work, he thought. Clean and simple, and it won't kill anybody. She wants me to work, but what could I do for a living now? Sell real estate or insurance? Get a job in a lab? Not after all those years of making gadgets. That's all I was ever good at, making those gadgets, and there I was the best. Sui generis, that's what they told me. There I am, Christ, only eighteen years old doing contract work for the Agency, and my control tells me that I'm sui generis, and of course I have to ask him what it means. Old Dick Wilenski, he says, "You're one of a kind, kid. You're some kind of a scientific freak, right up close to the genius level in what you know, but you only know one thing." And then he asks me if I want to go to college.

College? Me? I didn't know what to say. What good is college gonna do for a guy who figured out the Little Devil Blowback Silencer before he was nineteen? Genius, huh? Bullshit. It was just a kid's idea out of a fantasy world. All kids live in fantasy worlds, and I don't just mean jerking off three times a day. It's like you're sitting there watching a movie on TV or reading a comic book, and this guy has a pistol in his hand ready to shoot the hero. And you think, oh wow, what if the silencer on the piece is a fake and when he pulls the trigger he shoots himself instead? Every kid has fantasies like that. The only difference with me was that as soon as I got the idea, I went to work and made the gadget. It took me less than a week to figure out the theory and another week to turn it out on the lathe, and the next thing I know I'm doing business with AmerArmCo in Wilmington, and how the hell should I know that the Agency owned them lock, stock, and gunbarrel? A teenage kid and I'm doing business with the Agency, and Dick Wilenski tells me that I'm sui generis and asks me if I want to go to college.

College. I said, "Look, I already know enough to blow up

half of Moscow. What happens if I go to college? Will I learn enough to blow up the other half?''

"You shmuck," Eddie muttered to himself now. "The dumbest move you ever made. All those years making gadgets, and now what can you do?''

He looked in disgust at the Roman candle in his hands, finished off the plug, and pushed it aside. The movement brought his head up, and through the window he saw Ginger coming across the lawn toward the camper. Quickly, he began closing up shop, sweeping the candles into the storage bin, stopping up bottles and putting them away in place. Closing up took less than a minute. He checked the door of the toy closet to make sure it was secure, and when Ginger opened the camper door he was reading a copy of *Field and Stream*. He looked up when she came in, as if surprised, and she looked so lovely standing there in the doorway that he felt himself go soft inside at the thought that they would be sleeping apart in the night.

"You look terrific," he said, tossing the magazine aside.

"Thanks. Daddy says to come up for a drink and he'll put the steaks on the grill.''

He stood and came close to her. "What's the chance for a little romance before dinner?''

She was frowning. "No chance at all.''

"Something bothering you?''

"Plenty.''

"Your folks?''

"Yes, but not what you think. There's something I have to tell you.''

She told him in fifteen minutes what it had taken her father two hours to tell. At the end of five minutes, Eddie was bewildered. At the end of ten minutes, he was amused. By the time she was finished, he was terror-stricken.

The descending levels of the Emerson lawn, like tabletops of meadowland, formed a depression of terrain running northeast to southwest. As a result, Ginger's journey to the camper went unobserved by the two groups of men watching the house. Sasha sat with his head tilted back and resting against the front seat of the car, his eyes half-closed. The headache was worse. He had been popping aspirins like peanuts all day, but with no effective results. The booming of fireworks in the distance was no help, and he watched the house through a haze of pain. To distract himself, he reran in his mind the fantasy of the burning house and the daring rescue. He found both parts of the fantasy equally satisfying. The thought of Emerson trapped in the flames filled him with a profound pleasure, and the vision of himself as his father's rescuer was downright exhilarating. The fantasy and the satisfaction it provoked were no new things to him. He had been dreaming in various forms, asleep and awake, for as long as he could remember, long before there had been a face to attach to the name of the man he was sure was his father. Along with the headache, the fantasy was an old friend.

"Sasha." Nikolai's voice came from the speaker below the dashboard. "They're out of the car and heading for the house."

"Can you see them?"

"Not clearly. No lights back here, and it's dark now."

"Hold your position. I'll handle it."

"Don't you want me to follow discreetly?"

"Negative. Stay where you are."

"Sasha, those people aren't just out for a walk. They're making an approach on the house, using cover."

"Bunch of boy scouts," Sasha muttered.

"You sure you don't want me up there?"

There was silence as Sasha fought the pounding in his head. He knew that Nikolai was right and that he was being foolhardy. On the other hand, the intentions of the intruders were still uncertain, and even if they presented a threat it was *his* father who was being threatened, not Nikolai's or anyone else's, and if there was a job to do it was *his* job to do. After a moment, he said, "Negative, Nikolai, hold on where you are. I'll take care of this myself."

He clicked off, gritting his teeth against the pain in his head, and then he was out of the car and through the hedge, running lightly down the road toward the house. The countryside was still, not a sound except the distant rumble of fireworks, but

within his head he could see the whole of the house in flames
and hear his father calling for help.

"I had to tell you," said Ginger. "They told me not to, but I
had to."

"No, you didn't," Eddie said fervently. "And I wish to hell
you hadn't. It's none of my business."

"It is now. I just made it yours."

"Yeah, I guess you did. I've got it whether I like it or not."

Ginger sat on the edge of the bench in the tiny dining area of
the camper, leaning tensely across the drop-leaf table. Eddie sat
opposite her, his face closed and guarded.

I've got to get out, he thought. I've got to move quick. Christ
on a crutch, what lousy luck. The old man, a Soviet sleeper.
Who would ever figure that? I lay low for a year and keep my
nose clean, and then I walk into a mess like this. Shit!

All right, keep it cool . . . figure it out. Without emotion,
like a problem in chemistry. Forget that you like the guy; forget
that he's Ginger's father; forget your own problems for a minute. Add it up and figure it out.

OK, what have we got? A longtime sleeper who doesn't want
to play with his pals anymore. He wants to cross over, and who
does he go to for help? His old buddy, the DD5, Swan, that
sanctimonious, cold-blooded son of a bitch. OK, I said no emotion. So what kind of a deal does he make? Total immunity, a
new identity, government protection, and a fresh start in a small
town somewhere. A good deal? Sure, it's good, it's so good
that it stinks. They just don't work that way, not if they're still
the same cute and cuddly teddy bears I used to play with. They
can't let him live, even under cover. He's a liability; he's a
major embarrassment, a Red sleeper who made it right to the
top. If that ever came out . . . Christ, the heads that would roll.

So they have to extract him. Guys like that don't get plastic
surgery and a fresh start. They get accidentally dead. A little
VX gas in the air-conditioning system, that's all it takes, or any
one of a dozen other gadgets that I made for them over the
years. So he's gone. And so is Rusty. And so is the kid, and so
am I unless I move fast.

"Eddie, I'm worried. Is he doing the right thing?"

Ginger's question broke his reverie, and he started. The right thing? What difference does it make? Your father's a dead man. All he has to do is lie down, he's so dead.

"I suppose so," he said cautiously. "It doesn't sound as if he has much of a choice."

"No, he doesn't." She nodded sadly. "It seems such a shame to lose everything now. He never really did anything wrong. He's not a traitor. That's why he went to Swan."

"He's a victim," Eddie agreed, deciding to oversimplify. "Let's go get that drink."

He stood up and slipped on his jacket, smoothed the lapels and patted the pockets. Ginger, watching him, smiled faintly. "You don't have to wear a jacket in this heat," she said. "Daddy won't be wearing one."

"Your father is more socially secure than I am." He took a flashlight from a rack above the table.

"You don't need that, either," she pointed out. "I know every inch of this ground in the dark."

"More social security." Once outside the camper, he locked the door carefully and took her hand. "Lead on."

She was right. She knew her way across the darkened lawn unerringly, leading him over the velvety grass, past shadows that were trees and ghostly fences, and up the invisible rises of the tabletops with only the light of the house to guide her and the flicker of fireworks exploding on the horizon. She walked quickly, picking her way, and Eddie followed a half-step behind her. His mind still moved at a gallop.

I've got to get out of here and I've got to take her with me, but how do I do it? The father and the mother are finished; there's nothing I can do for them, but I can still get the two of us out. I don't know when they'll hit, and I can't wait to find out . . . I can't afford to be around when it happens. So she's got to take me on faith. I may lose her this way, but I've got to try it.

He tugged at her hand and stopped. She turned to him in the darkness and asked, "What's wrong?"

"Plenty. Part of it you know about, and part of it you don't.

Look, I'm going to ask you to do something now. No questions, no arguments. Just do it. Trust me on this, OK?''

She was silent for a long moment. "Eddie, I've been taking you on trust since the day I met you. I may have pushed you a little, but I've never asked questions."

"No, you haven't."

"Then why do you have to ask me now? What is it you want me to do?"

He took a deep breath. "We're going to go up to the house and wish your father a happy birthday. We're going to have one drink with your folks. Then we are very politely going to excuse ourselves and say that we're not staying for dinner and we're not staying overnight. Then we're going to leave."

"Leave?" Her voice went up a notch. "Just like that?"

"Just like that. Kiss them good-bye, walk out of the house, and get out of here."

"I can't do that," she protested. "Not on his birthday. No, the hell with his birthday, I just can't do it. Not after what he told me today."

"You've got it the wrong way around. *Because* of what he told you."

"But why?"

"That's the part that you take on trust."

"He's my father. I can't just walk away from him."

"Baby, you have to."

She pulled her hand away from his. "You're saying something, but I can't hear it. What is it? Is he in some kind of danger?"

"Jesus Christ—" He could swear he smelled it.

"But that's it, isn't it? Someone is trying to hurt him, and you want me to . . ."

The sound of a shot came clearly from the house. "Oh, my God," Ginger gasped. She broke away from him and ran.

He lunged, missed, stumbled, and took off after her. "Goddamn it! Wait a minute!"

She did not answer and she did not stop, running fleetly over familiar turf, heading for the house with Eddie behind her in frantic pursuit. Knowing the ground, she outdistanced him quickly, bounding up the last of the rises to the final level of the lawn while he scrambled awkwardly, the flashlight on now and helping him some, but not enough to overtake her. He was still far behind her when she reached the back door of the house, and he heard it slam, heard her footsteps inside; and then he was through the door himself and pounding across the veranda, through the darkened sitting room, and down the hall that led to Emerson's study. The door to the study was open, and the room was ablaze with light. Stumbling through the doorway, Eddie skidded to a stop.

Emerson and Rusty were tied to chairs against the book-lined wall, mouths gagged, faces contorted. Georgie Silk stood near them, pistol lowered. On the other side of the room, Pico was in the act of turning from the opened wall safe; a thin sliver of steel shone in his hand. Ginger stood frozen in motion, staring down at the slim figure of a man on the floor, his forehead dripping blood.

Silk's eyes widened. "Jesus Christ, it's Eddie Mancuso," he muttered, and his pistol came up.

"Georgie-boy."

The two men stared at each other, wonderingly, and then Eddie said, "Is that a gun you have there, Georgie? Do they let you play with guns now?"

Silk grinned. "Where you been keeping yourself?"

"Here and there. Around and about."

"Same old Eddie. People been looking for you."

"Yeah, I figured they might be."

"This is my lucky day. I go out on a job and I make myself a bonus the easy way."

"An open warrant?"

"Sure, what did you expect?"

"Had to be," Eddie agreed. "How much they paying?"

"Fifty large."

"I'm flattered."

"You made them pretty sore. Over a year now, and they're still sore. They want your ass bad."

"You going to give it to them?"

"Fifty large." The pistol was steady in his hand. "That's a lot to pass up. You know what I mean?"

Eddie sighed, then nodded at the man on the floor. "Did you do that all by yourself with your little pistola?"

"Watch your mouth." Silk shrugged. "He came in waving a piece. I put him down."

"Ah," said Eddie, as if a great truth had been revealed. "Who's your friend?"

"Pico?" Silk did not move his head. "Pico's new, but he's learning."

"Knife man?"

"Like I said, he's learning. I'm teaching him everything I know. Right, Pico?"

Pico grinned. "That's right, Georgie."

"Everything you know." Eddie laughed shortly. "That shouldn't take long. That should take about twenty minutes."

"I told you to watch your mouth."

"Georgie's OK," Pico said mildly. "He teaches me plenty."

"What did he teach you tonight? How to kill two helpless people?"

Pico shrugged. "All in the game."

"Well, I hope you've been taking notes. Did he ever teach you this one?"

Moving only one finger, Eddie pressed the button on the flashlight. A spring-loaded dart shot silently through the rim of the head. The dart hit Silk in the right shoulder, the venom-tipped point working at once to put the muscle into spasm. The pistol dropped from his fingers suddenly gone numb, and Silk fell, curled into a ball and moaning.

Across the room, Pico moved his right hand and the sliver of steel flashed in the light. He could see that Silk was down, but he could not see why. He could not see Georgie's face, the neck cords straining, the blood vessels engorged, and the features grotesquely twisted. The name Eddie Mancuso meant nothing to him. All he could see was a short, slight, unarmed man. He took three quick steps across the room and dropped into the practiced crouch of the veteran knife fighter. His lips peeled back, and with his left hand he made an inviting motion.

"Come on," he said. "Come on, *coño*."

Eddie shook his head, almost reluctantly. Pico feinted once and lunged. Eddie stamped the heel of his right shoe sharply on the floor. The explosive cap in the toe of the shoe flew up and forward, hitting Pico in the chest at a distance of six feet. The effect was the same as that of a double load of buckshot. Pico's chest disappeared, the muscles and bones hanging loose, the thorax shredded, the blood leaping in gouts. The body pitched forward through a fine, pink haze.

Without moving, Eddie looked down at the wreckage of Pico, then over to where Silk lay moaning helplessly. He nodded abstractedly, the way a master carpenter might in acknowledging the fine finish on a piece of furniture, expecting neither more nor less. He turned to Ginger, who still stood motionless in an attitude of frozen flight, her eyes shadowed in shock, her mouth open in a soundless scream.

With a forced lightness, he said, "Well, sweetheart, you now know what I used to do for a living."

Chapter 8

The sadness stormed up in him. In the past there had always been a moment so painful that at times he had been physically ill. It had made no difference to know, in those days, that he was fighting for his life and that the people whom he killed were after his blood. He killed, and then he sorrowed, and after a while his sorrow extended itself to encompass all of the suddenly dead, those few who had died by his hand and all of the untold others. Sometimes it seemed as if a pact of sadness bound together the killed and their killers. But he set aside the sadness now with an effort of will and strode across the room, brushing by Ginger to get to her parents. A blade dropped into his hand from the jacket scabbard, and he quickly cut them loose and whipped away the gags.

"They were going to kill us," said Rusty as soon as she could speak. There were grim lines in her face. "The bastards were actually joking about it . . ."

Facing Eddie, Emerson ran his tongue over his lips. "What did you do to them," he asked hoarsely. *"Who are you?"*

Eddie ignored them both and knelt beside Silk, who lay on his side curled up into a ball. Eddie tugged at a shoulder and rolled him onto his back. His face was purple, his fingers the size of sausages. His eyes looked up pleadingly.

"Eddie," he managed to croak, "for God's sake . . ."

Over his shoulder, Eddie said, "Come here, I want you to hear this."

Emerson knelt beside him. "My God, what's happening to him?"

"A highly concentrated dose of hornet venom, very

deadly." Eddie's voice was light and conversational. "I used to use real hornets, but they were too damn expensive. Used to cost me a buck and a half apiece, shipped up from Brazil. That was in the old days, of course. Now you can synthesize it using acetylcholine and serotonin. The combination hits the old myoneural junction just like a jolt of the real stuff. He'll be dead in twenty minutes." He raised his voice. "Did you hear that, Georgie? Twenty minutes. Then it's bye-bye, baby."

Emerson looked at him as if he were insane. "Will you please tell me what's going on here? Who are these people?"

"You mean you haven't figured it out yet, Colonel Volanov?"

Emerson did not react at once to the use of the name. Then he stared at Eddie and said slowly, "Ginger told you."

"What did you expect her to do?"

Emerson shot a quick, fierce glance at his daughter standing over them. She returned the look defiantly.

"It's a damn good thing I did," she said. "We'd all be dead if I hadn't." Her eyes were on Silk's congested face. "Eddie, can't you do something for him?"

"Eppy . . . eppy." Silk was making noises deep in his throat. "Eddie, you know, eppy . . . something."

"What is he saying?" Emerson asked.

"He's trying to say epinephrine hydrochloride," Eddie explained. "Georgie isn't very bright, but he knows that much. It's the antidote."

"Eddie, you gotta have some," came the pitiful croak. "You gotta give me some."

"Sure," Eddie said. "But why should I give it to you? You were ready to waste these people."

"That was just a job." Silk's voice was a strangled scream. "I'm just a mechanic, you know that. Eddie, the shot . . . please."

"Don't give him anything." Rusty stood over them, stern and forbidding, staring down with hard eyes. "Let the son of a bitch die."

"You hear that, Georgie? The lady says we should cross you off. That's one tough lady, tougher than I am." Eddie looked at his watch. "Maybe fifteen minutes left. Just enough time to give you the shot and call an ambulance."

"Please, Eddie . . ."

"I've got to hear some talking first."

"Anything. Whatever you want."

"Who made the contract for the hit?"

"The DD5."

Silk's words were beginning to slur. Eddie glanced at Emerson to see if he had heard. "Say it again."

"Swan, the DD5. He made the deal himself. Eddie, it's getting cold . . ."

"You heard?" Eddie asked. Emerson nodded slowly.

"What about backup, Georgie?"

"The shot. I can't move my fingers."

"Come on, come on, you don't work without a backup."

"A two-man team to check out the place. Only if I don't call in."

"When?"

"You've got less than an hour."

Eddie looked at Emerson again, and again received a slow, pained nod of understanding. "Anything else you want to hear?"

"No," said Emerson. "I've heard enough. Maybe too much. My oldest friend just tried to kill me. It's hard to believe."

"Believe it."

"Oh, I do. I have to believe it now." He shook his head, bewildered. "He said he would help. He said he would fix things. . . ."

"Oh, he's a great little fixer. He almost fixed you permanently."

"And my wife . . ."

"And anybody else who got in the way. From his side of the fence it was the only move to make."

"The only move to make." Emerson seemed intrigued by the words. "Yes, for Edwin. Oh, God! I should have seen that."

"Eddie!" Silk twisted his head violently. He was gasping for

air; his face was slick with sweat. "I leveled with you, didn't I? Give me the goddamn shot!"

Eddie leaned over and said into Silk's ear, "Hang in there, Georgie. It won't be long now."

"I can't see."

Ginger whispered sharply, "Does it have to be this way?"

Above them, Rusty's voice came like a tolling bell, saying, "Let the bastard die."

"You promised me," Silk gasped.

"I lie a lot, Georgie," Eddie said softly, "when I have to deal with people like you."

He moved from a kneeling position to sit on his heels, rocking back and forth. It took only a few more seconds. Silk's mouth suddenly filled with blood. His back arched and his feet drummed on the floor. His neck twitched once, twice, and he was still.

"Is he dead?" asked Rusty.

"Very."

She crossed the room to where Sasha lay bleeding on the floor. She knelt beside him, turning his head gently, then looked up and said, "This one isn't."

The two men stood up and looked at each other over Silk's body. Emerson said, "That wasn't any twenty minutes, not even close."

"I know. That stuff works in seven to ten minutes, at the outside."

"Do you really have the antidote?"

"No," said Eddie, lying again. "That was just to make him talk."

They joined Rusty kneeling beside Sasha's body. Silk's bullet had torn a gash across his forehead and down his left temple. The flap of skin hung loose and his eyes were closed, but he was breathing regularly. Eddie's fingers probed at the wound as he whistled tunelessly through his teeth.

"Typical," he muttered. "Very sloppy, Mr. Silk. That's why you never made the first team."

"How bad is he?" Emerson asked.

"He'll live. You know him?"

Emerson shook his head. "You?"

"I never saw him before, but I can guess who he is. The other side. Soviet protection for the valuable Colonel Volanov." He buried a smile as Emerson winced at the use of the name. "He wasn't very good at it, was he? On the other hand, neither was Georgie." He made a face of mock disapproval. "It's terrible, the quality of work these days. Nobody takes any pride anymore."

"Apparently you do." The two men regarded each other soberly. Emerson broke the brief silence. "What are the chances that he was alone?"

Eddie flipped his hand back and forth. "Hard to say. For all I know, the woods could be filled with them." He grinned wolfishly. "You're caught right in the middle, aren't you? The DD5 wants you dead, and the Reds want you wrapped up and delivered to Moscow. That doesn't leave you much of a choice, does it?"

"Only one choice. I have to run."

"There's always Moscow. You'll stay alive that way."

"I'll never do that," Emerson said. "I've learned to be an American and it means a great deal to me. If they won't let me stay an American, I'm not going to get petulant and play the traitor. I couldn't go back to Moscow and let the other side use me. Never."

"Better dead than Red?" Eddie chuckled.

"Not exactly."

"It doesn't matter," Eddie said. "I know what you mean. But then you have to run."

"Where? There's no airport that's safe."

Where? Eddie sighed. Mexico, of course. No airport necessary. An easy border crossing. A safe house waiting for me—and for them. It's the only place that I can get them to, keep them safe there, and get them ready for another life. So it's going to be Atotonilco after all. All those months of trying to make up my mind, and now a bunch of other people have made it up for me.

Filled with a cold joy at the prospect, he calculated quickly, figuring Washington to Houston in two days of steady driving in the camper, everybody switching off at the wheel, and then a day's layover in Houston while Sam Fusselman, the best in the southwest, cut some new paper for the Emersons: passports, drivers' licenses, and the rest. Then down to Laredo, over the border, and the long drive south; twelve hours in the saddle, through Monterrey, Saltillo, San Luis Potosí, and then cross country on the back roads until we're rolling into Atotonilco with the house perched high on the hill to the right.

"Where?" Emerson prodded urgently.

"I'll tell you once we're on the road. We've got to get out of here. And quick."

"We? Are you dealing yourself in?"

It was a frozen moment. In elapsed time the moment was measured in seconds, but in those few seconds Eddie saw it all before him, and he knew how it all would happen and how it would end. It was a losing battle, an idiot's joust with implacable windmills, for there was no way in the world that Emerson would ever escape the encircling arms that sought him. They were the two longest arms in existence, and if one didn't pluck him and cage him, the other would casually crush him dead. That was how it would happen. There was no other way.

Still, Eddie told himself, he wants to make a run for it, and he's entitled to try. He doesn't have a chance, but he deserves the best odds he can get; and I guess now I know why I never stopped playing with the toys, why I never stopped tinkering. There had to be a reason, and here it is. And now I know.

In the final part of that frozen moment he looked at Ginger and saw that all of his fears were written on her face. It was the face that he loved, and it was fine and firm despite the fear, but it was also the face of innocence lost. For all of her assumed sophistication she came from a world where good and evil came in plainly labeled packages, and people truly believed thou shalt not kill. It was a world of such staggering ignorance compared to his that he envied her having it, and it was a sadness to know that she had just lost it and would never have it again. No matter the rights and the wrongs, he had opened the cage and had shown her the beast.

Then the moment was over, time thawed, and he said, "Yeah, I'm in. All the way in."

Emerson said, "You still haven't told me who you are."

"Later. Right now we have to walk out of here, just as we are."

Rusty protested, "We can't just abandon the house."

"You can and you have to. Down the hill, into the camper, and off we go."

"We'll need a few minutes to put some things together."

"I'm telling you there's no time."

"But why the camper? We have two cars we can use."

"The camper," Eddie said impatiently, moving toward the door.

Without anyone's having noticed, Ginger had left the couch to sit on the floor beside Sasha. The wad of cloth in her hand was pressed against his open wound. She looked up at Eddie and said with quiet bitterness, "Are you running things now?"

"Somebody has to. I just elected myself." His voice rose angrily. "Goddamn, take it or leave it! I'm moving out."

"We'll take it," said Emerson, crossing swiftly to the wall safe that Pico had opened. He pulled out two thick stacks of currency, two blue passports, and an old, heavy Luger pistol.

"Do you know how to use that antique?" Eddie asked.

Emerson gave him a crooked smile. "I used to. I used to be pretty good. You don't forget those things."

The smile lasted a moment longer; for that moment Eddie saw not the middle-aged man with weary eyes, the worldly lawyer and pater familias, but a trace of the teenage Yuri Volanov, the cream of the NKVD, young, cocky, and capable. Then the smile faded, as if Emerson had remembered something unpleasant, even hurtful. He put the pistol away quickly.

"What about him?" said Ginger, nodding at Sasha. "We can't just leave him like this."

"We're not going to," Eddie said grimly.

It took a moment for the words to sink in, and then Ginger gasped. "No!"

"Get her out of here," Eddie said to her father. "You know we can't leave him alive."

Emerson hesitated, and in that moment Sasha stirred, moving his head against Ginger's arm and smearing it with blood. *"Atyets,"* he said, and the word came out like a groan from his lips. Emerson started visibly at the sound.

"Atyets, zdyes balit."

"Russian?" said Ginger. "What's he saying?"

The words came slowly from her father. "He says it hurts. He's in pain."

"He's in pain." Ginger cradled Sasha's head protectively and stared up at Eddie. "And you want to kill him."

"Ginger . . . look, you don't understand. It has to be this way."

"No, it doesn't," she blazed at him. "There's been enough killing. You've already done it twice tonight. Isn't that enough for you?"

Tensed with anger, she moved her arm, and Sasha opened his eyes. They were glazed and narrowed with strain. He looked up, saw Emerson standing over him, and with great effort, he said, *"Paidyom pasmatryet fudbolni match myezhdu kamandami dinama i spartak. OK?"* Then his eyes closed and he slumped unconscious again.

"He wants to go to a football game," Emerson said wonderingly. "That's what he said."

"Spartak against Dynamo," said Eddie. "Two good teams. I'm moving out of here in exactly sixty seconds, and I don't care who's coming with me."

Emerson was still wonder-struck by Sasha's words. "He said it like a child, like a little boy. He wanted me to take him to the game."

"Like a little boy," said Ginger, with bitterness. "And you're going to kill him."

Emerson looked at Eddie unhappily. "Maybe she's right."

"She's wrong. Thirty seconds."

"But . . . there's been enough killing."

Rusty said tentatively, "I know we said that you're running things, but this man was trying to help us."

"Eddie, please," Ginger pleaded. "Anything you say, but not this. Please."

Eddie looked up from his watch. His lips were set rigidly. He said to Emerson, "It's a mistake, a bad mistake if we leave him here alive."

Emerson nodded. "If so, it's a mistake I'll have to live with."

"If you're lucky. If you live." He shook his head disgustedly. "All right, let's go."

Without looking to see if the others would follow, he moved quickly across the room and through the door, half running down the hallway. Ginger, Emerson, and Rusty hurried after him. Outside on the lawn they saw the dim glow of Eddie's flashlight bobbing as he worked his way down to where the camper was parked. They started after him, Ginger leading the way. Rusty stopped to look back at her home. Emerson put his arm around her shoulder and tugged gently.

"Come on," he said. "One day, I promise, we'll come back."

"I don't believe that," she said, shivering, and then she followed him into the darkness.

III

Operation
Backfire

Chapter 9 _____

It came as no surprise to the night officer on duty at the Fun House to receive a call from the backup team operating at the Emerson residence in Princess Falls. He had been expecting the call all evening, for one of the functions of the backup team was the disposal of bodies, and he was prepared to give instructions for the final resting place of the Emerson family. Instead, he was told that the only bodies on the premises were those of Georgie Silk and Pico, and further instructions were requested.

"Jesus, the old man will have a fit," he muttered.

The team leader asked, "What about the stiffs?"

"Bring them in here for the time being. We'll have to figure a place to dump them."

He hung up the telephone and then, despite his reluctance, immediately dialed the number for Edwin Swan at the Hotel Coolidge. His reluctance was justified by Swan's reaction to the news, and when he hung up the telephone a second time, his hands were shaking and there were pinched lines around his eyes and lips.

If the backup team had arrived at the Emerson home as little as fifteen minutes earlier, there would have been three bodies to dispose of instead of two; but Nikolai, after waiting the obligatory twenty minutes for Sasha to check in, had made his own reconnaissance and had found the unconscious, bleeding body on the floor. A quick survey of the house showed him what had happened: two dead strangers, Sasha wounded, and the Emerson family gone. Nikolai was a big man. He had no difficulty in lifting the slightly built Sasha and carrying him down the hill to

123

the car. He then called in the other two team members, dismissed them, and drove quickly, but within the legal speed limit, to the nearest public telephone.

Anya Ignatiev was asleep when the call came in. The hour was still early, but hers was not the sleep of weariness, but of sexual exhaustion. Coming up from sleep, she reached blindly for the telephone, but she could not find it. She opened her eyes. There were two other people in bed with her, two young men lying between her and the bedside table. Groggily, she tried to remember who they were and where she had met them. Their bare, well-formed bodies were slick with sweat. The sight and odors aroused her at once, but the telephone called urgently. She slithered over their bodies to get at the instrument, enjoying the sensation. The men, awakened by the motion, thought that it was playtime again and responded with automatic caresses. Pushing their hands away, she picked up the telephone.

She was wide awake within seconds. She rolled out of the bed, away from the grasping hands, and stood with the receiver pressed to her ear.

After a moment, she asked, "How bad is he?"

Nikolai answered, "I don't think it's too serious, but he's lost a lot of blood and he needs a doctor quickly."

"Bring him here."

"Not a hospital?"

"No, you fool." Her voice squeaked on the words, and she fought to control herself. "I'll get a doctor from the embassy. Deliver Sasha here at once."

"*Nu kharasho.* Anything else?"

One of the men in the bed idly ran his hand up the inside of her thigh. Just as idly, she slapped it away. "What about Emerson? Are you sure he's gone?"

"No question about it. The house is empty."

She hung up the telephone and looked down at the two men on the bed. Rejected by her, they were amusing themselves with each other.

"Stop that, you pigs," she said. "You've got five minutes to get dressed and get out of here."

They looked at her in surprise. Earlier in the evening the same routine had stimulated her wildly.

"Out," she said. "I mean it. Five minutes."

They objected, they pleaded, but finally they went. Once they were gone she went to the kitchen, spooned instant coffee into a mug, filled the mug with hot water from the tap, and drank it down in three gulps. Then she went back to the bedroom, opened a recessed section of her desk, and took out a pad of one-time code forms. She sat at the desk with pencil and paper, laboriously composing a message and encoding it in a string of five-digit numbers. At the end of the message she added the uncoded word *doctor* and then dialed a telephone number. She said only one word into the telephone, but that word was guaranteed to bring her a messenger from the Soviet Embassy within thirty minutes. Only when she replaced the receiver did she realize that she was still naked. She put on a dressing gown and went back to the kitchen to make a proper cup of coffee while she waited for the messenger.

Anya's message, relayed through the cipher desk of the Soviet Embassy, reached Colonel Andrei Petrovich forty-five minutes after it left her home. It was shortly after 6:00 A.M. in Zhukovka then, and the colonel was fast asleep. In accordance with standing instructions he was awakened by his aide, who handed him the decoded message without comment. Petrovich, disheveled and sleepy, sat up to read it, screwing up his eyes against the light. The words came as a series of shocks as painful as physical blows to him.

So much for the sacred motherland, he thought bitterly. So much for the faithful Yuri Volanov. The son of a bitch, he's turned on us.

It was his worst moment in a long career as an intelligence officer. He had gambled on an agent, and he had lost. *Homefire,* for which he had taken full responsibility, was in jeopardy. His face composed, he took the pen that his aide offered and wrote just two words on the message form.

"Send that reply," he said and sank back down on the bed. He prepared himself to return to sleep. The sleep came slowly, but it came. There would be no tossing, sweating sleeplessness for Andrei Petrovich. Like most good intelligence officers, he was a cynic who, at the same time, nourished an incurable streak of optimism. Having placed his faith in Yuri Volanov, and having been betrayed, he now was ready to place an equal amount of faith in someone else. If Volanov refused to return to the motherland voluntarily, then he would be returned by force. One way or another, he would return.

The reply from Zhukovka took several hours to reach Anya, and by that time Sasha had been stitched and treated by the doctor and now lay propped up in Anya's bed, head swathed in bandages. Under the wrappings, his face was tense and drawn; dark smudges of strain showed under his eyes. Those eyes, normally dancing with humor, were still and solemn now, and when he spoke his usual bantering tone was gone. It was a weary voice, and sad.

"I fucked it up badly," he said.

"Why did you go in by yourself?" Anya asked. "That was inexcusable, Sasha—against all procedure."

He nodded and winced. "It was a mistake. I was foolish." The look on his face showed that he wasn't going to carry the subject any further. The relationship between mother and son was such that he felt that he could tell her anything, but he was not about to tell her about the fantasy of the burning building and his father's cries for help. Instead, he said simply, "How bad is it? Bottom line."

"It couldn't be any worse. We've lost him. He's on the run, and we don't know where."

"I'll find him." It was an effort to speak. The doctor had given him tablets for the pain, but they had only dulled the roar in his head. Despite this, he forced himself to think, trying to recall what had happened. There was little to remember. Into the room, the two of them tied to chairs, the other two wheeling around as he came, and then the shot. And then nothing. Until now. And somewhere in between, a fugitive fragment of childhood memory . . . a football game? He dismissed the thought. "I'll find him," he repeated. "Damn it, I had the feeling he might run. Have you notified Zhukovka?"

"Hours ago. Sasha, they're going to be furious."

"All my fault." He tried to smile. "Fear not, I'll get him back for you."

"How?"

"*Backfire,* of course."

"*Backfire.*" Anya said the word slowly, pronouncing the two syllables separately. "We were hoping never to have to use that."

"What choice do we have? Without *Backfire* we could look for him forever."

"We can't do it on our own," Anya said doubtfully. "We'll need authorization."

"Zhukovka will give it." He closed his eyes and sank back against the pillows. "Andrei Petrovich is no fool. He'll authorize it."

He was quite right. Less than ten minutes later, the messenger from the embassy arrived. A short, inconsequential-looking second secretary, he was accustomed to these nocturnal missions and he wasted no time. He delivered the message to Anya and then was gone into the night. Anya decoded the number groups rapidly, writing the results on a sheet of paper, and then brought the paper into the bedroom. She handed it to her son.

If Homefire *blown then strong chance House of Joy also blown. Deactivate House of Joy tonight. Joy #1 return to Center soonest. Joy #2 fall back to safe house and activate* Backfire.

"You were right," Anya said. "It's *Backfire,* and he wants you to run it."

"It had to be." Sasha raised his hand languidly and let the paper flutter to the bedclothes. "We have a chance now, a second chance for me. And you're going home."

She sat on the edge of the bed as they discussed plans for activating *Backfire,* for closing down the House of Joy, for moving Sasha to a safe house in Alexandria, and for Anya's exit from the country via Canada, the first leg of her journey back to Moscow. The plans were all of a contingency nature and had been laid down months before. When they were satisfied that all of the points had been covered, Sasha sighed and sank back into the pillows piled behind his head and shoulders. He closed his eyes and breathed deeply. He opened his eyes, and just for the moment they were dancing with the usual mischief. He turned his head and breathed deeply again, sniffing the pillow.

"English Leather cologne," he said brightly. "You sweet old harlot, you kicked someone out of bed just for little old me."

"How strange," said Vasily Borgneff. "Positively ironic. You want me, a former agent of the KGB, to extract this American Secretary for . . . what did you say he is?"

"Assistant Secretary of Defense," Edwin Swan repeated.

"Yes, this James Emerson, who is also a former KGB operative. One Russian eliminating another, and the CIA pays the bill."

"I didn't say anything about the Agency," Swan noted.

Vasily said thoughtfully, "Does that mean that I'll be working for your so-called Gang of Four?"

Swan did not answer. It was as if he had not heard the question, but the silence told Vasily what he wanted to know.

The two men stood in the main room of the bastion under the Fun House. It was almost four in the morning, but under the Fun House there was no day or night. Vasily, awakened from sleep by Swan's arrival, wore only jeans and a light shirt. The DD5, who had not yet slept that night, was dressed, as always, immaculately. The two men who had accompanied him out from Washington sat sprawled in armchairs on the far side of the room. They were both Orientals—Borgneff guessed Vietnamese—both short and wiry and dressed just a touch too carefully in black suits and white silk shirts without ties. Swan had introduced them only as Chuc and Van, and they sat together ignoring the conversation. The room was the same one in which, less than two days before, Borgneff and Swan had stood discussing frozen fish fingers and toaster waffles. Now they were discussing James Emerson and Eddie Mancuso.

"How sure are you that it's Eddie?" asked Borgneff.

In reply, Swan simply pointed to the two objects lying on the table beside him: a steel flechette and a U-shaped fragment of dull metal. Both had been brought from the Emerson home by the backup team. Vasily carefully picked up the dart by its fins and examined it closely, his hawklike face intent, his one eye gleaming brightly. He did the same to the piece of dull metal and nodded.

"Beautiful work," he said. "Yes, it has to be Eddie. Look at the flechette . . . see the lathe marks? This little beauty never came off a production line—it's hand-crafted. What did he use on it, some form of venom?"

"We don't have a lab report yet."

Vasily flicked the U-shaped piece of metal with his finger. "Vintage Mancuso. Marvelous! It's the rim of the charge that took out your other man. Eddie's famous toe-cap gadget. It's almost like a trademark."

"No question, then? He did the job?"

"He might as well have signed his name to it."

Swan sighed with a ghost of satisfaction. "Do you still think you can find him?"

"I'm sure of it. More so now than before."

"Why is that?" Swan inquired politely.

"Because you've flushed him out. He's running, and I know where he'll run to. What puzzles me is how he got mixed up with your man Emerson, or Volanov. What's the connection?"

"None that we know of," Swan admitted. "As you say, it's a puzzle."

It was a galling admission for the DD5 to make, but no more galling than the admission that two of his operatives had badly bungled an assignment, and that now he was forced to turn to a KGB maverick to finish the job. Coming to Borgneff this way, in the middle of the night and desperate, had punished his self-esteem badly, and he was seething inside. Only a firm resolve allowed him to maintain a calm exterior, for he knew that he truly had no choice. Before making the trip to the Fun House, he had, as usual, consulted by telephone with his associates abroad, and all four had agreed that Borgneff was the only man for the job. If Eddie Mancuso was involved, then Vasily Borg-neff was the logical antagonist to set against him. Still, it galled.

Swan reached into his jacket pocket and took out a thick envelope. He tossed it onto the table. Vasily opened it and examined the contents: a bound sheaf of currency, a U.S. passport, a Virginia driver's license, and three credit cards. He checked the names on the identification.

"Victor Barnum," he mused. "Yes, it's a name I can live with. What does the money represent?"

"That's twenty thousand you have there, a down payment on Emerson. The total price is fifty."

"And Eddie?"

"There's an open warrant out on him, good for another fifty. If you get him, it's yours." Swan hesitated. For a moment he looked almost embarrassed. "One thing more. The price for Emerson includes his wife and daughter."

Vasily grimaced but said nothing.

"What's the matter? Do you have qualms about the women?"

"Not as such, but I dislike overkill. Gratuitous slaughter tends to get out of hand."

"I can assure you that it's not gratuitous. It has to be that way, and it's an integral part of the assignment."

Vasily went to the sideboard, rummaging among half-empty bottles until he found a decanter of cognac. He poured them each a measure, raised his glass, and said formally, "To a successful conclusion."

Swan returned the salute, sipped appreciatively, and said, "You have one distinct advantage over Mancuso. He thinks you're dead. He'll hardly be expecting you."

"I'll need every edge I can get. I have a great deal of respect for Eddie."

"Any sane man would." Swan smiled wickedly. "Of course, there comes a time when respect turns to caution. You might decide that he's too much for you. You might just take the twenty thousand and disappear."

"The thought has already crossed my mind," Vasily said calmly. "But apparently you don't think that it will."

"No, I don't. For two reasons. Mancuso tried to kill you and damn near succeeded. He cost you an eye. . . ."

"He owes me more than an eye," Vasily said sharply. "We were like brothers once."

"Yes, and he turned on you. So you want Mancuso as much as I want Emerson, and if you get one you'll get them both. That's what I'm counting on. That's why you won't disappear."

"You said you had two reasons."

"Yes, I did." The wicked smile was back. He gestured across the room to where the two Vietnamese sat quietly. "Just to remind you where your loyalties lie, Chuc and Van will be working with you."

"I'm afraid that won't do," Vasily said coldly. "I always work alone."

"Not this time. Besides, as you said, you'll need every edge you can get."

"Those two?" Vasily looked at them contemptuously. Chuc was absently picking his teeth while Van stared at the ceiling. "If they're anything like the first two you used, I'll be better off without them."

"They're capable men," Swan insisted.

"For jungle work? I don't like this, Swan. You're imposing conditions that could shorten the odds."

"They're going," Swan said flatly. "You'll be in charge, but they're part of the team."

"And if I refuse?"

"You won't. Be sensible, man, two days ago you were begging—"

"Not begging!"

"Begging," Swan repeated, "for a chance to get out of here. This is your ticket out, and it's the only one you'll get. Don't be a fool . . . take it and be grateful."

"Grateful? Yes, I suppose I have to be." Vasily laughed bitterly.

"Good. How soon can you be ready?"

Vasily glanced again at Chuc and Van, and shook his head disgustedly. "Two days," he said.

"No sooner?"

"Not a minute sooner. I'll need at least one day in a good laboratory and another day with a first-class gunsmith. Can you arrange for that?"

"No problem." Swan looked at his watch. "We'd best get going right away. I'll brief you on communications procedure as we drive back to town."

"It's almost time for breakfast," said Vasily with an exaggerated politeness. "Would you care for something here before we go?"

Swan smiled gently. "I seem to recall a conversation about frozen fish fingers and toaster waffles. No, we'll breakfast in town."

Chapter 10

Mexico, for Eddie, was the smell of the jacaranda and the wood smoke mixing early in the morning as the *indios* passed through the streets driving burros impossibly laden with faggots of wood. It was the earthy odor of rotting fruit, the blaze of a salmon-colored sky at sunset, and the cascade of church bells that shattered each dawn. It was tortillas in the morning and margaritas at night; it was jalapeño peppers and chicken molé and bowls of ripe guavas and mangoes. It was the house built into the side of the hill high above the village of Atotonilco, rising from a walled courtyard in a succession of levels that topped the crest: levels of fountains and terraces, flowered gardens, intimate alcoves, and long, cool rooms floored with multicolored tiles. It was the harsh and drunken laughter that echoed from the cantinas; the soft laughter of young girls on paseo; and, best of all, now, the contented laughter that bubbled up in the back of his throat as he lay on the grass beside the swimming pool, warm and safe in the sun. Mexico was salvation, and that, for the damned, was something to laugh about.

"That's a wicked laugh," said Ginger. "What's so funny?"

She sat on the edge of the pool, her feet in the water, her fine, sleek body still stippled with dewdrops from her swim. The tiny flags of her bikini distracted him from the ripeness of that body, like a mustache scrawled on the Mona Lisa, and he was tempted to pull her to him and strip her bare. Impossible, of course, in the open daylight by the pool and with her parents wandering somewhere about . . . but still, he was tempted. He contented himself with reaching out to run his hand along the smoothness of her thigh.

"Nothing's funny," he said. "Nothing and everything. That was my fuck-you laugh."

"Oh? And whom are you fucking?" she asked politely.

"Whom? Christ, you're terrific. You're the only girl I know who can use fuck in a sentence and make it sound grammatical. Whom am I fucking? You'm, of course."

"That's nice," she said contentedly. "For both of us."

"Yeah, it is, but that's not what I meant," he explained. "That was my fuck-the-world laugh, nothing to do with sex. Like this." He raised himself up on one elbow and said loudly, "Hey, world. Fuck you, world, you can't touch us now."

"Don't say that," she said quickly.

"Bad luck?"

"Very."

"I'm sorry," he said when he saw that she was serious. Her eyes had been smiling and clear until then, but just for a moment he had seen them flash with fear, and he cursed himself for causing it. It was days since he had seen that look in her eyes, not since they had crossed into the magic of Mexico; but in the days before that, all during the drive from Washington to the border, her eyes had been filled with it.

It had been a trip of fear for all of them. Less for Eddie, who had lived with fear for so long and had learned to measure himself by his terror. Less, perhaps, for Emerson, who had willingly entered into a life of fear as a boy, and who had buried his fear under years of plenty, just as muscle is buried by fat. Less, in some degree, for Rusty, who had bought herself an interest-by-marriage in the fear game, and who had met every raise ever since. But for Ginger there had been no such shield against her fear, and she bore the full weight of it. Protected all her life, she was the least protected of them now as they fled in the night pushing south and west, running before winds of terror.

That first night set the tone of the trip, Eddie driving away from the house, piling on miles of back-country road, and making for the interstate highway below Front Royal. It was just before midnight when they reached the intersection of I-81, and he was tempted to keep his hands on the wheel and drive all night; but instead, he turned the camper into the parking lot of a darkened Burger King, slowed to a stop, and turned off the engine.

Then he told them where they were going. He told them about getting new papers in Houston, about Mexico, about the house in Atotonilco. He told it simply and without frills. He did not lie, but he did not emphasize the perils, and he did not show them the fear that he felt. After he told them, there was silence. They had been silent ever since leaving the house, but that had been the silence of tightly held breath. This was the silence of the same breath released, the silence of a sigh.

After a moment, Emerson said, "What's in Mexico?"

"Safety," Eddie told him. "Temporary safety. A place to hole up in, a place to make plans for the future. Right now, I don't think you could ask for more."

"I did ask," Emerson said bitterly, "and you saw what they gave me. All right, Mexico it is. How long will it take us?"

Eddie got out the maps and showed them all the route. "We drive in shifts of two," he explained. "Rusty and Jim, Ginger and me, and whoever isn't driving sleeps in the back. We drive straight through, no stops except for gas and food. If all the balls drop in the right holes, we should be in Atotonilco four days from now."

Emerson nodded his agreement. "One thought. Rusty and I should take the night shifts."

"Why?"

"If anybody comes looking for us, I've got the face they're looking for. Nighttime gives me some protection."

"Makes sense." Eddie slid out of the driver's seat and stood behind it. "That means you've got the wheel. Just lay it straight down I-81 for a couple of hours while I get some sleep."

He opened the door of the living quarters of the camper, looked at Ginger, and said, "Let's go, kid."

Ginger looked at her father and mother. She did not move. She looked back to Eddie and in a small voice said, "I don't think I want to go in the back with you."

Eddie felt his face grow hot. His first impulse was to grab her arm and pull her out of her seat. Instead, he kept his hands at his sides and said tightly, "Yeah, I know you don't, but you have to. Come on."

She did not move.

"What are you waiting for?" Rusty snapped. "You heard the arrangements. This is no time to get girlish."

Still, she did not move.

Emerson's gentle voice came out of the darkness. "Go ahead, Ginger. I'm sorry, baby, but this seems to be one of those times when personal feelings don't count."

She turned to peer at her father; then she sighed and said, "All right. For you."

They clambered into the back of the camper together, closed the door, and after a moment they felt the floor shift under their feet as Emerson edged the unfamiliar vehicle onto the roadway. Then the floor steadied as they picked up speed, and Eddie turned to her. He reached out a tentative hand, but she flinched and pulled away from him, her eyes dark and fearful.

"Look, kid . . ."

"No," she said wearily. "No looking. No talking. No nothing. Just sleep. Me over here, and you over there. That's all."

She dropped heavily onto the portside bunk, slipped off her sandals, and rolled over to lie facing the wall. Eddie shook his head sadly. He stripped down to his undershorts, bracing himself the roll of the road, and hung away his clothing carefully. Then he stretched himself out on the opposite bunk and stared at the ceiling. Well, I saw it coming he told himself. I saw it in her eyes back at the house. I'm the leper now, the man who kills.

He closed his eyes then and slept five good hours. When he woke he took the wheel, crossing into Tennessee as the sun came up over the rim of the Blue Ridge. Ginger made coffee and toast on the three-burner stove, Rusty and Emerson sank gratefully into sleep, and the pattern of the trip was set. Eddie and Ginger drove by day, and while they drove he tried to justify a lifetime. As they made the long haul south through Tennessee and into Alabama, he told her the tale of his Agency days, leaving out nothing and fighting for her understanding.

She no longer flinched from his touch, but the fear of him was still in her eyes, and at night they lay singly on separate bunks.

"You don't really listen to me," he told her on the second morning as they cut through bayou country on Interstate 10, the road a shining ribbon crossing swamp and cove, unwinding before them; and Jimbo and Rusty asleep in the back. "I've told you a dozen times so far. For as long as I worked for the Agency I was never operational, never in the field. My job was to make the gadgets, the UKDs, but other people used them, not me."

"Used them to kill people," said Ginger. Her voice was flat and accusing.

"Of course they did," Eddie said patiently. "That's why they're called UKDs. Unusual Killing Devices. You don't make a gadget like that just for the exercise. You make it to do a very specific job."

"A very dirty job."

"It was a job," he said firmly. "Look, how would you feel if I told you that for twenty years I was the chief designer for Remington, or Garand, or one of the other big arms outfits? Would you see anything morally wrong in that?"

She thought for a moment. "I wonder how good the comparison is. Somehow, designing a rifle seems . . . clean . . . compared to what you did."

"Oh? Nobody ever used one of my gadgets to kill a deer, or a whale, or a baby seal."

"Only people. And in the end you killed some yourself."

"They wouldn't let me retire. I wanted out—they said no. They sent people out to kill me. It was a question of them or me."

"Like the other night?" Her voice wavered. "I suppose I ought to be grateful. You saved my life. You saved us all."

"Gratitude is bullshit," he said. "It had to be done. I did it."

"Da, kanyeshna," said Emerson's voice behind them, softly, almost to himself. They turned. "Yes, of course it had to be done. Funny, how the Russian slipped in there. I haven't spoken Russian in thirty-five years, and now I find the words just crowding in."

He crouched to peer through the windshield. His face was drawn and his eyes looked weary as he stared at the road spinning out before them.

"How long to Houston?" he asked.

"Some time this afternoon. I made a phone call. We can get the papers done overnight and roll south tomorrow."

Emerson put his hand on Eddie's shoulder. "Forgive me, but I couldn't sleep, and I've been listening. I want you to know that I understand. As you said, it was something that had to be done. Thank God you were there to do it."

"Just something that had to be done," said Ginger. She looked up at Emerson, her face pale and her eyes questioning. "I thought I knew my father, and I thought I knew the man I love. Now it turns out that I knew hardly anything."

"Sometimes it's better that way," Emerson said gently. "To love without knowing too much."

"I don't agree with that," she said, and then suspicion hardened her face. "And you, Daddy? Did you ever do it?"

"Do what?" he asked, but he knew.

"Did you ever kill anyone?"

He remembered again, as he had remembered the night they left the house, and he clasped the old Luger in his hand. It was the Luger that had killed the real James Emerson. Radichek had given it to him and told him to say he had taken it from the body of a dead German.

"Only in the war," he said to Ginger, "and that's something no man wants to remember. Or talk about. I must try to sleep," he added, and closed the door.

They drove on through the morning, and for the rest of that day she sat silent and brooding.

The next afternoon they crossed the border at Nuevo Laredo, a party of four: Edward Angelotti, Jack and Rita Coleman, and Miss Pauline Rausch. Half an hour after clearing the internal control point they were booming south on the road to Monterrey, the sun high and hot, shards of rays bouncing off the roadway and breaking on the windshield in glitters. The air-conditioning in the Overlander was turned full on. Next to Eddie, Ginger looked cool and comfortable in a sunback dress of buttercup yellow, her long tan legs folded gracefully. It was then that he noticed that the fear had begun to fade from her eyes.

"I've been thinking," she said.

"Dangerous business."

"I think that what bothers me most about all this is the terrible waste."

"It happens," he said, shrugging.

"I mean the waste in you," she went on. "You're one of the brightest men I've ever met, but you're wasting yourself. What have you been doing with your life? Making gadgets that kill people. Even if I leave the morality of it aside, I can't understand how you ever got into such a business."

"What's a nice guy like me doing in a place like this?"

That brought a fragment of a smile to her face. "Eddie, I'm over the worst of it, and I'm ready to start with basics. Look, I love you. I loved you when I didn't know anything about you, and I love you now that I do. But I just don't understand it. With your talent you could have been anything, done anything you pleased. And you chose . . . this. Why? That's what I want to know. Why?"

He drove on, his eyes on the road, his hands gripping the wheel in the standard ten-to-two position. He pulled out to pass a lumbering truck, whipped the ungainly camper around it, and tucked back into the right-hand lane. He drove on for another mile in silence, thinking. Then he lifted his hands from the wheel and slapped them down again in futile exasperation.

"Every job was like a game to me," he said, "like a puzzle that had to be solved. They'd come to me and they'd say, 'Look, we need a gadget that's got to do such-and-such to so-and-so at a certain time and place, and it's got to look like an accident.' And I'd figure it out. I could do it. I could do it better than anybody else. But you see, you're wrong about me and what I can do. I guess maybe making gadgets is the only thing I've ever been really good at."

"I can't believe that," she muttered.

"That's love talking. You don't want to believe it. You want to believe that I could have been a doctor, or a bank president, or a lawyer like your father, or anything else because that builds up your love, that makes it worth more. . . ."

"Now, wait a minute. . . ."

"That's all right, I'm not knocking it. I guess I do the same thing sometimes when I'm looking at you and I see that absolutely great line of your hip and your thigh and that ass like a pair of apples, and I think to myself, hey, this kid's got it all. She's got a better body than a lot of the ones that you see in the movies or even the centerfold of *Playboy*. She's a beauty, and she's mine. You get that last part? *And she's mine.* That's the part that means that I'm kidding myself, because deep down I know that you're really not that great."

"Why, thank you," she said archly. "How sweet of you to say it."

"Don't talk cute that way; I'm trying to make a point. I don't have to tell you what you look like. You know that already. What I'm saying is that you're not a superstar. You're a beautiful woman, but you don't have that little extra unique something that would make you different from all the others. Christ, how many women have it? One in a million? Ten million? But most of the time you have it for me, because I *want* you to have it. Understand? I want you to have it because you're mine. And that's love talking."

He turned to look at her. All the fear was gone from her eyes, and something else was there instead. She said softly, "That's the most blatantly sexist statement I ever heard. It's also the straightest, finest thing that anyone has ever said to me."

She slipped out of her seat, stepped back to the door at the rear of the cab, and knocked on it sharply. After a moment, the door opened and Emerson put his head out.

"Sorry if I disturbed you," Ginger said. "Were you sleeping?"

"No, we're up. Neither one of us is sleeping very well these days."

"In that case," Ginger said brightly, "I wonder if you and Mother would mind switching with us for a while. Just for an hour or so. Eddie and I have some things to discuss."

"Discuss?"

Rusty's head appeared beside her husband's. "Discuss back here?" she asked querulously. "Why can't you talk up there?"

"It wasn't exactly talking that we had in mind. We have . . ."

Eddie snapped over his shoulder, "Ginger, cut it out."

". . . a lot of lost time to make up for." She smiled sweetly at her mother. "I'm sure you understand."

"But I don't," said Rusty, frowning.

"Well, I do." Emerson gave Ginger a wide grin. "Always glad to smooth the path of young love." He tapped Eddie on the shoulder. "Pull off the road—we'll switch."

"Look, this isn't necessary," Eddie said weakly. "I mean, you don't have to . . ."

"Don't argue," Emerson advised him. "Give in gracefully. My daughter is obviously a determined woman."

The camper rolled to a stop on the graveled verge. Rusty's lips were drawn in a thin line. Ginger grabbed Eddie's hand and pulled him through the door.

Ever since then the fear had been gone from her eyes, and now, three days later, lying beside the swimming pool in back of the house in Atotonilco, he cursed himself for bringing it back, if only for a moment. Then the moment was gone as she breathed deeply and stretched herself in the sun. The stretch turned into a wave as Rusty and Jimbo came out of the house, walking hand in hand along the path that led to the pool. They both waved back, but there was no gaiety to the gesture, no bounce to their step. Their heads were close and they were deep in conversation. Ginger followed them with her eyes.

"They look so . . . different," she said. "I know it's silly; it's only a few days, but they almost seem older."

Eddie nodded his agreement. The Emersons had not changed physically. Jimbo in bathing trunks still looked trim and hard, the model of a middle-aged man. Rusty's lacy bikini showed off a body that, lacking the ripeness of youth, still was glowing and handsome. Despite this, the pressure of the last days had worn them down badly, and it showed in their faces.

"What happens to them now?" Ginger asked.

Eddie wriggled luxuriously in the clean-smelling grass,

scrunching his toes in it. "A new life somewhere. They've got the papers and the money for it."

"What money?"

He grinned at her mockingly. "What do you think your old man's been doing all these years? He's been stashing it away in numbered accounts just like I have. I figure they'll want to head further south eventually, maybe Venezuela, or even Brazil. It'll take time to set up. Until then, our house is their house."

The use of the pronoun did not escape her, and she smiled her pleasure.

"Take a look at this," said Emerson, coming up beside them. He had a day-old copy of the English-language *Mexico City News*. He tossed it to Eddie and threw himself down on the grass. Rusty sank down gracefully beside him.

"Where did you get it?" asked Eddie, delving at once into the sports section.

"Over in San Miguel de Allende," said Rusty.

"I wanted to see how the Orioles were doing," Emerson explained.

"They lost." Eddie looked up from the paper. "The Mets won for a change."

"That's not why I showed it to you. Take a look at the bottom of page four."

It was a short item that could easily have been missed. The headline dealt with a forthcoming pan-American conference in Rio. The subject was interlinked defense systems for North and South America. Almost casually, in the final paragraph, the A.P. dispatch noted that the White House had nominated a special aide in place of Assistant Secretary of Defense James W. Emerson, who was ill and had taken an indefinite leave of absence.

"Ill!" said Rusty.

"Swan's work," Eddie explained. "He has to account for your not being there. If you wind up in the Soviet Union, even though he thinks that's unlikely, he'll change 'ill' to 'crazy.' "

"I don't like it." Emerson stared at the paper, then crumpled it up and tossed it aside. "I was just beginning to feel safe. Now I see this."

"Take it easy on the sports section." Eddie retrieved the paper and smoothed out the pages. "Look, stop worrying. This story doesn't change anything—it's just a cover."

"Swan wouldn't put out a story like that," Rusty said, "unless he thought he could back it up later."

"Back it up with my body," Emerson said morosely. "Found dead of some nervous disorder."

Ginger said nothing, but the fear was back in her eyes.

"You people break me up," said Eddie. He stood up and glared down at them in mock ferocity, like a drill sergeant. "I didn't bring you all the way to Mexico for this. Look at you . . . you look like the world just stopped turning because of that damn story. Now, I want to see some smiles on those worried little faces! I want to hear some bright and childish laughter! *I want you people to relax!*"

Rusty said, "But don't you see, it means that . . ."

Eddie roared, "Goddamn it, woman! You talk too much!"

He took a quick step, bent over, and lifted Rusty up in his arms. He turned and, in the same motion, threw her into the pool. She came up splashing and spluttering, wanting to scream, but speechless.

"That goes for you, too," Eddie said to Ginger, who had been totally silent. He put his foot in the small of her back and pushed. She went into the water with a loud smack, but she came up laughing.

Eddie turned to Emerson. "You're next."

"Think you can do it?" There was a slight smile on his face.

Eddie lunged and grabbed, but Emerson danced out of reach. He lunged again and this time got an arm lock in place. The two men strained against each other, struggling for footholds on the slick grass. Eddie grunted, slipped his hold, and tried for a leg. The next thing he knew, he was flat on his back and looking up at the faultlessly blue Mexican sky.

The man who had once been Yuri Volanov stared down at him gravely and murmured, "As I once said, there are some things that you never forget. Now, if you'll excuse me . . ."

He turned, ran to the concrete edge, and entered the water

with a flat racing dive. He came up stroking an easy crawl toward the far end of the pool.

Eddie rolled over on his belly and lay on the grass watching the scene happily. Ginger was floating on her back, eyes closed, accepting the sun. Rusty swam in small, contented circles, using an easy dog paddle to keep her head out of the water. Emerson reached the far end of the pool, did an awkward version of a racing turn, and came thundering back again.

Eddie raised himself up, resting an elbow on the grass, and called out, "That's a lot better. That's what I like to see. Everybody relaxed, everybody having a good time—"

He heard a soft *pop*, and a bullet dug into the grass a foot to the right of his head.

Chapter 11

Vasily Borgneff spent his first day of freedom accumulating supplies at a laboratory in downtown Washington, his second and third days working industriously with a gunsmith at Langley, and on the morning of the fourth day he boarded a flight at Dulles International Airport bound for Mexico City. There he rented a car and drove north for several hours until he reached the outskirts of Atotonilco, where, as one Victor Barnum, he established himself at the inn beside the mineral springs at Taboada. During those four days he was never out of the sight of the two Vietnamese, Chuc and Van, and by the evening of the fourth day he was ready to kill them. Literally.

It was not only because they clearly were evil, rapacious murderers. Vasily himself had done his share of killing, and as for evil, he had been around long enough to know that no sane man ever considers himself truly wicked, but only a misunderstood marcher to a particular drum. Nor was it because the two Vietnamese were so obviously his jailers as well as his associates. He could easily understand Swan's reluctance to let him operate alone, and, in truth, had he been given the opportunity, he might well have taken the twenty thousand dollars and disappeared happily into the night. Nor was it because the constant irritating presence of Chuc and Van had so far prevented him from making any social contact with any desirable female. It was not even because Chuc and Van were swinish boors with the manners of peasants and the pretensions of thugs recently raised to respectability. Over the years he had associated with worse and if the mission called for it, he had learned to accept

145

the dregs of humanity as bosom buddies. No, the fundamental reason why Chuc and Van exasperated him was that they were *stupid*. Anything else he could have borne . . . wickedness, boorishness, greed . . . but not this bovine stupidity, the nadir of which was their use of their language as a private code. They both spoke acceptable French and workable English, but when they wanted their conversation to be beyond his reach, they spoke to each other in Vietnamese.

As a KGB officer, Vasily had spent two years in Hanoi conducting classes in the construction of pinfire shotguns, plumber's-pipe pistols, homemade rocket launchers, and other forms of unconventional weaponry. By the end of those two years he had become fluent in the Vietnamese language. He did not, of course, reveal this to Chuc and Van. He was not about to surrender such an advantage, but in return for the edge he found himself forced to listen with a straight face to a boring and unending stream of recollections about the good old days with the Special Forces, the joys of tossing unredeemable Charlies out of low-flying choppers, and those carefree evenings sitting around the fire sharpening up bamboo slivers for the next day's interrogations. In addition, he was the recipient of their loutish opinions on every conceivable subject from the unavailability of American women to the indigestibility of American food. He was also required to listen to himself being described as a one-eyed weasel, a renegade Red, and a number-ten weary old man who didn't have the guts to kill a chicken on his own. By the end of the first day in Taboada, Vasily was cheerfully urging Chuc and Van to drink the clear, refreshing Mexican tap water.

On the afternoon of that first day, with the two Vietnamese in close tow, he drove up into the hills above the town, left the car parked on the side of the road, and worked downhill into a position above the house, the home he once had shared with Eddie Mancuso. It was the only house for miles around. It had been a dry summer, and the Guanajuato countryside was a succession of brown and rounded hills with only an occasional flash of green to mark a grazing spot, a stand of trees, or a hard-earned well. Across this featureless landscape marched the twin lines of rural electrification, the high-tension cables swooping from pylon to pylon in sagging arcs, this imprint of civilization on the countryside as out of place as a hat on a horse.

From a position below one of these cable-bearing towers on the hill overlooking the house, Vasily could view, through high-powered glasses, the top two levels of the building, the garden, and the swimming pool. Using the glasses was an irritant, for it reminded him forcibly that he now had only one eye, thanks to Eddie Mancuso, and the sight of Eddie disporting in the pool below did nothing to lessen the irritation. There were four people in the pool, two men and two women, and he realized that he had in view all four of his targets, as neatly grouped as ducks in a shooting gallery. All he needed now was the means to dispose of them.

"Wide open," said Chuc, who was watching through glasses of his own. "We could walk right in."

"Let's take them right now," Van said excitedly.

"Shut up, both of you," Vasily growled, his glasses still fixed on the scene below. "There's an alarm system, a good one. I designed it myself."

"Can you crack it?"

Vasily did not answer. He watched through the glasses with troubled eyes. The house presented a technical problem to be solved, penetration and execution, but it was also a place filled with memories for him. It was here that he had spent the happiest months of his life with Eddie and Chalice, two men in love with the same woman and living in almost absolute harmony. And then it all had fallen apart, both the brotherhood and the love degenerating into a clawing scramble for survival. Whose fault? There had been a time when his anger at Eddie Mancuso had been so strong and fresh that he would not have bothered to ask the question, much less answer it. But now he was not at all sure. Not that it made any difference. The end result was that Chalice was dead, that Vasily himself had come within a whisker of it, and that now it was Eddie's turn. The thought, which should have filled him with a long-delayed satisfaction, filled him with sadness instead.

That sadness was heightened by the sight of Eddie emerging

from the pool to stand dripping on the concrete lip, his hands on his slim hips and his chin jutting out as he surveyed his property with very apparent satisfaction.

"Cocky little bastard," Vasily murmured to himself and lapsed again into memory of the year before. That was the year when everyone was singing, "Bailando Loco," and dancing to it in the bars and cafés, the mariachis playing it in the streets and the plaza; and often that last summer they would swing through the night to the tune of it, the three of them laughing and singing and drinking the light, white, fourth-rate Mexican wine.

Bailando loco, dancing crazy to the wild, insistent beat that lit fires in the blood, an idiotic two-step meant to be danced at a lunatics' ball; and Eddie would hop around the floor like a demented cockroach with two broken legs, warbling, *"Como mis piernas, están roto los cojones. Como los cojones, están roto mi amor,"* while Chalice laughed delightedly and Vasily tapped the tips of his fingers together in affectionate applause. It had been a crazy time, indeed, for the three of them, and they had danced their way through it, *bailando loco,* in a crazy two-step all their own.

His reverie was broken by the sight of Ginger, who had come out of the pool to stand beside Eddie with her arm around his waist. Vasily caught his breath as his glasses played over the body of the young woman. Ten months of enforced continence pounded at his temples, and this time he murmured to himself, "Lucky little bastard."

But if the sight of Ginger affected his breathing, the sight of her mother caused a giant hand to squeeze on his heart. Rusty, clad in a white lace bikini, came up the ladder and out of the pool with Emerson close behind her. The lift of her chin, the tilt of her breasts, the casual go-to-hell roll of her walk defined her as his kind of woman, and he knew that he would soon have to do something about his social life.

As he watched, the four people turned and strolled up the path to the house. Vasily followed them with the glasses, parting from them reluctantly as the back door closed. He kept the glasses fixed on that door for a long moment, then shook his head sadly and turned his mind to the problem at hand.

Actually, there were three problems. The first was the alarm system, but the design was his own and he was confident that he could master it. The second problem was that, according to his mandate from Swan, the Emerson deaths had to appear accidental or, at the least, untraceable. It didn't matter how Eddie went, but the Assistant Secretary of Defense and his family had to slip out smoothly and without raising the fuss of an investigation. The third problem was Eddie—he had to be immobilized. The attack had to be mounted at a time when he was vulnerable, stripped bare of his formidable arsenal of death-dealing gadgets. Stripped bare? Vasily stared through the glasses at the swimming pool below him. He twisted to look up at the high-tension wires that curved above him. He did trigonometry in his head, estimating heights and distances, then took a pad and pencil from his pocket and confirmed the figures. He smiled grimly.

In Vietnamese, Chuc said to his partner, "The weasel smiles. He is thinking of his dinner."

Van answered in the same language, "No, he is thinking of women. The women down below. Did you see them through the glasses?"

"I saw them both. Unusual beauty."

"Two blossoms," Van agreed. "Both the mother and the daughter."

"It is a pity they must go."

"A terrible waste."

"Perhaps before . . . ?"

"Perhaps."

Vasily kept his face impassive. He lifted himself from his prone position and looked at Chuc and Van, their ferretlike faces turned up to him. He pointed to the cable-bearing tower that loomed above them.

"Can you climb that?" he asked.

Both of them looked up, then shrugged. Van spat contemptuously and said, "Sure, no sweat."

"A piece of cake," said Chuc.

"Would you need any special equipment? Shoes? Belts?"

"Nothing," said Van and spat again. He pointed to the rubber-soled sneakers that they both wore. "That's what these are for."

Chuc added, "Half monkey, half snake, that's us."

More hyena than either, thought Vasily as he led them back to the car, keeping close to the contours of the terrain. The drive to Querétaro, the nearest city, took less than an hour. On the outskirts, in the barrio behind the bullring, was a strip of automobile repair shops, junkyards, and several *ferreterías*. Leaving Chuc and Van in the car, he browsed around until he found what he wanted: two heavy-duty cable cutters. The blued cutting edges could go through all but the thickest cable, and the long handles were heavily insulated. He paid for them, stowed them in the trunk of the car, and drove back to their hotel, arriving there in the early evening.

"Up to my room," he told the others. "We have things to talk about."

Once upstairs, they disposed themselves around the room, Vasily in a wicker chair and the Vietnamese perched on the edge of the bed. Vasily took out his note pad and sketched a diagram of the house and of the high-tension wires that passed almost directly above it. He handed it across to the others without comment.

Chuc looked at the sketch. "You'll drop the cables?"

Vasily nodded.

"I don't get it. What good does that do?"

"Listen—" First, he explained, during the night both of the high-tension cables had to be weakened, not visibly, but enough so that one final clip would send them flying. Then it was just a question of waiting until the four people in the house were all in the swimming pool. A final cut of both cables would hurtle them into the pool. The result: instant electrocution.

The two Vietnamese listened carefully. Van frowned. "How do you know that the cables will hit the pool? You're guessing."

Vasily shook his head impatiently. "I never guess. It's my job to make sure they hit."

The other two looked unconvinced.

You're pushing them, Vasily told himself. Be patient . . . keep it simple. He managed a smile and said, "The cut ends of the cable don't have to drop straight into the water."

"Why not?"

"Because those cables are very heavy. Their own weight will drag them across the patio and into the pool in seconds."

"So!" Chuc and Van were smiling now.

"And what's our friend, Mr. Mancuso, doing while all this is happening? Swimming around as happy as a mackerel, and not even Eddie can hide a gadget in his swimsuit."

"Excellent. Ingenious." They were both fascinated. "And who cuts the cables?"

"You do. Both of you."

"And you?"

"I'll be on the ground to give the signal. Watch my left arm. When the arm comes down, cut the cables."

"Not so easy to see straight down from the tower," Van noted.

"I won't be under the tower. I'll be inside the grounds, close to the pool."

Chuc looked startled. "Inside? What about the alarm?"

"I'll be right on top of them before they know it."

"But they'll see you."

"I want Mancuso to see me. I don't give a damn about the others, but I want *him* to know who's killing him."

Van shook his head. "Bad business. I don't like it."

How do I explain? Vasily wondered. How do I explain a year's worth of anger still bottled up inside me? How do I explain loyalty? They would turn on each other for pennies, so how do I explain betrayal? If I told them the story of Cain and Abel, they would probably giggle and then applaud.

"This is important to me," he said slowly. "This man, Mancuso, tried to kill me. He thinks that he succeeded; he thinks that I'm dead. He gave me this." He tapped his eyepatch. "Now it's my turn. I'm going to kill him and all the others, but before I do I want him to know that it's me. I want him to look up and see me. I want him to fear me before he dies. I have to do this; otherwise, killing him is meaningless to me."

They both nodded solemnly, and Chuc said, "Every man understands revenge. It is part of the blood. But this will be dangerous. You might be hit by the cable."

"I won't be. I'll be watching for it."

He waited. They looked at each other, eyes questioning, then coming to a silent agreement. Van said, "OK, if that's the way you want it."

Vasily let out a breath. "It is."

"Swan said you're the boss, so we do it your way; but if anything goes wrong, we cut the cables anyway. Agreed?"

"Agreed."

"Good. When do we go in?"

"Tonight. The first step is to weaken the cables. We'll leave here around midnight, so get some rest before then. You've got a hard climb ahead of you."

They went down to dinner then. Vasily sent the other two into the dining room while he stopped in the lounge for an aperitif. The lounge was almost empty. Most of the hotel guests sat out on the lawn at tiny tables, and beyond them, although the sun was almost gone, an energetic group of teenagers still frolicked in the mineral springs and the warm-water pools for which the inn was famous. Vasily looked around the room. Several couples sat at tables; two business types huddled at the far end of the bar in earnest conversation; and at the near end sat a graceful woman in a simple white dress, masses of raven-black hair to her shoulders. Late thirties, he decided, and he noted the full figure, the good legs casually crossed, and the well-shaped hand that held her glass. He slid onto the next stool and ordered a Pernod from the stolid-faced boy behind the bar.

When the drink came he delicately added drops of water until the pale liquid turned milky, then raised the glass to his lips. He did not drink at once. He closed his eyes and breathed in the sharp aroma, conjuring up memories of other days and other drinks, overtones of roasting chestnuts and autumn smoke in other climes, fantasies of well-remembered flesh, familiar eyes and lips, and tapering fingers. He let the memories flood him indiscriminately, fragments of all his ages converging, and marveled at how many memories could be contained within a single glass. Then he opened his eyes, took the first sip, and sighed.

"*¡Válgame Dios!*" exclaimed the woman beside him in soft, unaccented Spanish. "You took that drink the way I take the wafer at communion. Are you praying, or are you drinking?"

Vasily took another sip before turning to face her. "A little of both, I suppose."

"Are you a priest of alcohol, then?" she asked, smiling with white, even teeth.

"Never," said Vasily, trying to appear shocked. "Do I look that holy? I am a priest of nothing, merely a worshiper."

"Very bad of you, *señor*." Her eyes were smiling as well, mocking him. "Such an elaborate worship should be reserved for a woman, not a drink."

"Ah, that." He waved casually at the room and the people. "That sort of worship one reserves for the private chapel, not the public church."

"*¡Mas mal!*" she said spiritedly. "Even worse. Is the worship of a woman such an occasion of sin that it must be done secretly?"

"A good point," Vasily conceded, taking another sip. "You called me a priest, but you speak like a Jesuit in disguise. Remember, however, that one must make a distinction between worship and ritual. To worship a woman publicly, well . . . *es muy caballero* . . . but the ritual must remain private or it loses all of its mystery." He slid from the bar stool to stand erect. He inclined his head slightly. "I am Victor Barnum, and your servant."

"Elena Castelnuevo."

She extended her hand. He took it and sketched a kiss over it, saying, "*Encantado.*" He was tempted to say more, to give gentle pressure to her fingers, to invite her to worship with him either in wine or in any other ritual that might move her. But he did none of these things. He knew what the night held for him.

"This has been delightful," he said regretfully. "Unfortunately, I am occupied this evening. Perhaps we could continue our catechism some other time?''

''Perhaps,'' she murmured, and as they parted there was surprise as well as regret in her eyes.

Chapter 12

On the same day that Vasily Borgneff lay on the side of a hill observing the house of Eddie Mancuso, Sasha Ignatiev spent part of the afternoon watching a young woman scrub the kitchen floor of his Washington apartment. The young woman started scrubbing shortly after noon and worked straight through until nearly two o'clock. The kitchen was not a large one and its tiled floor could easily have been scrubbed clean in fifteen minutes, but the girl performed the chore over and over again, working industriously on her knees with a stiff-bristled brush and a pail of soapy water. Just outside the kitchen door, Sasha lounged in a chair with a cold gin in his hand, observing the scene in comfort. He watched intently but for the most part silently, his only comments an occasional criticism.

"Over near the stove, you missed a spot, Marcella," he would say, or, "Try taking a longer stroke, sweetie."

Marcella's invariable reply was, "Whatever you say Sasha," and on she would go, dipping the brush, scrubbing and rinsing the already spotless floor. Each time she finished the task she would stand up, stretch, empty the pail of water into the sink, and look inquiringly at Sasha. A quick, impatient flick of his fingers would tell her to continue, and she would cheerfully refill the pail and set to work again.

Watching his floor being scrubbed was more than just an exercise in sanitation for Sasha; it was one of his favorite recreational activities, which accounted for three unusual facts about the girl who was doing the scrubbing. First, she was an unusually attractive young woman whose normal line of work was as a dancer at the House of Joy; second, she was totally nude as she worked away on her hands and knees; and third, she was being paid fifty dollars an hour to scrub Sasha's floor.

Since at one time or another most of the dancers at the House of Joy had been employed in this manner, the motivation behind the routine, and the gratification that Sasha derived from it, were a constant source of speculation among the girls. One theory held that Sasha, being gay, enjoyed the sight of a woman debasing herself on her hands and knees. This theory was contested by several girls who claimed that their kitchen sessions with Sasha had concluded with him leaping upon them and using them sexually. One girl, who had paged through Krafft-Ebing, was of the opinion that the man simply had a cleanliness complex; while another, who had picked up a little Freud, had come to the conclusion that Sasha as a little boy had observed his mother scrubbing floors and was only trying to recapture a childhood fantasy. A final group rejected the more overtly sexual explanations and opted for the premise that Sasha was really a frustrated sculptor who was madly obsessed with the female form divine.

If Sasha was aware of these speculations, he ignored them; but if he had been pressed to answer them, he would have been forced to concede a germ of truth in all of them. He found the sight of an attractive female on her hands and knees, breasts swinging and perky rump pointed skyward, a source of quiet satisfaction, subdued excitement, and an overwhelming contentment. Further than that he did not attempt to analyze its effect on him. He knew only that watching a naked girl scrub his kitchen floor was the closest approach to domesticity that his chaotic life would allow, and if the sight at times aroused the curious mixture of his sexual imperatives, why, that was just so much profit on the transaction. Within the limits of the kitchen routine he never saw himself as a debaser of womanhood, but on the other hand the thought of getting a boy to scrub his floor had never crossed his mind.

Marcella had been scrubbing for almost two hours, and Sasha, lulled by her movements and by the aphrodisiacal aroma of pine-scented detergent, was slowly approaching a state of satori when the telephone rang. Jarred from his reverie, he frowned, snapped his fingers at Marcella as a sign to take a break, and went into his bedroom to answer the call.

"Sasha, I want you down here right away," said Anya Ignatiev. The noises in the background were those of the House of Joy. "Right now, you hear?"

"Hmmmmm?" Still bemused and not quite himself, Sasha smiled into the telephone. "Can it wait a while, love? Half an hour or so?"

"No, it cannot. What are you doing that's so important?"

"Cleaning house, darling. You know how things pile up."

"Oh, that. No, I need you now." Her voice was rough and irritated. "And tell whoever it is this time to get her sweet little ass down here, too. She's being paid to dance on her feet, not scrub on her knees."

She hung up sharply. Sasha went back to the kitchen where Marcella was leaning against the sink, resting. Her lean dancer's body was covered with sweat. Sasha shuffled bills from his wallet and paid her.

"Game's over, sweetie," he said. "Time to go back to work. Just mop up and lock the door when you leave."

Twenty minutes later he sauntered into the back room of the House of Joy and found his mother behind her desk. When he saw the look on her face, he locked the door behind him before he settled into a chair and gave her a questioning glance.

Without preamble, Anya said, "We have a report from *Backfire*."

"Bloody well about time. Do we have a location for Emerson?"

"Mexico. A house outside a village called Atotonilco, which is out in the middle of nowhere in the state of Guanajuato. I have all the details."

Sasha grunted, and without thinking his hand went to his temple to touch the bandage that covered the tear in his skin. It was a small bandage, only a strip of gauze and tape, but the wound still throbbed on occasion. It bothered him painfully now as he thought of the night at Emerson's home and his failure to protect the man he thought of as his father. He was not a stranger to failure, but he had never learned to live with it; and although he enjoyed an easygoing relationship with Anya, he was not at all sure how much professional credit he still had left with her.

"What happens now?" he asked as lightly as he could. "Do I assume that I'm going after him?"

To his relief, his mother nodded without hesitation. "You'll go alone and pick up some people from our embassy in Mexico City. Make contact and bring him out. Those are your orders. Nothing less will be acceptable."

"I understand."

"I wonder if you do." Anya looked tired and, he realized, older. No, not older, simply her age. Her eyes were sunken, and violet shadows edged them. "There's no room for failure here, Sasha. What happened the other night was . . . barely allowable. But if something else goes wrong, I won't be able to protect you anymore." She thought for a moment. "And God only knows who will protect me."

"I understand that, too." For once his voice was level and serious.

"It won't be easy. He has an American with him, a dangerous man."

"The same one who . . . ?"

"The same." She hesitated, then said, "I want you to understand something else. Our priorities on this project have changed somewhat."

"What does that mean?"

"We still want him alive, of course. Alive and back in Moscow. But if we can't have him that way . . ." She shrugged.

He looked at her in disbelief. "You're talking about Yuri Volanov? James Emerson? My father?"

"I never said he was your father. I'm also talking about the man who was once my lover, but that's the way it has to be," she said wearily. "Those are the orders from Zhukovka."

"But why? It doesn't make sense."

"That isn't for you to judge. The question is, can you do it if you have to?"

He did not answer. He stared right through her.

"Tell me now, Sasha. It may never come down to it . . . I hope it doesn't, but it might. And so I have to know. If you can't do it, I'll send someone else."

He still did not answer. At the moment he was a long way from the House of Joy, parked on the side of a road and watching a house burst into flames, the inferno roaring and racing from room to room . . . destroying, blasting, burning. And he heard the sound of his father's voice calling for help.

"Sasha?" This time it was his mother's voice asking the question gently. "Sasha, I have to know. If you have to, can you kill him?"

And then it was his own voice he heard, removed from himself and echoing strangely, but unquestionably his own voice saying, "I can do it if I have to. Count on it. I can do it."

After leaving Elena Castelnuevo in the bar, Vasily joined Chuc and Van for a light meal, after which he napped in his room for two hours and met them again in the parking lot shortly before midnight. They made the same approach to the house as they had in the afternoon, driving up to the highway, leaving the car, and working down along the contours of the land to the hill and the tower. Vasily handed them the cable cutters.

"Remember, not too deep," he warned. "We don't want to cut it tonight. Use the edge of the tool to rub the cable, make it look worn. Nothing more, understand?"

They nodded, but for the first time they looked uneasy. They both glanced up. The night was cloudless, and the cables showed clearly against the starry sky. They seemed very far away.

"Not so easy at night," Van said nervously.

"Don't start that with me." Vasily's voice was angry. "You were the one who said it was a piece of cake. You were the one who was doing all the spitting."

"How much juice in those lines?"

"Enough to light up a small town. But those tools are fully insulated. It's an easy job."

"Easy for you. You stay on the ground."

"You're damn right I stay on the ground. I never said I could climb that bloody monster, but you did. You're the kings of the jungle, aren't you? Half monkey, half snake . . . so get your asses up there and get to work."

They were still unhappy, but they secured the tools to their belts with lengths of line, clenched pencil flashes between their teeth, and began the ascent up the latticework of the tower, moving gingerly at first, and then with more confidence. Vasily watched them go up until he could no longer see the tiny dots of light from the flashes; then he sat on the ground with his back braced against the lowest strut of the tower and looked down at the house below. There were no lights, the house was darkened for the night, and it was all too easy for him to place himself in his imagination within the shell of the building and wander through the halls and gardens, up and down the tiled stairways, in and out of the bedrooms filled with the silence of slumber. All too easy for an active imagination, but in that direction lay disaster, and when the sexual images began to flicker he forced himself to stop. The people down there were as good as dead, and he pushed his mind in other directions. He thought for a moment of Elena Castelnuevo, transferred the sexual imagery to her, let it build and mentally explode. Then, finished with imagery and ignoring the dark bulk of the house below, he centered down coldly within himself, blanked out his mind, and waited.

It was almost an hour later when he felt, rather than heard, the two men descending. Their descent was noiseless, he conceded in reluctant admiration. One moment he was alone on the ground, and in the next moment they were there beside him, breathing rapidly but otherwise at ease.

"How did it go?" he asked.

"No sweat."

"Piece of cake."

He collected the cutting tools from them. The insulated handles were clammy, and he could see now that their faces were covered with perspiration. "No sweat," he repeated. "Yes, I could tell. I could feel the tower shaking all the way down here. How much did you shave them?''

"Right down close," Chuc said smugly. "One more clip and away they go.''

Vasily nodded. He had little confidence in either of them and would have preferred to check the work himself, but he was not about to attempt the tower. Twenty years ago, perhaps, and with both eyes . . . he sighed. "All right, let's get back to the hotel and get some sleep. We have a long day tomorrow.''

It was a long three days, not one. For those three days they lay up in the same spot below the tower, observing the routine of the house below. The days seemed endless and the sun was merciless. They ate dry sandwiches, drank bottled water, and endured the dust and the flies silently. Chuc and Van rebelled at the procedure, but Vasily insisted, and by the end of the third day they had a rough idea of how the pool was used. Eddie was the first one out in the morning for a quick swim before breakfast. Rusty and Emerson used the pool around noon, he to thrash a limited number of laps and she to paddle about placidly. Ginger did not appear until late afternoon, when all four of them swam together. That was the only time the pool was full.

"That's it, then," Vasily said at the end of the third day. "It isn't much, but it's a pattern. As of tomorrow we go operational. We'll hit them around five in the afternoon when they're all in the pool. If they're not all together, we wait for the next day.''

They dragged themselves wearily back to the hotel. Once there, Vasily said, "I don't want you two hanging around me tonight. Do what you want, but stay out of my way.''

It was cocktail time as they walked across the close-clipped lawn, making their way through the maze of tiny tables. The last of the sun lay heavy on the hills, and the tables were filled with brightly dressed guests chattering gaily in a handful of languages. Two mariachis wandered over the grass singing softly, and white-jacketed waiters with broad Indian faces rushed drinks on trays with un-Mexican haste. It was that time of day when anything seems possible and anticipation rules. Still half an hour away from his first Pernod of the evening, Vasily could already feel the heat of it in the back of his throat. His eyes roamed the tables, and he wondered about Elena Castelnuevo.

"We stay together," Van said, frowning. "Those are the orders."

"Not tonight."

"Every night. Swan said so."

"Screw Swan. He's in Washington, and we're here. I don't want any nursemaids tonight."

The two Vietnamese looked at each other uncertainly.

"Go and amuse yourselves," Vasily said cheerfully. "Get yourself a drink, get yourself a meal, get yourself a woman." He gave them a mocking grin. "This would be a good chance for you to call your cutout number. Isn't it time for you to get in touch with Swan?"

Van said impassively, "We have no cutout number."

"*Merde.*"

"It is true. Our only communication is through you."

"Naughty, naughty. Didn't your mother ever tell you not to fib?" He reached into his pocket, found the car keys, and threw them over. "Here's your insurance that I'm not going anyplace. So don't let me see your faces tonight."

He went up to his room, bathed, and changed into a dark blue suit of shantung silk that he had bought off the peg before leaving Washington. He groomed himself carefully before the mirror, brushing the silver wings of his hair and adjusting the patch over his left eye to a rakish angle . . . the Moshe Dayan touch. After a complacent inspection, he left the room and went down to the lounge.

He was still on his first Pernod when he heard Elena's voice behind him, saying, "So there you are. I thought you might have retired to a monastery."

His one eye met hers in the mirror behind the bar. "I tried. They wouldn't have me."

"You're at your devotions early today, *padre.*" Her husky voice made a pool of pleasure inside of him.

"The wicked always pray early," he said, turning on his seat to face her. "There's always the chance that God is still drowsy."

She nodded approvingly. "Also, it leaves the rest of the day open to sinning."

"Still the Jesuit, aren't you? Will you join me in worship?"

"*Si, ¿como no?* A vodka tonic, please."

She sat beside him, settling down comfortably as if she had been there often before. They smiled at each other, sipped at their drinks, and began the ritual of identification, each telling the other a life in capsule.

He was the Baron Viktor Barnowski, a Polish expatriate and now an American citizen with the American name of Victor Barnum, an oil broker based in Dallas who often traveled south of the border to deal with Pemex, the state-owned Mexican oil producer. He was a lifelong bachelor, a collector of pre-Columbian statuary, and an unabashed lover of nineteenth-century Italian opera. Whenever he could, he stopped at Taboada to partake of its curative waters.

She, in turn, was Elena Castelnuevo León, a widow from Mexico City whose husband had died four years before and had left her with the dual responsibilities of a comfortable estate and a twelve-year-old daughter. Content in her widowhood, she divided her time between her home in the capital's Zona Rosa and a flat in Puerto Vallarta, and she was an unabashed lover of nineteenth-century Italian opera. She and her daughter—now sixteen—stopped often at Taboada to partake of its curative waters.

They had another drink while he complimented her beauty and she complimented his command of the Spanish language. They compared notes and found that they had friends in common in New York (the exquisite Carollinis; the two Lamont brothers; and the ancient pianist, Gina Lescower), in Bangkok (darling Paul and his ever-changing flock of boys), and in Paris (poor Carlotta Obregón and her alcoholic husband, and that terrible Linda Paternoster, who was always in trouble with the police). They smiled comfortably at each other, destroyed two bowls of salted almonds, and fended off the approaches of the mariachis with a twenty-peso note. He told her wearily of the difficulties involved in brokering petroleum in today's chaotic market, and just as wearily she told him of the difficulties involved in the raising of a teenage daughter in today's permissive society.

The object of her concern appeared just then, the sixteen-year-old daughter, Isabella, bursting into the lounge and running the length of the bar calling to her mother. Fresh from the mineral pools, the girl wore a next-to-nonexistent string bikini and a terry-cloth cover-up, which she had not bothered to tie together. The temperature went up sharply in the lounge; heads turned and eyes were riveted on firm flesh bouncing, buttocks and breasts ajiggle as Isabella jumped up and down in excitement and begged *Mamacita* to please, please let her stay at the pool during dinnertime and have hamburgers and beer with the other young people.

"Cover yourself," said Elena.

"What? Oh." She had been casually indifferent to her near nudity, but now she tugged the terry cloth closed. "May I, Mama, please?"

"I was about to call you to dress for dinner."

"Just this once, please? It's so boring in the dining room."

"The sun is down, you'll be cold out there," Elena said.

"No, I won't, really. See?" She hugged the terry cloth close to her body and shivered to show how warm she would be. Everything jiggled again.

"*Basta*, we don't need an exhibition," her mother said resignedly. "All right, but not too late, understand?"

"Thank you, Mama!" Isabella jumped with excitement again. She kissed her mother three times quickly on the cheek, then turned to run down the length of the bar and out the door. The terry-cloth robe fell open again as she ran, and necks craned and eyes narrowed as her passage was followed.

Elena laughed with a touch of embarrassment. "You see what I mean about problems?"

"She is a lovely child," Vasily said gravely.

"Child? She's a teenage volcano." This time Elena's laughter was natural. "I saw what your eyes were doing, you and every other man in the room."

Vasily smiled easily. "One would be less than human not to

admire, but she is still a child. With some luck she may grow into a woman as lovely as her mother.''

Elena acknowledged the compliment with a nod. ''And you called me a Jesuit. Still, she's at a difficult age. There are times when she embarrasses me badly.''

''Such as now,'' Vasily pointed out. ''She has deserted you at the dinner hour.''

Elena waved the thought away. ''Not important at all.''

''But it is, and I was thinking of remedying the situation by asking you to dine with me.''

''I was hoping you would,'' she said simply.

Three hours later, Vasily lay flat on his back in Elena's bed, the perspiration cold on his skin as he stared at the ceiling and wondered at the fragility of the male ego. The bedroom was part of an elaborate suite, its walls ornately decorated with tapestries of hunting scenes. Vasily glared at a slavering wolfhound and dared it to glare back. Beside him, Elena; all soft pink undulations and comforting noises, cuddled close. Vasily gritted his teeth and made a despairing sound deep in his throat.

''Be easy, *hombre,*'' murmured Elena. ''Rest, and we'll try again soon.''

''The hell we will,'' snapped Vasily. ''Enough is enough. I'm getting out of here.''

He rolled over on his side, preparatory to jumping out of bed. Elena caught his arm to stop him, then gently pulled him to her. He groaned as he sank back into her arms.

''Rest,'' she commanded. ''It would demean us both if you left now.''

''Dearth before dishonor,'' he muttered, and he meant it.

The climax of the evening had proved to be anything but. All else had gone well: the dinner of lightly curried shrimp followed by a baked red snapper with braised celery, and a chocolate mousse; a quiet walk around the grounds of the inn, a pause to admire a gibbous moon, a cognac at the bar, half an hour of gentle dancing; and then the long, confident walk, arm in arm, down the darkened corridors to Elena's suite; the key in the door, the tender disrobing, the tumble into bed . . . and then disaster. After a year of enforced continence, a year of sensual yearnings so sharp that at times he had thought he would die of them, Vasily now found himself staring at his limp and uncooperative phallus.

"These things happen," said Elena, consoling.

"Not to me, they don't," he growled.

"Never?"

"Never."

She shrugged at such obvious hyperbole and in the motion of the shrug managed to press even closer, her breasts a cushion for his arm and one of her legs thrown over his loins. She waited for a moment and then began to move herself against him, rubbing his body with hers while her fingers worked dexterously.

"Stop that," he said. "It isn't going to work."

She shrugged again and stopped.

"Besides, I thought we were going to rest for a while."

"Very well, we rest." She hesitated, then asked shrewdly, "Tell me, *querido*, has it been a long time since you were with a woman?"

Teeth clenched, he closed his eyes and said, "Yes."

"A very long time?"

"Yes, damn it, a *very* long time."

"Ah, I thought that might be it. The expectation was too much."

"Perhaps," he conceded.

"And of course, there was the girl."

"Who?"

"Isabella. My daughter. She distracted you."

His eyes popped open. "Nonsense."

"Not nonsense at all. She put an image in your mind, and for the moment that is all you can see."

"Elena, I assure you . . ."

"Please." She put a finger on his lips, then took it away and kissed him there lightly. "It is not necessary to assure me of anything. I am in no way insulted." She was silent for a moment, as if in deep thought; then said, "Come. There is a simple way to fix this."

She sat up and got out of bed, coming around to stand over him. She reached down to take his hands, saying, "Come with me now."

He looked up at her, mystified. She was an imposing sight from that angle, the strong hips, narrow waist, and high-riding breasts like those of a clipper ship's figurehead; and he was the fish in the sea. He shook his head and said, "What is all this?"

But he let her take his hand and pull him from the bed, lead him across the bedroom and into the sitting room, conscious of his nudity and hers as they padded across the carpeted floor. At the door to the other bedroom she turned to him and smiled. She put a finger to her lips for silence.

He whispered hoarsely, "Elena, this is crazy."

She only shook her head. Still holding his hand, she opened the door and led him inside. Isabella's bedroom was smaller than her mother's and more simply furnished. No slavering wolfhounds, he was pleased to see, only flowery prints. A single lamp acted as a night-light, casting a pale pool over the bed. Isabella slept deeply, her body sprawled at all angles, and only a sheet covered her. Elena sat on the edge of the bed and ran her fingers lovingly through the thick hair, which was spread over the pillow like a cape. The girl did not stir.

"Observe," said Elena.

She put her hand to the top of the sheet and very gently drew it down, exposing her daughter's body. Vasily stared, a thickness in his throat. This was a loveliness that had only been hinted at earlier in the lounge. It was not that the girl was now totally nude—the few wispy strings had been nothing more than a legal masquerade—but the sprawl of her body in the abandonment of sleep made an aphrodisiac out of vulnerability. As if to emphasize that vulnerability, Elena cupped one of the girl's breasts in her hand and caressed it with her fingertips. With a moistened finger she rubbed the nipple erect, and Isabella stirred in her sleep.

Elena's eyes were dancing as she looked at him. "Lovely?"

"Lovely." He barely got the word out. His throat felt full of plums.

"This was what you saw in your head . . . this is what you wanted."

"No, I wanted you."

"Oh yes, but you wanted this, too, and the vision got in your way."

He watched, fascinated as her hand wandered lower on the girl's body, circled softly on her belly, and then slid down to dive into the delta. The shadows there concealed the movements of her fingers, but he did not need to see them to know what they were doing. Isabella moaned in her sleep, and her lips formed a circle of protest, then softened. Elena increased the pressure, and the girl moaned again.

"Yes, that feels good, *guapa,* doesn't it?" Elena murmured. "Yes, I know it does. Right there, just like that."

"Enough," said Vasily, "you'll wake her."

Elena looked at him over her shoulder. "And so?"

"I don't want this."

"Of course you do. Just look at yourself."

He did not need to look. Still, he persisted. "I'm ready for you. Leave her alone and come back inside."

She looked at him reproachfully. "And leave the poor child all excited? What terrible creatures men can be." Her fingers never stopped moving. She put her lips close to her daughter's ear and whispered, "Hey, sleepyhead, wake up."

"Mmmmmmm."

"Come on, darling, look at the present I've brought you."

Isabella opened her eyes and looked up at her mother. Elena kissed her tenderly on the forehead. In a tiny voice, choked with sleep, the girl asked, "What present?"

"Look for yourself."

Isabella shifted her gaze and saw Vasily standing at the foot of the bed. Her eyes widened. "For me?"

"All for you."

"Thank you, Mama." She could have been thanking her mother for a new dress or a ten-speed bicycle. "Is he nice?"

"He smells wild and strong, the way a man should. *Venga, guapa,* go to him."

Elena slipped her hand out from between the girl's legs.

Isabella arched her back and stretched, her eyes still fixed on
Vasily. She lifted up her arms to him in invitation. He stared
down at her, blood pounding, unable to move. Elena was suddenly at his side, her breath hot in his ear.

"Take her," she said hoarsely. "Go ahead, man, I've done
all the work for you."

"You know, I've always considered myself a sophisticate,"
he muttered, "but now I'm beginning to wonder."

Elena chuckled. "There's always something new to learn.
Go."

"What about you?"

"Don't worry about me. I'll be here when you want me. And
believe me, you'll want me."

During the next two hours Vasily repaid himself for a year's
worth of celibacy. The sex was mindless and seemingly endless, pure animal rutting as he went from the girl to the mother
and back again, over and over, with the earlier impotence replaced by an unbreakable ability that he had never known before. The sex was also nearly silent. There were no endearing
murmurs, no compliments to be savored later, no high-pitched
screams of passion . . . only the never-ending creaking of the
bed, the liquid sounds of lust, and an occasional grunt of gratification. Time spun round, and flesh spun with it; time stood
still, but the flesh never stopped. After a while, drained and
sated, and completely contented, he slept.

He awoke from a dreamless sleep as contented as when he
had closed his eyes. Memory came flooding back, all of it
clear, all of it warm, none of it displeasing. He felt flesh beside
him, grinned, and opened his eyes to find Isabella tucked in
next to him in sleep, as neat as two spoons. He awoke without a
sense of time, and his eyes searched for a clock. They found
one on a bedside table. It was not yet 6:00 A.M., and he winced
at the sight of Mickey Mouse on the face of the clock, happily
signaling the hour. His eyes traveled further. The light was
burning as before, the room was still, and the door was closed.
He looked for Elena, but she was gone. He disengaged himself
from the sleeping girl and padded into the sitting room. She was
not there. He looked into her bedroom, but that was empty as

well. He noted with satisfaction that his clothing, which he had discarded frantically the night before, had been neatly hung on hangers. He felt in his jacket pocket for a cigarette, debating what to do next. There was the familiar morning-after temptation to extract himself from the situation as quickly as possible, but there was equal temptation in the thought of the mound of nubile flesh asleep in the other room. Debating the point with himself, weighing the temptations, he found the cigarettes in his jacket and was about to light one when he heard the voices coming from the patio outside the bedroom window. Two of the voices belonged to Chuc and Van; the other was Elena's. They were speaking softly, but clearly, and he could understand every word they were saying. Elena's Vietnamese was as pure as her Spanish, rapid and colloquial.

He stood there and listened without moving, his body inclined toward the window and the sound of the voices, his face intent, the silver wings of his hair disheveled. As he listened he began to smile, and after a while he nodded his head twice, abruptly, as if in agreement with some private understanding. When he had heard enough, he went back to the other bedroom and lay down beside the sleeping Isabella. He kept his eyes open, staring at the ceiling.

A few minutes later Elena came in. She wore a robe, and her hair was brushed and knotted into a neat bun. When she saw that his eyes were open, she smiled and came to sit on the edge of the bed beside him.

"Pues, ¿qué tal, caballero?" she asked. "Feeling better now?"

"I'm feeling bloody hungry, that's how I feel."

"Very understandable." There was mischief in her smile. "You were very active last night. It builds the appetite."

"Do you think we could order up breakfast this early?"

"I'm sure of it. What would you like?"

"Scrambled eggs and sausages," he said after a moment's thought. "Those tasty little sausages that come in cans."

"Canned sausage?" Elena did not think much of the idea.

"Humor me, *guapa*, I adore them. And ask the nice people to chill a bottle of Piper as well."

Elena clapped her hands in delight. "How lovely."

"The occasion demands it."

"But none for Isabella." She gazed fondly at the sleeping girl. "She is much too young for champagne at breakfast."

"Much too young," he agreed.

Chapter 13 _____

At the sound of the first shot, Eddie rolled hard to his left, hoping to make the cover of the stone bench beside the pool before another shot came. He flipped over on his back, rolled twice, and then he heard another *pop*. The second bullet was carefully placed on his other side. The warning was clear; he stopped rolling. He lay facedown on the grass, his arms spread helplessly. The hot sun beat down on him, but the pit of his stomach was ice cold.

"You look ridiculous that way," said a disembodied voice. "Sit up . . . but do it slowly and carefully."

In the space of seconds came fear, then anger, and finally confusion. The fear came and went quickly. The anger lasted longer, directed at himself for being virtually defenseless. The confusion lasted longest of all, because the owner of that voice was supposed to be dead. He raised his head, then pulled himself up to a sitting position. Twenty feet away, a pistol in his hand, Vasily Borgneff sat atop the low wall that separated the patio and the pool from the fields behind the house.

"You're dead," Eddie said flatly.

"You exaggerate." Vasily's voice was controlled and polite. "A bit older, a good deal wearier, a touch wiser, but very much alive."

"I killed you."

"You certainly tried." Vasily jumped lightly from the wall, but the pistol in his hand never wavered. It was a Browning 9-millimeter, all the gun that he needed. He was dressed in black trousers and a light shirt, and his black eyepatch was set at a jaunty angle beneath the frame on his silver wings of hair.

He turned his head slightly so that his one eye could also take in the three people in the pool. They floated there helplessly, staring at him.

"You folks stay right where you are," he said to them. "I don't care if you swim, tread water, or drown. Just stay in that pool." He shifted his gaze to Eddie. "Mr. Mancuso and I have some talking to do."

Eddie realized that he was calm, and that pleased him. He had never become accustomed to violent death; it had never become a commonplace to him. For twenty years the creation and manufacture of lethal gadgets had been the center of his concern, but death had never become a commodity to him, like pork bellies or grain futures to be traded one for the other. After all those years he had come to know that every man's life is unique, and that the passing of even the most unreconstructed is mourned by someone. Because of this, even though he had been on speaking terms with death for most of his adult life, he had never sat down and supped with the grim old bastard. His familiarity with violence had brought him only one conviction: that he himself would someday die by the tools of his own trade. There was no morbidity in this conviction, only an acceptance of circumstance, just as a sailor recognizes the high possibility of a wet death, and a fighter pilot a flaming one.

He took another look at that unstained blue sky, breathed deeply, and said, "The people in the pool, they've got nothing to do with this. Let them walk."

"On the contrary, they have a great deal to do with it."

"I see," Eddie said slowly. "That means you're working."

"Clever fellow," Vasily said. "Quick as ever."

"Swan?"

"Swan."

"Since when did you hire out as a gun? That's not your style."

"All things change." Vasily's voice was smooth and amused. "Besides, I owe Mr. Swan a great deal. He saved my life when you left me for dead. He fed me, clothed me, kept me safe, and let me go on living."

"A regular Salvation Army."

"Not quite. I have an obligation to him. It was his idea that I combine a little business with pleasure. The Emerson family is the business."

"I see. And I'm the pleasure."

Vasily shrugged gracefully. "Try to see my side of it. I have it coming, don't I?"

Eddie did not answer. While he was mouthing easy words his mind struggled to figure the angle. The gun was a threat, but only that. There was no profit in it for Swan if a bunch of riddled bodies were found floating belly-up. Then what was the gadget? Not a gas, not outdoors. No sign of any explosive device. Nothing ingestible, not unless he poisoned the pool, and that was not likely. The pool? Something to do with the pool?

He tried not to look at the pool as his mind clicked through the possibilities, but he could not blank out the sight of Ginger's terror-stricken face as she clung to the nearest ladder. Just within his vision he could see Rusty standing in the shallow end of the pool, water to her knees, every line of her body tensed. Emerson . . . where was he? Then he caught sight of the head moving slowly through the water. He was using only his legs, showing nothing as he carefully worked himself toward the side of the pool.

He'll never make it, Eddie thought. One splash and he's finished. The gadget, what is it? What the hell could it be?

Vasily laughed. It was not a cheering sound. "Figured it out yet?"

Eddie just stared at him, giving away nothing.

"The tower." Vasily gestured with his free hand. "Look up."

Eddie raised his eyes slowly, following the soaring lines of the structure to the very top. He saw the two dots there, dots that he knew were men, perched precariously at the point where the cables formed the top of a T. His eyes narrowed as he estimated distances, running figures through his mind, doing the same trigonometry that Vasily had done days before. Then he nodded abruptly in understanding.

"Neat?" asked Vasily, obviously proud.

"Neat," Eddie agreed. The professional part of his mind had

to admire the concept. His eyes registered Emerson's movement; he was closer now to the edge. Working for time, he asked, "Who are your friends up there?"

"Pawns, nothing more," said Vasily, shrugging, and without turning his head he added casually, "I may have only one eye, Mr. Emerson, but if by chance you make it to the side of the pool I will definitely put a bullet through your head before you can clear the water. Please stay where you are."

Emerson stopped moving. Rather than tread water, he put up his legs and floated on his back. In that position his eyes stared up at the men on the tower. He was still not sure what was happening, but he knew that those men held his life in their hands. He kept his eyes on them, wondering.

High above, and off to the side of the pool, Chuc and Van braced themselves against the cross struts of the tower, their cable cutters open and ready. They clung to the structure with a casual agility, unconcerned by the height and able to survey the imposing countryside and the scene beside the pool without vertigo. They did not hear the sound of the shot from their perch, but they saw Vasily go over the wall, a stick figure leaping, and they saw the action at the pool freeze into a tableau. They watched and they waited.

After a while, Chuc said, "Can you see his arm? Is it up?"

"Not yet."

"What is he waiting for? He takes too much time."

Van grinned. "Revenge is a song to be sung slowly. He wants to enjoy every note."

"He should make the sign and get it done with."

But Van was enjoying himself. The air was cool and refreshing at the top of the tower, and a slight breeze caused the cables to hum pleasantly. He was looking forward to cutting the cables, imagining how they would fall in a grand swoop to the pool below. In his mind he could already see the people in the water leaping in uncontrolled spasms as the current passed through them. His only regret was that in doing it this way there would be no opportunity to use the women beforehand.

"An operation like this," said Chuc, "should be done quickly, like a knife in the dark. This is no time for Borgneff to be dramatic. He hooked his left arm around a strut and managed a look at his watch. "I'll give him five minutes more, that's all."

"And then what?"

"We cut the cables and get out of here."

"Against orders. We're supposed to wait for the signal."

"I warned him that we'd cut them if anything went wrong. Every minute that he wastes down there increases the risk. Five minutes, that's all."

"He could be hit by the cables," Van pointed out. "He won't know that they're coming."

"What difference would that make?" Chuc asked.

"True." Van nodded thoughtfully. "What difference?"

Below them in the pool, staring up at them through space, Emerson now knew what he had to do. The details were not clear to him, but he knew that sometime soon death would come swooping down from that tower, and he also knew that he could not stay still and wait for it passively. A move had to be made, any kind of a move that would give his wife and his daughter some kind of a chance. He decided on a loud and splashy diversion that would draw the intruder's attention away from the women. He hoped only that they would have the sense to clear the pool as soon as he made his move.

He was gathering himself for that move when he heard Eddie's voice say quietly, "Don't do it, Jimbo, it won't work. Stay cool and stay exactly where you are."

"Excellent advice," Vasily told Eddie. "It's a lovely day, just right for a dip in the pool. Why don't you join your friends in the water?"

"Only if you'll go with me. You used to enjoy this pool."

"Indeed, I did. Many good times we had here." He made an apologetic gesture with his free hand. "But you see, I'm not dressed for the occasion."

Eddie shook his head. "And, I've already had my swim for today."

"I'm afraid I must insist."

"And if I don't?"

Vasily's lips twisted in more of a grimace than a smile. As an answer, the tip of his pistol described a tiny circle, a zero, a cancellation.

Eddie's chin came up and his lower lip came out. He looked exactly like what he once had been, and in many ways still was: as he would have put it, a kid from the streets of the Lower East Side who had been taking shit long enough and wasn't taking any more, not from anyone.

"Go ahead," he said hoarsely. "If you're gonna do it, then do it now. I'll take it right here."

"Still the tough little monkey." Vasily raised his free hand slowly into the air until it was above his head. "When my hand comes down, those cables get cut."

"So what am I supposed to do? Crawl on my belly? Beg for my life?"

"I was rather hoping for something like that."

"Keep on hoping."

Vasily looked at him thoughtfully. "I suppose I was also hoping for some words of regret."

"You mean for Chalice?"

"For Chalice, and for me."

Eddie said angrily, "You can take your regret and shove it. Chalice did it to herself. She was trying to kill me and she pressed the wrong button, literally. The same with you. You were OK as long as we were fighting just to stay alive, but then you went kill-crazy that day in Williamsburg and you had to be stopped."

"You almost stopped me permanently."

"Nobody's perfect," Eddie said.

Vasily frowned. "Easy, old friend. You're walking a thin line. I've had a year to think what I'd do to you if I had the chance."

Eddie nodded. "You've had a year, and so have I. A year of thinking I'd killed my best pal. A lot of sweat in the night, if you know what I mean. A bad year. But now I know something I didn't know before. Standing here, right now, I know."

"And what is it that you know?" Vasily asked curiously.

"I'm glad you're not dead. I never hated you. I always thought you were a pretty good guy. But when I clobbered you with that rock, in case it's slipped your mind, you were trying to blow up half the CIA . . . and that included secretaries who didn't know an extraction order from a toothache. I was trying to stop you, *and you were trying to kill me.* If it happened again, I'd do it again. Except this time I'd use a machine gun instead of a rock.'' He shook his head disgustedly. ''Now pull the goddamn plug if that's all you can think of. Pull it and get it over with.''

Vasily nodded. His arm came down in a broad gesture, as if he were hauling down a flag. Several things happened at once.

Emerson's arms and legs began to flail in an attempt to reach the side of the pool.

Rusty, at the shallow end, tried to run through the knee-high water but tripped and fell, pitching forward.

Ginger, one foot on the lowest rung of the ladder, reached for the second rung, barked her shin, and fell backward.

Eddie and Vasily stood still, looking upward.

Chuc and Van each laid the sharp edge of his cutter onto a cable and applied pressure. The grip of that pressure was never completed. The instant that the metal of the cutters touched bare cable, twenty thousand volts of electricity shot through each of them, killing them instantly. The force of the jolt bounced them back against the steel tower, and then, hair aflame and their clothing smoldering, they pitched forward and fell, their bodies performing two slow rotations before hitting the ground.

The thud of the bodies hitting was followed by silence. Emerson reached the side of the pool and hung there, gasping. Rusty picked herself up and stared. Ginger surfaced, looked around, and started again for the ladder.

Vasily smiled and slipped the pistol into his pocket. Eddie looked at him inquiringly.

''The insulation on the cutters,'' Vasily explained. ''I pulled it all out this morning and replaced it with steel wool.''

''Naughty,'' Eddie observed. ''And nasty.''

''But necessary,'' Vasily said. ''They were going to kill me after this job. Swan's orders.''

''That sounds like his style.''

"And so I decided that it was time to come home. I was never very happy on the other side of the fence."

Eddie stood stiffly. There was a weakness in his legs that he was determined not to show. He made a vague motion toward the tower and the two bodies crumpled at its base. "That was one hell of a homecoming present you brought with you."

Vasily made a modest bow. "I didn't have a chance to do any shopping, and I thought it might amuse you."

"Amuse me? I nearly died laughing." Eddie's eyes were still on the tower, narrowed and reflective. He tore his gaze away and looked at Vasily. He grinned and put out his hand. "You are one crazy son of a bitch. OK, I'm amused. Welcome home."

"That bastard Swan has to die," roared Vasily. He slammed his fist on the table and wine bottles jumped. "There's no honor left in this business anymore."

"None," Eddie agreed glumly. He refilled his glass.

"I had a contract with the man and he ordered me killed. He has to be extracted, and quickly."

Eddie said, "So stop talking and kill the prick."

"He tried to kill me, too." Emerson's thick, sad voice confirmed Swan's infamy.

"That's different." Vasily emptied his glass. "It made sense for him to kill you. But I was working for him. There was a point of honor involved." He put his hand over his heart and declaimed, "My honor is dearer to me than life. Who said that?"

"Mick Jagger?"

"Cervantes, my illiterate Italian chum. *Don Quixote*, part one."

"Which page?"

Vasily ignored him. "For a man such as me, honor is everything. After all, what is left when honor is lost? Who said that?"

"Richard Nixon? Al Capone?"

"You're close," Vasily conceded. "Actually, it was Publilius Syrus, a very noble Roman."

"Another Italian illiterate," Eddie said.

"My most sincere apologies." Vasily tried to bow. Being seated, all he did was bump his forehead on the table. He recovered quickly and said, "Please don't misunderstand. My respect for Italians goes all the way back to the Borgias."

The bottle of wine in his hand, Eddie looked around the table for takers. Emerson held out his glass. Ginger smiled but shook her head. Rusty was not drinking at all.

They sat at the round table in the *sala* on the first floor of the house. The room was dimly lit, the heavy oak and walnut furniture looming in the shadows. The table was burdened with plates of cold meats and cheeses, slabs of bread, and over a dozen bottles of wine, most of them empty. It was after midnight, and, aside from Rusty, everyone was drunk in varying stages. Ginger was tipsy, Emerson was high, Eddie was owlish, and Vasily was roaring.

It was a strange celebration. Part of the gaiety around the table came from the near-hysterical relief that follows a close escape from death, part of it from the desperate humor of people who face an uncertain future, and part of it from the quiet understanding that passed between Vasily and Eddie at the resumption of their old relationship. It was the nature of this relationship, and Vasily's sudden switch from enemy to ally, that confused the Emersons and made the celebration less than perfect. Rusty kept her eyes fixed on Vasily at all times, as if convinced that he was about to produce a weapon and assassinate them all. Ginger was suspicious as well, but her suspicions centered on the obvious bond between this intruder and her man, and womanwise, she was on guard against it. Only Emerson, as a onetime soldier, seemed to understand the comradeship involved, but he, too, had his reservations.

"The bottle, please." Vasily raised his glass to eye level and inspected the straw-colored wine. "Here's to Swan, that swine. A devious man with a devious plan. He hires me to take out all you lovely people, and after I've done my job his two little Oriental thugs eliminate me. All very neat and tidy." He belched.

"A contract on *me*. You have no idea how shocked I was to hear it. Betrayed! By a so-called gentleman. 'Keep honor, like your saber, bright.' Now, who said that? Never mind. Don't try to guess. George Washington Patten, a minor poet, but a gentleman." Vasily looked curiously at Rusty. "Do we offend you with our levity, madam?"

Rusty ignored the question. Her face was set in hard lines. She asked, "When did you find this out about Swan?"

"This morning." He belched again. "I regret to admit it, but I was eavesdropping."

"And if you hadn't been eavesdropping we'd be dead by now. Isn't that right?"

The question cut through the alcoholic haze in the room. There was an embarrassed silence. Eddie started to say, "Rusty, I don't think you understand . . ."

Vasily cut him off. His voice, for the moment, was steady. "I don't owe you this explanation, madam, but I'll give it to you anyway. The answer is no, you would not be dead. Not if it would have involved any harm to my curly-headed little buddy over there. You see, I had a year's worth of hate built up in me when I came to Mexico, but . . ." He paused, looked at Emerson, and said something in Russian. Emerson smiled understandingly. "I just said to your husband in our native tongue that, like all Russians, I am a sentimentalist. A weakness, perhaps, but part of my Slavic soul. All it took was the sight of this house, the sight of my old friend with your lovely daughter, and memories came flooding back to me, memories . . ."

"Come on, cut the bullshit," muttered Eddie.

". . . of happier times, tender memories that washed away all the anger and hate. I decided several days ago that I could not possibly harm him, although I had not yet decided on a course of action. And since harming you would have meant harming him, ergo, you were not going to die."

He pointed a long and bony finger at her. "But barring his presence? If you had been on your own? Yes, madam, you would have been dead, all three of you. I can assure you of that."

Rusty gasped, and Emerson looked unhappy.

"Why are you surprised?" asked Vasily. "Five days ago you people meant nothing to me. Why should I have spared you?"

"No reason, I suppose," said Emerson. "And now?"

"A different situation." Vasily speared a morsel of Chihuahua cheese and took a delicate bite. "Now I've crossed over. My connection with Swan, as you might imagine, is irrevocably broken. You have nothing to fear from me anymore." He looked down at his wine glass pensively. "Not that it makes any difference at this point. You don't have a . . ."

He stopped when he saw Eddie making small signals for silence, but Emerson wanted to hear more.

"What were you going to say? What don't we have?"

"Let it go. The wine was in and the wit was out."

"No, I want to hear it."

Vasily chewed cheese without relish. Reluctantly, he said, "You don't have a chance in the world. Do you think I'm the only one he'll send after you?"

Which was exactly what he had said to Eddie earlier that day, after the two of them had buried Chuc and Van. The burial came before anything else, of course, in the same fashion that a fussy housewife will insist on doing the dishes after dinner despite the temptation to linger at the table and savor the aftertaste of the meal. As soon as the danger was over, the three Emersons were hustled out of the pool and into the house to dry themselves off, dress themselves up, and calm themselves down, while Eddie and Vasily found tools and sacks and made the trek across the barren countryside to the base of the tower.

After a brief inspection of the remains, Vasily asked, "The cave?"

"Good a spot as any," Eddie agreed.

It was the work of half an hour to lug the laden sacks down to the split in the rocks that concealed the mouth of a cave cut deep into the hillside, and another fifteen minutes to maneuver them into the back of the dark cave where the rock floor dropped away sharply to form a pit. They rolled the sacks over the lip of the pit and waited. They did not hear the sound of their striking bottom, but they had not expected to.

They went back out into the sunlight to sit on the rocks and rest. They both lit cigarettes, drew deeply, and looked at each other and grinned.

"Steel wool," said Eddie, shaking his head in admiration. "What a beautifully wicked mind you have."

"Don't think it was easy. It took me over an hour to get the insulation out of the handles, repack them with the steel, and then work enough points of the metal up to the surface to ensure contact." He looked up at the sun and down at his watch. "Perhaps you'd best fill me in on the situation here. After that, I'll give you my side of it."

The exchange of information was quick and concise. It was made on a professional level and without emotion. When Vasily came to the part about Elena Castelnuevo, Eddie interrupted him.

"She was reporting to Swan?"

"She was the link between my two scheming sidekicks and the DD5. She was passing information back and forth, positions reports to Swan and instructions from Swan to Chuc and Van. I heard it all this morning, including the son of a bitch's final instruction to get rid of me." He stared out over the treeless terrain. "You realize that you're backing a lame horse, don't you? Emerson doesn't have a chance, now that Swan knows where he is."

"I wonder." Eddie thought for a moment. "The woman reported in this morning, right? When would her next check-in be due?"

"From what I could hear, it sounded like she was on a three-day schedule with a one-day fallback."

"Standard."

"So Swan will expect to hear from her again in four days, five at the outside."

"Shit, that means we're on the run again."

"Eddie, face it. Your man is dead. He can't run forever, and Swan will never stop trying."

"Maybe so," said Eddie, not convinced. With obvious reluctance, he added, "I hate to say this, but you'll have to do something about Señora Castelnuevo."

Vasily looked surprised. "I took care of that this morning at breakfast. Their bodies were probably found a couple of hours ago."

"Both of them?"

"Certainly." This time Vasily looked irritated, rather than surprised. "What choice did I have? Besides, they were both professionals. The girl was no more her daughter than Lenin was my grandfather."

Eddie laughed. "And I was worried about you getting sentimental about them."

"Fear not, I had my moment of sentiment this afternoon. It should last me quite a while."

Professionally curious, Eddie could not help asking, "What did you use?"

"Clostridium botulinum."

Eddie stared at him, unbelieving.

"I picked up some of the active bacillus in Washington, a handy little ampule sewn into a trouser cuff. It seemed like a good idea at the time. Everybody knows how dangerous it is to eat canned sausage in Mexico."

"Botulism?" Eddie jumped up and stamped on his cigarette. "Jesus, if I didn't know you better I'd think you were losing your touch. That stuff takes forty-eight hours to kill."

"Not when you use a one-milligram dose."

"One milligram?" Eddie almost screamed. "Just for the two of them?"

"One milligram *apiece*."

"My God," said Eddie in awe. He did some rapid calculations. "That's enough to take out a small town, maybe forty thousand people."

"I've never believed in half-measures," Vasily said primly, "any more than I've ever believed in eating canned sausage."

They started walking back to the house then, Vasily adjusting his long strides to Eddie's short ones. It was a silent walk for the most part, each man occupied with his thoughts.

They were almost home when Vasily said, "This may be so obvious that it doesn't need stating, but there's a way out for Emerson. An easy way."

"The Russians?"

Vasily nodded. "They'd still welcome him as a hero. It's the only sensible choice. A hero's life on one hand, certain death on the other."

"You don't know him. Jimbo probably recites the Pledge of Allegiance every morning in front of the bathroom mirror—and means it."

"Patriots! I loathe them. They're like adolescents in love."

"Yeah, but Jimbo is different. He doesn't make a lot of noise about it, but he really means it. Once he made up his mind that he wasn't going to Moscow, that was *it*. There's no changing the stubborn bastard."

"A man of principle. I can't say that I adore that type either."

Eddie shrugged. "He's an old-fashioned kind of a guy, that's all. You know the kind I mean."

"Indeed, I do. He's a patriot, and a walking anachronism to boot."

"Actually," said Eddie, "I think he's some kind of Methodist."

Vasily stopped short and looked down happily. "Delightful, now I know I'm home. Come on, I'm dry enough to drink a barrel of wine by myself."

He did not drink a barrel, but he tried. They all tried, except Rusty, and the four of them managed to put a considerable dent in the supply of Chablis and Rioja laid down the year before. They drank with a frenzied gaiety, the conversation galloping wildly as the wine whipped the words, with only Rusty sitting solemn and silent, a ghost at the feast. They might have gone on that way all night, but then Emerson asked the question and Vasily, reluctantly, answered it.

"You don't have a chance in the world. Do you think I'm the only one he'll send after you?"

The party came to a sudden halt right there. Frenzied gaiety has a value only when the obvious is left unstated. Once it is out in the open, no amount of graveyard whistling, desperation drinking, or witty words will serve to mask the terror. The terror came down to sit on their shoulders then, and the taste of the wine was suddenly sour.

"Hard words," said Emerson. "You really believe that?"

Vasily nodded. Uncharacteristically hesitant, he said, "I'm sorry that I put it so bluntly." He shrugged. "But it's true."

"Of course it's true," snapped Rusty. "We're not idiots; we realize that. The question is, what are we going to do about it?"

"That exactly is the question, madam." Vasily was struggling to rebuild his façade. "And that's why we are gathered here around this table. You might call it a council of war."

"I call it a convention of drunks, and stop calling me madam. I haven't been impressed with old-world charm since my junior year in high school." Rusty stood up abruptly. "Nothing is going to get accomplished here while you people sit around and swill cheap wine. I'm going to bed."

Vasily protested, "The wine is anything but cheap. I laid down these bottles myself."

"The Chablis is second-rate and the Rioja I had at lunch was definitely corky." She turned to her husband. "Are you coming, Jim?"

Emerson looked apologetically at the two other men. "Maybe some sleep is what we all need. The morning is the time for decisions."

Vasily watched the Emersons leave with a sour look on his face. "Corky," he muttered. "And to think that through a pair of Zeiss binoculars that woman looked like a goddess."

Upstairs in their bedroom, Emerson and Rusty undressed quickly and in the warmth of the night lay uncovered on the bed. Moonlight slipped through louvers and painted stripes on their bodies, but they did not notice them. They lay silently, side by side, right hand clasping left, and stared at the ceiling. Over the hills, a coyote called and was answered.

Rusty asked in a small voice, "How scared are you?"

"Plenty."

"Me, too. It's funny. I wasn't scared this afternoon in the pool. Everything was frozen. But now . . ."

"I know."

"It all seems so hopeless. We thought we were safe, and now this. I hate it, Jim. And I don't like the people we're mixed up with."

"Eddie's all right. We owe him a great deal."

"Eddie is a killer, no matter what we owe him. He's no better than the other one, Borgneff. We've put ourselves in the hands of two professional thugs."

"They're hardly thugs." He forced himself to laugh. It was a short one. "Besides, I don't see what choice we have."

She was silent for as long as it took the distant coyote to place another call, ring five times, and hang up. Then she said, "There is another choice."

She saw him nod in the darkness. "There always has been. The Russians. I thought we had pretty well covered that subject."

"Things have changed since then. Then we had an option; now we don't. We're backed into a corner."

"A man always has an option," he said slowly.

"A man does. Did you hear what you said? You're talking about machismo ideals. I'm talking about life and death."

She propped herself up on an elbow so that she could look down at him. "I said before that I was scared, but I didn't say of what. I'm not too much afraid of what could happen to me, Jim, but I'm scared silly of being a widow. I don't think I'd make a very good one."

"What are you asking me to do?"

"I'm not asking you anything. I'm telling you how I feel."

"You're asking me to go over. You're asking me to call Anya Ignatiev in Washington and tell her that I'm ready to go. You're asking me to give in."

She sighed. "If anything, I'm asking you to make a choice between life and death."

"Downstairs, just now. You didn't like all that talk about honor, did you?"

Instead of answering, she ran a finger over his lips, touched his cheek with her fingertips, reading his features in the dark. He caught her hand and held it, forcing a reply.

"It's a male concept," she said. "It doesn't move me much. I'm far more concerned about the life of the man I love."

"Enough to ask him to do something dishonorable?"

"If necessary, yes."

"*I could not love thee, dear, so much, lov'd I not honor more.*" He chuckled. "Richard Lovelace. Let Vasily cap that one."

"Is that an answer to my question?"

"For the moment, I'm afraid, it will have to be."

He drew her down to him and held her. There was no more talk, but sleep did not come quickly. After a while he realized that she was quietly crying, as she had on the night he had said good-bye to his paintings. His last thought before sleep was the uncertain hope that Eddie would think of something.

Such thoughts are sometimes best born of wine, and the idea came after another hour of drinking and reminiscences, the two old warriors trading stories of other, better times, while Ginger listened avidly and tried to drink along with them. Both tasks were difficult. The men were into the wine with muscle now, making no pretense of savoring aftertaste and bouquet, and at one point she had the feeling that had she not been there they would have been drinking the stuff straight from the bottles. Their conversation, too, was difficult to follow, laced as it was with references to exotic chemicals, toxic gases, and explosive devices. Even though the technical aspects of it defeated her, she was fascinated by the dialogue. The two men spoke casually, almost disparagingly, of adventures that seemed to her to represent the height of daring, laughing the loudest as they recalled each other's failures. After a while she had the floating feeling of being transported in time to some pirates' den of long ago, listening to the buccaneer captains recounting their exploits as they gnawed on greasy bones and flung bottles crashing into walls. The scene swam in front of her, and with a muttered excuse she left the table and barely managed to make it to the couch, where she curled herself up and was instantly asleep.

Vasily looked at the sleeping girl with approval. "A lovely creature. It's a pity that the two of you can't stay here and enjoy the house."

"That's finished. Got to run again."

"When? And where?"

Eddie shrugged. His eyes were heavy and his head was low.

Vasily said carefully, "I take it then that you are committed to staying with Emerson?"

Eddie's head came up. "Yeah, I'm committed, all right."

Vasily nodded toward the couch. "Because of her?"

"Mostly."

"It's suicide, you know. Anybody who stays close to that man is bound to get caught in the line of fire."

"Maybe." His lower lip came out and muscles twitched along his jaw.

Vasily said quickly, "Please don't give me the tough-kid act; I've seen it before. You know as well as I do how these things work. He's going to get hit. Maybe next week, maybe next month. His car will crash, or his plane will go down, or he'll catch a whiff of VX gas . . . something that looks like an accident. But it's going to happen, and if you're in that car or that plane you're going to get it, too. You know that, Eddie. It's not a question of odds anymore. It's a sure thing."

"I don't believe in sure things. I'm sticking." He looked away, and, in a voice so low it was barely audible, he added, "I was sort of hoping that you'd stick, too."

As if he had not heard, Vasily said, "When I was in Washington I heard some news of Benny Zahn. Remember Benny?"

"The Israeli? Didn't he do that car job in Oslo?"

"Yes. He's in Colombia now, working on his own out of Bogotá."

"So?"

"I heard he's doing very well making gadgets for the South American trade. It's a big market now."

"Benny's a field man. He doesn't know shit about UKDs."

"That's just my point. If a slob like Benny is doing well, we could clean up."

Eddie shook his head. "I don't need the money."

"It isn't just the money, my friend. New sciences, new horizons, the other side of the mountain."

"Is that where you're headed?"

"Maybe."

"If you do, you'll be going alone."

"Going down with the ship?"

"The ship isn't sinking. I've got plans of my own."

"Plans of your own! You are a very stubborn son of a bitch. You're as bad as that man upstairs." Vasily threw up his hands in disgust. One of those hands held a bottle, and wine spilled across the table in a pale yellow arc. He ignored it and shouted, "All right—stick! Stick to him like glue, and you'll get blown away when he does. Of all the idiotic, quixotic gestures! If you think you can take on the entire Central Intelligence Agency and get away with—"

He stopped speaking abruptly, a look of surprise on his face. That look was replaced by a fixed set of concentration, and as if to aid that concentration he closed his eyes. Seconds went by, stretching; then he pursed his lips in a soundless whistle. He opened his eyes. Eddie was grinning at him.

Vasily said, "Actually, it isn't the whole CIA, is it?"

Eddie shook his head, still grinning. "It's just the Fifth Directorate."

"Not even that much." Vasily smiled, too. "Just the Gang of Four. Swan, Krause, Andriakis, and Wolfe. Christianson and the rest of the Agency probably don't know anything about it."

Eddie grunted, "Your brain is finally beginning to work. The Director—that guy Christianson—would never issue a contract on Jimbo. He's under too much pressure from Congress. Only Swan and his friends would have the balls to try it, which means that they're the only ones who know that Emerson is *Homefire*. Eliminate them and our boy walks free."

"And so you're going to extract them." It was a statement, not a question.

"We are."

"Oh? *We* are?" Now it was very definitely a question.

"That's right, we. You and me. A couple of hours ago you were yelling for Swan's ass. The son of a bitch has to go, that's what you said. Bye-bye, Swan. Well, I'm gonna give you a chance to send him on his way. What do you say?"

Vasily stared at him silently.

"Come on, what about it? Was that just a lot of noise, or do you really want to take him out?"

"I want it, all right."

"Then let's start figuring how to do it."

Vasily yawned, stretched his arms, and was surprised to find that he still held a bottle of wine in his right hand. He set it down carefully and said, "I think someone had best make some coffee."

"That's me. Your coffee tastes like a UKD in disguise."

Two hours later Vasily stretched again, reached for the coffee pot, shook it, and found it empty. He grimaced and drank what was left in his cup. It was cold, and he grimaced again. He looked down at the four sheets of paper in front of him. They were covered with closely written notes and were headed: *Swan—Washington, Krause—Brissago, Andriakis—Corfu, Wolfe—Barcelona.* Under these headings he and Eddie had listed everything they knew about the individual involved: every professional fact, every personal foible, every rumor that had ever reached their ears.

"Difficult, almost impossible," he said. "The trouble is we would have to get them all. Even three out of four would be no good. As long as one of them is alive, your boy is as good as dead."

"It can be done." Eddie had built himself a monster of a cheese sandwich, and he nibbled away at the edges of it. "I've done tougher ones. So have you. We've done them together."

"It's not the hits I'm talking about. Four separate hits in four different parts of the world . . . difficult but not impossible. But there are two time factors that are going to beat you.''

''How so?'' asked Eddie, chewing.

''Time factor number one. Five days from now Swan doesn't hear from the delightful Elena, and he knows the contract here has gone wrong. At that point he has to figure that his life is in danger, and he heads for the Fun House. Do you know about the Fun House?''

''I've heard about it.''

''They had me there for seven months, and I can tell you that once he dives for cover in the Fun House we won't be able to touch him. That place is impregnable. And once he's inside he'll alert the other three. Each one of them has a Fun House of his own, a place where he can run for cover. Once they get into their holes, the game's over. Emerson is finished.''

Eddie was unperturbed. ''That just means that the jobs have to be done within the next four days. I've seen operations mounted in less time than that.''

''I question that, but let's assume it.'' Vasily looked distastefully at the window and the grayish light that was just beginning to show through the trees outside. ''Christ, it's daylight already. All right, assume it. At that point we're beat by the second time factor. These four people run a close net; they're constantly in touch with each other. So assume that we hit Swan first. As soon as the network is broken, the others go into their Fun Houses, and what have we got? We've hit one out of four, but the ball game is over.'' He turned his hands palms up. ''It's impossible.''

''Few things are impossible to diligence and skill,'' Eddie quoted smugly.

Vasily raised an eyebrow. ''Montaigne?''

''Samuel Johnson.''

''My Lord, she's civilizing you.''

Eddie ignored the thrust. ''Look, it isn't impossible. The answer is to hit all four at the same time. The same day, the same hour if we can.''

''And how are we supposed to do that?'' Vasily asked icily.

"Washington, Greece, Spain, and Switzerland . . . all on the same day?"

"I haven't got that part figured out yet," Eddie admitted. "We're a little short of hands."

"Just a little. It would take four people to make the hits simultaneously. We only have two."

"You have three," said Emerson, standing in the doorway.

He came into the room. He was wearing a robe and his hair was tousled. "I couldn't sleep. I've been listening. Is there any more of that coffee?"

"We can make some," said Vasily. "Did I hear you correctly?"

"You did." Emerson sank into a seat, his robe flapping loosely around him. His eyes were clear, and he looked at both of them sharply. "What you're trying to do makes sense. It would work. And if you people are willing to do this for me, the least I can do is join the team."

Vasily looked embarrassed. He turned his eyes away and let Eddie say the words. "It's no good, Jimbo. Thanks for the offer, but you're a civilian."

"At the moment. I wasn't always. I'm sure I know enough to follow instructions." He turned to Vasily. "I was trained at Gaczyna. Does the name mean anything to you?"

Vasily nodded. "It means a great deal, but that was over thirty years ago. Also, one hates to sound elitist, but this business of killing . . ."

"I'm no stranger to killing," Jimbo said coldly, remembering once again, with dreadful clarity, that night in the barn when he was Yuri Volanov confronting the real James Emerson. "As I've told Eddie more than once, there are certain things that one never forgets. I'm not asking in, Borgneff, I'm dealing myself in whether you like it or not. It's my life that you're playing with. Remember that."

Vasily looked at Eddie, who shrugged and said, "Who knows? If he follows instructions, it could work."

"I'll accept your judgment . . . but it's academic, of course." He looked regretfully at the empty coffeepot. "We still need four people. We only have three."

"You're wrong," said Ginger from the couch. She sat up and pushed back her hair with her hand. The signs of sleep were still with her, and she looked particularly young and vulnerable. "You have all you need. You have four."

Chapter 14

The island is called Kérkyra in Greek, Corfu in English, and it lies scythe-shaped and verdant in the Ionian Sea just off the mainland of Greece. It also lies just off the mainland of Albania, for the border between the two countries, if extended across the water, would cut through the curve of the scythe, and so the northeastern tip of the island is only a little over a mile from the towering mountains and sparsely inhabited coastline of Europe's most isolated country. The juxtaposition of Communist Albania and carefree Corfu is dramatized by the contrast in terrain. Albania is brown and sere; Corfu is green and lush. Albania lies closed and forbidding, while Hellenic Corfu lies sprawled in the sea with its arms opened wide. In Corfu the silver leaves of three million olive trees tack gracefully to every breeze, orange and lemon groves puff incense, and vibrantly colored flowers cloak the land; yet over it all loom Albania's somber peaks.

Aware of the contrast but indifferent to it and blinded to beauty by a single-minded concentration, James Emerson arrived on Corfu on Monday, July 14, by way of the afternoon flight from Athens. The incoming customs check there had been no more than cursory, justifying the Athenian reputation for the loosest airport security in Europe. The inspectors had never suspected the odd pieces of plastic hidden beneath the liner of his suitcase, pieces which, when properly assembled, would form a modified version of the PPK Walther pistol. They were also indifferent to the small piece of clay statuary, a priapic Pan, that lay nestled between his shirts. Had he been leaving Greece, not entering it, the inspectors would have been interested, indeed, in the statuette, quick to suspect yet another theft of a national treasure, but Emerson anticipated no such problem on his departure. He had no intention of taking the Pan with him when he left.

Following directions and driving an airport rental car, he drove into Corfu town, parked on the Avenue Voulgareos, and visited four real estate agents in quick succession. The first three assured him that there were no villas of any kind available at this, the height of the season. The fourth, influenced by a substantial stack of drachmas, allowed that he did have a hovel of sorts, certainly nothing suitable for such a gentleman, but possessing a stall shower, a decent bed, a working refrigerator—

Emerson interrupted, asking, ''Does it have an oven?''

''It has a stove,'' said the mystified agent. ''And, of course, underneath the stove is the oven.''

''Good. I'll take it.''

By early evening he was installed in a stucco cube of a house perched among olive trees above the town of Ipsos. With bread and ham and cheese laid by, and a gin and tonic in his hand, he sat on the front porch looking out over the darkening Gulf of Kérkyra. He breathed deeply, savoring the scent of oleander and lemon that was subtly altered, as always in the Mediterranean, by the musty odor of olives. Directly across the gulf lay the Albanian shore and the winking lamps in farmhouse windows that seemed as close to his touch as fireflies. Down the island shore to the south the streetlights of Corfu city cast a disturbingly urban glow against the sky, while to the north he could follow the curve of the gulf by the lights of Pyrgi, then Nissaki, and finally Kalami, the closest point on the island to the Albanian shore. He stared longest at the lights of Kalami, wondering which lamp shone from the house of Peter Andriakis, the man he had come to kill.

After a while his eyes drooped and he began to drowse. He had been traveling for almost twenty-four hours and his body cried out for rest, not only from the activities of the past day, but from those of the two days before that. Those last days in Mexico had been filled with detailed planning, cram-course training, and an ongoing discussion about assignments. In the end they had decided to hit the four men simultaneously on Wednesday, the sixteenth. Emerson had drawn Andriakis in Corfu, Ginger was assigned Krause in Brissago on the Swiss-Italian border, Vasily had elected Wolfe in Barcelona, and to Eddie had gone the responsibility for Swan himself. Which had left them with the question of what to do about Rusty.

"She can't stay here," Vasily had said. "Too risky."

Eddie had agreed. "There's always a chance that Swan makes a move before we get to him. She has to change houses."

"Mexico City?"

"A hotel?"

"Why not? Safest place in the world, a large hotel. What do you think, Jimbo?"

"Sounds good to me," said Emerson. "Is that all right with you, Rusty?"

"Oh, don't worry your heads about little old me," she said breezily. "I adore Mexico City; I'll have a wonderful time there. I'll just lie around in the sun and oil the body while you people go jazzing around the world bumping off the baddies."

Her tone did not reflect her feelings. From the beginning she had been unalterably opposed to the idea of going over to the attack. At first her objections had been angry and resentful, but the others had stood firm in the decision and she soon saw there was no way of changing their minds. Now she had abandoned anger for sarcasm, but her attitude was still the same. She thought the idea was insane.

"I suppose that sounds very selfish of me. I really should contribute something to the cause. Now, what could I do?" She put a finger to her lips, considering. "I could do some sewing, run up a few shrouds. Feed the rattlesnakes? Milk the tarantulas? Polish your pistols? Anything else I can do to help?"

Emerson sighed. "Not very funny, Rusty."

"Isn't it?" she asked sweetly. "I think the whole thing is hilarious. Actually, my love, I don't give a damn what happens to these so-called professionals, but what about you? A fifty-three-year-old adventurer who hasn't fired a weapon in anger in thirty-five years! That's not funny?"

"I suppose it depends on your point of view. I don't see what choice I have."

"I do, but I suppose you're entitled to your burst of machismo—it goes so well with the male menopause. But what about your daughter? Did you have to get her involved? She can't step on an ant without throwing up. And you two are going to go out and kill people? Tell me again that it isn't funny?"

Eddie and Vasily looked at each other uneasily; there was a core of truth in what she said, but Ginger pushed herself in front of her father and stared at her mother with level eyes.

"Let's stop all this crap," she said evenly, all of the girlishness gone from her voice. "We're not talking about ants, we're talking about people. I don't like the idea of killing people either, but these sons of bitches are trying to murder my father, and I'm not going to let them do that. I'll do anything I can to prevent it, including killing, and I promise you, Mother, that I won't throw up when it happens."

"Take it easy," Emerson said softly.

"I'm sore," Ginger told him, "and I don't care who knows it. You should have had a son—he'd be doing this for you now. But I'm all you've got and I'll do what I can. And if my mother loves you as much as she says she does, she'll stop the bitching and moaning and get off her ass and give us a hand."

She had turned away then, but not before she had seen the silent applause in Eddie's eyes; and after that there had been no more arguments.

Sitting on the porch and watching the Ionian waters darken to the deepest blue, Emerson smiled as he thought of that scene. He had never been prouder of his daughter, but the stricken look on his wife's face had brought him to her side, and he had held her.

They each love in their own way, he thought, and I'm the lucky man in the middle.

He breathed deeply again of the oleander and lemons, finished his drink, and went inside to prepare for bed. Sleep did not come easily. There was too much to think about, too many things that could go wrong, and he stared at the unfamiliar ceiling as he fought to order his mind.

Take it slow, he told himself, one step at a time. You have all day tomorrow to survey the ground, and then you hit him on Wednesday.

He smiled in the darkness as he thought of what his Washington colleagues would think of him now.

All those years practicing law, he thought as he finally closed his eyes. All those years in government playing the game. All those good, rich years, and now I'm finally about to do what I was trained for as a boy.

It was an oddly comforting thought.

On that same Monday afternoon, Ginger drove north out of Milan, leaving behind the permanent cap of brown industrial smog that hung over the city, breathing deeply with relief as she swung the rented Fiat onto the autostrada that led to the lake country and the Swiss-Italian border. The flat, unattractive countryside was strange to her, but the road signs were clear and Vasily's instructions had been explicit. Follow the signs to Sesto Calende, then up the western side of Lago Maggiore and over the Swiss border just north of Cannobio. The first town on the Swiss side would be Brissago, and there she would find Gerard Krause.

As she drove along at a steady one hundred kilometers, a speed that drew derisive toots from passing sportsmen, she reviewed what she had been told about Krause.

"First of all, don't make the mistake of underestimating him," Vasily had told her, "just because he's stuck in a backwater like Brissago. He may not seem to have much power, but he has Swan, and that's all he needs. He's like Andriakis and Wolfe, an extension of Swan, and you can't take him lightly."

"I won't," she had promised. "What does he look like?"

"About fifty-five, short and chubby with a pencil-thin mustache. He has a certain amount of what your mother would call continental charm—the kind she claims doesn't impress her. For a cover he plays at being a retired American insurance executive living the good life in northern Italy and Switzerland."

He turned to Eddie. "Frankly, I could never understand the lure of northern Italy. Magnificent scenery, but the people are so dour. What part of Italy are you from?"

"I was born in Manhattan," said Eddie. "In my family, a northern Italian was anybody who lived above Fourteenth Street. What else do you know about this guy?"

"He eats well, drinks well, and he thinks of himself as a ladies' man. Who knows, perhaps he is. I believe that's why he got posted to a place like Brissago."

Eddie had confirmed that with a nod. "Yeah, I heard that. Some kind of scandal in Bangkok. Man, you really have to work at it to cause a scandal in Bangkok. Some kind of kinky sex routine."

"Sounds like a charmer," Ginger had said, then, seeing the look of concern on his face, had touched him lightly on the cheek. "Take it easy, I'm going there to kill him, not seduce him."

She had seen the look of concern on his face replaced by one of wonder at this newfound attitude of hers, this apparently casual acceptance of the need to kill. She wondered at it herself now as she drove over the noisy, ill-bolted bridge that spanned the River Ticino at the bottom of the lake. Only she knew that it was not casual at all. Tough words and an aggressive stance did nothing to change the hollowness she felt within her whenever she thought of what she had to do. But she also knew that she was going to do it.

"I'm going to drop him in his tracks," she promised herself, using words on loan from Eddie, as if by using the words she could borrow strength and confidence, too. "He's gonna fly like a bird and drop like a rock."

Beyond Sesto Calende she began to notice the dreary landscape giving way to impressive tree-covered slopes of deep green and silver. She drove with the water below to her right, and rising high on her left the sub-Alpine peaks that pocketed the lake like the setting of a jewel, and beyond them the immense display of the Alpine arc itself. The sun fled fast behind those peaks, and in the late afternoon long shadows lay across the land. Then she was negotiating the hairpin turns above Cannobio with the border coming up ahead.

At the border she produced her passport, the Houston special in the name of Pauline Rausch, first to the Italians and then to the Swiss, and stood by the car showing no apparent concern while both her suitcase and the Fiat were carefully searched. The lack of concern was real. Unlike her father, she carried no weapons, either whole or disassembled, none of Eddie's death-dealing devices, gadgets, or toys. She had made that clear when she had volunteered. No guns or knives, no explosives or gases, or anything like that.

"I'd be helpless," she had told them. "There simply isn't enough time for me to learn about those things. I'd either shoot myself in the toe or stab myself in the butt."

Now she watched with satisfaction as the meticulous inspection was made of her belongings, the examination showing nothing more exotic than a two-pound box of chocolate creams and a box of penicillin-based flu tablets that she had purchased in Mexico City. Told that she could pass, she tossed the guards a jaunty, *"Grazie,"* and minutes later was tooling down the main street of Brissago. She found the Pension Valentina without any trouble on one of the winding side streets that pitched up from the lake at a seemingly impossible angle, registered there with the Rausch passport, and went to her room to unpack. She hung her clothes away carefully, stored the penicillin tablets in the top drawer of the armoire, then turned to the telephone. She breathed deeply several times, then picked up the receiver and placed a call to Gerard Krause.

She heard the sound of ringing, and a man's voice said, *"Pronto?"*

"Signor Krause?"

"Si."

"Hi there, you don't know me, but my name is Pauline Rausch, and I'm a very dear friend of Mary Jo Betterman. From Mobile, Alabama? I'm sure you remember Mary Jo?"

"Well, actually, I'm not quite . . ."

"You mean you don't remember Mary Jo?" She rushed her words, trying for a breathlessness in her voice. "Tall girl with jet-black hair and a terrific figure? Just about my age, twenty-two? Come on, nobody forgets Mary Jo. She certainly didn't forget *you*."

There was a chuckle on the other end of the line. "That's very complimentary but . . . you see, I do meet a lot of people, especially during the tourist season."

"I just can't believe this. Wait till I get back home and tell Mary Jo. As a matter of fact, I won't do anything of the kind; the poor girl would just die of embarrassment after all she said about you."

"What did she say?" he asked calmly.

"I don't know if I should tell you, since you don't even remember her."

"One moment. Mary Jo? Tall girl with a southern accent and big . . . um?" He broke off, chuckling.

"That's right, big . . . um." She laughed with him. "At least you remember part of her."

"Rather difficult to forget that aspect. It's all coming back to me now. Dear Mary Jo Betterman. I don't know how she could have slipped my mind that way. Indeed, we had a splendid time together last year."

"Now, that's exactly what she said. She said, Pauline, if you pass through Brissago you absolutely *must* call that darling Gerry Krause and give him my love. So I just had to call because she'd never forgive me if I didn't and . . ."

Five minutes later, when she hung up, Ginger had a date to meet Gerard Krause at the café on the Via Cantonale at eleven the next morning. She offered a thank you to the fictional Mary Jo Betterman, debated having something to eat, and decided that she wasn't really hungry. Like her father, she had had a hard day's journey, and all she really wanted was sleep. She bathed, brushed her hair exactly one hundred strokes, and got ready for bed. As with her father, sleep did not come quickly; but unlike her father, her head was not filled with fears of failure, plots, and counterplots. She considered her task a simple one.

Tomorrow, Tuesday, she would meet Gerard Krause. On the next day, Wednesday, she would kill him. He was one of the men who wanted to murder her father. She would kill him without a gun, without a knife, without any of Eddie's fancy gadgets.

Vasily had been able to provide little information about Krause, only that he was a sensualist, a womanizer, and that there had been a second reason for his transfer from Bangkok. The risk of disease had been too great for him there, and unlike other people he lacked the usual defenses against it. Gerard Krause was abnormally allergic to penicillin. One shot of it was enough to make him comatose. Two shots would kill him.

On that thought, Ginger closed her eyes and slept.

Barcelona was a city of memories for Vasily Borgneff, most of them happy ones, but one of them so sad that even now, ten years after the event, it brought him melancholy moments when recalled. In a way it seemed unfair for the city to be burdened with this memory. He loved the town too much, and what had happened to Josefina Carillo years ago should have happened somewhere else. Madrid, perhaps, or Valencia. He had no feelings for those cities, but Barcelona was a special place to him. The elegant squares and plazas, the tree-lined streets, the busy port, the bustle of hard-working Catalonians, and some of the most chic women in Europe all combined to remind him of another city he once had loved: New York back in the days before the garbage took over the town. The New York of yesterday and the Barcelona of today both were cities that he could happily claim as his own. He still felt that tie to Barcelona, although New York was finished for him, and the comparisons were painful.

On that Monday afternoon when he arrived there he tried to imagine a Barcelona street filthy and littered with trash, but he couldn't. He tried to imagine a Metro subway car covered with inane graffiti, but the image would not come. He tried to imagine a gang of kids roaming the Ramblas de Capuchinas snatching gold chains in the night, but the concept was impossible.

But don't carry the comparison too far, he warned himself. Barcelona pickpockets are the slickest in the world.

Standing at his window in the Hotel Colón, he looked out at the enormity of the cathedral on the other side of the square. He tried to keep his gaze steady, but he knew that he was blinking to compensate for the presence of the artificial eye in his left socket. The familiar eyepatch was gone, sacrificed on the altar of anonymity, and he rather missed it. The cathedral was the essence of Barcelona to him; the restless vitality of the mass of gray stone spoke of medieval masons drunk on the logic of form. Later that evening he would touch those stones for luck as he passed by into the *barrio gótico*, there to have two Pernods before the roast duck at Tinnel's. Then would come a stroll on the Ramblas in search of a coffee, and perhaps even a journey to the other side of town for a nighttime view of Gaudí's Catedral de la Sagrada Familia. To call it a cathedral was a misnomer, for no bishop resided there, but half of Barcelona thought of it as such. If the cathedral across the square was a soaring vault built for the storage of vibrant spirit, the Sagrada Familia was a burning, melting surreal candle offered up daily to God. That Barcelona should have two such monuments to the imperishability of the divine spark often seemed like aesthetic overkill to him, but that was one of the reasons why the city meant so much to him.

"It's a great town," he mused, looking down at the crowds in the square surging in waves that lapped on the great stone steps of the cathedral. But, as always, his warm thoughts of Barcelona were altered by the memory of what had happened ten years before. Again, as always, he wished that it had happened somewhere else. Of course, it never should have happened at all, but before the death of Francisco Franco such happenings were commonplace in Spain.

That was the way he had explained it to Eddie during those last few days in Mexico when the assignments were being divided up. There was no question about where Ginger and her father were going. Krause was the girl's natural target, and the setup on Andriakis was simple enough not to put too much of a strain on Emerson's faded skills. The decision lay with the other two, and Vasily had opted for Wolfe in Barcelona.

"I thought you wanted to take care of Swan personally," Eddie had said, surprised.

"It would give me the greatest pleasure, but it can't be done. For two reasons. It may be necessary to get close to Swan, and he knows my face well. He knows you only by reputation."

"That makes sense. What's the second reason?"

"That one is personal."

Eddie grunted impatiently. "We can't afford personal secrets. What is it?"

Vasily had thought for a moment, sighed, and then had told him.

"You have to remember what it was like in Spain ten years ago. The country was a Fascist dictatorship. There was only one official political party, the Falange, and the Communists were banned, of course. Even a milk-and-water Socialist had to keep his opinions to himself. If he didn't, he wound up behind bars, or worse."

"Could you leave out the history lesson and get to the point?"

"Don't push me; I don't find this easy to tell. In those days the CIA was plugged in tight with the Spanish authorities, and the man who ran the show over here was an American everybody called the Chessmaster. It was a fitting name for him. Aside from intelligence work, chess was his major passion. He was good at it, a life master. There were some who said that if he had devoted himself exclusively to chess he could have played on the international level, but the Chessmaster was content to be a very big fish in a small pond. That pond was the Sociedad de Ajedrez, the Barcelona chess club, and he played there every night from early evening until they put out the lights. Within the confines of that small club he was virtually unbeatable, and every year he won the club championship easily. Then Martín Carillo came along."

Vasily paused for a sip of wine. "Am I boring you?"

"Chess isn't one of my favorite games."

"A massive understatement. At any rate, there was Martín Carillo ten years ago, a natural chess genius at twenty-three. Untrained, untutored, but he was on the way up. For the last two years he had faced the Chessmaster in the finals of the tournament and had lost. This was the year he was expected to win. What else can I tell you about Martín? He was a fine young man, a dockworker who drove his body hard all day and drove his brain just as hard at the chessboard. He was also a Socialist, a member of a small discussion group that met once a month. Highly illegal, of course, but hardly a threat to the stability of the state.''

''I'm beginning to see it.''

''I doubt it. Martín had a sister.''

''*Now* I see it.''

''You'd have to have known Josefina Carillo to see it all. She was seventeen that year and . . . Eddie, do you know what I mean when I say that she had a sultry innocence?''

''Sexy, but untouchable?''

''That's another way of putting it. She was also blind.''

Eddie grunted. It was hard to tell if he was affected by the story or simply impatient to get to the end of it. ''How did you fit into all of this?''

''I was passing through Barcelona at the time.''

''Bullshit. You must have been working.''

Vasily shrugged. ''Some people needed some instruction, and Moscow Center thought I might be able to help. I met Martín through those people, and through Martín I met his sister.''

''And there went the innocence.''

''Strangely enough, no.'' Vasily's eyes had a faraway look. ''Actually, I never touched her except to take her arm when we walked in the streets. She affected people that way. She and her brother lived together in the *barrio chino,* their parents were long dead, and I would take her to the club when Martín was playing in tournaments. We would walk along the Ramblas and I would describe the colors of the flowers in the stalls and the antics of the monkeys in their cages, and then we would go to the club and I would tell her what was happening on the board. She was very proud of her brother. It was just before the tournament finals, and everyone was saying that this was the year that Martín would finally beat the Chessmaster. But the Chessmaster was obsessed with that championship. It was his private property, and nobody was going to take it away from him. And he knew that Martín had reached the top of his form.''

"So he blows the whistle on the kid. A true sportsman.''

"It was easy for him. He was CIA. All it took was one telephone call to the right man in the *policia secreta*. Just the name, the address, and the fact that he was a Socialist. That's all they needed in those days. The *policia* came for the boy in the middle of the night, three days before he was due to face the Chessmaster. Unfortunately, they took the girl as well. No reason. They didn't need a reason. They just took her.''

"What happened?'' The question came softly.

"The inevitable. The Chessmaster won his tournament.''

"And Martín? The girl?''

"They kept him for over a month. Routine questioning. They broke both his legs and most of the bones in both hands. They did a pretty good job on his mind, too. He wasn't much good for chess after that. As for Josefina, they made Martín watch. That's what blew some of his fuses. Sometimes they didn't bother to rape her. Sometimes they used sticks, or bottles, or—''

"That's enough.''

"Yes, you're right—quite enough. It was enough then, and it's enough now. They let her go after a week, and she made her way back to that pathetic little apartment in the *barrio chino*. She dragged herself up the stairs, locked herself in her bedroom, and hung herself from a steampipe. I was there when they cut her down.''

Eddie waited for more, and when nothing more came there was a question that had to be asked. "Why didn't you kill him?''

"I was on assignment. Under discipline from Moscow Center. I couldn't.''

"Screw discipline. You should have dropped him.''

"No doubt you're right, but I was younger then. I was a great one for following the rules in those days. I missed my chance, and I never thought I'd get another one. But now I have it. I want him, Eddie. Joseph Wolfe, the Chessmaster.''

"Yeah, you've waited long enough. He's all yours.''

* * *

On Monday afternoon, Eddie drove from Dulles International Airport on his way into Washington, looking for a motel. He passed several Ramadas and Great Westerns and Holiday Inns, without stopping. He wasn't looking for that kind of motel. He was looking for one called Happy Hours, or Fun and Games, or something similar. A motel where every room had a circular water bed, a television equipped with video games and X-rated movies, and black satin sheets that had been scrubbed to a rusty purple. He found one halfway into the city. It was called the Cinq à Sept, and the room he was given smelled heavily of antiseptic. It was just what he wanted.

As he unpacked his few belongings, Eddie reviewed all that Emerson had told him about Swan's personal habits. The pattern was that of a meticulous man who lived on a rigid schedule and demanded satisfaction for all of his creature comforts. He had eaten the same breakfast for twenty years, left his suite at the Hotel Coolidge at the same time every morning, and returned there promptly to dress for the evening. He conducted the rest of his life on an equally organized basis. He was an ideal target.

The last item out of Eddie's suitcase was the flat, square metal box that was his traveling laboratory. He set it carefully on the floor of the closet, swung the switch near the handle through a ninety-degree turn and heard the mechanism click into place. An unauthorized attempt to break open the box would now be met by a confined but lethal explosion. Satisfied, he changed clothes quickly, putting on a pair of rough denims, heavy shoes, and a moderately clean T-shirt. He exchanged his Concorde wristwatch for a cheap digital number, tucked his star-sapphire pinky ring into a pocket, and ran his fingers through his hair to loosen the carefully nurtured wave. He felt his jaw, debated shaving, and decided that the one-day growth would help, not hinder, him.

It was midafternoon when he drove the rental car into downtown Washington and parked it in a garage several blocks from the Coolidge. The delivery entrance to the hotel was on a narrow side street lined with parked cars. He picked a spot opposite the entrance and lounged against a car, waiting. During the next half hour three trucks pulled up to make deliveries to the hotel. He let a bakery wagon and a butcher's van go by. The sign on the third truck read G. MARTINELLI, FANCY FRUITS AND VEGETABLES, and Eddie moved quickly to be at the curbside when it double-parked in front of the entrance. When the driver got out to open the back of the truck, Eddie was right beside him. He reached inside and grabbed the first box his hands touched, a crate of celery. He hoisted it onto his shoulder.

The driver stared at him in surprise. He was wide-shouldered and heavy through the chest. He had a belly of solid suet. He said flatly, "Put it the fuck down."

"Sure thing," said Eddie. He set the crate on the pavement. "It's too fuckin' hot to work anyways."

"Who the fuck are you?"

"Chef sent me out to help with the fuckin' crates."

"No shit!" Now the driver looked truly surprised. "It's a fuckin' miracle."

"It's a fuckin' pain in the ass, that's what it is."

"You new here?"

"First fuckin' day," said Eddie, his bona fides established. "How do you wanna handle it?"

"We'll split it up even," said the driver after a judicious moment. "I'll stack the crates on the sidewalk. You haul 'em inside."

"Some fuckin' even," said Eddie, but he bent down and hoisted the crate back on his shoulder.

He spent the next twenty minutes lugging crates of celery, lettuce, and tomatoes into the hotel and down a flight of clanging iron steps to the kitchen. On his first trip he came through the kitchen doors yelling, "Delivery from Martinelli. Where do you want it?" A shocked aristocrat in faultless whites, his chef's toque stiff and starched, looked up from the sauce he was stirring and silently pointed a ladle at the door to the refrigerator room. After that it was easy. He used each trip through the kitchen to familiarize himself with the physical plant, the layout of the kitchen, pantries, elevators, and halls. He noted the traffic of the uniformed waiters, where they placed their orders, where they picked up the food, where they submitted their slips to the checker. His eyes searched for the inevitable time clock and found it just inside the employees' locker room. By the time he had hauled his last crate, he was satisfied with what he had found. When he was finished, the truck driver handed him a receipt to be signed by the chef. Eddie scrawled some initials on it.

"You work too hard, friend," Eddie told him. "You could get a fuckin' hernia that way."

Downstairs once again, he picked up the first crate he saw, put it on his shoulder, and paraded through the kitchen with the familiarity of experience. When he came to the locker room, he looked around quickly and ducked in. The room was empty. He checked the time cards in the slots and found the one for Swan's personal waiter, Bernard Randall. Then he found a place to rest behind the last row of lockers and settled down to wait for the shift to end.

Mama, he thought, grinning to himself, I'll never say that nasty word again, I promise.

The shift at the Coolidge changed at five fifteen. When the first of the outgoing waiters came into the locker room, Eddie was standing in front of a washbasin lovingly combing and recombing his hair. No one paid any attention to him. He kept his eyes fixed on the mirror that reflected the time clock, watching the waiters punch out. Bernard Randall turned out to be a mousy man in his fifties whose maroon and gold livery hung on him loosely. Eddie fixed the man's features in his mind, gave a final lick of the comb to his hair, and left the Coolidge. Half an hour later he was back in his sleazy motel room talking to Rusty at the Hotel Princesa in Mexico City.

"You're the second one to call in," she told him. "The man with one eye was the first."

"Does he have any problems?"

"He says he's in place and ready to move on the day. But I haven't heard from the other two. *My* two."

"They're still traveling. You'll hear from them in the morning."

"I know, but I can't help worrying."

"You've got the toughest job of all, sitting it out down there. Just hang in until we get this circus operating. Then you'll be able to relax."

"Yes." There was a silence on the line. "You and I have never gotten along very well." It was a statement.

"No, we haven't."

"Basically, I don't like you. I don't like your style, I don't like what you do, and I don't like the fact that you're much too old for my daughter. But you're a good man to have around. I should have said that before, but I never got the chance. When all this is over . . ."

"Yeah, I know, but we've still got a long way to go."

"All right, but I thought I should say it."

"I'm glad you did. When the others call in, you tell them that the balloon goes up right on schedule."

"You're set then?"

"Ready to roll. Seven o'clock Wednesday morning, local time. No changes in plan."

"I'll tell them."

"Good. And hang loose, Mom, you hear?"

"Don't you dare call me that," she said, suddenly furious.

"Why not?" he asked, laughing. "When all this is over, you're going to be my mother-in-law, aren't you?"

"I'm exactly six years older than you, and you know it. Don't you ever call me that again."

"You're the one who started getting sentimental. I'll check in tomorrow, same time." He was still laughing when he hung up.

Rusty put down the telephone and shivered. Outside her hotel room, Mexico City throbbed with its particular brand of nighttime vibrancy, but she got no pleasure from the rhythm. Outside, the night was hot and sticky, but inside the room the air conditioner hummed, and she felt a chill. She also felt very much alone. In all the years of her marriage she could not recall more than a dozen nights that she and her husband had spent apart. In retrospect, the statistic seemed incredible, given the nature of the times in which they lived and Jimbo's occupation. Still, it was true, and what she felt was less a sense of loneliness than of being incomplete. She wandered aimlessly about the room, trying to think of something to do. She knew that she should take two Valium and a glass of warm milk and try to get some sleep, but there was still a chance that Jim or Ginger might call. In the end she decided on a long bourbon and water, and stretched out on the couch near the telephone.

After all these years it's come down to this, she thought. Kill or be killed. And my family is out there doing the killing.

She closed her eyes, as if closing them could shut out her thoughts. The air conditioner hummed, and she shivered again.

Sasha Ignatiev arrived in Mexico City on Monday evening aboard Pan American flight #67 out of Washington. His step was jaunty and his eyes were bright as he cleared the formalities of immigration and customs, and came out into the rotunda. Waiting for him was the personal limousine of the Russian ambassador, and he was driven at once to the embassy. There he was taken to a drab room on the second floor of the building, where he was met by the embassy's military attaché, a KGB officer named Dorenkin, who handed him a sealed envelope. Inside the envelope was a teleprinted message.

FROM: *A. Petrovich*

TO: *S. Ignatiev*

RE: *Operation Homefire/Backfire*

1   Current phase of this operation is now code-named Seafire.

2   Soviet submarine E434 will arrive off reference point C-2683/Grid 43/Pacific Plate 11-No. Calif. night of 19/20.

3   Beach rendezvous with motor launch from E434 at 0200 PDT plus/minus 20 minutes. Fallback rendezvous plus 25 hours 10 minutes.

4   At time of rendezvous you are instructed to deliver Colonel Yuri Volanov, aka James Emerson, aka Homefire, to the launchmaster for transportation to the USSR.

5   On board E434 to welcome Colonel Volanov and ac-

company him on his voyage home will be Colonel Andrei Petrovich, Major Boris Radichek, and Captain Pavel Kolodny.

6   Upon receipt of this message you will at once communicate with me aboard E434 through embassy facilities.

Sasha's eyes narrowed as he read the message. The presence on board the submarine of the original team that had launched *Operation Homefire* all those many years ago came as a surprise to him.

Christ, they must be edgy, he thought—to come all the way out to escort him home. And I don't blame them. If this works, and if I get him, they're going to have one hell of a reluctant hero on their hands, and I'd hate to be him on that sea voyage back to Vladivostok. They'll work on him with everything they've got to make him cooperate. First the old buddy routine, then the appeal to his socialist conscience, and if that doesn't work they'll apply the persuaders. That's going to be one bitch of an ocean cruise for my dear old daddy. By the time they get him on Russian soil either he'll be brainwashed into the ideal Hero of the Soviet Union, or he'll be so lit up on drugs that he'll say anything they tell him to. They're not taking any chances with all three of them on board. The only card they aren't playing is the grand old harlot, mother mine.

Sasha raised his eyes from the paper and said to Dorenkin, the KGB man, "You've read this, I trust. Can you get through to Colonel Petrovich on board the sub?"

"It will take time, but yes."

The two men went up a flight of stairs to the embassy code room where Sasha consumed a pot of tea and two sandwiches while he waited for the connection to be made. Finally, at Dorenkin's signal, he picked up the handset and spoke his name. In reply he heard Petrovich's voice, distorted by static, in his ear.

"Fraternal greetings, Sasha," said the colonel. "And greetings from your mother as well. I've been advised that she returned safely to the Soviet Union the day after we sailed. Otherwise, she would be with the rest of us on this journey.''

That explains that, Sasha thought as he returned the greeting mechanically, then said, ''How does it look to you? Do you confirm your ETA at the rendezvous?''

''Affirmative. What about your end?''

''It all depends on *Backfire*,'' Sasha said cautiously. ''If we get full cooperation, I'll have Colonel Volanov waiting for you on the beach the night of the nineteenth.''

''Listen, Sashinka—I know you since you were a baby, and I'm trusting you to pull this off. No slip-ups like the one in Virginia. Don't fail me, Sasha.''

Petrovich broke the connection abruptly. Sasha grinned at this breach of procedure and thought: Christ, the old man must really be nervous. As he gave the handset back to Dorenkin he glanced at the clock on the wall and decided that he had time for a few hours' sleep before the wheels began to turn.

Chapter 15 _____

On Tuesday, July 15, the day before the scheduled assault on the Gang of Four, Eddie Mancuso and his colleagues prepared themselves for Wednesday in varying fashions. Ginger Emerson went sailing, her father went dancing, Vasily played chess, and Eddie sucked eggs. These were not recreational exercises. All four of them were working.

Ginger reclined in the cockpit of a twenty-two-foot Luchesi sloop, her body displayed in the briefest of bikinis for the pleasure of Gerard Krause, who lounged against the transom with his arm hooked over the tiller. The transition of invitations from the café on the Via Cantonale to luncheon at the marina to a sail on the lake in his boat had been made smoothly enough. That was the word, she decided, for Krause. He was smooth in every way, from his light line of patter to his slick mustache to the easy way with which he handled the boat in the capricious breezes that swirled around the bowl of Lago Maggiore. They had run before the wind over to the Verbania side, then down-lake into Italian waters as far as Luino before pointing up into the prevailing northwest winds to complete the triangular course. Ginger, who had done her share of sailing on Chesapeake Bay during college days, had to give the chubby little man full marks in seamanship. In fact, she had to give him top marks in all of the social graces, which bothered her somewhat. She would have preferred to have found a less charming victim.

Actually, she admitted to herself, she would have preferred to have found him to be a monster. She was aware, of course, that in many ways he was. She knew too much about the man to be deceived by his surface. He was an irrational fanatic whose

215

hands had been bloodied many times over, and he was one of the four men who had decided that her father must die.

I'll manage, she told herself. I'll manage it very nicely.

She realized that he was smiling at her, and she smiled back automatically. He reached out his free hand to touch her ankle and stroke it.

"You're very quiet," he said.

"Just enjoying myself." She breathed deeply, arching her back, and saw the appreciation in his eyes. "The lake, the Alps, the forests . . . I didn't believe it at first. Fir trees and palm trees growing side by side."

"Lago Maggiore is a jewel that has been polished by craftsmen for centuries."

"It must be wonderful to live here all the time."

"One gets tired of it after a while. I spend about half my time here, and half in Milan."

"Why Milan? It's such a dirty, ugly city."

He shrugged, his eyes on the luff of the mainsail. "A man can't always choose the places he does business."

"I didn't know you were in business. Mary Jo didn't tell me that."

"Mary Jo again." He seemed amused. "Are you going to insist on maintaining that fiction?"

"Fiction?"

"We both know that Mary Jo Betterman doesn't exist."

His fingers tightened on her ankle. She felt a touch of ice in the pit of her stomach, but she kept her face calm.

"You made a small mistake." He was smiling broadly now. He released the grip on her ankle as he hauled on the sheet to point the sloop closer into the wind. "You said she called me Gerry. Nobody calls me Gerry, I don't allow it. The name is Gerard."

"I . . . I probably misunderstood her," she said faintly.

"Come, admit it. Why pretend?"

She stared at him, not knowing what was coming next. They were closing up quickly on the stone jetty at Brissago, close enough to shore that if she had to swim for it, she could. She braced herself to move quickly.

"Not that I mind, you understand." He was not looking at her. His eyes were on the jetty, calculating when to tack and lay the boat alongside. "This isn't the first time that a girl has tried that routine on me."

"Routine?" she managed to say.

"I assure you, I'm not offended. In fact, I'm flattered." He gave her a happy wink. "You wanted to meet me and you managed it very cleverly. But now that you have, let's forget about Mary Jo Betterman, shall we?"

She made a confused gesture.

His hand was back on her ankle. "I'm aware that I have a certain reputation with models. I enjoy beauty, and I pay well for what I enjoy. Where did you hear about me? In Milan?"

Models, she thought. Good Lord, he thinks I'm trying to hustle him. She said vaguely, "Oh, here and there."

"Cherubino's, no doubt, or Calvin's. That's where those bitches hang out." He suddenly giggled; it was shockingly out of character. "Well, you mustn't believe everything you hear. What agency are you with? Eileen? Wilhelmina? Johnny C.?"

"I'm not connected right now."

"And so you decided to meet the notorious Gerard Krause. Not that I'm sorry you did. You're remarkably lovely." He looked at her reprovingly. "You American girls, you come over to Milan to do one spread for Italian *Vogue* and you get sophisticated much too quickly."

She buried a smile as she remembered her words to Eddie: *Don't worry, I'm going over there to kill him, not seduce him.*

Krause turned his attention to the boat, coming up into the wind deftly and letting the way drop off her until they drifted neatly alongside the jetty. Two of the boys from the marina were there to fend off and take lines. Krause hopped ashore, giving instructions to the boys, then held out a hand to help her. Standing next to her on the jetty, some of his charm dropped away. His head came only to her shoulder.

"Do we go on from here?" he asked.

She hesitated, just long enough.

"Come," he said, with a touch of impatience. "Don't make

me repeat myself. I enjoy beauty, and I pay well to keep it around me.''

I'll bet you do, she thought. I'd love to see your expense sheets.

''How about dinner at Il Giardino tonight? It's three stars, the best in Switzerland.'' When she did not reply, he took her silence for agreement. ''I'll meet you there at seven thirty.''

''Let's make it eight. I have some things to do first.''

She went back to the Pension Valentina and did those things that she had to do. She crushed and then pulverized eight penicillin tablets into a smooth powder. Then, following Eddie's instructions, she packed the powder into two tiny plastic bags and secured them in her purse. Then she was ready for dinner.

While Ginger was sailing on Lago Maggiore, Vasily was playing chess at the Club de Ajedrez in Barcelona. The chess club was located in an old building off the Plaza de Cataluña, a long and narrow room with three dozen tables. Everything about the club was old but serviceable. The carpet on the floor was heavy but worn; the chairs were well padded but faded; and behind the coffee bar the espresso machine babbled a constant complaint. The prevailing odors in the room were those of stale coffee and tobacco, for the windows to the street were sealed against both sound and light, and tiers of smoke collected around the green-shaped lamps that hung over each table.

At four in the afternoon the club was almost empty, with no more than half a dozen tables in use. Vasily paid the visitor's fee to a bored ancient at the door, bought himself a *carajillo* at the bar, and stood sipping the anise-flavored coffee appreciatively as he watched a game in progress. When he had finished his coffee, he went to one of the empty tables and sat down. He dug his hand into the box of wooden chessmen and fingered the pieces absently. After a while a young man with long hair came over and asked if he wanted a game.

''If you're prepared to be patient,'' said Vasily. ''It's been a while.''

The young man shrugged and sat down. They chose for

color; Vasily drew white and opened with a conventional Ruy
Lopez that brought him to defeat in twenty-two moves. In the
next game, playing black, he used a Queen's Indian Defense
but did no better. In the third game he reached back into his
memory and opened with the rarely used Nimzovich Attack.
His opponent looked at him curiously but said nothing. After
the forty-third move, the young man resigned.

"You may not have played for a while, but you know what
you're doing," he told Vasily. "Are you new here? I don't remember seeing you before."

"I used to come here years ago, but the place looks the same.
Ready to fall apart. Does the Chessmaster still play?"

"Wolfe? Of course, every night. The club wouldn't be the
same without him."

"Does he still play simultaneous games?"

"Twice a week, Wednesdays and Saturdays. He limits himself to twenty opponents these days." He brightened as he
added, "I've drawn with him twice."

"Something to be proud of," Vasily assured him. "I might
try him myself. That would be tomorrow?"

"At noon." The young man got up to leave. "Try that
Nimzovich on him. You might get away with it."

After the young man had left, Vasily sat for a while at the
table, apparently lost in thought. His eyes stared absently at the
ceiling, and his fingers toyed with the chessmen in the box.
Once in a while his hand went to his pocket. When he got up
from the table to leave he had collected and secreted six chessmen, all white, one of each rank: one pawn, one rook, one
knight, one bishop, one queen, one king.

Back in his room at the Hotel Colón, he laid out the pieces on
a table and set up his traveling lab kit, which was virtually the
same as Eddie's. He made exact measurements of the pieces
with a caliper and rule, and traced their outlines on a sheet of
paper. Then, using a minute jeweler's drill, he bored a hole in
the head of the pawn. The hole, on the surface, was barely visi-
ble. He used a second tiny drill with a burr tip to enlarge the interior of the hole, forming a hollow space in the top of the
pawn. He worked slowly and cautiously, and when he was fin-

ished only the thinnest shell of wood was left. The procedure
had taken over half an hour. He then did the same with the other
five pieces. It was eleven o'clock before he was finished with
that stage of the operation.

After a ten-minute rest he went back to work. As a precaution, he coated the outside of the pieces with Vaseline. Working with extreme concentration, using a triple-zero pipette with
a diameter no greater than that of a needle, he filled each hol-
lowed piece with a special solution of almost pure nitrobenzine. Finally, he sealed off each entry hole with white wax,
smoothed and sanded to the color of the chess piece. By then it
was two in the morning.

He regarded his handiwork soberly. Once the Vaseline coat-
ing was removed, each chess piece would be transformed into a
lethal weapon. Anyone touching the head of the piece would receive, through osmosis in the wood, a substantial amount of
nitrobenzine on his fingers. As a contact agent, this form of
nitrobenzine was unbeatable. It bonded on contact with the
blood, inhibited oxygenation, and resulted in death by suffoca-
tion within minutes.

Staring down at the row of white pieces, Vasily smiled
grimly and murmured four words. "Josefina. Martín. Wolfe.
Checkmate."

On that same Tuesday, Eddie Mancuso slept late. When he
finally left his motel room for breakfast it was past eleven, and
the fogginess in his head told him that he could have slept even
later. A while back he had decided that he used sleep as a shield
against the reality of certain things he had to do. Stay in bed,
don't think, just dream, and maybe tomorrow will go away. As
a theory it was comfortable; it made him feel more human,
more vulnerable, and less like a life-taking machine. But if it
was a comfortable theory, it was also a dangerous one, and he
tried not to take it too seriously.

"I'm just a precious little wildflower bending in the breeze,"
he sang to himself as he tooled the rental down the Interstate
looking for a place to have breakfast. "Too fragile and delicate
to survive in this cold, cruel world. No shit, really I am."

He found an open Pancake Heaven and settled in for a meal. This would be breakfast and lunch combined (he had never been comfortable with the word brunch), and he had eaten lightly the night before. He ordered grapefruit juice, a four-egg omelette, and a pile of sausages, and then remembered what he would be doing for the rest of the day. He called the waitress back.

"Hold everything. Make it a double order of corned-beef hash, toast, and coffee," he told her and just in time remembered to add, "No poached egg on the hash."

When his breakfast came he ate it with a copy of the *Washington Post* propped up in front of him and leaning against a bottle of ketchup, feeling the pleasurable guilt of a man who has been somewhat tamed by a woman and knows he is reverting to bachelor habits. Finished with breakfast, he drove back toward the motel looking for a supermarket and found one just beyond the traffic circle. In the dairy section he loaded his cart with three dozen of what now passed for extra-large white eggs. Each was somewhat larger than a Ping-Pong ball. He looked at them distastefully.

They'll have them down to the size of marbles soon, he thought. Shmuck, buy something else. Who the hell buys three dozen eggs and nothing else?

He knew that it was unnecessary, but as a sop to his professional conscience he added flour, sugar, and a box of plastic cake frosting to his cart. At the checkout counter he debated going back for a cake of yeast but decided that he was verging on paranoia.

Uncle Eddie is baking today, kiddies. First one home from school gets to lick the pot.

Back in the motel room he laid the eggs out on the table, set up his lab kit, and stood for a moment staring at the setup. There are unpleasant aspects of every occupation, and this was one that he disliked intensely. He knew exactly what was going to happen. First he would try to do it the easy way, and then, after he had failed with the first dozen eggs, he would do it the hard way, but the right way.

First the easy way. He took from his kit a hypodermic syringe and the finest needle available. Sitting crouched over the table, he punctured the shell of the egg with the needle and very slowly and carefully began to draw out the contents. The albumen came out easily. It always did. The problem came with the yolk. The viscous yellow substance clogged the tip of the needle at once. He withdrew the needle, washed it, and tried again. The same thing happened. He tried a third time, and this time the needle enlarged the hole so badly that the egg was useless. He sighed, discarded the egg, and reached for another one. The result was the same. It continued to be the same through the first dozen eggs, just as he had known it would be.

So much for modern technology. He moved a carton of eggs into the bathroom. With an ordinary straight pin he punctured a tiny hole in the round end of an egg. He made a face at himself in the mirror over the sink, put the egg to his lips, and began to suck with an even pressure. The contents of the egg came out smoothly, filling his mouth. With considerable effort he kept himself from gagging and spat out into the sink. He sucked again until the shell was completely empty. He examined the result of his labor and found it perfect: a clean, empty shell with a tiny pinhole. He rinsed out his mouth and started on another egg. In no time at all he had six perfect specimens, but his mouth tasted like the inside of a chicken coop.

"There's got to be a way," he said to himself in the mirror. "A smart guy like me should be able to teach his grandmother how to suck eggs."

He moved the six empty eggs back inside. From his lab kit he took a dark, tightly sealed bottle, a lightweight gas mask, a tablet of amyl nitrate, and an amyl nitrate capsule. He swallowed the tablet dry and popped the capsule under his nose, trying to ignore the rush of pleasure that coursed through him. He had nothing against the rush, but this was business, not fun. Adjusting the gas mask around his face, he then proceeded to transfer the prussic-hydrocyanic acid from the dark bottle to the hollow eggs, injecting it drop by drop through the pinhole. Finally, he sealed off the pinhole with a calcium-gum compound and finished the exterior so that no sign of entry showed. He repeated the procedure with a second egg.

Enough, he told himself. No sense mass-producing the damn things.

He packed the loaded eggs into a padded box and cleaned up the mess. By the time he had finished, it was early evening. He knew that he should be hungry again, but he could not face the thought of food. He rinsed his mouth out with bourbon, built himself a proper drink, and settled down to watch television. At midnight he turned off the set and slept for two hours. Shortly before three in the morning, his bill already paid, he packed up and left the motel, driving the deserted highway into the city.

James Emerson's mission had been, from the beginning, different from that of the others. Eddie had explained that to him during those hurried briefing sessions in Mexico.

"You're going into a blind situation," he had said. "We don't know as much about Andriakis as we do about the other three. Generally, in a situation like this, we look for a weakness in the target. Either that, or a habit pattern that we can use against him. That's the whole point when you're using UKDs; it's not like potting a guy with a rifle and running for it. The takeout has to look either like a natural death or like an accidental death. If you can't make it look that way, then it has to look like part of something bigger, something that draws attention away from the actual target. That's why we hunt for the weaknesses. Is the target a junkie? Maybe he OD's. Is the target a drunk? Maybe he drives off a road. Things like that.

"But with Andriakis we have a problem. It was easier to figure the angle with the others. With Swan it's his regular eating habits, his rigid schedule. With Wolfe it's this obsession he has about chess. With Krause it's even simpler. The shmuck is a fool for anything in skirts, which is why we gave him to Ginger. But Andriakis? We just don't know that much about his personal life. There's a weakness in him somewhere, either that or a habit pattern. There has to be; everybody has something like that. But you'll have to find it by yourself, and you won't have much time. You'll have to find it quick and then make your move."

By Tuesday evening, after a day of surveillance on Peter Andriakis, Emerson had come to two conclusions. The first was that he had been set a task that was preordained to failure. There was no possible way to discover the weaknesses of a man's character, much less the habit patterns of his life-style, in one day of observation. By Tuesday evening he knew no more about Andriakis than he had known on Tuesday morning. The second conclusion was that he was going to use the pistol and kill the son of a bitch anyway.

I'm not cute like Eddie or Vasily, he thought. They have the minds of fiends, and they've been around this business for twenty years. My mind doesn't work that way. I'll shoot him, run for it, and take my chances.

It had been a frustrating day. He had kept a discreet tail on Andriakis from early morning onward. From a distance he had seen the man confer with a farmer about the purchase of olives, seen him shop for fish at a local market, and had watched him drink three cups of sugary Greek coffee while chatting with friends in a café. He had gone without his own lunch, camping outside a *tavérne* in Pyrgi, while inside Andriakis consumed skewers of lamb and a mound of rice, and then had followed him across the island to the beach at Aghios Górdis where his target had done nothing more startling than lie in the sun for most of the afternoon. Then had come the return trip to the house in Kalami, where Andriakis had disappeared inside and had not emerged since. Staked out on a deserted section of road that overlooked the house, the hood of his car up in a pathetic attempt to simulate a stranded motorist and sustained only by a sandwich grabbed on the fly, Emerson kept watch while his spirit weakened and his resolution waned. By ten o'clock he had been on the job over twelve hours, the night was dark, and he knew that he had accomplished nothing.

So he likes to lie on the beach . . . how do I arrange for a tidal wave? He likes shashlik for lunch . . . do I stab him with a skewer? Setting this up the way they want me to do it would take weeks, and they expect me to find an angle in one day. It can't be done. Even if Eddie or Vasily were here it wouldn't work. They wouldn't see any more than I did.

He was wrong about that. Either Eddie or Vasily would have

noticed the tiny strip of beach below the Andriakis house, the sailboat moored offshore, and a second boat that had been run up onto the beach under cover of darkness. They would have noticed the way Andriakis drove the hairpin turns of the hilly island roads, cutting corners so sharply that a blowout on a turn would mean disaster. They would have noticed the suntan oil that he spread on his body so liberally and would at once have started their chemical calculations. But Emerson saw none of that. He saw only a bland man in a bland routine, and he decided that he would have to shoot him.

I'll wait another hour, he thought miserably. If he doesn't come out, or if nothing else happens, I'll go home, and tomorrow I'll take him out with the gun. After that I'll just have to take my chances on getting off the island. It's the wrong way to do it, but what else can I do?

While Emerson asked himself these questions, Peter Andriakis sat across a heavy wooden table from a bulky man with a weatherbeaten face. Between them, on the table, rested a bottle of retsina and a bowl of olives, both of them untouched. The two men had been talking steadily for over an hour with no time for food or drink. The contrast between the two was notable. Andriakis, the Greek-American who was fifty and looked forty, was slim and elegant in white linen, his shirt open to the waist and a bronze medallion gleaming on his chest. Lex Enhora, an Albanian who was fifty and looked over sixty, was dressed in jeans cut down to shorts, a tattered cotton vest, and a pair of ancient sneakers. Despite the disparity of dress, the two men conversed as equals. Andriakis' job with the Agency was to run agents inside Communist Albania, and of those agents Enhora was the most important.

The proximity of the northeastern tip of Corfu to the Albanian mainland had been a problem for the Tirana government for years. Obsessed with internal security, more secretive than even the Russians, and very much aware of their anomalous position as China's only Communist ally in Europe, the Albanians had lined their borders with steel and their Adriatic coastline with patrol boats. The result had been a state hermetically sealed off from the rest of the world, save for the tender spot at

Corfu. With only a mile and a half separating the Greek island from the Albanian mainland, it was impossible to maintain a truly integral border. Fishing boats from both countries "accidentally" fetched themselves up on the wrong side of the passage, other boats easily eluded the patrols at night, and strong swimmers were known to negotiate the strait without the benefit of any boat at all.

One of the Albanians who regularly made the surreptitious trip to Corfu was Lex Enhora. To his farmhouse outside of Buthroton on the mainland came intelligence reports from a network of agents throughout Albania, and once each week he slipped across the water to run his sailing dinghy up onto the beach below the house at Kalami and transmit this information to Peter Andriakis. On this particular occasion his report had been a long one dealing with the new construction at the port of Durres, and the hour was late when the two men finally rose from the table. Business over, Enhora then proceeded to the second reason for his trip to Corfu that night: to collect a priest for his daughter's wedding the next day.

"Where is this priest that you found for me?" he asked.

"He's waiting down at the beach," Andriakis told him. "He's a good man, Lex, but he's young and he's nervous. This is his first trip across, so take good care of him."

"As if he were my brother," Lex promised. "I'll have your priest back here safely two days from now. By God, but I wish you could be there for the wedding."

"We've gone over this before. It would be too risky."

"No, it wouldn't, I promise you. The only people there will be close family, people I can trust."

Andriakis shook his head. "I can't take the chance."

"A shame. My only daughter gets married, and my best friend won't be there for the wedding."

Like some 20 percent of his fellow countrymen, Enhora was a member of the Greek Orthodox faith living in a predominantly Muslim country. At least, he would have been a member of the faith and the country would have been Muslim had not the Tirana government closed down every church and mosque in Albania years before in a move to create what it called "the first atheist state in the world." Ever since then religion had flourished only underground in Albania, which, for the Greek Orthodox community there, had meant the clandestine celebration of weddings, christenings, and the holy days—always at night, and always in some secluded spot away from the eyes of the police. It had also meant the secret importation of priests from Greece to preside over these rites, and Enhora had come to his good friend Andriakis for just that purpose.

The two men walked down to the tiny beach of sand and shale below the house where the priest was waiting. For this occasion he had discarded his cassock and stovepipe hat—they lay packed in the canvas bag at his feet—and only his full black beard indicated his calling. He was clearly nervous, and Andriakis knew he had reason to be. The three men pushed the sailing dinghy back into the water, and the priest climbed aboard. With wavelets curling around his knees, Enhora put a hand on his friend's arm.

"Are you sure you won't cross over tomorrow?" he asked plaintively. "It would mean a lot to all of us, especially Melina."

Andriakis hesitated, tempted. He knew what the next day would be like. In the afternoon Melina Enhora and her bridegroom would be married in a civil ceremony in the state office in Buthroton, but that night in the privacy of the Enhora barn, cleaned and decorated for the occasion, the marriage would be properly celebrated in the old-fashioned style. After the ceremony with the priest there would be feasting and drinking, the bouzoukis would play, and the men would dance. It was the sort of evening that Andriakis enjoyed more than any other, and he was tempted to say yes. He had stayed at the house before, but this would mean exposing himself to people who were strangers to him, close family or not. He shook his head again.

"I'm sorry, old friend, but it can't be done. Give Melina a kiss for me, and take good care of my priest. Watch out for the sharks on the other side."

Enhora showed his teeth in a grin to indicate what he thought of the Albanian patrol boats, and then he climbed aboard to hoist sail.

"*Yassas*, Peter," he called. "See you next week."

Andriakis watched until the dinghy, running under sail and without lights, merged with the darkness and was gone. He went back to the house, poured himself a tiny measure of retsina, and threw it down. The report had been a good one, and he was pleased with the evening's work. He looked at his watch. It was just past ten, plenty of time for him to hear the new bouzouki player at the *tavérne* in Pyrgi. Other than his work, the music and the dancing of Greece were his twin passions, most particularly the music of the eight-string mandolin called the bouzouki. In Corfu the word "bouzouki" stood not only for the instrument, but also for the dance and for the way of life it engendered. To go "bouzouki-ing" meant to bounce from tavern to tavern drinking the wine and dancing the stately *syrtáki*, the wildly energetic *naftikós*, the butchers' *chasápikos*, and at the end of a long night, flushed with wine and joy, to dance alone in the *zeïmbekikos* to the admiration and applause of the onlookers. The appearance of a new bouzouki player of repute was an irresistible lure to Andriakis, and fifteen minutes after he had seen off Lex Enhora he was on his way to the *tavérne* at Pyrgi.

The tavern was crowded; too many tourists, of course, but enough of the regulars to preserve the legitimacy of the occasion. The new player was a boy named Yanis, still in his teens but with impeccable technique and a born affinity to the music. He played *Koritsaki Mou*, and the Greeks in the room nodded nostalgically. He played *Frangosiriani*, the dance from Piraeus, and the tourists in the room murmured, "Never on Sunday." He played *Samiotisa*, and *Froso* and *Yerakina*, and the tempo of the dancing picked up, the tempo of the drinking kept pace, and wild yips of exultation echoed from the walls of the *tavérne*.

Then, without a pause, he segued into the choppy rhythm of the *zeïmbekikos*, and the women on the dance floor drew away and sat down, for this dance was for men only. One of the men was Andriakis, standing arrogant and straight, eyes and heels flashing, clearly the most impressive figure on the floor. The Greeks in the room recognized him, called his name, and applauded. The music grew faster and wilder, Yanis' fingers flashing on the bouzouki, and one by one the other men dropped away to give Andriakis the floor to himself. He danced alone, seemingly indifferent to the cries of encouragement that came from the tables. From one of those tables a hand offered a glass of ouzo. Without breaking step or spilling a drop, he saluted the donor and gulped down the fiery stuff. He tossed the glass away casually; it crashed on the floor. As if on signal, someone else tossed an empty glass, and it also shattered. Another glass, another, and then the plates began to fly and crash, Greek and tourist alike smashing crockery, hurling the dishes in a passionate frenzy as the music built to a climax with Andriakis dancing alone, accepting the tribute. From the back of the room the owner of the *tavérne* looked on happily. The cost of the crockery was included in the price of the drinks, and he considered it a bad night for business when plates were left unbroken.

Emerson watched the scene in amazement from a table near the door. He had never seen anything like it, and it had taken a while for him to realize that the plate breaking was part of a local tradition. Now, with the *zeïmbekikos* over, the owner of the tavern stood in the middle of the dance floor holding up his hands for silence. When he got it he made an announcement in Greek, then repeated it in English.

"Thass all for now, everybody. You drink, you dance, but no more throwing. We got no more dishes."

The crowd groaned.

"You come back tomorrow. Tomorrow we got more dishes. Tomorrow Yanis plays bouzouki. Tomorrow my good fran, Mr. Andriakis, he comes back and dances."

The crowd cheered. The owner flushed happily.

Emerson got up abruptly and left the tavern, ignoring the rush around him for the free drinks. He drove back to the house in Ipsos as fast as he could. Once there, he took the statuette of the god Pan from his suitcase and filled the sink with water. He immersed the statuette in the water and left it there. Then he turned on the oven and sat down to wait.

It took twenty minutes, just as Eddie had said it would, for the claylike substance of the statue to become pliable. Once he was able to mold it, Emerson set to work pressing and flattening the material until he had formed it into a thick disk about six inches in diameter. He made an indentation into the underside of the disk with his thumb, then began to shape it, running his fingers around the edges, working it into the form of a plate. He had to do it over several times before he had it right. Satisfied, he put it into the hot oven to dry and to bake. The baking process, again as Eddie had explained, took another thirty minutes, and when it was done he had an acceptable-looking dish, somewhat lumpy, slightly gray, but not too unlike the common crockery of the countryside.

"It's all I can give you," Eddie had said when he handed him the statuette. "Anything else would be too complicated. You'll have to pick your spot and use it when you can. Once you've found your angle."

The statuette, which was now a plate, was composed of a mixture known in the trade as Aunt Jemima, 25 percent ordinary baking flour and 75 percent cyclotrimethylenetrinitramine, or RDX. Together they made a potent explosive. The mixture could be baked, molded, pounded, even cooked into pancakes without exploding. For that a detonator was required. Emerson now fixed a number-six detonator into the indentation in the bottom of the plate and covered it over with a dab of Aunt Jemima. He now had a UKD that would explode on contact.

It had taken all day, but he had finally found the weakness. Andriakis was a dancing fool.

"Dance, Andriakis," Emerson murmured. He caressed the plate lovingly. "Tomorrow when you dance I'll be there to show my appreciation."

Chapter 16 _____

Edwin Swan, like many men of his age, slept only for a few hours each night. Because of this he had developed the habit of working late in his suite at the Coolidge, but even this did not keep him from waking promptly at six thirty. On Wednesday he was up at the usual hour. He collected the newspaper from outside his door, and thirty minutes later was bathed, shaved, dressed for the day, and seated at the table by the window, ready for his breakfast. Breakfast for Swan was an ascetic meal: two three-minute boiled eggs, whole-wheat toast, and tea; and it was served to him promptly at the same time every morning. While he awaited its arrival he made the first of his many telephone calls of the day, this one on the scrambler phone to Gerard Krause in Brissago.

"*Pronto,*" Krause answered.

"Good morning, Gerard. Edwin here. Or rather, good afternoon."

"And a lovely one at that. Sunshine, blue water, and a bunch of silly birds singing their heads off just for the joy of it."

"How nice for you."

"You should see the Alps today, Edwin. Still a touch of snow on the peaks, as white as cream cheese. and when the sun comes up it turns them a delicate pink, just like a slab of smoked salmon."

Lox and cream cheese, thought Swan. Once a New Yorker, always a New Yorker. "It sounds enchanting."

"What's on the agenda today? Make it quick; I'm off to a luncheon date shortly. A magnificent redhead."

"I'm sorry to interfere with your social life," Swan said dryly, "but we have to make a decision about Emerson today."

"Still no word from Mexico?"

"Total silence. Nothing from Borgneff, nothing from his team, nothing from the Castelnuevo woman, and today is the last day for contact. I don't like it at all."

"How do you see it? Does the other side have him?"

"Emerson? That wouldn't account for the silence. Unless I hear something today, I'll have to assume that Borgneff either failed or he's switched sides."

Krause gave a low whistle. "If he's switched it may mean that he's extracted his entire team. Both men and both women."

"Let's not jump to conclusions . . . we may hear something by the end of the day. But if we don't, I'm afraid it means sending in someone else."

"Can we get away with that, Edwin?"

"Just barely," Swan admitted. "If Christianson gets wind of this . . ."

"It's your decision, Edwin."

"Yes, it always seems to work out that way, doesn't it? We'll speak again tonight."

He hung up and was about to call Wolfe in Barcelona when a knock on the door announced his breakfast. His eyes on the front page of the *Washington Post*, Swan said, "Come in."

The waiter smoothly wheeled in the serving trolley and placed the dishes on the table. Without looking up, Swan asked, "What's the weather like, Bernard?"

"Not bad," said the waiter. "Maybe a little rain later."

Swan looked up sharply at the sound of the voice. The waiter was a stranger to him. He asked, "Where's Bernard?"

"Called in sick. Can I get you anything else?"

"No, nothing." Swan waved him away testily. He was a man who treasured habit and convenience, and he was irritated by the sight of a stranger at that hour of the morning. He waited until the waiter was out of the room, then poured his tea and took an appreciative sip. He took away the metal shell that covered the soft-boiled eggs in their cups and reached for the silver clipper beside his plate. It was his custom to open his eggs as they lay in their cups, neatly incising the pointed tip. He picked up an egg and was about to clip the tip when his eyes narrowed. He set the clipper aside and looked closely at the egg. He opened his hand and let it rest in his palm, moving the hand up and down in a weighing motion. He frowned, rotated the egg, and weighed it again. He set it down and did the same with the other egg. Then, very gingerly, he put the egg back in its cup. With equal care, he pushed his chair back from the table and slowly stood up. There was a telephone on his desk, but he went into the bedroom and used the extension there. The number he dialed rang only once before someone answered.

"Weather Control," said the voice.

"This is the DD5," said Swan. "I'm in my suite at the Coolidge. I'm not sure, but I may have a thunderstorm here."

"Hold, please." Swan heard the voice say in an undertone to someone else, "I have the DD5 in a possible storm. Roll car number one to the Coolidge." The voice came back on the line. "Details, please."

"I was having my breakfast, two boiled eggs." Swan paused for a moment to gather his words.

"Sir?"

"The eggs . . . they don't feel right. They're much too light."

"Hold, please." Again in an undertone, the voice said, "That's a confirm on the storm at the Coolidge. Roll car number two with a chemkit and a crash box." To Swan, he said, "On the way, DD5. Please leave your rooms at once. Go directly to the office of the manager of the hotel and wait for us there. Move out now." There was a click as the phone went dead.

Swan laid the telephone down, and without undue haste he crossed through the sitting room and went out of the suite and into the corridor. He left the door open. He considered walking down the three flights of stairs but forced himself to wait for the elevator. Downstairs, he crossed the lobby to the manager's office and had himself admitted. He had known the manager for twenty years, and a favor was not out of line.

"I'll need your office for half an hour," he said. "Would that be asking too much?"

The manager had a fairly good idea of who Swan was and what he did for a living. Without hesitation he nodded, stood up, and made for the door. He stopped there and asked, "Have you had your breakfast? Can I get you anything?"

"Tea and toast would be fine, thank you."

He settled himself behind the manager's desk and waited. Within minutes there was a knock on the door and six quietly dressed and purposeful young men filed in. He recognized one of them as Frank Patricio from Weather Control.

"Good morning, Frank," said Swan. "It's suite Three-B. The door is open."

Patricio nodded to the others, who filed out again. He stayed behind, his face marked with concern. "I'll stay here with you," he said. "The squad will handle it."

They sat facing each other, waiting. Swan's tea and toast arrived, and he looked at Patricio apologetically. "You'll excuse me," he said. "As you know, my breakfast was interrupted."

Patricio smiled politely. Without invitation, he broke off a corner of Swan's toast, chewed it, and followed that with a sip from the teacup. Swan looked on, horrified, shaken to his fastidious core. He wondered swiftly how he could avoid drinking from the same side of the cup. As if reading his mind, Patricio gave him a wicked grin.

"The food's all right," he said. "Go ahead and eat."

"Thank you," said Swan in a choked voice. "You're very thorough."

"My job."

They sat in silence after that. Swan ate the second piece of toast, the untouched one, and drank his tea holding the cup in his left hand. He did it casually, almost naturally, but he was sure that Patricio was silently laughing at him. Twenty minutes later they were joined by one of the other agents, a shorter, plumper version of Patricio named Stanley. He declined Swan's offer of coffee. He looked as weary as Patricio.

"It's a gadget, all right," he said. "They're loaded with

prussic-hydrocyanic. No wonder they seemed light to you. I'm surprised the damn things didn't float up to the ceiling.''

"Toxicity?" asked Patricio.

"Absolute."

"Remind you of anything?"

"Cassavetes in Stuttgart. Manlicher, three years ago. That other guy in Turkey. Same routine. The Reds took out three of our best that way."

"The Reds." Patricio gnawed at his underlip. He looked at Swan. "That doesn't make any sense. You know what I mean?"

"I think so," said Swan. "Why me?"

"I've been doing Weather Control for over ten years, and I've never seen anything like this. The Reds'll hit an operational, especially a unilateral, but not someone like you. Not a top administrator. It breaks all the rules. It invites reprisal."

Swan stared at him steadily. "Which leads you to what conclusion?"

"The egg trick. The Russians picked it up from us, but who invented it in the first place?"

Swan lifted his teacup, forgetting to use his left hand. He took the last swallow of tea and noted with disgust that his hand was shaking. He willed some control and set the cup down with a rattle.

"The one and only," he said. "Eddie Mancuso."

"You didn't recognize him?"

"I've only seen his photo on the files. My God . . ." His eyes opened wide. "The man served me my breakfast!"

"It was almost your Last Supper," said Stanley. "We found your regular waiter, Randall, tied up in the third-floor linen closet."

Patricio cut in quickly. "Look, Mr. Swan, I know this may be a delicate area, but is there any reason why Mancuso—"

Swan stopped him. "Yes. There are reasons."

"Then I'm afraid we're headed for the Fun House."

Swan nodded. Patricio turned to Stanley and snapped, "I want a four-by-four box around the DD5 from here to the cars.

He rides in car number one with me; you handle the crash car. Let's move.''

"One moment," said Swan. "There are three telephone calls I absolutely must make before we leave here. I'll need the scrambler phone upstairs."

"No way." Patricio's voice was flat. "There's a scrambler in the car if you need it."

"I'd prefer to—"

"Mr. Swan, I said we're moving. When all this is over you can have my ass, but right now it's my job, and I say we move. Now, let's go. *Go, go, go.*"

Outside the Coolidge, sitting in his car parked on N Street, Eddie had witnessed the screeching arrival of the Weather Control cars, and after that he had waited only for the confirming sight of a body bag being carried out of the hotel. Instead of that, now, he saw the seven men exit in a controlled trot, two of them forging ahead to open the cars, the other four in a protective box around the tall, gray figure of Edwin Swan.

Oh, Jesus, I screwed up, he thought. I blew it. I'm getting old. He's going under—he's headed for the Fun House. And right this minute he's getting on his scrambler and telling those other three to do the same thing.

The Agency cars sped away from the curb. Eddie tried not to think of what might happen to Ginger, Vasily, and Emerson once those calls were made and their targets alerted. I can't reach them, he realized. They're on their own.

Edwin Swan sat hunched over the scrambler phone in the backseat of the speeding car, his voice controlled but urgent as he gave instructions to the relay operator at Langley. The need for speed was clear to him. An operation mounted against him by Eddie Mancuso could only be part of a counterstroke from Emerson, and any attack on him would be meaningless unless it involved attacks on his three associates. As he waited for his calls to go through, he reviewed where the other three would dive for cover once they got the word.

Andriakis had his equivalent of the Fun House in the home of Lex Enhora, and would simply cross over into Albania and hole up there, paradoxically seeking safety in a Communist country. Krause's Fun House was the bordello of Katerina Felluci in Milan; he spent half of his time there anyway, and the delightful Katerina would bury him so deep in flesh that not even a battalion of agents would ever uncover him. As for Wolfe, Swan admired the foresight that had led him to develop his relationship with the Order of San Vicente, that offbeat offshoot of the brotherhood that had flourished for centuries in the foothills of the Pyrenees. As a tertiary of the Order, a secular member who had made substantial contributions over the years, Wolfe was free to visit the monastery in the mountains near Puigcerdá whenever he wished, to bury himself in the monastic life and participate in the daily rituals. Swan shuddered at the thought of some of those rituals but had to admit that the walls of the abbey provided Wolfe with the safest sort of redoubt.

The Langley operator broke in then to shatter his reflections and announce that his calls were ready. He spoke first with Brissago. Krause was not at home—at lunch no doubt with his magnificent redhead. Swan left a two-word message to be delivered at once. It was the same at the Barcelona number; Wolfe was at his chess club, and Swan left the same message. Only Andriakis was at home.

"It's time to head for the Fun House," Swan told him and outlined the situation quickly. "Get across as quick as you can."

"It's early afternoon here," Andriakis said slowly. "I can't cross over until it gets dark."

"Peter, you're in danger every minute that you stay on that side of the water."

"I realize that, but I'll have to sit tight until nightfall. There's no way I can make it during the day."

"That's up to you. *Sauve qui peut:* I've done the best I can."

He replaced the receiver and closed his eyes. He was still hungry, and he wondered if he would ever be able to eat a soft-boiled egg again.

Gerard Krause leaned across the table to inspect Ginger's plate. "You aren't eating your fish," he noted. "Is there anything wrong with it?"

"No, it's fine," she said, moving a morsel with her fork.

"It comes directly out of the lake, so it has to be fresh."

"I'm sure it is. I'm sorry, Gerard, but I don't seem to be very hungry today."

"Not like last night. Last night you had the kind of appetite that I love to see in a woman. It appeals to the sensual side of me."

She gave him a faint smile.

"And today you can't finish a tiny piece of fish," he said with mock reproach.

Last night I didn't have to kill you, she thought. Today I do.

But it was easier to oblige him, and so she finished the last of her fish while sailboats swooped on the waters of the lake, a ferryboat tooted, a gentle sun stippled the surface of Lago Maggiore with a handful of golden coins, and on the terrace of the Ristorante Pesche d'Oro the waiters paraded ceremoniously. It was a glorious summer day, but it was lost on Ginger.

I could have done it three times so far between the soup and the fish, she thought.

One of the two tiny plastic bags of penicillin lay under her hand, enough to do the job, and at least three times she could have loaded it into his wine as he turned his head to nod at people he knew at the other tables. But she had not done it. Not from fear of being seen, but out of a last-minute reluctance that she could only think of as buck fever. She had prepared herself to kill with hearty words and thoughts, but now that her finger was on the trigger her mind shied away from action and she could feel the faint sheen of perspiration on her forehead. Buck fever.

This man is evil, she reminded herself. He is totally evil and he wants to kill your father.

The familiar pep talk failed to move her this time. The short, chubby man with the slick mustache who had wanted her to finish her fish was a mortal animal, and in the twenty-four hours that she had known him, despite all his talk of buying beauty and his suggestive stories, he had treated her with exquisite politeness. He had yet to press himself upon her or indicate an obligation on her part. Even the night before, after a memorable dinner at Il Giardino, when she had expected him to make a move, he had simply escorted her back to her pension, taken her hand, and asked her to lunch on the next day. Now the plastic bag was beneath her fingers . . . and she had buck fever. She remembered something that Vasily had said back in Mexico, something about no sane man ever considering himself to be truly wicked, but only a misunderstood marcher to a particular drum.

That's the trouble with this business, she thought. Dividing the world up into us and them, good guys and bad guys. Gerard probably thinks that killing my father is nothing more than an ethical solution to a problem of national security. And because of that I have to kill him. If I can.

"Is something bothering you?" Krause asked softly.

"A bit," she admitted.

"I've confused you, haven't I?"

She was surprised by his perception. "Yes, you have."

He smiled broadly. "I've paid you a great deal of attention, a twenty-four-hour whirlwind, and I haven't tried to climb into your bed. Pretty rare for this freewheeling day and age, and now you're trying to figure out if I'm impotent, or gay, or what. Right? As a matter of fact, I'm neither. It's just that I have other plans for you."

"Plans?"

"I'm going to introduce you to Katerina Felluci." He paused expectantly. When he got no reaction, he asked, "Doesn't the name mean anything to you?"

"I'm afraid not," she said, puzzled. "You make it sound like being introduced to the Pope."

"How could you bounce around Milan and not know about Katerina? Didn't the other models tell you about her?"

"Gerard, I really haven't done that much modeling. And even less bouncing."

"I see." He smoothed his mustache with a forefinger. "Katerina Felluci runs the finest house in Milan."

"House?"

"Bordello, if you insist."

"Good Lord."

"Actually, Katerina's place is more like a private club. She gets only the top people there, and her girls are all either models or actresses. Believe me, I could mention some names that you'd recognize who once worked for Katerina."

"Name one."

He named several, one of whom had just married Middle Eastern royalty.

Ginger said slowly, "I'm impressed, but whatever made you think I'd be interested in something like that?"

It was Krause's turn to look puzzled. "Because you're young, you're extremely attractive, and you're a model out of work. What else would you do?"

"I can think of several things better than whoring in Milan."

"Don't use words like that. Katerina runs an exquisite operation. You wouldn't be doing anything there that you wouldn't do on your own, and you'd be getting paid very nicely for it. Aside from meeting the right kind of people." He seemed genuinely distressed. "I thought I was doing you a favor. There are plenty of girls I wouldn't recommend to Katerina, you know."

"Now I'm meant to be flattered."

"You should be."

Suddenly she realized that he must have done this with dozens of other girls, and she wondered if his superiors in Langley knew that their man in Switzerland was moonlighting as an Italian procurer. Suddenly the chubby little man with the slick mustache seemed substantially less endearing.

"Is that why you left me alone last night?" she asked. "Were you saving me for Milan?"

He shook his head and looked away for a moment, almost shyly. "No, not at all. You see . . . you're a beautiful girl, but I have rather . . . particular tastes in women, and you don't fit into the pattern."

She wondered if he was going to tell her about his particular tastes, but before he could say anything else the headwaiter was standing over him, bending in apology, and saying, "Il telefono, Signor Krause. Urgente."

Krause excused himself. She watched him work his way through the tables to the telephone booth at the rear of the restaurant. He slid closed the door of the booth and she could not see him anymore.

Now, she thought. Do it now, get it over with.

He's just another marcher to a different drum, thought another part of her mind.

I can't, she screamed silently. But while she was screaming her hand reached out and passed briefly over Krause's wineglass. Her fingers flicked open the plastic bag and dumped the powder. The crushed penicillin settled into the wine without a trace, and then the plastic was back in her handbag. She looked around; no eyes were on her. She looked down at her fingers approvingly. They had done the job without conscious command, as if they had been practicing the gesture for years. While her mind had been involved in debate, her hand had known exactly what to do.

While Ginger was congratulating herself, Krause took the telephone call in the booth and got the two-word message from his housekeeper: "Fun House."

He hung up at once. His hands were sweating, his face was pale. His first instinct was to run, but he sat for a moment, thinking. He had no idea what lay behind the Fun House order and had no time to find out. It could signify anything from an international crisis to a shakeup within the Agency itself. He had no way of associating it with the Emerson affair—as far as he knew, Emerson was dead—but he had been in the business too long to ignore an apparent coincidence. Yesterday a girl had marched into his life unannounced, and today came the order to get under cover. Coincidence? He toyed with the idea in his mind. There was no question about where he would go to hole up. Katerina Felluci would seal him into a private room and tend to his every whim for as long as he wished. If he took the girl along . . . ?

If it's just a coincidence then there's no harm in taking her along, and I get a fat commission from Katerina.

If it isn't a coincidence, if she's involved somehow and I leave her here, I'm leaving a loose end that can work against me. And if I take her with me that's the best way I have of keeping an eye on her until I can find out what this is all about.

And if I do find out, and if something has to be done, Katerina has more ways of disposing of people than the Borgias had.

His decision made, he went back to the table and announced that they were leaving for Milan at once.

"Don't be silly," said Ginger. "Sit down and finish your wine."

"Something's come up and I'm needed in Milan right away. Why don't you come with me? It might prove entertaining."

"Gerard, you look awfully pale. A sip of wine might help."

"No time for that."

"Of course there is; there's always time for wine," she said, thinking, damn it, I finished my fish like a good little girl. The least you can do is finish your wine.

"No, really, we've got to get going. It's a business emergency."

"And you want me to come along?"

"I thought you might want to. It will give you a chance to meet Katerina Felluci."

"Is that where you're going? I thought you said it was business."

"Business is a broad word. I have all sorts of dealings with Katerina. Are you coming?"

"Do you really want me to?"

"I wouldn't have said so otherwise."

She grabbed her handbag and stood up. If he wasn't going to drink his wine, he wasn't going anywhere without her. Not so long as she still had another plastic bag full of penicillin. She took his arm and forced a gay smile.

"You sure know how to show a girl a good time," she said. "On to the bordello."

Late Wednesday afternoon, Emerson dressed himself in a pair of shorts, an open shirt and sandals, and examined himself in a mirror. Satisfied that he was indistinguishable from the hundreds of hiking tourists on the island, he packed a light haversack with bread and cheese, a bottle of mineral water, and some extra handkerchiefs. On one side of the handkerchiefs he wedged in the stripped-down PPK Walther and on the other side, reverently wrapped, he secured the plate he had made the night before. Then he locked the door of the rented house, left the key in the lock, and set out in the car for the hills behind the Andriakis house in Kalami.

The decision to stake out the house had been a difficult one to make. One set of instincts told him to keep out of sight, to stay away from Andriakis until bouzouki time that night in Pyrgi. Another set of instincts, based on long-ago training, told him that by lying back and waiting he might lose his target. There was no guarantee that Andriakis would appear that night in Pyrgi, only a promise, and one which could be easily broken.

In the end the human fear of losing his man overcame the animal instinct to lie low, and it was late afternoon when he turned off the coast road and drove up through the winding turns into the hills. He left the car at the edge of a meadow and then worked his way downhill, going overland between the horseshoe bends of the road, until he came to the observation point he had used the day before. From there he had a clear view of the Andriakis house gleaming like a sugar cube on the edge of the sea, the beach below it, and running out from the beach the two stone jetties that provided a breakwater for the motor sloop moored offshore.

He unslung the haversack and settled down with his back against a slanted olive tree, a hiking tourist relaxing in the last of the sun. But he did not really expect any questions in easygoing Corfu.

Joseph Wolfe moved his rook to the bishop's square, setting the piece down precisely. He looked up from the board. His round, fleshy face was expressionless, and his bald head glistened under the clubroom lights. His eyes, from behind thick glasses, met Vasily's blankly. There was no sign of emotion or concern. It was like playing chess with a machine.

Vasily stared back. In the old days he had known the Chessmaster only slightly, and he had no fear of being recognized after ten years. Having made his move, Wolfe nodded abruptly and went on to the next table. Vasily watched him go, conscious of no anger, no outrage, no yearning for revenge for

what had happened to Martín and Josefina. He was at the chess
club to do a job, and, as always when he worked, he suppressed
all emotion in favor of an overwhelming concentration on the
technical aspects of his trade. At that moment he was as much a
machine as Wolfe was.

The room in the chess club was quiet, only occasional murmurs breaking the silence. At fourteen different tables fourteen
players studied their boards as Wolfe went from one to the
other, playing fourteen games simultaneously. There had been
twenty players to begin with, but six had already gone under.
Of the remaining players, it could be expected that one or two
would manage a draw and one, perhaps, even win. The others
would certainly lose.

Vasily, from his position at table twelve, watched Wolfe as
he continued up the line studying each board briefly, making
his move, nodding once, and then moving on. Aside from his
skill, the Chessmaster had only two slight advantages over his
opponents. At each board he played the white pieces, which
had given him the opening move, and at each table it was required that the challenger have made his next move by the time
that the Chessmaster returned. Slight edges, nothing more.

Vasily studied his board, prepared to move *P-Q6*. He was pleased with his position after twenty-eight moves, pleased to see that he had retained some of his onetime skill. His technique, such as it was after long disuse, was dramatically opposite to that of the Chessmaster. Wolfe played a hypermodern, technical game, dull and colorless, with clearly charted lines of defense and a logical progression of attacking moves. Vasily, on the other hand, played chess with élan in the classical fashion, constantly attacking and happily sacrificing material for an advantage in position. The clash of styles was stimulating to him, and he realized that he had allowed this game to capture his imagination too strongly. He was there for a purpose, and he should have made his move, his professional move, long before this. The carrying case in his pocket, with the six loaded pieces, pressed against his hip, reminding him. He turned his attention to the board again and advanced his central pawn a space: *P-Q6*.

When Wolfe returned to the table, his next move, given his style of play, was obvious. It would be *PxP*, the white pawn taking the black pawn just advanced. Thus, Vasily's move, his professional move, was to substitute the loaded pawn in his pocket for the one that Wolfe would have to touch. But he hesitated. Once Wolfe touched that pawn, he was a dead man and the game was over. His hand in his pocket, Vasily studied the permutations of play. If he kept the loaded piece in his pocket, then *PxP* would be followed by *Q-Q5*, after which Wolfe would be forced to move his rook to *QB3*, and then . . . yes, he could see the progression. Wolfe would be forced to resign, his position hopeless, within five moves at the most.

I've got him, he thought with quiet satisfaction. Just a few more moves and he's finished.

He laughed quietly to himself, knowing that the game would never be ended that way. He had an end game of his own in his pocket. Slowly, he moved his hand in that pocket, reaching for the loaded pawn, gripping it by the base so as not to touch the lethal head. He looked around the room. The attention of the players and the spectators was concentrated on the boards.

Wolfe was in motion on the far side of the room, approaching table number three. Using only his fingertips, Vasily began to extract the pawn from the case. Then he saw something that made him stop, the motion frozen.

The president of the chess club had come up to Wolfe and was talking to him in an undertone, motioning toward the telephone on his desk. Wolfe shook his head. The president said something insistently. Wolfe, frowning, went to the desk and picked up the phone. He listened briefly, then replaced it. His usually expressionless face was suddenly drawn and strange.

By this time Vasily was up and moving, the loaded pawn still in his pocket, heading for the door. Only the severest emergency could have interrupted Joseph Wolfe in the middle of a simultaneous match, and from the look on the Chessmaster's face, Vasily had a clear idea of what that emergency was. Something had gone wrong with one of the hits. The alarm had been given and his target was about to run.

He was almost out the door when he heard Wolfe's flat, incisive voice announcing, ''Gentlemen, I regret that I must cancel the remainder of this exhibition. My apologies to you all.''

Vasily ran down the steps quickly, leaving behind him the babble of protest from the disappointed players. Out on the street, he raced for his car and was behind the wheel with the engine turning over when Wolfe emerged from the building flanked by two husky young Spaniards. The three men hurried into a dark blue Lincoln Continental parked at the curb, Wolfe in the back and the others up front, and pulled out into traffic with a squeal of rubber. Vasily followed, easing back to leave a five-car distance between them. He maintained that distance as the Lincoln turned left along the port, then left again past the railroad station, heading north out of town on the road that led to Vich and beyond. Vasily drove with tight concentration, his eyes on the road and on the car up ahead; but a part of his mind was still back at the club, observing the board. He could still see the ending as clearly as if it had been marked on a score sheet.

White	Black
PxP	Q-Q5
R-QB3	P-N5
R-N3	B-Q4

Wolfe, playing white, is helpless. He resigns.
Vasily sighed and drove on.

It was a long and boring watch for Emerson, perched on the deserted hillside. The sugar-cube house sat silent against the sea with no indication of life inside it. The shutters were slatted closed and the garage door was down. At various times a rooster crowed, a donkey brayed; but he heard no human voices. Out on the water the daytime fishermen chugged down the coast, heading for home, while out on Andriakis' sloop a wiry young Greek padded about the deck doing the chores that seem never to end for seamen: polishing fittings, scrubbing planks, checking lines, and tending to the dinghy that was run out astern. The sun wore down, and Emerson waited patiently for a sign of Andriakis.

At twilight time the lights came on in the house, the first indication to Emerson that his target was at home, and the first confirmation that he had not been wasting his time. He relaxed a bit then, prepared to wait through the evening until he was sure that his man had left for the tavern in Pyrgi. He ate some bread then and washed out his mouth with water. It was just after eight, and the night was quiet.

At nine o'clock he decided to shift his position. Based on what had happened the night before, he reasoned that Andriakis would leave for Pyrgi sometime within the next hour, and he wanted to be closer to his car when the time came to follow. He worked his way back up the hill in the moonlight, scrambling across the rutted fields that lay between the bends of the road. He was halfway up when he heard the sound of an engine starting. He whirled around, looking back and down. The lights in the house were off; the garage door was up; and Andriakis' car, a red Lancia, nosed out onto the driveway. Emerson froze, undecided. One part of him wanted to race for his car, but another, older, well-trained part told him to wait.

Wait, said the voice from his past. Never assume, always confirm.

Wait, he told himself. There's always time to get to Pyrgi.

He waited. The Lancia pulled out onto the road and roared away, heading south for Pyrgi.

He waited. He saw moonlight on the water and . . . he looked again. He saw the dark bulk of the moored sloop and the slighter shape of the dinghy moving away from it, silently heading in toward the beach with the young Greek at the oars. And then he saw the unmistakable form of Peter Andriakis hurrying out of the house, across the terrace, and down the stone steps that led to the water.

He started running then, bounding downhill in giant strides, the heels of his sandals thudding into dirt each time he landed. He ran mindlessly, knowing that he would be too late. He was still pounding downhill when the dinghy reached the beach and Andriakis climbed aboard, still forcing his stride and panting when the Greek turned the boat around and began the return journey. He stumbled as he ran, sharp stones nicking at the soles of his sandals. The haversack bounced against his back, and he knew that he should throw it away but he could not take the time. He was almost to the bottom of the hill when he heard the sloop's engine starting up and then the distinctive clank as the mooring cable was slipped. He lurched, skidded the last ten feet, and then was racing across the highway, past the house, and toward the beach as the sloop came round and headed out on a course that would take it past the nearer of the two jetties that extended out into the sea.

It was hopeless, but he kept on going, plowing through sand now. He was only at the base of the jetty as the sloop approached the tip of it, but he did not stop. His mind was turned off and only his body was functioning. Wheezing and creaking, but it was functioning as he raced down the concrete strip and threw himself into the water. The sloop was past the jetty by then, but the dinghy trailing astern was there. Three frantic strokes, legs pumping, brought him close enough to grab, miss, grab again, and this time hold on to the heavy metal pintle at the stern of the boat. He hooked his arm around the rod and turned on his side, gasping for air as the water rushed past him, and let his body rest as his mind began to work again.

Rusty Emerson awoke Wednesday morning to a feeling of overwhelming helplessness. She knew that she had nothing in her power to control the events of the day. Thousands of miles away the two people whom she loved the most were doing things she dared not even think about, and there was nothing that she could do to help them. After she had bathed and had breakfasted in the sitting room of her suite at the Princesa, she looked the day dead in the eye and knew that the only way she would get through it without climbing the walls would be to submerge herself in a trivial round of sightseeing and shopping. It was a remedy she had used before at difficult times in her life, although never so difficult a time as this.

Well before noon she set forth in a taxi hired for the day, armed with instructions from the concierge of the hotel, and went first to the Anthropological Museum in Chapultepec Park. After an hour of delighted wandering, she went on to the National Palace on the Plaza de la Constitución, and then made the rounds of the Palace of Fine Arts and the National Preparatory School to view the murals of Rivera, Orozco, and Siqueiros.

By then it was well into lunchtime, and she had her driver take her, again on instructions from the concierge, to La Trucha Vagabonda in the Zona Rosa. She told herself that she wasn't at all hungry, but she finished an order of snails with ease and then disposed of a plate of the tasty white fish from Lake Patzcuáro. By now the game was beginning to pall on her, but she forced herself to linger over coffee before being driven to the Reforma. There she instructed the driver to wait for her and plunged into the web of side streets off the Reforma for an orgy of shopping.

In a shop on the Calle Hamburgo she found a blouse for herself and one for Ginger, and the expedition was fairly launched. In the next two hours she bought four dresses and two skirts; a feathered poncho for Ginger; a sweater for Jimbo; a hand-tooled leather belt for Eddie; and, in a moment of whimsy, an oversized sombrero for Vasily, guessing at the size and smiling at the thought of how it would look perched on his aristocratic head. Thoroughly pleased with herself, she ordered the packages delivered and had herself driven back to the hotel through the jam of evening traffic.

As she took her key from the desk clerk she congratulated herself on having handled the day, and decided that she would indulge herself now with a long bath and then would take her time dressing. She would have exactly two Rob Roys, order up dinner, watch television for a while (it sounded so much less dreary in Spanish), and go to sleep early.

And tomorrow?

Tomorrow would be all right, she decided. Tomorrow she would hear good news. There was no other way it could be.

With this comforting philosophy in mind she rode the elevator to the third floor, walked down the corridor and opened her door, flicking on the light switch as she came into the sitting room. She stopped and stood motionless. Lounging casually in the deep chair facing her was a slim young man with an engaging smile. Three other men were in the room. One of them closed the door behind her.

The young man beamed at her. The last time she had seen him he had been lying on her living room floor, bleeding from a head wound.

"Dobri vyechir, Mrs. Emerson," he said. "My name is Aleksander Ignatiev. Most people call me Sasha. The last time we met I never got a chance to introduce myself."

She stared back at him, stiff and unbending, and said, "You haven't said what I'm supposed to hear."

"Ah yes, the magic word. *Homefire.*"

"Backfire," she replied.

"Seafire." He laughed and snapped his fingers. "There, the formalities are complete. *Backfire* may now commence."

Rusty sank into a chair with a sigh of relaxation. "It will have to commence after I've had a bath and a drink. I'm exhausted."

"Don't get too comfortable," Sasha warned her. "We're leaving shortly. You see, I've come to abduct you."

Chapter 17

The bordello of Katerina Felluci occupied the first four floors of an old but well-preserved building on Milan's Via Manzoni, a respectable neighborhood of dwellings, offices, and shops. The building was much like the others on the street, a sturdy granite structure with a spacious courtyard that could be entered only through a narrow archway. The façade was well kept, the courtyard tidy, and each of the doors was varnished to a black sheen. The interior of the building, however, was considerably different from the others. On the first floor what once had been a sitting room had been converted into an elegant bar, and the former dining room was now a miniature cinema. At the back of the floor, the kitchen was occupied eighteen hours a day by a team of Calabrian cooks turning out platters of *antipasto di mare, carciofini all'olio, peperoni arrosto*, and fried baby squid covered with soul-searing sauces.

Above the ground floor were three stories, each with four bedrooms and two baths. The bedrooms were furnished simply and functionally. The bathrooms were furnished with adjustable rubbing tables and Jacuzzi baths. The medicine cabinets in all of the bathrooms contained a supply of Vaseline, baby oil, contraceptive foam, and vaginal jelly large enough to stock a small gynecological clinic. Twelve girls worked in the house, nine regulars and three interns-in-training, plus four maids, the two cooks, and two others in the kitchen—all of them under the benevolent fist of Katerina Felluci. Architecturally and logistically, Katerina's bordello was a model of its kind, and if *Better Homes and Gardens* had ever thought to devote an issue to the whorehouses of Italy, hers would have been the first to be featured. Her prices were outrageous, but her clients were restricted to the fortunate few who could afford them, and her girls were considered well worth every Eurobuck spent. The House of Felluci represented a standard of excellence in the trade, and Katerina was determined to keep it that way.

"We're number one in Milan and we're going to stay number one," she was saying. "And the only way to do that is to improve the efficiency around here."

It was six in the evening, with the daytime customers gone, the nighttime customers still to come, and it was time for Katerina's weekly sales conference. Attendance was obligatory, and the bar was filled with girls, some dressed for the evening in wisps of flimsy nothingness, others dressed for the street, and the uniformed maids and kitchen staff in spotless whites. Some had finished the daytime shift, others had just awakened, and all of them sat slumped in their seats, eyes glazed, heads nodding.

Katerina held the floor in front of the bar, an attractively plump woman in her forties, sedately dressed in a beige linen suit, her dark curls framing a heart-shaped face. On the bar behind her were propped two charts with plastic overlays. One was a multicolored time-and-motion analysis, and the other was a weekly production graph with each girl's name slotted into a column. Katerina was a passionate believer in American-style efficiency, and she was convinced that every business could be reduced to its essentials through the intelligent application of graphs and charts.

"I don't know of any other industry that would tolerate such a low level of efficiency," she was telling her benumbed audience. "According to my figures, the average girl in this house has an on-bed percentage of only fifty-four point two. That means that during a given hour a girl here spends only slightly more than thirty-two minutes performing the functions for which she gets paid. The rest of the time is spent in servicing and resupply, and I'm sorry to say, simple laziness. Now, there is absolutely no reason why a girl should take twenty-eight minutes in turnaround time between one customer and the next. It simply does not take that long to wash and freshen up."

Katerina paced up and down, swinging a rubber-tipped pointer in arcs through the air, her voice firm and commanding as she spoke in the precise accents of the northern Italian. "Yes, I know what you're thinking," she continued. "We run a quality operation here, but nobody ever made money by turning business away, and that's what wasted time amounts to. Now, girls, I'm going to ask you all, regulars and interns alike, to try for a lower turnaround time. I'm setting twelve minutes as the maximum, and I want you to make it your goal. Next week we'll compare figures and . . ."

She went on and on, exciting not a single soul to the goal of higher productivity and impressing no one except Ginger Emerson, who sat on a couch at the far end of the room between a failed opera singer from Liverpool named Shirley and a girl from Naples who once had done a shoe commercial on TV. Ginger was impressed mainly because the inside of a high-class brothel was not very much what she had expected it to be. She had anticipated the furnishings, the overstuffed upholstery, the flocked wallpaper, and the rich-piled carpets, but she had not expected the girls to be such decent types. True, there was an awful lot of flesh flashing about, but that was what they were there for, and the overall atmosphere was not too different from that of the Kappa Kappa Kappa house of her college days. And there was also the undeniable fact that simply being in a place like this produced in any girl a certain sense of wonderment, of . . . *what would it be like to . . . ?*

Dismissing that tingling thought from her mind, she wondered what had happened to Krause. Upon their arrival at the house on the Via Manzoni, he had turned her over to Signora Felluci and then had disappeared.

"You won't be seeing me for a while. But Katerina will look after you."

So far the looking-after had consisted of an introduction to the two girls sitting beside her, an invitation to look over the establishment with a view toward future employment, and then Katerina had launched into the weekly sales conference, leav-

ing Ginger bemused and impressed by the older woman's grasp
of the essentials of her business. What was she talking about
now?

Orgasms?

". . . very likely that some of you girls have been having orgasms. Now, I realize that this is an occupational hazard, but at
the same time, in our business an orgasm is wasteful and
counterproductive. First of all, it saps your strength and increases your turnaround time. Second, it plants a seed of personal involvement with the customer, which is something that
should be avoided. So remember, girls, if you feel one coming
on, stomp on it, stifle it, save it for after hours. In other words,
come on your own time."

Some of the girls were openly yawning now, and one of the
maids was asleep in her chair. When Signora Felluci laid down
her pointer and picked up a thick stack of handwritten notes, a
collective groan rose up from her listeners. She looked at her
watch and shook her head.

"All right, it's getting late," she said reluctantly. "That's all
for now."

The meeting at once broke up, with the kitchen staff heading
for the back of the house, the maids upstairs, and the working
girls gathering into small groups of relieved and animated chat-
terers. The girl from Naples, whose name was Sofia, turned to
Ginger and asked, "What do you think of our Signora Felluci?"

"She's very . . . businesslike," Ginger said cautiously.

"She's a silly old cow," said the other girl, Shirley. "She
doesn't know a bloody thing about it with her bloody charts.
You don't make a man happy with charts."

Sofia nodded, agreeing. "*É vero* . . . but still it is a good
place to work." She looked at Ginger. "Do you come here to
work?"

"Actually, I'm not sure. I came with a friend to look the
place over."

"Some friend," said Shirley, stretching. Both she and Sofia
were dressed for work in baby-doll nighties and nothing else.
"I saw you come in with him. Bleedin' Gerry Krause, wasn't

it? Oops, 'scuse me, not supposed to call him Gerry. Mr. Gerard Krause himself.''

"You know him?" Ginger asked.

Both girls laughed, and Shirley said, "Bloody few girls here who don't. Most of us came here the same way you did. With Gerry, just to look the place over. Not that I'm complaining, mind. I do myself nicely here.''

"I see," said Ginger, pleased that her suspicions were confirmed. "Then he must be very close to the Signora.''

"Like this," said Sofia, holding up two fingers close together.

"But not like *this*," said Shirley, doing the same, but crossing one finger over the other.

Both girls laughed again, and Ginger looked around the room. "I don't see him," she said in what she hoped was an innocent voice. "I want to talk to him about this before I make up my mind.''

"No chance of that," said Shirley. "No chance at all.''

"What do you mean?" Ginger felt the pit of her stomach go hollow. "I have to see him.''

Shirley stood up and scratched the inside of her thigh, apparently unconcerned about her near-total nudity. "Nobody sees Krause while he's here, sweetie. He stays locked in that room of his on the top floor. Nobody goes in, nobody comes out.''

"He once was here for a week," Sofia offered. "All that time he stayed locked in the room.''

Casting for ideas, Ginger asked, "What does he do for food?''

"The Signora." Shirley grimaced. "Takes the food into him herself, she does. Nobody else allowed to touch it. Treats him like bleedin' royalty; wouldn't be surprised if she tastes it for him, too.''

"With all these girls around," Ginger said hopefully, "you'd think he'd want . . ." Her voice trailed off as she saw the other two exchange knowing looks.

"Krause doesn't have much use for us," Shirley explained. "He's never touched me, nor any of the others.''

"Except for Anna," said Sofia, giggling.

"But she doesn't really count," Shirley said.

"Anna?"

"That one over there."

Shirley nodded at a woman sitting by herself in a corner. Ginger had noticed her before. She was attractive enough, with a well-featured oval face, but she was older than the others, perhaps thirty, and her full-breasted body was thick through the waist. She wore a somber, simple dress and flat-heeled sandals, no makeup and no jewelry save for a tiny gold crucifix at her bosom and a wedding band. She looked less like a whore than a countrywoman who had come into town on market day.

Ginger shook her head. "*She* sees Krause?"

Shirley nodded. "His one and only. She's not a regular, you see. She comes here only when Krause is due. You wouldn't believe what they do together."

"Nasty," said Sofia.

"No, not nasty, but it's unnatural." Shirley was trying to be fair. "I guess some women have no pride; they'll do anything for the old lolly."

"She doesn't have much else to offer," Sofia said judiciously. "You really can't blame her, I guess."

"But what is it they do?" Ginger asked.

Shirley told her.

"I don't believe it!"

"God's truth. Not that you don't see everything in a house like this. I knew one girl here a while back who got paid ten thousand dollars just to . . ."

Shirley went on, but Ginger wasn't listening. Her eyes were fixed on the woman, Anna, and her mind began to calculate.

The midway of the All-American Amusement Park was crowded. Under the steaming sun the throngs sauntered idly, searching for fun, munching cotton candy and ice cream while children tugged and demanded and adults conceded indulgently, for it still was early in the day. Young girls strolled in protective pairs, young men eyed them hopefully, and older couples walked arm in arm. Mechanical noises rang harsh and loud, the cries of the barkers were louder, but loudest of all was the carnival music blaring from speakers on poles.

Eddie sat in his car in the parking lot, staring at the plywood reproduction of a Scottish castle that formed the façade of the Fun House. He tried to remember everything that Vasily had told him.

"I would have to consider it virtually impregnable against anything except a total wipeout. There are three checkpoints before you even get close to the heart of the place. There's the Mirror Maze, the back of the Wax Museum, and then the voiceprint identification. And even if someone got past all three he'd still have to crack the nut down below. No, the only way to assault the Fun House is to destroy it completely. A canister of VX gas in the air conduits, or a fire bombing."

Eddie shook his head impatiently. There was no way that he could attempt a massive assault on the Fun House with dozens of people wandering about inside it and hundreds more passing by on the midway. Of course, it could be done at night, after the park had closed, but that was twelve hours away and he had to act now.

He opened his lab kit on the seat beside him and stared for a while at its contents. Eventually he filled his pockets with an assortment of tubes and flasks, half a dozen steel pellets, an electronic oscillator, and an HDM pistol with a Bell Labs silencer. He hesitated over the pistol. He disliked such weapons and did not consider himself adept in their use, but he knew he had to take it with him.

He locked the lab kit in the trunk of the car and then strolled onto the midway, heading for the concession stands. There he bought an oversized trucker's cap, a pair of sun glasses, a jelly apple, and a stick of cotton candy. He found the nearest men's room, fed a machine a quarter, and locked himself into a stall. He was in the stall fifteen minutes working on the jelly apple and the cotton candy, and when he came out he was wearing his cap and his glasses.

Back on the midway he waited until he saw a group of young people approaching the Fun House, the boys loudly describing the horrors inside and the girls feigning an obligatory reluc-

tance to enter. He fell into casual step behind them. He had his
cap low over his eyes and the jelly apple up in front of his face
as he paid his admission, and he was still attached to the group
as they all staggered through the Barrel Roll entrance, the girls
squealing wildly as they tumbled and sprawled on the revolving
floor. Eddie stepped around them, smiling.

He stayed with the group through the Tunnel of Love like
somebody's goofy brother tagging along in his crazy cap, one
hand busy with the cotton candy, the other with the jelly apple.
When they entered the Mirror Maze he hung behind, letting
them stumble and shriek and bump their way through before he
entered cautiously.

A giant Mancuso glared down at him; he turned, and Eddie
the mouse stared back. He moved again and the image decom-
posed into dozens of fragments, then coalesced into a Mancuso
impossibly squat and broad. He turned left and hit glass, turned
right and hit glass again, walked straight ahead and the glass
seemed to melt away before him. He turned right through an
apparently solid wall, turned right again, and came face to face
with a smiling uniformed guard.

"Wrong way," said the guard to the funny little guy with the
crazy cap and his hands full of goodies. "You made the wrong
turn, friend. You go back that way."

He reached out a hand to guide Eddie around. Eddie
nodded gratefully and said, "I got a little mixed up back
there."

"Don't feel bad; plenty of people do that," said the guard,
and then the cotton candy was under his nose, the sticky fibers
clogging his nostrils, the ether vapors flooding his brain. He
pulled back his head, but the cotton candy stayed with him,
stuck to his face like strawberry jam. He opened his mouth for
air, but the sticky tendrils were there as well. He struggled to
breathe, tried again, and then folded down, unconscious as he
hit the floor.

Eddie stepped over him and raced down the corridor clutching his jelly apple. He burst into the storage room of the Wax
Museum and almost broke stride as he was stunned by the real-
istic statuary: Lizzie Borden with her ax, Jack the Ripper and

his knife, the Little Princes cowering in the Tower. Across the room the two guards jerked around at the sound of his running feet, hands reaching for the pistols at their belts. Eddie threw the apple directly at them and flung himself face down on the floor. The apple, loaded with magnesium oxide, landed between the two guards, detonating on contact. The resultant noise was no louder than a door being slammed, but the brilliant flash of green was blinding. The two guards dropped, unable to see and out of action. Eddie ran by them without pausing, cutting hard right and down another hallway, heading for the third checkpoint.

The abbey of the Order of Saint Vincent of Ferrer perched on a crag high in the eastern Pyrenees, as massive and as formidable as a medieval fortress. Behind and above it rose higher peaks still, stepping up to the mountain enclave of Andorra. Below it the valley fell away so sharply that the switchback road winding up from below, when seen from above, resembled the coils of a snake about to strike. The abbey stood alone, removed from the world by the solitude of mountains, removed from the nearest town as much by centuries as by miles.

Self-contained and self-sufficient, the brothers of the order dwelt behind the heavy monastery walls much as they had done for hundreds of years. Originally an offshoot of the Beghards, that unpopular and mistrusted society that was condemned by the Council of Vienne in the fourteenth century, the present order had drifted over the Pyrenees from France to find a home among the crags and tors above Puigcerdá. Not until two centuries later was the present abbey built, and by then the brothers of Saint Vincent had settled into a way of life designed to last the ages, a life devoted to contemplation and prayer, to the making of fine wine, and to the constant purification of the body and the spirit through a daily scourging and flagellation of the flesh.

For this practice of self-inflicted punishment the order was indebted to its founder, Saint Vincent of Ferrer, who had encouraged flagellation as the ultimate expression of the ascetic

ideal, and for centuries the succeeding generations of brothers
had scourged themselves twice daily. At the canonical hours of
lauds and compline they marched in a loose circle round the
narthex of the church, chanting plainsong as they beat their own
bare arms and shoulders with bristling scourges, whipping
themselves with a quiet passion. The blood that they drew at
those times was the only blood allowed to be spilled within the
confines of the abbey; even a chicken had to be slaughtered in
the fields beyond the walls. The brothers of San Vicente led
well-ordered lives, and it was to their abbey, and within those
walls, that Joseph Wolfe, the Chessmaster, had fled to sanctu-
ary.

Vasily Borgneff stared up at those walls from a field below
the abbey. He had seen Wolfe's car disappear behind them after
a tortuous trip up from Barcelona, the dark blue Lincoln Continental edging through the narrow entryway hung with solid
oaken doors, which had promptly closed behind it. Vasily had
driven his own car on beyond the monastery, two miles further
up the winding road to a bend where it could be safely left, and
then had worked his way down through the fields to a point below the abbey. Now he stared up at those walls, his one good
eye squinting against the lowering sun, the false eye an unac-
customed weight in the other socket.

Strong Cluniac influence, he thought, admiring the double
transepts that crossed the nave of the church and the echelon of
apses clustered at the turreted east end.

His eye traveled from the walls to the acres of cultivated land
below the abbey, all of them devoted to the production of the
grape that was used to make the distinctive Vino San Vicente.
Much as the Carthusian and the Benedictine orders produced
their own liqueurs, the San Vicente was the exclusive property
of the brotherhood and was fermented and bottled only within
the monastery walls. Now, at the height of the growing season,
the vines were full and glossy under the late-afternoon sun. In
the middle of one of those fields, Vasily could see the brown
habit of a toiling monk, the only human in sight for miles, moving down the row, pruning and tending the vines. Smiling, Vasily sauntered through the field to wait at the end of the row. He

seated himself on the ground with his back against an algaroba tree and, to pass the time, took from his pocket the latest in portable electronic chess games. He set up an ending, and the lights in the squares flickered on and off as he positioned the pieces. He studied the board, moved a piece, and the battery-operated computer made a countermove. He nodded approvingly at the sophisticated response.

A handy gadget, he thought, folding up the set and patting it affectionately. He slipped it into his pocket as he saw the monk approaching.

"Buenas tardes," he said as the monk came up to stand in the shade of the tree. "How are they growing?"

The monk did not answer, but he threw back the cowl of his habit, which had been protecting his neck and his head from the sun, and gave Vasily a happy grin. He was a young man with an open, friendly face, and in his work-hardened hands he carried a pruning hook and knife. He used one of those hands to describe how well the vines were growing. It was a gesture of pride.

Vasily looked at him curiously. "You do not speak?"

The monk shook his head, still smiling.

"Do your vows prohibit speech?"

Another shake of the head, and another smile.

"Are you able to speak?"

A nod.

"Ah, then you *prefer* not to speak," said Vasily, who had heard of orders whose members were free to exercise such an option.

The monk nodded enthusiastically.

"An excellent way to live," Vasily told him. "I can think of many who would profit by it."

The monk made it clear with signs that there was entirely too much chatter in the world, although he seemed delighted to be part of this one-sided conversation. Vasily was about to ask him when the grapes would be ready for harvest when the abbey bells began to ring, the peals bounding down the valley like boulders set free.

"The Angelus?" asked Vasily.

A nod.

"Angelus Domini nuntiavit Mariae."

The monk's nod was solemn this time. He pointed to himself, and then to the monastery walls. It was time for him to go, time to join with his brothers in prayer, and then to sit with them at the long refectory table to eat the thick *potaje*, the bread, and the fruit that formed their staple evening meal. All this he conveyed in a series of delicate gestures.

"Momentito, hermano," said Vasily as the monk turned to leave. He reached into his pocket and felt the ampule there. "Before you go, I should like you to forgive me."

The monk turned back, a puzzled look on his face. After a moment of hesitation, he spoke for the first time. "I am not a priest, my friend. I cannot hear your confession, if that is what you mean."

"No, not confession, only a forgiveness. I wish you to forgive me for something I must do."

"Only that?" The monk shrugged. "That is easily done. Everything is forgiven within the grace of God, and so must you be, too."

"Grácias, hermano." The hand holding the ampule came out of his pocket. He snapped the thin plastic sheath under the monk's nose and seconds later caught him gently as he fell. Equally gently, he dragged him further into the covering shade of the algaroba. He looked down at the young man's face. There was still a hint of a smile on his lips. Almost reluctantly, Vasily stripped him of his robe and sandals, and put them on.

"Rest well, brother," he said quietly. "You have a solid six hours of sleep ahead of you. You probably can use it."

Ten minutes later, with the echoes of the Angelus still settling over the valley, he entered the monastery of Saint Vincent of Ferrer through the almoners' gate, the cowl of his habit pulled closely round his face. Keeping his head down and his body bent forward as he walked, he passed through an open cobbled courtyard, down a dank alleyway, and out into the quiet of a cloister carpeted with velvety grass, wall-hung with ivy, and bordered by square-cut hedges. Conical fir trees and leafy planes gave shade, and on all four sides a mass of fragrant oleander tinted the walls with purples and blues. He slowed his step in the cloister as his path crossed those of other monks on their way to the evening meal. Some of them were cowled, others were not. Some saluted him with a nod or a word, others only hurried by. To all his only response was an inclination of his head as he passed in the other direction. The temptation was to hurry, but he kept his pace slow. He knew exactly what he was looking for and how to find it, but he knew that he hadn't much time.

Spiro Dodonis was a mainland Greek who lived in Corfu, both loathing and loving the island. The island was easy to love. The white beaches, the blue Ionian sea, the tranquil olive groves in the uplands . . . who could help but be at ease in such a place? But the people of the island were something else. Spiro had lived among them now for almost five years while working for Peter Andriakis, and he still had not accustomed himself to the Corfiotes. They were, he felt, a foolish people. Spiro himself was from Piraeus, that fast-dealing, tough-talking port of Athens, where a man turned a drachma in any way he could and an instinct for hustling a profit had been bred into him early. Not so the Corfiotes, those amiable people who seemed to think more of their pleasures than of filling their pockets.

They were also ridiculously honest. Not that Spiro was not an honest man. He would fight to the knife anyone who said otherwise. But these Corfiotes carried it to an extreme. There was more than one case, he knew, of a tourist losing his wallet in the street only to have some inanely grinning islander find it and come running up to return it intact. He himself had seen automobiles parked in the public streets without fear of theft, the windows wide open and the seats loaded with luggage, radios, typewriters, and other such temptations. This may have been honesty to the Corfiotes, but to Spiro it was an indication of a lack of fiber in this island race and an almost sacrilegious indifference to the gifts that the gods bestow. He estimated that the average Corfiote would last about three hours on the streets of Piraeus.

For all of his dual feelings about Corfu, however, Spiro counted his five years on the island as profitable ones if only because of his connection with Peter Andriakis. As general factotum of the household and informal skipper of the forty-foot motor sloop *Athena,* Spiro found his work enjoyable and his pay more than adequate; but most important, he worshiped the man he worked for. Andriakis was, to him, the ultimate symbol of Hellenic aspirations, a Greek-American who had made good and had returned to the old country. And then there was his dancing. When Andriakis danced, Spiro was in heaven; nobody danced in the Greek style the way his boss did. Spiro had his own bouzouki and could play well enough, and often a moonlight sail on the *Athena* with a couple of tourist girls for guests would end with Spiro playing and Andriakis dancing the *zeïmbekikos* in the early hours of the morning.

Because of this affection for his employer, Spiro was neither annoyed nor surprised when he was told on Wednesday afternoon that they would be making a crossing that night, and making it secretly. It was not the first time he had received such orders, and he rather enjoyed the secrecy of the preparations, the standard decoy of sending the houseboy off in the Lancia, and the zigzag run across the gulf, avoiding the Albanian patrols. Such nights were the spice of his ordinary life; they gave meaning to his days, and so he was calm, but alert, at the helm when he heard the splash. They had just cleared the small harbor formed by the double jetties, he had just laid the boat on a course due east, when over the chugging of the engine he heard the sound of what might have been a large fish breaking the surface of the water. His head came up, and he looked around. Andriakis stood at the mast, his eyes on the opposite shore. Astern, the dinghy bobbed along in the wake. Spiro hesitated. It could have been a large fish. It could have been a piece of driftwood slapping alongside. It could have been a lot of other things, but you don't survive in Piraeus by wondering. He gave a low whistle that brought Andriakis astern on the run.

"Take the wheel and circle back," Spiro said. Neither of them thought it incongruous that he was giving orders. "I think I got a fish on that line."

He plucked a wrench from the toolbox by the wheel and shoved it through his belt; then he kicked off his sandals and went over the side. He kept his head up as he hit the water, ignoring the engine noise and the foul exhaust, his eyes on the dinghy. Staying still in the water, he let it come up to him, let it slide by. As the transom of the small boat passed he grabbed for it and held, and found himself staring into Emerson's eyes.

Both men reacted in the same moment and in the same way. They each let go of the dinghy and reached for the other, grappling. Emerson's hands went for Spiro's throat and gripped hard. Spiro's hand went to his belt and grabbed the wrench while his knee came up into Emerson's groin. It was a blow that should have broken the grip on his throat, but it didn't. Those hands were firm, the fingers pressing to crush small bones. He saw Emerson's contorted face only inches away from his own, and he knew that those hands would never let go, not while there was strength left to squeeze. Those hands were part of his neck now, flesh bonded to flesh, and squeezing the light from his eyes. His right arm came up out of the water gripping the wrench. He swung it alongside Emerson's head, and the fingers at his throat went limp. The man went limp as well. Gasping for air, Spiro shoved the wrench back in his belt; it was too good a tool to lose. Then he grabbed the other man's shirt and held his head up out of the water.

"Over here, boss," he called to the circling sloop. "I got me a fish."

Minutes later they were back on course, due east across the gulf, with Spiro again at the wheel, Emerson unconscious on the deck, and Andriakis squatting beside him, staring at his face.

"You know who he is?" Spiro asked. His throat hurt badly and it was difficult for him to talk.

"Yes," said Andriakis, shaking his head in amazement. Ever since the Fun House call from Edwin Swan that afternoon he had wondered who would be coming after him. He had never expected it to be Emerson himself.

Give the son of a bitch credit, he thought. He was doing all right for a man his age. He just made too much noise.

Spiro reached into the toolbox and came up with a long, thin knife. He held it delicately by the point, flipped it in the air, and caught it by the hilt. He looked at Andriakis meaningly.

Andriakis said, "Why the hell didn't you take that with you when you went after him?"

Spiro shrugged. "I was going fishing, not hunting." He spat over the side. "Deep water here. Plenty deep enough."

Andriakis nodded. "Yes, but not yet. There are some questions he has to answer first."

"Six thousand lira for a chicken," said the woman named Anna. "A thousand for milk, eight hundred for bread, a thousand here, a thousand there, and God forbid the baby gets sick . . . you know what a doctor costs? I could buy a new Fiat with my doctor bills." She threw up her hands in the timeless gesture of abandonment. "Holy Mother in heaven, how can you bring up a family these days with those prices?"

It was past eight o'clock, and the bar in the House of Felluci was filled with well-dressed men and barely dressed women. The atmosphere was calm and correct. Katerina's customers did not come to her house to whoop it up. They came to relax in the sort of atmosphere to which they were accustomed, an atmosphere that went well with boardrooms and corporate jets, Kashan carpets, triple-A bond ratings, a villa in Cannes and a ski lodge in Aspen. The girls of the house were well aware of this, and their demeanor was as correct as that of the men. No coarse language, no ribald jokes, only quiet conversation over a glass of wine until the gentleman was ready to go upstairs.

Off in one corner, Ginger sat talking to the plainly dressed, thick-waisted woman who looked more like a farmer's wife than a big-city hustler. Her conversation was as prosaic as her appearance, her one apparent concern being the high cost of living in Italy today. The conversation did not flow easily. Anna's

English was about on the level of Ginger's Italian, but Sofia was there on a break between customers to help in translation.

"What is she saying now?" Ginger asked Sofia as Anna went off in a string of Italian that was meaningless to her.

"The same old crap," said Sofia, looking unutterably bored. "All about how she wouldn't be working in a place like this if it wasn't for the new *bambino,* and the big *bambino,* and the in-betweensy one and the husband out on strike and no money in the house . . . it's like a record with her; it never changes."

Ginger said sympathetically, "Well, after all, it must be tough for her with a new baby and everything."

"Come on, sweetie, she's lucky to be working at all. Just look at her. It's just her pure dumb luck that she's got what Krause wants."

And just what I want, too, thought Ginger, her eyes on Anna's drink. The woman had been sipping Coca-Cola all evening.

She felt fingers on her shoulder and looked up to Katerina standing there. The older woman smiled down at her and asked, "What do you think of our operation? Are you ready to go to work?"

"It's really . . ." Ginger hesitated, searching for a word to fit the persona. "It's really super, but I was hoping to talk to Gerard about it first."

Katerina shook her head. "He's unavailable now; nobody sees him. You'll have to make your own decision." She fixed Sofia with an icy look. "Where were you when I was talking about turnaround time before?"

Sofia made a face. She looked as if she wanted to stick out her tongue, but she got up without a word and went over to join a table of men.

"I never push a girl to work for me," Katerina told Ginger. "I don't have to. Take your time and make up your mind. If you decide that you want to work there's plenty of business to-night. One of the girls will show you where to change your clothes."

"And me?" Anna asked softly.

"You, *cara?* Of course you'll work." She touched the woman's cheek with a gentle finger. "He's eating his dinner now, but he'll want you later tonight. About eleven o'clock. What's that you're drinking?"

"Coca-Cola, *signora*."

"Good. Make sure you stick to it."

When Katerina had gone, Anna looked down at her glass and said softly but passionately, "Oh, how I'd love a whiskey."

"But you can't," Ginger said with understanding.

"No, it wouldn't be proper. Not now."

"Well, at least I can get you a fresh Coke." Ginger stood up and took her glass before Anna could object. "I want another drink myself."

At the bar, Ginger ordered a Coke and a glass of wine, and while she waited for the drinks she slipped the plastic bag of penicillin from her purse and palmed it.

It can't be right to mess around with someone's body that way, she thought, but it's the only way I can get to him. I don't even know if it will work, but I have to try it. It won't hurt her, I'm sure it won't. Maybe it's even good for her . . . and I'm tired of figuring right and wrong, I just want to get it over with.

The drinks came then, and she dumped the full load of penicillin into the tall, bubbling glass of Coca-Cola. She took the two glasses back to the table and handed the tall one to Anna.

"Here you go," she said. "Bottoms up."

"*Grazie*, Geen-ger," said Anna. "I got such a big thirst. All the time I got a big thirst. It's always the same thing with me after I have the baby."

Then she lifted the glass and emptied it in three convulsive swallows.

Jim darling,

I am writing this with a gun at my head. Literally. The writing is mine, but the words are being dictated to me by a man who does not want his name mentioned. He says to tell you that the last time you saw him he was lying on

*our living room floor with a head wound. That should
serve to identify him.*

*Jim, they are taking me away from here. I don't know
where they are taking me, but they tell me it is someplace
outside of Mexico. The point of the exercise seems to be
that if you want to see me alive again you are going to
have to conform to your original orders and return to the
Soviet Union. (The man with the gun prefers the phrase
"your homeland.") I'm afraid that there is no room for
compromise in this. The man is very definite. Either you
follow orders, or I've had it.*

*The man says that the orders will come to you in the
following manner. He is taking me from here tonight and
will leave this letter for you with the manager. Starting
tomorrow, he will call you here at the Princesa every
evening at seven o'clock. When he makes contact with
you he will tell you where we are and how to meet us.
From that point on he has made arrangements for our
transportation to the Soviet Union. He makes it very
clear that you are to tell no one where you are going. No
one. He has made some rather ugly threats about what
will happen to me if you don't show up alone.*

*So there it is, my darling. I can't tell you how sad I am
that things have worked out this way. I know how much
you wanted to stay in the country of your choice. But
then, I wonder how many of us today are truly free
agents, able to afford the luxury of choice. We, you and
I, certainly seem to have lost that luxury long ago.*

*I am being urged to finish this now. Kiss Ginger for
me; tell her not to despair. I hope and pray that we will
be together again soon.*

> *All my love,*
> *Rusty*

She put the pen down and rubbed her stockinged feet. Her
arches hurt from a day of shopping, and her shoes were
off. Sasha, who had been reading over her shoulder as she
wrote, picked up the thick, embossed stationery of the Hotel

Princesa and read the letter once again. He nodded his approval.

"Excellent. This should do it nicely."

"It should," Rusty agreed. "My husband is very devoted to me." She paused, frowning, and added, "As I am to him. That must be understood."

"It is," Sasha assured her.

"I have a very good marriage," she said defensively. "I don't want you to think that it's just a part of my job."

"Believe me I don't. Which is why I must ask you a personal question."

She nodded.

"You say that your husband has no idea that you are also a sleeper. How sure are you of that?"

"Totally."

"Not even a suspicion, not even a random thought that you might be connected to the service?" He rattled the letter in his hand. "Because if he has even the slightest doubt, then this approach becomes worthless."

She shook her head firmly. "I'm sure it's never even crossed his mind."

"Forgive me, but how can you be that sure?"

She permitted herself a smile. "It's a trite phrase, but it applies. A woman always knows. I've been married to Jim for twenty-five years. There's nothing about him that I don't know. You can rest assured of that. He has no idea that I'm a sleeper."

"I'll accept your judgment." Sasha slipped the letter into an envelope and looked at her curiously. "Tell me, during all those years, weren't you ever tempted to tell him?"

"Certainly not. I had my orders."

"And yet he told *you*."

She shrugged. "Jim is a man. The finest man I know, but he's still a man. It wasn't the kind of burden he could carry alone."

"And a woman could?"

It was Rusty's turn to look curious. "How much do you know about women?"

"Apparently not as much as I thought I did." He looked at his watch. "The car will be waiting. Time to go, Comrade."

Chapter 18

The cells provided by the Order of Saint Vincent for visiting lay brothers were larger and airier than those of the resident monks, and they were also located in a lovelier part of the abbey. The monks' cells, forty of them, occupied a low, mean, barrackslike structure set hard against the southern wall of the monastery. On one side of the barracks was the cemetery, and on the other side were the ancient latrines. Generations of novices had sought to find some philosophical justification for this placement, but with little success.

The visitors' cells, however, were located next to the graceful scriptorium, directly over the cool wine cellar, and their windows opened onto the cloister and the masses of oleander that grew along the walls. There were only two such cells, for visitors to the abbey were rare, and both were occupied at the moment: one by Joseph Wolfe and the other by the two young Spaniards who had escorted him out of the chess club and up to the abbey.

Vasily stood in the doorway of Wolfe's cell. It was a clean but simple room, freshly whitewashed, and furnished with a narrow bed, a washstand with pitcher and basin, and a table and chair. A crucifix hung on one wall, and on another a sepia-toned print of Saint Vincent of Ferrer. On a third wall, as if in a position of honor, hung a wooden scourge—actually only a bundle of sharpened twigs bound with a leather thong—for use in the order's ritual of flagellation.

Vasily moved quickly into the room. The window onto the cloister was open, and from across the way came the sounds of the brothers at their evening meal, the clashing of crockery and the low rumble of conversation carrying from the refectory. He calculated that he had ten minutes and he would need only five. He lifted the scourge from the wall and laid it on the table, then dug under the monk's robe into his own pockets and came up with a small brown bottle and a fine-pointed brush. Working carefully but quickly, he brushed the colorless liquid from the bottle onto the sharpened tips of the twigs. He held the scourge up to admire his work with his one eye, imagining the scene that evening at compline with the circle of chanting monks swinging the scourges up and over their shoulders and down their arms, lacerating their flesh.

The boomslang venom should work in less than five minutes, he thought happily. And then farewell to the Chessmaster. A silly business, this flagellation. Self-defeating, just like all self-abuse.

He laid the scourge on the table and turned to the chessboard. There was no reason not to purchase a little insurance. Once again he dug under the robe, this time coming up with the carrying case containing the loaded chessmen. He studied the problem on the board, working out the most likely move that the white side would make next. In the end, he abandoned elegance and did the job wholesale, replacing the white queen, a rook, a knight, and a bishop with the loaded pieces. Again, he stood back to admire his handiwork happily. He was so taken up with the complex beauty of the scheme that he did not hear the footsteps behind him. He was still lost in admiration when he felt the prick of the knife in the small of his back.

"Stand very still," said the voice of Joseph Wolfe. "Carlos has a nervous hand. He'll kill you if you move."

Four minutes, Vasily thought. I was wrong. I must be getting old. "You're back early from your meal," he said pleasantly. "Too much salt in the gruel?"

Wolfe and one of the Spaniards came around from in back to face him across the table. They both wore the coarse brown robes of the order. The point of the knife remained steady on his spine. Wolfe reached across the table to flick back his cowl. The two men stared at each other.

Wolfe said slowly, "Table number twelve at the club this afternoon. You used the Queen's Indian defense."

"I thought you might like to continue the game."

Wolfe made an impatient gesture, and the knife point pressed harder into Vasily's back.

"Tell your man to go easy," Vasily said. "There's only one way that blood can be drawn within these walls."

"You know a lot about our order," Wolfe said with a grunt. "Those are the rules, but I'd be willing to make an exception in your case. Who are you, and what are you doing here?"

"Who I am isn't important, but what I'm doing is. I've come here to kill you."

"Others have tried, but I'm still alive," Wolfe said, unimpressed. His cold eyes swept over the table before him. "You've been busy. What would have happened if I had used this scourge?"

"A painful death from the venom of a boomslang snake."

"And these?" Wolfe made a motion toward the chessboard, then drew his hand away quickly.

"An apparent but unquestionably fatal heart attack. They're loaded with pure nitrobenzine."

"I take it that you intended using them this afternoon?"

"I never got the chance."

"Amazing." Wolfe looked up, his usually impassive face animated for the moment with interest. "Then you must be Vasily Borgneff."

Vasily inclined his head a fraction.

"Which means that you're working for Emerson now. How much did he pay you to do this to me?"

Vasily ignored the pressure of the knife at his back. "I'm not working for money on this job. I have my own reasons for wanting you dead."

"Indeed? And what might they be?"

"Martín Carillo. Josefina Carillo."

"That was a long time ago." Wolfe seemed truly surprised. "You knew those people?"

"I knew them well. I remember them well. By the time I'm finished with you, you'll remember them, too."

Wolfe suddenly smiled. His face was not meant for smiling and the effect was not a happy one. "You're quite an optimist as well as a murdering son of a bitch. We'll see who remembers what."

Through the open window came the pinging sound of the small bell that signaled the end of the evening meal, and across the cloister the first of the monks issued forth from the refectory. The sound of the bell moved Wolfe to action. He turned to the man beside him.

"Barto, put the scourge and the chessmen into that pitcher of water," he instructed. "That should keep them from doing any damage. You heard what this man said, so handle them carefully if you cherish your life."

He watched while Barto did it, working gingerly. Then he turned back to Vasily. "With the brothers wandering about, we'll need a less public place to continue this conversation. The wine cellar will do. Just out that door and down the stairs, if you please. Carlos will be right behind you."

"We have nothing to talk about."

Wolfe tried the smile again. It still didn't work. "You're quite right; we have little to say to each other. But I promise you, it won't be a long conversation."

It was almost like going home, home to the childhood of forty years before. There was the familiar tickle of straw beneath his back and neck, and the honest smell of horses, long forgotten but remembered now: horse sweat and the ammonia odor of horse piss on straw, the mustiness of moldering leather and the penny-bright taste of metal in his mouth. Horses and straw, earth odors rising up from the barn below, and close to his face the sweetness of the hay in the loft. He remembered all that from childhood, and then there were the music and the murmurs of the people down below. That was part of childhood, too, the memories of music in the barn and people dancing there on feast days. It would have been so pleasant just to smell the hay and listen to the music, if it had not been for the pain.

In the beginning the pain in his hand had seemed almost bearable, like the pain of an aching tooth. It was intense pain, and piercing, but localized. Bearable. Just tough it out and hang in there, and after a while it will go away. For a while it was that kind of pain, and then suddenly it was like no pain he had ever believed could exist. It was terrifying in its intensity, every nerve end screaming. He became pain, he breathed pain and sweated pain out through his pores as Spiro probed delicately with a long, thin knife at the complex of nerves under first one fingernail and then the next. He tried to scream, but his mouth was gagged. He tried to kick, but his feet were bound. One hand was tied to a wooden post, and the other hand belonged to Spiro.

"Mr. Emerson, all you have to do is nod," said Andriakis. "Then Spiro will put his knife away, and we'll take out the gag and talk sensibly. Sensibly and quietly. We don't want to disturb our friends downstairs."

Emerson closed his eyes. He did not want to see Andriakis' cool, inquiring eyes. He did not want to see Spiro's sweaty face intent upon his work. He did not want to see his left hand. It wasn't much of a hand anymore. With his eyes closed he did not see the look that Andriakis gave to Spiro, but a fresh wave of pain rolled over him and he tried to scream again.

"Two names, that's all I want from you," said Andriakis. "Then we can stop this primitive butchery."

Emerson kept his eyes closed. He was trying to listen to the music through the pain.

"We know that Mancuso went after Swan, and we know that you came after me. That leaves two of my associates unaccounted for, and I have to know whom you've sent after them. You can see that, can't you? I simply have to know."

The music was familiar, the sharp plinking of the bouzouki. The pain in his hand throbbed to its rhythm.

"You see, Emerson, this is just the beginning. Spiro can keep this up all night. When he starts on some of the other parts of your body, you'll think this first sequence was like your mother's kiss. So there's absolutely no sense in trying to be a hero."

Which song were they playing? Did he hear it last night at the tavern in Pyrgi?

"He's right, mister," said Spiro, leaning forward intently. "Most people got the wrong idea about things like this. Nobody ever holds out—everybody talks. So why don't you make it easy on yourself?"

Listen to the music, he thought. That's the only way. Concentrate on the music and don't think about anything else. Don't think about Ginger, don't think about Eddie and what must have gone wrong with Swan. Just listen to the music.

He tried to remember why there was music. Something about a wedding. In Albania. He knew that much. He remembered coming to on the deck of the sloop, dizzy with pain from the blow on the head, and he remembered the secluded cove where they had moored the boat. He remembered the overland hike, stumbling along a narrow, rocky pathway with Andriakis leading and Spiro at his back. He remembered the farmhouse and the surprised look on the face of the man who had greeted them . . . *Peter, so you came after all!* . . . a look of surprised pleasure that had turned quickly to dismay when he saw Emerson. He remembered all that, and he remembered the hurried, whispered conference at the back door and behind the man a kitchen filled with bustling women and the fragrances of roasting meats. *Peter, it's impossible, not now, not here,* and then they had hustled him into the barn and up into the loft by an outside ladder, and there he lay while down below there was music and a wedding.

"Peter, how much longer is this going to take?"

"I have no idea, Lex. Mr. Emerson is being particularly stubborn."

"Very foolish of him; just causes more pain."

"I've been trying to convince him of that. All I need are the other two names and then he can rest."

"Melina was asking for you downstairs. She knows you're here. Come and congratulate her."

"I'm sorry, old friend. This has to be done. I'll come down as soon as I can."

Even through the pain Emerson sensed the weird incongruity

of the conversation: social apologies while a man was being tortured. But *he* was that man. He opened his eyes. Andriakis stood near the door to the hayloft. In the doorway was the one he called Lex. Spiro crouched nearby, one hand still grasping Emerson's wrist, the other ready to go back to work with the slender piece of steel. Lex looked at the scene distastefully.

"Is this really necessary?" he asked.

As if to provide an answer, Andriakis looked around for Emerson's knapsack and found it on a pile of straw. He turned it upside down. Out tumbled the PPK Walther, the box of ammunition, the wadded handkerchiefs, the homemade plate, and all the other odds and ends. Emerson's eyes widened when he saw the plate, but Andriakis was interested only in the pistol. He picked it up and showed it to Lex.

"A nice little toy," said the Albanian, inspecting the piece. "I don't suppose he was going to shoot rabbits with it."

"No, he was after bigger game. Me. So you see, it's really necessary."

"I see. But leave it for a while, Peter. Come downstairs, have a glass of wine. Kiss the bride." He looked at Andriakis shrewdly. "Give the man time to think for a while. Let him think about pain. Maybe he'll come to his senses."

Andriakis nodded in understanding. "It might work."

"It often does with these tough cases." He put his arm around Andriakis' shoulder. "Come, let's go down. Melina will be delighted."

"All right." As they turned toward the hayloft door, Andriakis said to Spiro, "Stay here while I'm gone. Don't touch him, you understand? I want him to think a while."

"Yeah, sure."

When they were gone, Emerson closed his eyes again. There was nothing to think about. Andriakis would kill him, and all that there was left for him to do in life was to keep from involving Ginger. He wondered if he would be strong enough for that and knew that he had to be.

Listen to the music, he instructed himself. No matter what they do to you, just listen to the music and keep your mind blank.

It was then that he realized that Spiro was still gripping his hand. He opened his eyes again. Spiro grinned down.

"The boss says you should think," said the Greek, "but the boss don't know everything. I think you're gonna talk for Spiro. You gonna do that for me? Sure you are. You're gonna talk for me right now and make the boss happy."

Emerson saw the steel blade come closer. He closed his eyes and screamed into the gag as he felt the first shock of pain. Then he felt nothing at all as he passed out.

He came back to consciousness hearing the music, swimming up from the depths with strokes that were timed to the beat of the bouzouki, the sounds of revelry from the floor below, the clapping of hands, the stamping of feet, the cries of joy that came from straining throats: *"Ee-la! Ee-la!"*

He lay on the floor breathing shallowly through his nose, the taste of the gag sour in his mouth. He opened his eyes slowly, expecting to find Spiro crouched over him, but the Greek was gone. He looked down at his left hand. The end finger was pulped ruin. He tried to move the fingers and almost fainted again from the pain.

"Ee-la!"

This time the shout of joy came from closer by. He shifted his eyes and saw Spiro standing at the hayloft doorway, looking down at the scene on the barn floor. In the sharpness of pain his mind registered details. The Greek was drinking, so someone had brought him a glass of wine. He had been fed as well, for at his feet was a greasy plate. His face was shiny with sweat, and he slapped one hand against his thigh in time to the music.

"EE-LA!"

Emerson recognized the music now, the choppy rhythm of the *zeïmbekikos,* the dance for men alone that he had seen Andriakis do the night before in Pyrgi. He remembered how the other men on the floor had dropped away to give him room, and how he had danced on alone, indifferent to the cries of praise that came from the onlookers.

Spiro called loudly, "That's the way, boss! You show 'em how!"

So Andriakis was dancing again. The music grew faster and

wilder as the climax approached, and Emerson thought bitterly of how his plans had been twisted out of shape. Just about now, with the music flaring, was the time he had intended for the destruction of the man who had helped to order his death, and instead he now lay helpless, forced to listen to that same music while the same man danced on. They were cheering now down below, these Albanian Greeks as much in awe of the dancing Andriakis as the Corfiotes had been, and there, yes, there came the first of the glasses thrown to burst in a tinkle of admiration. The sound of another glass breaking, and another, and still another as Spiro hurled his wineglass in glee, straight down twenty feet to the barn floor.

"Ee-la. Ee-la," came the happy chant, and now they were throwing the dishes as well, heavier thumps as the crockery crashed on the hard-packed earthen floor.

"Ee-la, Andriakis,'' shouted Spiro. He picked up his greasy dinner plate and threw it.

The noise of the clapping and the stamping was deafening now, the yipping cries of joy continuous. Spiro turned away from the door, a rapturous look on his face, his eyes alight as he searched for something else to throw. Those eyes passed over Emerson, unseeing, and fastened on the homemade plate lying next to the knapsack on the straw. He pounced and grabbed it, ran back to the door. He raised his arm as Emerson watched in disbelief, fear welling up within him.

"Ee-la, Andriakis,'' Spiro screamed, and hurled the plate at the feet of his idol.

Emerson closed his eyes as the barn heaved up under him.

Eddie crouched low against the wall of the corridor deep in the recesses of the Fun House. At the far end of the corridor, about fifty feet away, was the third checkpoint, but unlike the first two there were no guards in sight. There was only a massive metal door and, beside it on the wall, a loudspeaker and a microphone, both mounted on brackets. Breathing deeply, he collected himself, reviewing in his mind what Vasily had told him.

"Assuming that anybody got that far, the third checkpoint

is unbeatable. It's got a door on it like a bloody great bank vault, and that door opens only in response to a computer-coded voice-identifier. If the voice doesn't check out, the people inside don't open the door. Nobody can beat that kind of setup.''

''Why can't the door be blown?'' Eddie had asked.

''It can be. Any door can be blown. The problem is with the voice-identifier. The people inside request a verbal statement in order to check the voice pattern. They make the request three times. Unless there's an answer after the third request, and unless the voice checks out, some very unpleasant things begin to happen.''

''Oh.''

''Exactly. There's no way in the world of blowing a door like that in thirty seconds, unless you can figure out how to bring a cannon down into the basement of the Fun House.''

''One other thing. Do the people inside hear the response through earphones or over an open speaker?''

''A speaker, but what the hell difference does it make?''

''Plenty.''

Crouched against the wall, Eddie measured the distance to the door with his eyes. Call it fifty feet—six seconds to get there from a standing start. Figure that whatever sensors there were in the walls would pick up his presence about halfway down the corridor. Three seconds, plus one second for the sensor to react . . . another second for the relay made five, and then thirty seconds for the question to be asked three times. Thirty-five, total.

From his left pocket he took a pencil-shaped, battery-operated electronic oscillator with a quartz crystal hooked into the feedback loop. From the same pocket he took a tiny screwdriver and a roll of sticky black tape. He tore off two strips of tape and attached them to each end of the oscillator. Gripping the screwdriver between his teeth, from his right pocket he took an ordinary kitchen sandwich bag filled with plastic RDX explosive. It looked like a ball of gray putty. The oscillator in his left hand, the RDX in his right, the screwdriver clenched between his teeth, he crouched like a runner under the gun.

He checked the second hand of his watch and took off.

He raced down the hallway to the speaker-microphone complex, dropped the bag of RDX at his feet, took the screwdriver from between his teeth, and went to work unscrewing the shell of the microphone.

Above his head the loudspeaker spat static, and then a quiet voice said: "This is an electronic check of your voice pattern. Please use the microphone and speak a complete sentence of not less than ten words."

Eleven seconds gone, twenty-four to go. Damn, the screws were tiny and they were tight. He wrestled with the last one.

"This is the second request for voice identification. It is essential, for your own physical safety, that you make your statement into the microphone."

Last screw off, he stripped away the outer shell of the microphone, discarded it, and inserted the oscillator next to the diaphragm. Two quick twists of the tape secured it there.

Twelve seconds to go.

"This is the third request for . . ."

He twisted the bottom of the oscillator and flicked the switch to the *on* position. There were six seconds to go.

". . . voice identification. No further requests will be made. Speak into . . ."

The voice stopped abruptly. Eddie smiled. The ultrasonic oscillation fed into the microphone at 200,000 vibrations per second, or ten times the upper limit of the human ear, had effectively spiked the sound-based programming of the computer in control of the voice-identification system. He also had a pretty good idea of what it had done to the two men on the other side of the door who had heard the signal amplified over an open loudspeaker.

Working quickly, but without the pressure now of a time-table measured in seconds, he packed the RDX around the wheel-shaped handle of the door, inserted a ten-second-delay detonator into the putty, and retreated down the hall. The wheel blew off with a dull, almost muted explosion, and the door swung open.

Inside he found what he had expected: two technicians sitting at a control panel, a bit of blood trickling from their ears, eyes glazed and staring straight ahead in shock. He passed his hand in front of those eyes. There were no reactions. They would recover, but for now they were helpless.

He looked around the room. It was just as Vasily had described it—small steel self-service elevator on the far wall and, on the other side, the mouth of the old Fun House drop chute. Swan's bunker was thirty feet below, an efficiency apartment with living room, bedroom, kitchenette, and bathroom. The elevator doors would slide open in Swan's living room. The chute went straight down into Swan's kitchen.

I hope the son of a bitch is alone, Eddie thought, as he emptied his pockets. He had two smoke grenades and half a dozen high-explosive Beanos, each the size of a golf ball. He pulled the pins on all of them and sent them clattering down the chute, smoke bombs first and then the Beanos. The *crump crump crump* of the explosions echoed and died away.

There comes a time, Eddie told himself, when there are no more gadgets to use, no more tricks to pull. Like a World War II movie, after the bombardment, when the squad of tired soldiers has to enter the town on foot—you have to fight.

I hate that time, he thought, but it sure as hell looks like it's here.

He drew his pistol and headed for the chute.

"There was a sound reason for the biblical injunction against nakedness," said Joseph Wolfe, "and it wasn't just prudishness. A man without his clothing is something considerably less than a man."

"You might at least give me back the shoes," Vasily complained. "This floor is too cold."

"I think not. From what I've seen so far, those shoes of yours could be as deadly as a machine gun."

Stripped naked and shivering, Vasily leaned against an open

wine cask and strove for a nonchalance that he hoped would be convincing. The wine cellar of the monastery was low-ceilinged and vaulted, built of slabs of stone, and even in July it was damp and chilly. To add to his discomfort, the fumes of sour wine rising from the cask behind him were making him dizzy, and he had to shake his head to clear it. Both Barto and Carlos stiffened at the motion, then relaxed. They stood at opposite corners of the room, their knives exchanged for pistols, and they watched him closely. Wolfe, too, had produced a pistol, but it lay on the old refectory table before him as he examined the clothing he had taken from Vasily: trousers, shorts, shoes, shirt, jacket, and the robe of the order. To one side of the clothing was a pile of his personal possessions: billfold, card case, keys, and the electronic chess set. To the other side was a far more imposing pile.

"Absolutely amazing," said Wolfe, looking over the collection of weapons, gadgets, tubes, and vials that he had found secreted in seams, linings, hidden pockets, flaps, collars, and cuffs. So far he had uncovered two lengths of serrated steel wire, two incendiary pencils, six miniature grenades that looked like cigars, a throwing knife complete with arm sheath, a plastic bag of RDX, an assortment of detonators, a one-shot pistol concealed in a fountain pen, and two ominous-looking bottles of dark liquid. He held one of the bottles up to the light and asked, "What's in this one?"

"The boomslang venom that I put on the scourge," said Vasily, shifting his feet.

"And this?" Wolfe held up the other bottle.

Vasily looked embarrassed. "My cough medicine," he confessed. "I'm subject to head colds this time of the year. Look, Wolfe, just let me have the robe back. It isn't even mine; I borrowed it from one of your monks."

"Cough medicine?" Wolfe couldn't believe it. "How do you tell them apart?"

Vasily shrugged. "The medicine smells bad. What about the robe?"

"Not a chance You're safer naked."

"You mean *you're* safer."

Wolfe nodded. "That's exactly what I mean. I don't even feel safe with this arsenal in the same room with you. Carlos, get these things out of here. Put them in my cell and lock the door."

Carlos shoved his pistol into the pocket of his robe and gathered up the weaponry. He was about to go when Wolfe stopped him. He pointed to Vasily's personal belongings.

"Take this stuff, too. Mr. Borgneff won't be having any use for it now."

Vasily raised an eyebrow at this. "Since you're robbing me of my personal property, you might try your hand at the electronic chess. I find it amusing."

Wolfe glanced down at the black case and dismissed it with a grunt. "A toy, nothing more."

"Perhaps for you," Vasily conceded. "I find that it has its uses."

When Carlos had gone, clanging shut the heavy doors behind him, Wolfe said, "I suppose I should feel flattered. All that sophisticated weaponry just for me."

"Not really. They're just the normal tools of my trade."

"Your trade." Wolfe made a sneer out of the word.

"A poor one, but my own. A while back you referred to me as a murdering son of a bitch. I prefer to think of myself as an avenging angel."

"The Carillo business?" Wolfe looked at him wonderingly. "All this for something that happened ten years ago. And you're supposed to be a professional. Professionals don't carry grudges."

"I'd argue that point, but I don't have the time. I didn't come here to debate with you, I came to kill you."

Wolfe's eyes traveled over Vasily's lean, naked body. "With what? Your bare hands?"

"If necessary."

Wolfe stroked his chin thoughtfully. "You seem extraordinarily confident for someone in your position. I hope that you're not counting too much on the Rule of the Order you mentioned before. About not spilling blood within the monastery walls."

"I was rather hoping that you'd keep it in mind," Vasily admitted.

"As I said before, I'd be willing to make an exception in your case, but actually I don't think it will be necessary."

Vasily looked perturbed. His eyes narrowed and searched around the room. Then he felt the open wine vat at his back and his lips twisted in a grimace. "*Richard the Third?* You're going to play the hunchback to my Duke of Clarence, is that it? Drowned in a butt of malmsey wine, by God."

Wolfe pursed his lips and nodded. He seemed to be enjoying himself. "An interesting end for a professional assassin, wouldn't you say? And not a drop of blood will be spilled. As soon as Carlos returns . . ."

There was a dull *crack* above their heads that echoed through the thick walls of the wine cellar. Wolfe and Barto looked up instinctively.

"What was that?" Wolfe asked.

"Oh dear," said Vasily. "Oh dear, oh dear. That must have been Carlos."

"Carlos?" Wolfe repeated, uncomprehending.

"I have the feeling that there's been a terrible mistake."

"Mistake?"

"I really should apologize, but it wasn't supposed to happen this way. That electronic chess game was meant for you, but I imagine Carlos just couldn't keep his hands off it. You see, it's been programmed to explode when White checkmates Black."

Wolfe's hand jerked and his pistol came up. "You mean that Carlos . . ."

"It probably took the top of his head off."

"You're lying," Wolfe shouted.

"Afraid not. I'm really very sorry about this."

"Barto!" Wolfe wheeled and made a gesture toward the door, then shouted, "No, wait . . . !" He looked back and forth wildly between Barto and Vasily.

Vasily extended his arms out, palms up, his naked body posed against the wine vat in the attitude of the crucified. "Are you afraid of dividing your forces, Chessmaster? You have me pinned here, totally helpless.''

Wolfe hesitated, considering. Then, over his shoulder, he said, ''Barto, go. Find out what's happened.''

This time the door was left open, and they heard Barto's footsteps scurrying up the stairs and then fading away as he ran down the hallway. Wolfe breathed deeply, but the hand that held the pistol was steady.

''I hope for your sake that you're lying,'' he said. ''Those boys mean a lot to me, and if anything has happened to Carlos you're going to die very badly. There won't be any talk about spilling blood, either. You'll wish you . . .''

The second *crack* was louder than the first because of the open door. Again Wolfe jumped and looked around.

Vasily said conversationally, ''That was Barto. It's a two-stage gadget, you see. The second explosion comes ninety seconds after the first.''

Wolfe wheeled around, his face contorted, his pistol coming up, but by that time Vasily had moved. He jumped in back of the wine vat and crouched down low behind it. Wolfe fired, and the bullet plunked into the side of the vat. Vasily laughed and did four things very quickly.

He took a deep breath, bent his head over, and plucked his artificial eye from its socket.

He pressed the brown iris of the eye with his thumb, and it depressed with an audible click.

Still holding his breath, he tossed the eye out from behind the vat in Wolfe's direction. As he released his thumb the eye began to hiss.

Then, in one quick motion, he rolled over the side of the vat and under the murky surface of the wine until he was wholly submerged. The wine slopped over the sides of the vat.

Wolfe stared in horror at the disembodied eye bouncing at his feet. The eye regarded him, unblinking. The hissing sound was louder now. He kicked wildly at the eye and missed. He kicked again and then a third time, breathing deeply. A lethal dose of the gaseous nitrobenzine hissed out of the eye. The effect on

Wolfe was the same as that of a massive coronary attack. He felt a single sharp pain in his chest, and then he fell to the floor, dead.

Vasily held himself under the surface of the wine by bracing his hands against the side of the vat. He counted off thirty slow seconds, the dispersal time for the nitrobenzine. Then he forced himself to count off thirty more before he rose up out of the wine like Bacchus at harvest-time, the rich, red liquid running from his head and shoulders. He stepped out of the vat and looked around for something with which to dry himself. There was nothing. Without even bothering to look at Wolfe he padded up the stairs, dripping wine from his naked body, and ran down the hallway. At the door of Wolfe's cell stood a group of horrified monks peering in at what remained of Carlos and Barto. The monks fell away when Vasily appeared, opening a path for the wine-soaked apparition.

Inside the cell, he used the coarse brown robe of the order as a towel and quickly dressed in his own clothing, retrieving his wallet and keys. Wolfe's own chessboard lay on the table. On impulse, he took fresh pieces and set up the end position of the game they had played in Barcelona. He studied the board, shaking his head.

"He has to resign; he doesn't have a chance," he murmured, and then added brightly, "Of course, he never did."

No one tried to stop him as he left; the monks regarded him silently as he passed by. At the end of the hall he looked back. They were still staring at him, just as they might have stared at an elephant that had suddenly appeared within their monastery walls.

"You make an excellent wine," he told them. "Vivid, dramatic, authoritative, and with a definite lilt to the aftertaste. But I don't suggest bathing in it."

They looked at him as if he were crazy. He decided that at the moment he probably was.

Instead of driving back to Barcelona, he took the precaution of going north over the border into France. It was a needless precaution—the monks would bury their own—but he felt better for taking it. Seven hours later he bought himself a new eyepatch in Marseilles and boarded a flight, by way of Paris, for Mexico City.

The drive from Mexico City to the U.S. border took fifteen hours with only five ten-minute stops for gas, food, and rest rooms. The three men from the Soviet Embassy did all the driving; Rusty and Sasha sat in the back of the Lincoln for the entire trip. As they drove through the night Rusty found herself responding to the young man. He was anxious about the operation, concerned for its success, but he also was cheerfully inpudent and without any of the conventional stuffiness that she would have expected from such a man. He joked with her, told her outrageous stories, gave her coffee from a Thermos flask, but most of all he coaxed her to talk about herself. She needed little coaxing. There was a quarter of a century of conversation dammed up inside her.

"I'm not one of your big-city people," she said, leaning back into the softness of the seat. "I come from farming country just outside Orel. Do you know Orel?"

"Only from reading Turgenev," Sasha admitted.

"Then you know Orel, at least the way it used to be. Turgenev captured it perfectly. Such a fine, fair land, and the river . . . to me the Oka will always be the loveliest river in the world. How I hated to leave there to go to Gaczyna."

"You trained at Gaczyna?"

She nodded in the darkness. "Just like Jim did. Of course, I was five years behind him and so we never met. It's strange, thinking back on it now, but I fought so hard against the assignment. It wasn't just leaving the motherland, perhaps forever. That was bad enough, but the idea of marrying a man I had never seen seemed horrible. And spying on him for the rest of my life, being a watchdog as well as a wife . . . well, I was a romantic girl, only nineteen, and you know what girls that age can be like."

"Yes, that much I know about women."

"So romantic. I begged my control for another assignment, literally begged, but you can guess how much good that did me. In the end, I went. I knew my duty and I did what had to be done. Infiltrated through Canada with an American birth certificate and set out to marry James Emerson.''

"Advance my education on women, please. How does a woman make a man marry her? How were you so sure that you could do it?''

"Why, Sasha, that's nothing. You certainly do need educating. A good-looking woman can always do that. There's no great trick in getting a man to marry you; the hard part is to keep him in love with you. And to love him. I hated him at first, hated him because he was the man other people had chosen for me. It wasn't prudishness, understand. If my control had ordered me to seduce a stranger, or something like that, well, it's all part of the job. But to marry a man, to bind myself to him for the rest of my life . . . on orders. Can you understand why I hated him at first?''

"Yes, I think so." They were passing through treeless desert, but the moon was up and there were shadows on the rocks to mark their speed.

"If you can understand that, then perhaps you can understand what a miracle it seemed to be when I realized that I was falling in love with him. It was after we were married. Yes, I admit that, I married him as cold as a fish, without the slightest feeling for him. I thought I had signed up for a life without love, and then . . . it's funny how it happens. You wake up one morning and you think to yourself, you know, I may not be in love with him, but he's such a thoroughly good man, he's so decent and tender, and later that day he calls to say that he'll be working late at the office and you think, good, that gives me a chance to wash my hair before he comes home. Only you don't wash your hair. You sit in the kitchen staring at the clock, watching the hands crawl. Six, six thirty, seven, seven thirty, and all you want to hear are his footsteps in the hall, the click of his key in the lock, and all you want to see is him walking in the door, that night and every other night for the rest of your life. And just about then you begin to laugh at yourself, just a giggle at first, and then louder, and pretty soon you're laughing like a crazy woman because you know what's happening to you. Love, that's what's happening, love for that good, thoroughly decent man who suddenly means more to you than anything else in the world. You can feel it rising up in you like water in a well, and it's like nothing that you ever felt before. And there's your miracle. Love where it never should have been, love where you never thought you'd find it. It started that night, and it's been the same that way for me ever since. Twenty-five years, the finest years a woman could ever have.''

She stopped suddenly. She closed her eyes and put her head back.

Sasha said softly, "Until we came along to mess up your lives.''

"I've been talking too much," Rusty said, her eyes still closed. "Don't confuse my personal life with my professional obligations, and don't make the mistake of confusing me with Jim. America never seduced me. I left Russia over twenty-five years ago as a convinced Marxist-Leninist, and my convictions are the same now as they were then." She opened her eyes and looked at him directly. "So don't talk about messing up my life. I'm a loyal daughter of the socialist revolution, a member of the Communist Party of the USSR, and a serving officer in the KGB. I am not only doing what I was trained for, I am doing exactly what I want to do. I'm going home.''

He absorbed that, then asked, "And your husband?"

"It will take time. He's wearing emotional blinders now, but once he gets home, once he stands on Russian soil, once he breathes Russian air again . . ." She finished lamely, "It will take time, but it will work, I know it will. We have a good life ahead of us. Back home.''

"I hope so," said Sasha.

They had left Mexico City at nine in the evening, and they came into the border town of Nuevo Laredo at noon the next day. The man driving the Lincoln dropped them off a block away from the International Bridge and turned the car around to make the return trip to Mexico City alone. Rusty, Sasha, and the other two embassy men walked over the bridge to the Texas side of the border. There they were met by a car from the

Houston consulate that drove them north to San Antonio. A chartered jet was waiting for them at the airport there. At five in the afternoon they landed in San Francisco and headed north in a rented car along Route 101. Just short of twenty-four hours after leaving Mexico City they arrived in Point Balboa, California.

Chapter 19

The plate that Spiro Dodonis threw might have transformed the gaily decorated Albanian barn into a slaughterhouse if Andriakis had not been dancing alone. Andriakis had no chance at all. The plate exploded directly in front of him and opened him up from groin to sternum. He was dead within seconds, and so was Lex Enhora, the man nearest to him, his scalp laid open to the brain. Spiro Dodonis himself was pitched out of the hayloft by the force of the explosion; when he struck the floor below, his neck snapped. Three other men were wounded. The explosion also blew out every light in the barn, and in the resulting chaos the groans and yells of the injured were mixed with the cries of others searching for flashlights and lanterns. When light was finally restored the scene resembled the aftermath of a wartime air raid. No one except James Emerson yet realized what had happened.

He was dazed, but not for long. Spiro's long thin knife, that recent instrument of unbearable pain, lay close to hand, but the hand that it lay close to was maimed almost to the point of uselessness. But he gripped the haft of the knife, shut his mind to pain, swore he would neither scream nor faint, and sawed his right hand free. It was easier after that, using his good hand to unbind his feet, and then he stumbled down the stairs. He stared in disbelief, the pain in his hand almost forgotten for that moment.

He saw the body of Andriakis, and he nodded to himself with satisfaction. He saw Spiro's body, and he nodded again. He saw the body of Lex Enhora.

My God, he thought—what did Eddie give me? *"An antiper-*

sonnel weapon," he had said. *"Limited range. Good for taking out a single target . . ."*

None of the survivors commented on Emerson's presence. They were all contained within envelopes of shock and grief. Besides, with his bloody hand and tattered clothes, he looked like one of the wounded. *A single target?* If they had been a few steps closer, any one of those wounded men might be as dead as Andriakis.

And as dead as Lex Enhora, the man who had tried to stop Andriakis from torturing him . . .

It was the priest—his cassock torn and stovepipe hat crushed in—who saved him, tugging at his sleeve, firing incomprehensible Greek at him. Only one word came through—Kérkyra, the Greek name for Corfu.

"Corfu?" he asked. "What are you saying? You want to go to Corfu?"

"Corfu, yes," said the priest in surprise, switching languages. "I must get away from here at once."

The barn was filled with a whirlwind of imploring voices, the wounded men begging now for help. Emerson looked at them quickly, but long enough to assure himself that none of them had suffered more than a deep cut.

"I can't help anyone from a jail cell," the priest said. "Perhaps you don't understand. I am a priest from Corfu, and I am Greek, and this is Albania. I came over here to perform the ceremony. After such an explosion the police must come shortly. When they do, I am finished." The priest looked at him shrewdly. "You are certainly not Albanian, either."

Emerson nodded. "Let's go outside . . ."

Outside, under the stars, he said, "I know where there is a boat. However . . ." He held up his left hand, and the priest sucked in his breath. He had not seen the extent of the damage before. "I'll need help handling it," Emerson continued. "Do you know anything about boats?"

"I am from Corfu," the priest said. "We learn to sail before we can drive a car."

Emerson let out his breath and sucked air. "In that case, Father, let's get the hell out of here."

The priest led the way down the steep and rocky path that led to the sea, pushing the dinghy off the sand and into the water, and rowing them out into the cove where the sloop was anchored. Once on board he got the mainsail up while Emerson steadied the helm, then slipped the anchor for speed and silence, and ran up the jib. He came aft then to take the helm. He kept the boat under sail until they were well past the point of the Albanian patrols and the lights of Corfu were dead ahead.

"We can use the engine now," he said and went below. The engine chugged into life, and after a while the priest came topside carrying an old shirt and a slab of something soft and yellow.

"Butter from the galley," he explained. He tore the shirt into strips, greased each strip well with butter, and wound them around Emerson's hand in a makeshift bandage. When Emerson winced, he apologized for his clumsiness.

"It will have to do until we can get you to a doctor."

"Where are we headed for?" Emerson asked as the shore lights came closer.

"Anywhere you wish. I know this coast the way I know my beard."

Emerson hesitated before saying, "I have a car in the hills above Kalami. The keys are in it. We'll need it to get me to a doctor."

"Kalami. Where Mr. Andriakis lives. Lived."

"Yes."

"And this is his boat, is it not?"

"Yes."

The priest looked out to sea and said nothing.

It all seemed to go very quickly after that: getting the car and the drive to Ipsos to pick up his clothes and papers; and then into Corfu town, where the priest roused a doctor who complained bitterly about the hour but who tended to Emerson's hand. He took one look at the maimed fingers and asked the priest a question in rapid dialect. Whatever answer the priest gave seemed sufficient. The doctor shrugged and went to work, and when he was finished he accepted payment reluctantly.

"What did you tell the doctor?" Emerson asked later. It was

nine in the morning and they sat in the airport restaurant, eating grilled cheese sandwiches and drinking sugary Greek coffee. They made an incongruous-looking pair: the priest in his torn cassock and dented hat, and the American with the bandaged hand dressed in smooth gray worsted. "Whatever you told him, it certainly worked."

The priest blew on his coffee before sipping. "I told him that we no longer live in an age where every question has an answer."

Emerson looked at him silently. He did not trust himself to speak. His bloodstream was so full of painkillers that his brain was humming.

"I don't even know your name," said the priest, "and I don't want to know it. But you probably saved my life last night and I probably saved yours, and we'll never see each other again. In a few minutes you'll be on the plane to Athens and wherever else you're going and I'll be on my way home to my wife and children . . ."

"Your wife . . . ?" Emerson caught himself. He had forgotten that these priests marry.

"But before I do, there is still a question that I have to ask. Even if there is no answer to it."

"Go ahead."

"I'm not asking you as a priest. You're not of my faith, and my office means nothing to you. But I'm asking you as a man. Were you responsible for the horror that happened last night?"

"I was."

The priest winced, as if he had been struck. Emerson looked away for a moment, and then looked back, directly into the priest's eyes.

"Father," he said, "there are many questions about me that will have to remain without answers. But I can tell you this much, as God is my judge. Two of those men deserved to die. The third, Lex Enhora, did not."

"Then you carry the burden," the priest said slowly.

"Yes."

"And what now?"

"I don't know, Father."

"More killing?"

They called his plane then, and he left the priest sitting there with his half-eaten sandwich and the sugary dregs of his coffee. He walked away without having answered the question, but he knew what that answer had to be. Once the killing starts, it never stops.

Gerard Krause felt warm and comfortable. He always felt that way at Katerina's house: protected against the world. His room on the top floor was like a vault into which he could lock himself safely, bounce around from wall to wall and emerge only when it was time to show himself again. In that room he was fed, nurtured, and catered to like a royal infant. It was the most trouble-free place he had known since his childhood, and although fear had sent him to the Fun House this time, it was a delicious sort of fear, tinged with the pleasure of naughtiness.

He watched as Katerina collected his dinner dishes onto a trolley and wheeled it to the door. That same flood of warmth and comfort flowed over him as he watched the neat manner with which she handled the plates and cups. She reminded him so much of his mother, so tall and erect and full-breasted that he wondered for a moment if . . . and then discarded the thought, for she lacked the one ingredient he needed. Sitting slouched in a chair with his hands jammed into the pockets of his lounging robe, he smiled up at her. She smiled back, as if she knew what he had been thinking.

"Do you want me to send Anna up?" she asked.

"I'm ready for her now."

"You look it," she said, chuckling. "What about the other one, the redhead you brought? What shall I do with her?"

"Is she working?"

"Not that one. She just sits in the corner. Not very enterprising."

Krause thought for a moment. "Keep an eye on her. Don't let her go wandering off."

Katerina nodded in understanding. "She won't be going anyplace. I'll send Anna right up."

Once she was gone he undressed quickly, lowered the lights,

and got into bed. He lay flat on his back, pulled the covers up under his chin, and closed his eyes. He breathed deeply several times, letting his mind go blank, spiraling back and down through the years to simpler times and simple pleasures, long-remembered tastes, touches, and smells: the particular flavor of the strawberry ices he loved as a boy, the odor of baking bread, the stroke of his mother's hand on his cheek. Thinking of that, he turned on his side, his knees came up and his arms went down to grasp them. He lay that way, suspended in time, as the door opened and Anna came in. The door closed and was locked behind her.

She had changed from her somber dress into an equally somber dressing gown that rippled and flowed over her full hips and breasts. Her hair was pulled back into a bun at the nape of her neck, and her face was scrubbed clean of cosmetics. She smelled of plain soap and of lilac water. She came to the edge of the bed and sat there, and when she spoke it was in a soft, almost whispering Italian.

"Ah, little Gerry, are you sleeping? Yes, you are, I can see that you are. You look so cute curled up that way, so precious that I hate to wake you, but it's that time, you know, time to feed, time to drink Mamma's milk and grow up big and strong. Come, my little one. Wake up and drink."

She opened her robe to reveal the full, white, blue-veined, slightly pendulous breasts of the nursing mother, the aureoles dark and the nipples protruding. She slid her left arm under Krause's head and moved him gently toward her, holding her left breast in her right hand, offering him the nipple. His lips brushed against her hesitantly, once and then again, and then with his eyes still closed he took the nipple into his mouth and began to suck the thin, rich milk from her. He swallowed greedily and sucked again.

"Good, that's a good boy," she murmured. "Drink it all up, there's plenty of milk for little Gerry."

He gurgled contentedly, and as he sucked she slipped her hand under the blankets, down over his belly and in between his legs. In rhythm with the in-and-out motion of his lips and the tug at her breast, she began to stroke him to hardness. As always when she did this with him, she felt a rush of warmth inside her, a feeling not so much of excitement as contentment. Aside from the money that he paid her there was nothing about the little man that excited her, not even the rapidly hardening shaft between her fingers, but she was contented to know that she could offer to him the one service that no other girl in the house could supply. After a while she said gently, "Wait, wait now, baby. Time to change over."

She moved to the other side of the bed and gave him the other breast as she resumed her stroking. She was a big woman with an ample supply of milk, but whenever she did this with Krause she was always amazed at how much of it he could drink. And the more he drank, the harder he got.

His eyes were open now and his hands were at her breast, clutching it, pressing it into his face as he sucked. His breathing grew rapid, the air whistling in and out of his nose; his face grew flushed and she knew that he was close to climax. She quickened her stroke, murmuring to him, urging him on, and then his body stiffened; he arched his back and ejaculated over her hand. Then he went limp.

"Good Gerry," she said. "That's a very good boy."

When she was sure that he was finished, she waited a moment and then tried to move away. She could not. His lips still gripped her nipple, his hands still clutched her breast. Patient, she waited for him to release her, but he did not move.

"Gerry?" she said tentatively and then, remembering that her role playing was over, said, "Signor Krause?"

When he did not answer, she took his hands in hers and slid them from her breast. His hands fell limply. She took the nipple from his mouth with a faint *plop*, and his jaw fell open. Alarmed, she jerked her supporting arm away and his head fell back on the pillow. His eyes stared up, unseeing.

It was then that she began to scream.

Ginger heard the screaming in the downstairs bar as she toyed with her fifth glass of wine for the evening. Everyone else heard it, too. First it was only Anna screaming, two other female voices joined in, and then the bar emptied out as cus-

tomers and girls alike dashed for the stairs and the tiny elevator
to see what was happening upstairs. Ginger sat perfectly still,
listening to the pounding feet and the screaming voices above
her, listening for one word. She didn't know much Italian, but
she knew the word that she wanted to hear. And then she heard
it.

"*É morto, morto.*"

"What happened? Who was it?"

"A customer. Dead!"

"God save us! How?"

"Have they called a doctor?"

"Too late! He's gone. Gone!"

Ginger smiled faintly as the words swirled down the stairs.
She was alone in the bar. She gathered up her purse and, without apparent haste, strolled to the door and walked out of the
House of Felluci. Out on the Via Manzoni she hailed a late-
cruising taxi and told the driver to take her to Malpensa Airport.
There was the rental car up in Brissago and her clothing in the
pension, but she was willing to write all that off.

She sat back and closed her eyes as the taxi sped through the
deserted streets, wondering what the coroner would say when
he found that Gerard Krause had died of an overdose of
mother's milk laced with penicillin.

In the bunker deep inside the Fun House, Edwin Swan leveled his pistol and stepped cautiously from the bedroom closet.
He had been alerted to danger at the moment of the second request for voice identification at the microphone complex on the
floor above. That second request automatically triggered a
beeper and a blinking yellow light on the display of the living
room computer terminal. The third request, and its abrupt,
unprogrammed termination, had switched the yellow light to
red and sent Swan rushing from his desk to the bedroom with a
speed that belied his seventy-three years.

Swan was alone in the apartment. He had designed the system himself, years ago, when the Fun House had been set up as
the Agency's prime hideaway. A little foresight, he thought,

that may now save my life . . . How rare it is that we plan ahead and are so richly rewarded.

He had immediately ducked into the clothes closet and slid shut the six-inch steel door. About a minute later, through the transparent bombproof panel, he had seen his apartment destroyed.

The scene that he now observed as he edged quietly from the closet resembled that of a wartime village devastated by artillery. The wooden furniture was reduced to splinters and rags, the government-issue desk had been pulped, and the Swedish metal chairs looked like twisted paper clips. The smoke still billowed in the close confines and the air stank of cordite.

Yes, Swan thought again, an artillery barrage—that was an apt analogy. And such a barrage is usually followed by an infantry attack. He wondered who it would be. Mancuso again? Borgneff? Perhaps even James Emerson himself, now that their friendship was in ashes equal to those in this room. No, not likely. It was daylight up above at the carnival site, and Emerson's face and gait were too recognizable. Ditto for Vasily Borgneff, he realized. The penetration had probably been by one man alone. So it's the little one, the nervy one who had tried the first time in the hotel room with poison . . . the streetwise Italian . . . the one whom they had never been able to catch and who was now attempting to repay them for their lack of doggedness.

"Well, yes . . . we shall see," Swan murmured to himself, gripping his pistol. He drew back a step, crouching behind what remained of the desk. He waited. Whoever the visitor might be, he had proved himself both resourceful and ruthless. He must therefore be respected.

And what next? If I were he—not knowing what damage the Beano explosives might have wrought, not knowing with any degree of certainty if my target was alive, wounded, or dead— what would I do? Swan analyzed that for a moment or two. He tried to glide into Eddie's mind. Mancuso: define him as impetuous, talented, determined—but with a limited imagination. Place him in a hostile, alien territory. He would surely be tempted to follow the Beanos down the chute . . . but then he would hesitate, wouldn't he . . . he would wonder if there was a reception committee. Yes, he would mull it over, but not for too long. And then . . .

The two technicians at the voice ID center would be either dead or neutralized. Swan smiled. Yes, of course, he decided. The technicians . . . that's exactly what I would do if I were Eddie Mancuso—smart and stubborn, but not smart enough to do the job right the first time.

Almost on cue, as if he had willed it, Swan heard the swift whooshing sound of someone tumbling down the chute. He raised the pistol and waited. Mancuso would be thinking, *If Swan's alive down there, and that's what I've got to know, he'll shoot first and worry later.*

"No, my friend," Swan murmured between clenched teeth, "I worry beforehand, and shoot only when I know my target . . ."

The body tumbled from the chute, groaning. For a shadow of a moment Swan was tempted, his finger beginning to tighten on the trigger of the Colt Woodsman pistol. But he stopped in time. The body on the floor twitched a few times. The eyes were open. There was a bit of blood speckling one earlobe. The technician, thought Swan. I was right.

Before he had time to congratulate himself for foresight and restraint, he heard the faint whine of the elevator descending. So he's coming down that way, in style. He can assume now that I'm dead.

No, Swan decided. I'm not giving him enough credit, and that's a mistake that could be fatal. He knows whom he's up against—he'll use a fail-safe device. The second technician will be in the elevator. If this second time there's no reaction from me, he'll be coming down the chute to gloat over the body. Smart, thought Swan. Yes, he's certainly smart. At least, not stupid.

The whine of the elevator ceased. The steel doors parted in the center. Again, Swan almost fired as a man seemed to step into the room, arms waving awkwardly. But he was not stepping, he was falling. The second technician had been propped cleverly at a forward angle against the inside doors. As the man struck the carpet Swan wondered how Mancuso had done it. Probably an electronic oscillator in the diaphragm of the microphone. Hardly lethal, but enough to put even a horse out of action for an hour. Clever boy.

Swan settled in a crouch, his back to the elevator now, slightly to one side of the chute so that he would not be immediately seen by the descending man and yet would have a clear line of fire. This time, when the body hurtled down, he knew who it would be. A grand entrance, like a children's play or a game. *Surprise!* He only wished there would be time for him to see the expression of shock on Mancuso's face.

Behind him, Eddie silently slid open the thin oiled metal panel in the ceiling of the elevator and dropped from darkness to the floor, body weight nicely cushioned by the thick soles of his New Balance running shoes. Eighty-five bucks they'd cost, he remembered, and worth every nickel.

He saw Edwin Swan. Well, I'll be damned . . . the son of a bitch is still alive! How about that?

In his youth—his childhood, really, for it seemed to Eddie that he had somehow skipped the time that most people call youth—he had hated everything about so-called amusement parks. He had been dragged against his will by his parents and his friends to Coney Island, Rye Beach, and Palisades Park. He was nauseated for at least an hour after every stomach-bending ride on the roller coaster. In the bump-'em cars he was slammed from side to side until his eyeballs ached. In the Fun House he recoiled from skeletons that popped from dark corners and banshee howls, and he dreaded the sudden opening of floors that dumped his thin boy's body on poorly stuffed mattresses. Once, at the age of nine, hurtling down the slide, he had caromed off a railing, overshot the padded landing, and sprained his wrist so badly that he couldn't play stickball in the street with the other kids for two weeks. As a boy he had borne with all that lest he suffer the tag of "Chicken!" But now he was a man. In theory he didn't have to do anything he didn't damn well want to do.

And damned if I'll slide down one of those mothers even now, he had decided. Call me chicken—I don't care. A quick inspection of the little elevator had given him his surreptitious method of entry . . . just in case there was some kind of booby trap that he hadn't thought of. And there was Swan—alive. *Surprise!*

He hated to shoot a man in the back, even a man like Edwin Swan, who had been ready to kill Ginger and Rusty along with James Emerson. "Swan," he whispered.

As the DD5 turned, Eddie fired twice into the look of total shock that whitened the man's features. Two blue-black holes appeared in the wrinkled forehead just above the left eye. Swan sprang backward as if he had been jerked by the noose of a rope. But when he struck the floor he stayed there, without life, without even a residual twitch.

Smart guy. Smarter than me, but his luck ran out. Any day of the week, Eddie thought, I'd rather be lucky than good.

He made his way up the stairs, past the helpless guards and the man sleeping peacefully with cotton candy all over his face. Outside the Fun House, the midway was packed with people searching for something new or exciting to do or to see. Sousa marches spurred them onward. Eddie wiped sweat from his forehead, then looked up just in time to see the cars of the roller coaster flash by in a tight, screeching, sickening turn.

"Not for me," he said aloud, and headed for the car that would take him to the airport.

They straggled into Mexico City on different flights, arriving at the Hotel Princesa within hours of each other; Eddie first, then Ginger, Vasily, and finally Emerson with his hand freshly bandaged and lines of both weariness and pain etched deeply into his face. They told each other what had happened and then, with Emerson's arrival, they read the letter from Rusty to her husband, instructing him what to do.

In the living room of Emerson's suite they stared at one another. Swan, Wolfe, Andriakis, and Krause were dead, but Rusty's letter made it all meaningless.

Eddie went to the bar and found the vodka. He sloshed some over ice and stared down at the swirling liquid in the glass. "Double zero," he said bitterly. "Those guys were rotten and they deserved what we did to them, but we forgot that someone else was in the game." He raised his glass to Emerson in a mock salute. "Bon voyage, Colonel Volanov. Give my regards to Moscow."

"He's right," said Vasily, stretching his legs wearily. "It's the only move you have left."

There was no reaction from Emerson. He stared straight ahead and his lips were slightly puckered, as if he were whistling a tune they could not hear.

Eddie raised his voice slightly. "Do you understand what he's saying? There's nothing more we can do for you. We tried. We were lucky, but not lucky enough. We failed."

He was about to say something else, but Ginger gave him a warning look. She got up and went over to her father. She put her hand on his shoulder, and he looked up.

"You're tired," she said. "Why don't you lie down for a while?"

In a thin voice, he said, "Do you think I can relax when they've got Rusty?"

Vasily looked at him narrowly, leaned forward, and said, "They may have her, but they won't hurt her. You don't have to worry about that part of it. They want you sweet once they get you. They want you happy."

Again, Emerson seemed not to have heard him. He picked up Rusty's letter and read it through again. "She says that they'll call at seven," he said. "Another hour to wait."

"You could wait lying down," said Ginger. "Come on, Daddy, please."

Eddie said, "They'll call and set up a *treff*, and you'll be back with Rusty before you know it."

"And then homeward bound," Emerson said bitterly.

Ginger rubbed the back of her father's neck. "Daddy, you should rest."

Emerson gave her a faint smile. "I don't see how putting my feet up will help the situation, but if it makes you happy . . ."

He rose, and with his arm around her shoulders they walked to the bedroom door. Eddie started to follow them, but again Ginger gave him a warning look, and he stopped.

"I'll just turn down the bed for you," she said, and the door closed behind them.

Eddie went to the bar, added a splash of vodka to his glass, and built a scotch on the rocks for Vasily. "What do you think?" he asked, handing the drink to the Russian.

Vasily shrugged. "End of the game. Check and mate."

"I meant Jimbo. That thousand-yard stare."

"Yes, I saw it. I don't like that, either."

"I saw it a couple of times in my outfit, down in Williamsburg. That's the way they look when they can't handle it anymore, when they're about to go kill-crazy. It's showing in his eyes."

"Take it easy," Vasily said. "It's almost over."

Ginger was in the bedroom with her father for fifteen minutes. When she came out, quietly closing the door behind her, Eddie said, "What the hell was that all about? Since when do you have to turn down the bed for him?"

"Make me one of those, would you?" She pointed at his glass. "I wanted to be alone with him for a while. Eddie, he scares me. He's like a different person."

Eddie looked at Vasily swiftly but said nothing. Ginger took the glass from his hand, sipped, and then leaned against him, the top of her head against his cheek. "He's lying in there," she said, "staring at the ceiling and talking. Not really talking, sort of mumbling. I couldn't understand half of what he was saying." She pulled away to look at him. "Has he told you what happened when he went after Andriakis?"

"Only that he took him out. He wouldn't say any more than that."

"From what he's saying now, it was a lot more than that. Someone else seems to have been killed, too. It doesn't sound very pretty."

Eddie's lips tightened; he could think of nothing to say. From across the room, Vasily said, "Ginger, let's concentrate on one problem at a time. Right now the job is to make sure that your mother is safe. After that, we can worry about your father."

"But he's acting so strangely."

"He'll come out of it. He did what he had to do and now he's feeling it, that's all. It won't last long."

He did not sound at all convincing, and Ginger looked to Eddie for confirmation. Eddie nodded. "He's right—it's a natural reaction, that's all." He did not try to explain why the same reaction had not hit any of them.

They settled down to wait then, and they waited for almost an hour, Eddie and Vasily drinking steadily and Ginger just sipping. It was three minutes after seven when the telephone rang. Eddie made a move for it, but Ginger stopped him. "Let him take it in the bedroom," she said.

The ringing stopped as Emerson picked up the phone. They waited again, and a few minutes later he came out of the bedroom, the lines around his lips deeper than before. Ginger jumped up as he came in.

"First of all, your mother is all right," he said to her. His voice was fuller than before, and he seemed more in control of himself. "I couldn't speak to her, but this man Sasha says that she hasn't been harmed and that she won't be harmed . . . as long as I do as I'm told."

Ginger sank back in her seat and nodded gratefully.

"Did he give you instructions?" Eddie asked.

Emerson was about to answer when Vasily held up his hand. "If he gave you instructions he probably told you not to repeat them to anybody. Isn't that correct?"

"Yes—"

"In that case, I don't wish to hear them."

"What the hell's eating you?" Eddie asked sharply.

"I no longer care to be involved," said Vasily, "in anything that isn't my business and over which I no longer have any control."

Eddie looked at him with anger. "If you don't want to listen, stick your goddamn fingers in your ears. Go ahead, Jimbo."

Vasily frowned, said nothing more; but he turned his back.

"They're in Point Balboa, California," Emerson said. His eyes once again seemed glazed, unseeing. "He gave me directions to the Reynolds house on Scotsman's Bay. I'm to be there by tomorrow night. Alone."

"This Sasha," Eddie said, "has a flair for the dramatic. What the hell's behind it?"

"I don't know. He said that he thought it would be the perfect place for me to end my American odyssey. Those were the words he used. He may be right. I once had that idea myself . . . but under different circumstances."

A wave of weariness swept over him. Suddenly too tired to talk straight or think straight, he closed his eyes and in a flick of time went tumbling back to the barn in Albania with that tickle of straw beneath his neck and the honest smell of horses, horse piss on straw, and the mustiness of moldering leather in his nose. And then knew that the smells were right but the barn was wrong; it was a German barn so long ago in the last days of the war when he sat behind a wooden stall and listened to the thrashing sounds of love on straw, and in the aftermath of passion heard the reedy voice of an eighteen-year-old reciting the brief, pathetic, and soon-to-cease story of his life. The story that had formed the core of the American odyssey of James Emerson, the story that he knew so well and which now unrolled itself across his mind like Bible verses well recalled.

 . . . all kinds of things we used to do together, Chub and me. There's always good fishing in Scotsman's Bay, and crabbing, too, if you know how to look for them. Sometimes we'd get a couple of dozen out of the bay, take home half, and sell the rest for a nickel a crab. Old Mr. Reynolds always used to take a dozen from us, has that little old house on top of the cliff up over the bay, so Chub and me would stow those crabs in gunnysacks and go climbing up to the Reynolds house, right up that cliff. Could have taken the stairs, of course, but it wasn't any fun that way. There's this crazy zigzag staircase Mr. Reynolds built right down the side of the cliff. It's the only way to get down to the beach from his house unless you're good at climbing cliffs, which is what we used to do. Wasn't much of a climb 'cause it wasn't much of a cliff, just a real sharp slope with plenty of bushes and vines to grab hold of, and halfway up there's a sort of a cave where we could rest. Yep, that was our secret cave. We used to climb halfway up and sit there for a *while where no one could see us, just looking out over the water. . . .*

He opened his eyes and realized that the others were staring at him, concerned. He smiled faintly to reassure them. "Just memories. The old Reynolds house on Scotsman's Bay. I've never seen it, but I know that house. Smack on the water, a secluded bay no bigger than a cove. Does that suggest anything to either of you?"

Eddie cocked an eyebrow at Vasily. "Submarine?"

Vasily looked away.

"That's my thought, too," said Emerson. "They can't take me out through any public transport, so maybe the choice of Point Balboa is more than just dramatics. A sub would make sense."

Vasily was shaking his head unhappily again. "I don't want to hear any more of this. When are you leaving?"

"Tonight. As soon as I can."

"Alone?" Eddie asked the question, then threw back his drink and went to the bar to make another. He turned and looked at Emerson over the rim of his glass, and repeated, "Alone?"

"That depends on you people. I have a course of action to propose."

"That's what I thought," Vasily said. He put down his glass and stood in front of Emerson. "I don't know what you have in mind, but it has to be something unintelligent. Your options have run out, don't you understand that? For God's sake, man, do as they say! Get your wife—go back to Mother Russia—live the Soviet equivalent of happily-ever-after. There's nothing else you can do . . . unless you want to abandon the woman whom you obviously care for more than anyone else in this world. I'm not a sentimental man. But you are. Now, my dear fellow, you have to pay the price."

"I think there is something else I can do," Emerson said quietly.

With a touch of impatience, Vasily turned on Eddie. "Are you really going to get involved in this?"

"I'm going to listen to what the man has to say."

"Then you're as insane as he is. We just took on the CIA and barely got away with it. Are you going to start throwing rocks at the KGB, too?"

"It won't be the first time."

"Quite so, but this time you'll be doing it without me. This is turning into a family affair, and it's not my family." He turned and walked out the door. Eddie ran after him and caught him in the corridor near the elevators.

"What the hell do you think you're doing?" he said angrily.

"Saving my valuable skin. I suggest you do the same with yours. I don't know what happened to that man back in Albania, but he's turned into a suicidal fire-eater. I won't work with people like that. The risk is hardly worth the satisfaction."

"He wants his wife back. You said so yourself—he loves her."

"He can have her back and live in peace for the rest of his life. All he has to do is go home and be a hero. But no, he'd rather go up there, wherever it is, and snatch her away from the KGB. That's self-destructive, and I won't have any part of it."

The elevator door opened, and Vasily stepped in. Eddie said, "Where are you going?"

"Remember Benny Zahn in Bogotá? He'll know where I am. If you get out of this idiocy alive, look me up." The elevator doors closed.

Eddie went back to the Emersons' suite where Jimbo and Ginger were sitting just as he had left them. He sighed, sat down, and said, "All right, let's hear it."

The house was ten miles north of Point Balboa, overlooking the sea, an old house that had lasted past its time. It had a brick foundation, but the rest of it was made of clapboard weathered by sun, wind, and salt. Small and without pretense, it was furnished with the kind of wickerwork and spare rugs, outsize vases and improbable tapestries that most people save either for garage sales or summer homes. Everything was old about the place, the only new item being the transceiver that Sasha had set up in the living room. There were bedrooms on the second floor for Sasha and the two embassy men, and on the first floor a cramped but secluded room for Rusty. What saved the house from total tackiness was its cliff-hanging perch above Scotsman's Bay and a sweeping view of the ocean. A rickety wooden staircase zigzagged down the face of the cliff for over a hundred feet, leading to the crescent-shaped beach that rimmed the bay below.

Rusty stood at the edge of the cliff near the top of the wooden staircase, staring out to sea and into the setting sun. The air was warm, but she shivered in the slight breeze blowing in off the bay. Somewhere out in that sea an E-class Soviet nuclear submarine was running submerged on a course set dead for Scotsman's Bay, and tomorrow night a launch from the sub would creep into the bay in the secret hours after midnight, pick up two passengers, and return. After that would come the trans-Pacific haul to Vladivostok, and then the supersonic flight to Moscow. The arrival of the launch would mark the successful end of her mission. She was very much aware that it could also mark the end of her marriage. She shivered again at the thought.

Sasha's voice behind her said, "They tell me that sometimes you can see the whales offshore. Frankly, I don't see the attraction, but people come for miles. I've just spoken to your husband."

She wheeled around at the sound of his voice. "Is he coming?"

"He's agreed to everything. He'll be here tomorrow, and you'll leave tomorrow night. I'll make contact with the sub this evening."

"I see," she said softly. "Not that I'm surprised. He wouldn't have done anything else. How did he sound?"

"Concerned about you. I assured him that you were unharmed. The important thing is that he's coming."

"So you've won, Sasha, after all."

"We," he said pointedly. "We have won."

"Yes, I suppose so. But I've lost, too. I won't have much of a marriage after tomorrow."

Sasha looked away, unwilling to meet her eyes. He muttered, "Perhaps it won't work that way."

"Of course it will." Her voice was sharp. "How would you feel if you found out that the woman you loved had been lying to you for more than twenty years?"

"Not very happy about it," he admitted.

"So my marriage becomes a casualty of war," she said, still staring out to sea. "I knew it would happen. I knew it as soon as I was activated. Unfortunately, knowing doesn't make it any easier."

"Once he's back home," he said hopefully, "once he's had a chance to adjust to a different way of life, once he becomes a Russian again . . ." His voice dropped off and he finished lamely, "Maybe then he'll be able to see your side of it."

"You don't know Jim."

"I know *about* him. He's a soldier, and you were following orders. That's something he should be able to understand."

"Possibly. I'm hoping that Petrovich will be able to make him see it that way."

"The colonel can be very persuasive," Sasha said cautiously.

"And the other two, Kolodny and Radichek, his old comrades on board to welcome him home. Once they talk to him, remind him of the old days . . . it might help, Sasha, don't you think?"

"It might," he said, keeping his voice neutral, but at the same time thinking: Christ, how naive can she be? She doesn't have the faintest idea of what her man is in for once he sets foot on that sub. First the soft persuasion, then the hard, and then, if they have to, the drugs. She makes it sound like a reunion of old soldiers sitting around the campfire and trading war stories.

"It might help," he repeated, then added slowly, "I admit that I don't know much about marriage, but from what you've told me yours is one of the good ones. It seems to me that a marriage as good as yours should be able to survive any kind of shock, even one as heavy as this."

"Do you really think so?" For the first time she gave him a faint, hesitant smile. "Oh God, I hope you're right."

"I think it's very possible." He was forcing confidence into his voice. "Look, it's going to be a hell of a blow to him, and it's going to take a very unusual man to absorb that blow, but from what I understand, that's exactly what your husband is. A very unusual man."

Her smile broadened. Impulsively, she put her arm through his. "I know that you're just trying to be kind, but you're saying all the right things. You're good for me, Sasha. I'm glad it's you I'm here with."

"All part of the service," he said airily. "Always try to look on the bright side of things, I say. For instance, you're going home. That's something *you* want, isn't it?"

She sighed. "More than I can tell you. I've had to listen to an awful lot of bad jokes about the motherland these past weeks. Herring and black bread, lumpy shoes, that sort of thing. That's Jim's sense of humor, but isn't mine. I don't care how lumpy the shoes are—I'm going home."

"They really aren't lumpy at all . . . at least not the ones that you'll be buying."

"It's going to be so strange. I'll have to learn Russian all over again."

"One never forgets."

"I know, but look at the two of us. We're both Russian, but we've been speaking only English."

He shrugged. "It's easier that way. Always drink the wine of the country."

"Still, back home I'd know your patronymic by now."

"No, you wouldn't. I don't have one."

"I don't understand. Every Russian has a patronymic."

"Not if he doesn't know his father's name," he said casually.

"Oh, I'm sorry." Confused and embarrassed, she took her hand from his arm. He laughed and tucked it back in again.

"Call me Aleksander Yuriovich," he told her. "It's as good a name as any."

"Aleksander, son of Yuri. Your father had the same name as my husband." She felt she had to comment, if only to acknowledge that she was no longer embarrassed by the revelation of his bastardy.

"Yuri is a common enough name," Sasha muttered.

"Do you know if he's still alive?"

"I'll find out soon," he said.

"Soon . . . ?"

"Yes. A little sooner than any of us might care for."

They looked at each other silently for a while, then turned to walk back to the house, their eyes on the ground, their feet scuffing dirt. Behind them the sun bounced brass off the sea, sinking lower. The silence continued until Rusty looked up.

"Sasha, are you saying what I think . . . ?"

He stopped and swung her around so that they were facing each other. "Are you sure you want to know the answer to that?"

She nodded slowly, her eyes wide.

"Don't look so grim," he said and gave her the smile that he had used all his life to smooth his way. "All I'm saying is that it's entirely possible that your husband is my father."

"I'm afraid . . . I don't understand."

"It's really quite simple," he said and told her the story. The telling took only a few minutes, and then he asked, "Does it bother you, knowing about my mother? It was long before he met you."

"Of course not." She shook her head impatiently. "Does Jim know? About you?"

"No, and I don't want him to. Not yet. Someday, perhaps, but not now." He smiled again. "Besides, there's no way of really knowing, is there? My father might well have been the real Emerson."

She reached out to touch his cheek with the tips of her fingers, and her eyes were sad again. "How strange this all is. It was strange enough to start with, but now it's getting to be a family affair. Your mother must be a remarkable woman."

"My mother is a—" He laughed and stopped himself. "Yes. A remarkable woman."

Rusty missed the overtones in his comment; she was thinking of something else. After a moment she said, "That means that you and Ginger are half . . ."

"Only possibly," Sasha interrupted.

Rusty shook her head. "No. Looking at you now, and knowing . . . You're his, I'm sure of it. Back in Virginia, when you were hurt, Eddie Mancuso said that we couldn't afford to leave you alive. But Ginger wouldn't let him kill you. She saved your life. She must have felt something.'' She saw him shake his head doubtfully. ''Don't you think it's possible?''

''I don't believe in things like that.''

''I do. She must have felt it deep inside, that you were her brother.''

''Half. If that.''

''Still, I believe it.''

He laughed. ''Because you want to. It's a very Russian way to think. We're all of us determined to forge our own destinies. Life rarely permits that.''

They went into the house.

IV

Operation Seafire

Chapter 20

There are a dozen ways to destroy a man. Killing is only one of them, and a generous one at that. There are other forms of destruction much crueler. You can shatter a man with terror, robbing him of his manhood. You can strip him of ideals and leave him naked in the wilderness. You can stake him out and lift up the rocks of his life to show him what crawls underneath. And at the very end, if all else fails, you can always betray him with the instrument he treasures most, usually the woman he loves. Compared to these more subtle forms of destruction, a bullet in the brain is a blessing.

Rusty Emerson destroyed her man in all these ways, using a string of words spoken softly and sadly. In the weary hours just after midnight she sat in the cramped living room of the house above Scotsman's Bay and poured out the story of twenty-five years of deception. She gave him all the details, leaving out nothing, not trying to spare herself. She started with her orders years before to meet him and marry him; carried the tale down through the decades of their marriage; and finished with the submarine lying offshore with Petrovich and the others on board, ready to welcome him and carry them both back to the Soviet Union. She told him all this, and by the time she finished he was as close to being gutted as a live man can be. His face was gray and his deep-set eyes were filled with pain. He was close to total destruction, but not quite there yet, for the sanity-saver within him refused, for the moment, to accept what she was saying.

"I don't know how to believe it," he said.

"Darling, I'm afraid you'll have to."

"You?" He could barely manage the word.

"Me."

"Jesus, Rusty, not you."

"Sweetheart, I know it's difficult to accept, but try. I'm a KGB officer, just as you are. I'm under orders to return you to the Soviet Union, and I intend to carry out those orders."

"You . . . a sleeper." The words came wonderingly. "Another sleeper."

"Again, just like you. I didn't want you to know it, not ever, but it's too late for that now."

"And you got me to come here knowing that—" He stopped, struck by a sudden hope. "They forced you to write that note. They made you do it, didn't they?"

She refused the offer. "Nobody forced me to do anything. It was the only way to get you here. I did what I had to do." She looked away from him. "I hope that someday you'll understand that. And forgive me."

"Then all these years . . . ?"

"All these years," she repeated, but her voice was pleading now, "I have been exactly what you are—a sleeping spy. But all these years I've also been the woman who loves you. And I still do. You have to believe that, Jim."

"I don't know what to believe anymore." He shook his head dumbly. "I don't know how to believe any of this."

But as he said the words, he had already begun to believe. A man's disbelief is a fragile shield, easily shattered. There is the disbelief in his own mortality that vanishes with the first sharp pain in his chest, the disbelief in the frailty of a friend that crumbles with the first betrayal, the disbelief in the chaos of life that is whisked away when the fist of random chance first raps him rudely in the ribs. *I don't believe it,* he says, but he does. Deep down in the primeval place where everything human is known to be possible, there is room for belief; and as Emerson stared across the room at his wife he began to believe. It happened quickly. The shield of his disbelief shattered; he believed it all, and in that moment his destruction was complete. The light went out of his eyes like a campfire quenched by a sudden storm.

All right, that's it, he thought. *That's it, that's it, that's it.* End of the road, nothing more after this, and keep on going . . . where? Does it make any difference? Down those rickety stairs, I guess, down to the beach and whatever happens . . . happens. Whichever way it goes, I don't much care anymore. If I could call it off now I would, but I can't. No way in the world I can stop Eddie from making his move, and so more people are going to get hurt. More blood. I've been wading in blood ever since this began, starting with that poor homesick kid who had to die so that Andrei Petrovich could have his sleeping spy . . . and ending with Lex Enhora. Too much blood, or maybe not enough. Maybe once it starts, it takes an ocean of blood to wash things clean. Maybe that's what it takes, and maybe that's what I'll get, but either way I don't give a damn anymore.

Rusty said hesitantly, "Jim . . ."

He shook his head. "Don't bother. No matter what you say, it doesn't mean anything now."

She turned to Sasha, seated at a small blond-wood desk in a corner of the room. On either side of him, lounging against the walls, stood the two embassy guards, the pistols in their hands dangling casually. In the same pleading voice, she asked, "Could Jim and I have a few minutes alone? Is that possible, Sasha?"

"I'm afraid not." Sasha stood up, and the two guards shifted position slightly to keep him clear of any line of fire. He looked at his watch. "We leave for the beach in twenty minutes. Until then, everybody stays in place."

"Please, Sasha, there are things I have to tell him."

"Can't be done, love, that's the drill. You'll have plenty of time to talk once you're at sea."

Rusty accepted it. She leaned forward, staring across the room at her husband. Her eyes met his but could not hold them; his vacant gaze slid off into space. In a low, urgent voice she said, "Jim, listen to me. This isn't something I want to talk about in front of people, but I have no choice. I have to say this now, and so I'm going to pretend that no one is listening, that we're alone. Because before we go down those steps to the beach, before we get on that boat, you have to believe me when

I tell you that no matter what else I did, I never stopped loving you.''

She paused, hoping for a response. But Emerson sat slumped in his chair, uncaring. Her words came down on his head like raindrops on the surface of a pond. Sasha grimaced and said, ''Rusty, enough. This is embarrassing.''

She ignored him and went on. ''Do you hear what I'm saying, Jim? The love was always there. I did what I did because of the love, because it was right for you. And for me. It was right for us and for our country, and one day you'll know that and you'll thank me for it. Not now, I don't expect that now. You're hurt and betrayed now, and that's my fault, too . . . but that was the duty part of it. I had my job to do, but my job had nothing to do with my love. The love was always real. You believe that, don't you?''

He was silent.

''We're talking about twenty-five years of loving now. Do you think I was faking it all that time?''

It was as if he had not heard her.

''Do you think that every time I kissed you, every time we made love—I was doing it under orders?''

His head was down and he was staring at the floor.

''The baby we made, the child we raised . . . do you think I did that because somebody told me to?''

His head still down, he crossed his arms over his chest and hugged his shoulders as if he were cold.

''Is that what you think?''

He started to shake his head, then stopped.

''Answer me,'' she said fiercely. Leaning forward in her chair, every line of her body was tense. ''Is that what you think? Is that the kind of bitch I am? Is that the kind of whore you married?''

She stopped abruptly, breathing heavily. For a moment she looked as if she were going to cry, but she held the tears in, the tips of them glistening on her lashes. Sasha stirred uncomfortably and turned away.

Emerson raised his head, and for the first time his eyes met hers. "Don't cry," he said gruffly. "For Christ's sake, whatever you do, don't cry."

"I won't."

"You know how it pains me when you cry."

"I know."

"Then don't do it."

"I won't. I promise."

"You always promise, but you do it anyway."

"This time I won't. Really."

She sat back in her seat, her eyes on his, and made sure that she did not cry.

"Ten minutes to go," said Sasha, looking at his wrist. He perched himself on the edge of the desk, watching the two Emersons carefully. Oh Lordy, but she's good, he thought. She's going to turn him around; she's going to make it work. First she took him apart, and now she's going to put him back together again. Not right away, not today or tomorrow, but sometime between here and Vladivostok she's going to have him licking her fingers again. Yes, she's good, all right, so good that she almost had me crying there myself. It was either that or throw up. Or is Sasha being his silly old cynical self again? Maybe so, but that lady is one high-class, machine-tooled piece of work. Not taking anything away from her—she's the key to the whole operation—but she sure knows how to handle a man. I thought I was immune to that particular brand of horseshit, but she even had me going for a while, yesterday out in back of the house and that time in the car when she told me about her romantic girlhood and how she didn't want to take the American assignment. She's so good that you have to believe her at first, but then you begin to think. Postwar Russia with everything in ruins and people dropping like flies from typhus and starvation, and what young girl wouldn't have sold her soul to get out of there? But not our Rusty; she didn't want an assignment to the land of the hamburgers and the nylons. What kind of a twit does she think I am to swallow that crap, or does she really believe it now? Could be. Time, the great editor. But whether she wanted the assignment or not, she got it and she did well with it. Parlayed it into a good marriage, a soft life, and now she's heading home with his scalp in her belt. The most important defector since Philby. She devoted herself to a lifetime of deceit, and the man she deceived still adores her. Look at him sitting there. She just ripped his guts out, and all he can do is ask her not to cry. I'm beginning to wonder if he's my dear old daddy after all if he can be such a sucker.

Not that it matters anymore. If he is or if he isn't. Spent too much of my time worrying about that, too much of my life wondering what it would be like to have a father, grow up holding someone's hand. There weren't all that many hands available when I was growing up. Half the kids I knew had no fathers in the house, but theirs were buried in Poland and the Ukraine, while mine was on assignment in the land of soap and sunshine. So what? Comes a time when you have to shove all that behind you. There's no need for it anymore. The game is over and, Lordy, it was close. Sweet Sasha's nookie was really on the line this time, but we made it, thanks to Rusty. In the homestretch now; just get them on board and the job is done. Petrovich has his triumph, and Sasha's stock goes up again. Just walk through it nice and slow; don't screw things up at the very end. The boat should hit the beach just before three, so we start from here at two thirty sharp. Out the back and down the steps, Anatoly first, then Emerson, then me, then Rusty, and with Marko in the rear. Straight down to the beach, guide the launch in and load them aboard. Wave bye-bye, and there they go, the colonel and his lady, homeward bound.

And there goes my old man, out of my life again. Well, so what? I found him, I met him, and that's enough. He's a pretty nice guy. A little slow, maybe, and a little innocent, but a decent person. If he really is my father . . . I'm not unhappy about it. And if he isn't . . . again, so what? It doesn't mean anything now. Right now, for me, he's a body I have to deliver, that's all. He's Colonel Yuri Volanov, and he's got a date on that beach at exactly three o'clock.

Eddie and Ginger came in over the spur of land to the south of Scotsman's Bay, a rough and hilly piece of ground that rose up to a hogback ridge and then dropped away sharply to the water. It was a long and messy hike in the darkness, stumbling over unfamiliar terrain, through scrubby stands of second-growth timber and bramble patches, and sliding over loose-packed shale. They traveled light, a knapsack apiece, but still they were hot and breathing hard by the time they crested the ridge and worked their way down to the beach below. They got there just before midnight, a dark night of stars with the moon still down. Off to the right, on top of the cliff, the glow of the Reynolds house was the only light for miles. Below the house the zigzag staircase showed only as a faint white cross-hatch of lines against the dark face of the cliff. They trudged down the beach hugging the base of the cliff until they were close to the foot of the staircase, and then unslung their packs and sat down to rest. The quiet was as intense as the darkness, and all they could hear was the lapping of waves on the sand. After a moment they reslung their packs and started up the slope, moving silently on rubber-soled shoes, Eddie first and Ginger following, her hands in his footholds. They did not speak. They had worked out the procedure hours before, based on what Emerson had remembered about the bay, the cliff, and the house. They knew what they were looking for, but it took them a long time to find it. The cave was where it was supposed to have been, about halfway up and to the right of the staircase, but the entrance had been overgrown with brush and vines.

They found it almost accidentally, Ginger stumbling against the matted growth, feeling it give under her and catching herself before she could fall in. She hung there, clutching, and clicked her tongue twice. Ten feet away, Eddie looked up and then made his way across the face of the slope to her. She pointed. He nodded and went to work parting the vines and silently clearing away a section of the brush. He peered in and risked a quick shot with the pencil torch shielded from above by the overhang. The cave was narrow, but it went back about twenty feet, a slash of fissured limestone in the slope. He rolled up and over the edge of it and beckoned for Ginger to follow.

Once inside, he put his head close to hers and said softly, "We can talk in here if we keep it low. Let's get it set up."

He placed the torch on the ground and adjusted it to throw a low-powered glow, then he rolled over on his side and opened one of the knapsacks. He took out what looked like two large fountain pens, an assortment of wooden pegs, a coil of wire, heavy tape, and a wire cutter. Ginger looked around the cave. The ceiling was of clear stone, but the dirt floor was strewn with an assortment of rubbish and animal droppings.

"It stinks in here," she whispered.

He looked up from sorting his equipment. "Get used to it. If they don't go tonight, we stay here until they do."

"It smells like goats."

"What do you know about goats?" he asked as he worked a loop into the end of the wire.

"I had one as a pet when I was little," she said defensively.

"No kidding? When I was little, we ate goat for Easter. Here, hold this."

He handed her the looped end of wire and ran the coil around his wrist. He stuffed the rest of the equipment into his pockets and crawled to the lip of the cave. "Just hold on tight to that," he told her. "This will only take a few minutes."

Outside the cave, he pressed himself into the face of the slope and edged across it to the staircase twenty feet away, paying out wire as he went. The stairs were set on wooden piles driven into the earth, each length of riser supported by six of the piles. At the point where the stairs doubled back across the cliff, extra piles supported the landing. He chose the landing that was as close as possible to a horizontal plane with the mouth of the cave and crawled underneath it, barely clearing the latticework of slats around the piles. Working quickly, he taped one of the fountain pens high up on the piling where it joined the under-side of the landing. He ran the end of the wire through the trigger rings of both pens, doubled it back on itself, tied it off, and snipped it. Then he worked the wooden wedges between the pens and the surface, securing them there. With the safety pins still locked, he tugged cautiously at the wire; the pens held in place. Breathing deeply and easily, he slid out each of the safety pins and dropped them in his pocket. Then he made his way back to the cave, following the wire and making sure that it lay slack along the ground.

Back inside, he lay flat on the ground at the mouth of the cave and made sure that the wire ran freely through the underbrush. He peered outside. There was no sign of the wire along the ground, no telltale glint. He grunted with satisfaction and called Ginger up beside him. He placed the loop of wire in her hand.

"Now tell me what you're going to do," he said.

"I wait until I hear them coming down the steps. I wait until I can see them. I wait until the first man is on the landing—"

"Not on the landing, just before it. Look, they'll be coming down single file, and the odds are that the first man will be one of theirs. But we can't take the chance. They may have your father out in front."

"Sorry. All right, just before he steps onto the landing. Then I blow it. I haul back hard on the wire. I don't tug at it and I don't twitch it. I lean back and haul for all I'm worth."

"Right. Remember, we're not trying to kill anybody with the explosion, not with your folks there. I want to freeze them on the staircase, immobilize them. Those pens are loaded with low-kick juice—all they'll do is snap the supports and drop the landing. That's all the edge I want. Whoever is on those stairs won't be able to go down, and they won't go up either. I'll be above them."

"Where will you be?"

"On the other side of the staircase, above the landing. I'll have them cold from that angle."

He felt her move beside him, heard her hesitant voice. "Eddie, it sounded good before, but now . . . it seems awfully risky. We don't even know how many there are."

"Your father knew the risks when he set this up. It's the way he wants it. You know damn well I wouldn't be doing it all by myself if Vasily hadn't walked out on me, but that's the way it is. All right, what do you do after you pull the wire?"

"I move to the back of the cave and stay there until it's all over," she said in a small, bitter voice. "It was all right to send me into an Italian whorehouse, but you're keeping me out of this."

"I didn't send you. You went by yourself. And don't knock

Italian whorehouses, they're not bad . . . I hear. I hope to hell you learned something there.''

"You pig."

"Look, you admit yourself that you can't handle weapons, and that's all this is. There's nothing cute about it. Either I get them out or I don't, and I don't want to worry about you while I'm doing it. You just do your job and sit tight. All right?''

"All right," she said in an even smaller voice.

He struggled into the straps of the second knapsack and twisted around to kiss her briefly. "Stay awake and eat chocolate. If nothing pops tonight I'll be back in here before dawn, and we'll sit out the day.''

"Luck," she said. He nodded in reply.

He went silently across the slope, past the landing, and began to climb. Fifty feet above the landing and to the right of it he found what he wanted: a rocky projection that was shielded from the staircase by a run of spikey brambles. He eased himself onto the rock in a sitting position, unslung his pack and laid out his weapons. He picked up the HDM flashless, frowned as he weighed it in his hand, then put it back in the pack and took the Safari Special instead. Shit, why not, he thought. There's been enough killing already. Too much. He checked the action on the Safari and inspected the tranquilizer dart loaded into the barrel, carefully avoiding the gummy substance layered onto the tip. The dart was loaded with enough narcotic to put a hippo to sleep for an hour. Satisfied, he took a chocolate bar from the pack, bit off a chunk of it, and settled down to wait. He did not wait easily, relaxed and ready for action. There had been other times when he had been forced to wait this way and he had always been able to blank out his mind in total concentration. But not this time. There were too many things that could go wrong. He knew what they were, and they frightened him.

At least the kid is safe, he thought, if she stays put in that hole. She's got the Walther if anybody stumbles in there and she knows enough to use it if she has to. So she'll be all right. All she has to do is pull the wire and I make my move. *Tick*, *tock*, just like that. And then another *tick*. No more than that. Please God, no more than that. If I'm fast and if I'm good I can handle three. Fast, good and lucky. But if there are any more than three I'm fucked. Christ, for all I know they could have an army, and what do I do then? Punt, I guess, and let's take it easy, keep it in perspective. There isn't any army up there in that house. Not for a job like this. Two or three, the most. But please, not four. If that son of a bitch hadn't run out on me I wouldn't care if they had half a dozen. But not now. Not four.

He heard them coming then, heard first the murmur of voices above him, and then their footsteps on the wooden stairs. He cocked his head, trying to count numbers from the sound of the footsteps, but he could not tell. He picked up the Safari, checked the safety and, still in a sitting position, eased himself across the rock until he was directly behind the brambles. Through the gaps in the twisted branches he could see the staircase clearly. They passed in front of him in single file, only fifty feet away. Someone first, then Emerson, someone else, then Rusty, and then a heavy-set bull-necked man bringing up the rear. A total of five.

Three, he thought joyfully, only three.

The single file passed him by, approaching the landing, and then they were below. The three Russians all carried pistols, but they carried them casually at their sides, as if as a matter of form. Emerson kept his eyes on the steps as he moved, his good hand sliding along the railing. Rusty negotiated the steps awkwardly, not using the rail but clutching her purse with both hands. The lead man was three steps from the landing. Eddie raised the Safari and breathed deeply.

Pull it, he said silently. Pull it now.

Ginger pulled it just as the lead man stepped onto the landing, the sharp double *crack* sounding as one. The landing collapsed, tearing a gaping hole in the staircase, and the man went with it, shouting in surprise as he tumbled down the steep incline. He did not tumble far. His head hit an outcropping of rock that laid his scalp open. He flopped over once, and lay still.

As soon as the landing dropped, Eddie shot the rear man in the back of the neck with the Safari Special. The Russian went down in instant narcosis, his feet going out from under him. His body hit the back of Rusty's legs and then jammed in the stairwell.

Rusty gasped and wheeled around, Sasha turning with her. Emerson, only feet away from the gap in the stairs, pivoted on the balls of his feet. His bad left hand smashed down on Sasha's wrist, knocking the pistol free and sending shocking pain from his fingers to his shoulders. Then his good right arm, braced by the left, was around Sasha's neck and choking. Rusty, her face set in hard lines, grabbed at his arm, trying to loosen it. She struggled with him silently as he braced himself and heaved.

"Shit," Eddie muttered. He had no clear shot. The two men were too closely twined, and there was Rusty hanging on for some reason as well. Any shot could easily have hit any one of the three. He shoved the pistol into his pocket and broke out of the cover of brambles, sliding and thrashing his way down the slope toward the staircase.

Emerson strained to increase the pressure on Sasha's neck. The Russian's head came back, his face distorted, his eyes wide. They were sad eyes, and pleading, but his lips were twisted into what might have been a smile.

Rusty pulled frantically at her husband's arm with both her hands, but she could not move him. "Jim, don't do it," she said breathlessly. "You don't know what you're doing."

Sasha's back arched into a bow and his feet kicked futilely. Emerson looked down into those pleading eyes, staring into death. The spark of life was still there, and still on the lips that were trying to form words. A message? A plea? Something said once before in what seemed like a long time ago? Something about a football game? *Paidyom pasmatryet fudbolni match myezhdu kamandami dinama i spartak?* For the moment he was tempted to ease his grip, hear the words, but he felt the strength going out of his arms, felt the muscles going slack. From somewhere above him he heard the scrambling sounds of Eddie sliding down the hill, but the sounds were still far away and he knew that he had to do it himself. He braced himself for a final effort.

"Damn it, let go," said Rusty, her voice a hiss.

Her face was inches away and her eyes were locked on his.

They were hard eyes, and he had never seen them before. Her lips were drawn back over her teeth and he had never kissed those lips. The hands that once had caressed him were tearing at him now, and the body that once had been his oasis was pitted against him. He heaved once more and heard a distinct click as the hyoid bone in Sasha's neck snapped. His head rolled loosely and the spark left his eyes. Emerson released his hold and the body slid down. Rusty stared at it in horror.

"Sweet God, you did it," she breathed. "You killed him."

"He sure as shit did," said Eddie as he came crashing through the brambles, his heels dug in against the pitch of the slope. Standing on the side of the hill above the staircase he was no more than ten feet away from them.

"Three out of three," he said. "Now let's get the hell out of here."

Rusty turned at the sound of his voice. "You son of a bitch, you spoiled it all," she said tightly. "Nobody's going any-place."

Then in one swift motion she bent over, picked up the pistol that Sasha had dropped, and before Emerson could make a move to stop her she pointed it at Eddie and fired.

Ginger, lying on her belly at the mouth of the cave, saw the landing collapse when she pulled the wire. She saw the lead man tumble down the slope and she saw the rear man fall from Eddie's shot. She saw her father struggle with Sasha, and at that point she shot out of the mouth of the cave, scrambling across the slope with the brambles whipping at her ankles as she ran to join her parents. She ran leaning into the tilt of the hill, placing one foot higher than the other, and she saw Eddie come crashing out of his cover, half sliding, half crawling downhill. She saw Sasha die, saw the body slide from her father's arms and saw the grin on Eddie's face as he slid to a stop above the staircase. Then something jolted her under the heart as she saw her mother bend over, come up with a pistol and fire it directly at Eddie. He sat down as if he had slipped, punched back by the force of the bullet and clutching his shoulder. He stared at

Rusty accusingly, as if she had just pulled a tasteless practical joke. Her hand came up for a second, final shot.

"No!"

Ginger heard herself scream, and in that flick of time knew that something was terribly wrong if her mother was shooting at Eddie, something so wrong that the world was out of whack; but there was Eddie helpless on the ground and then her own hand was moving, the Walther in it, swinging up. Even as it swung she knew that she could never pull the trigger but her hand was moving just the same, leveling and sighting it in on her mother, and she knew that it had to be done but she never could do it, never and had to, and she never did find out if she ever could have pulled that trigger. She never had to. Somebody did it for her as Vasily stood up in the long grass under the staircase, leveled a shotgun at Rusty, and pulled the trigger.

"Last I heard you were on your way to Bogotá." Eddie lay on his side in the grass, propped up on one elbow, as Vasily worked on his shoulder.

"That's right, I was."

"Going to work with Benny Zahn."

"Uh-huh. Stay still while I do this."

"Didn't want part of a suicide mission."

"Still don't."

"Then why the hell did you deal yourself back in? You said it was a family affair."

Vasily tied off the make-shift dressing and sat back on his heels to admire his work. The flesh wound was bandaged neatly and the bleeding had stopped.

"Maybe that's why," he said slowly. "You're a stubborn son of a bitch and you drive me crazy at times, but when you get right down to it you're the only family I've got."

Eddie grunted and sat up. He felt a rush of dizziness that steadied and passed as he looked around. The night was unchanging, still and dark. Rusty lay where she had fallen from the staircase; Emerson and Ginger knelt next to her. They had covered the lower part of her body with a coat taken from one of the Russians. She was speaking, and Emerson's head was close to her lips. Ginger looked up, and when she saw Eddie sitting she came over to kneel beside him. Her face was tearstained, but dry. Her tears had come in one flash flood, and now they were gone.

Eddie asked, "Is she still. . . ?"

"Just barely. She can't last much longer." She looked at Vasily, who turned away from her gaze. She put her hand on his arm and said, "No, it's not going to be that way. You saved his life and that's all I'm going to remember."

Vasily's somber voice was low in the night. "You understand that I had no choice?"

"I told you, I understand."

Eddie winced as he shifted position. "She was one of them, wasn't she?"

"All the time," said Ginger bitterly. "All her life, just like my father. She told him up there in the house."

"The second sleeper. An insurance policy for Moscow Center." Eddie whistled tunelessly between his teeth. "Go back to her. No matter what else she is, she's still your mother."

"No, I'll stay here."

"You should be with her."

"You don't understand—they want to be alone. It's as if I don't know either of them anymore. They're speaking Russian together."

The Russian that they spoke was slow and halting, neither of them at ease in the language anymore, but both of them determined to use it now that they had it together. Rusty's eyes were glazed, but she was past pain and though her words came slowly, they were clear.

She was saying, "All those things I said up there . . . they were true, every word."

"I know that."

"The duty had nothing to do with the love."

"I know that too."

"Yes, now you know, but it doesn't matter anymore. Everything's wasted."

"Not wasted," he said. "Not all those years."

"Yes, wasted. All the dreams and secrets we could have

shared in our own language. All the words of love we could have said without translation. That was the waste. I never said 'I love you' in my mother's tongue.''

"Yes. And I never knew your name. I still don't.''

She tried to smile but it did not work. "How strange to think that. My name is Olga Aleksandrovna Kuznishev.''

"So.'' He murmured the name to himself. "I love you, Olga Aleksandrovna. I always have, and nothing will change that.''

"Even after this?''

"Even so.''

"Then it wasn't wasted, none of it was.''

"No.''

She reached a hand to touch his cheek, but her strength was gone and she could not make it. "I wanted to go home. Do you understand that? No, you don't. You were always at home here and I never was.''

"And I never knew it.''

"That's all it was; I just wanted to go home. With you.''

Her voice was faint now, and he bent close to hear the words. ". . . back to Orel in the summer . . . flowers in the meadows now . . . on the banks along the Oka . . . but we never . . .''

"Never what?'' When she did not answer, he said in English, "Never what, Rusty?''

"Never got there,'' she murmured, and then she was gone. He closed her eyes gently and kissed her. He rose, came over to his daughter and took her hand.

"That's it,'' he said, and Ginger nodded. Vasily moved away from the group, separated but still a part of it. They stayed that way, silently, until Eddie said, "There it is, I can hear it.''

They all heard it then, the faint *putt-putting*, and their eyes went down to the entrance of the bay. It loomed there as a darker part of the darkness, the thin silhouette of the launch nosing round the southern arm of the crescent and making for the beach.

"Time to get moving,'' said Eddie. "They'll probably just turn around and go back when nobody meets them, but I'd just as soon not be here. Let's go.''

"Somebody will meet them," said Emerson. The lines that had marked his face for days were gone, and he was smiling faintly. "You three get going. I'm heading in a different direction."

Alarmed, Ginger got to her feet. "What do you mean? Where are you going?"

"I'm taking your mother home."

She started to protest, but he stopped her. "It's too late in the game for arguments," he said gently. "You're going one way and I'm going another, that's all. That was bound to happen eventually. It always does with parents and children. Go with Eddie and stay with him. It's an insane world that you're living in and he's one of the few who knows how to cope with it."

He fondled the back of her neck, and then rubbed it briskly with his knuckles the way he would do it to a child or a pet. He turned to Eddie, and said, "I want a minute with you alone."

He put out a hand and helped Eddie to his feet. They moved away from the others, and Emerson said softly, "I want a favor from you."

"No."

"I want some RDX."

"Yeah, I thought that's what you had in mind. No way."

"I'll say the same thing to you that I said to Ginger. It's too late for that kind of talk." His voice was suddenly angry. "For God's sake, Eddie, what kind of a life have I got left? I'm finished wherever I go, and Rusty's gone. She was gone a long time ago, but I didn't know it."

Eddie rubbed his eyes wearily. "You're talking about taking out a Russian sub with a hundred young sailors on board. What the hell did they ever do to you?"

Emerson did not answer. He was staring at the launch coming into the bay. After a moment, he said, "Not the sub, Eddie, just the launch. Petrovich is on that boat, I'll bet on it. Radichek and Kolodny too. The welcoming committee, they wouldn't miss it for the world. This is the high point of their careers. They're on that launch, I'm sure of it."

"And so are maybe half a dozen sailors."

Emerson conceded the point with a shrug.

"Does six make it any better than a hundred?" Eddie asked. Emerson was silent.

"What if there was only one sailor on board? A bosun to steer, and three evil old men. Would that make it any better?"

Emerson still did not answer. He was thinking about two barns, one in Germany so many years ago and one in Albania just a few days past. Barns and blood, the cold and casual murder of the real James Emerson and the blood that had been spilled on a wedding-feast floor. He wanted to tell Eddie about those two barns and how they had twisted and reshaped his life, but there was little time and he could not find the words. Instead, he said, "I have a debt to pay, and this is the only way I can do it."

"Maybe so," said Eddie, "but it's your debt, not mine. I won't help you."

Vasily rose from the grass and came over to them leaving Ginger sitting alone on the hill, her head down and her arms around her knees. He asked Eddie, "What is it? What does he want?"

Eddie told him, and Vasily smiled coldly. "It was predictable. He's more Russian than he thinks he is. He has that Slavic tilt toward self-destruction. Did you give him the stuff?"

Eddie shook his head firmly. "I don't want any part of it. I've got no feud with the Russian Navy."

"Yes, you always were the moralist on this team. It's a luxury I've never been able to afford." He reached into his pocket and came out with a plastic bag filled with a ball of the grayish, putty-like RDX explosive. From another pocket he took a detonator and slipped it into the bag.

Eddie stared at him in disbelief. "You're giving it to him?"

"He has a right to roll his own dice," said Vasily, and his voice took on an edge. "Stay out of this, Eddie. This is just between us Slavs."

He handed the package to Emerson who shoved it into his pocket. Eddie scowled, and looked away unhappily. Emerson put a hand on his shoulder and, mistaking the scowl for sadness, said, "Don't look so unhappy, you knew how it was going to end. We all knew, we just wouldn't admit it. I've been dead for weeks now. This is just a formality."

He squeezed Eddie's shoulder, then went over to his daughter who rose to meet him. He put his arm around her and she pressed her head to his chest, just once, then stepped back, giving him up. Emerson turned to Vasily and said several quick words in Russian. Vasily nodded in reply, and in English said, "You'd better hurry. Your boat is almost there."

Emerson scrambled along the steep pitch of the slope to where Rusty's body lay. He picked her up in his arms. It must have been difficult with his hand the way it was but he made it seem easy. Then, sometimes sliding, sometimes stumbling, sometimes at a run, he made his way down to the beach and was waiting there when the launch nosed in against the sand. He passed the body over the gunwale into waiting arms, and then clambered aboard. He did not look back as the launch circled around to head out to sea.

They drove along the cliff road beyond the Reynolds house heading south, Vasily doing the driving, Ginger beside him and Eddie resting in the back seat. The shoulder had started to throb again and he wanted to get to a doctor.

"I know a quack I can trust in Oakland," said Vasily. "If you can hold out that long."

"I'll make it."

"And after that, what?"

"You still thinking about Bogotá?"

"It seems like the next logical step. Coming along?"

Eddie nodded in the darkness, and said to Ginger, "That all right with you?"

"Whatever you say," she said absently. "Would we be able to see it from here?"

"See what?" Vasily and Eddie said it at once.

"Stop it," she said impatiently. "He's my father, isn't he? I should know what my own father is going to do and I sure as hell know what RDX is after hanging around with you two. Would we see it?"

Vasily shifted uncomfortably in his seat. "No way of telling."

"Pull over," she said. "Over there, off the road."

Vasily looked at her sharply, and then did as she asked, swerving onto the grassy verge. He pulled the car close to the edge of the cliff and set the brake. Below them the ocean crashed against the base of the rocks and sent spume flying. The sea was as dark as the night and the stars were obscured by scudding clouds. An onshore breeze brought the acrid odors of kelp and seasalt as they waited.

"This is foolish," Vasily said after a while. "We don't even know. . . ."

"We'll wait," said Eddie. "It's all right."

"You need that doctor."

"We'll wait."

It came quickly, a greenish-white light that started as a pinpoint and rapidly expanded into a fireball that glowed on the horizon. It hung there, suspended, then collapsed again, green and gold fading into black. The glow was gone by the time they heard the roar come rushing over the water, and then the roaring faded and was gone as well. The night was dark again.

Vasily started the engine and maneuvered the car over the bumpy ground, back to the road. Ginger touched his arm lightly, and said, "Just before he left he said something to you in Russian. What was it?"

"He said that he forgave me."

"I'm glad." She was still for a moment, then asked, "When they were talking in Russian before she died. Could you hear them?"

"Yes."

"What did he say to her."

Vasily considered that as he pulled the car onto the paved surface of the road. "Pretty much the same thing," he said finally. "He forgave her, too."

"That's all right then," she said in a tight, tough little

voice as the car picked up speed and they headed south into the night.

"It isn't all right," said Eddie. "But it's as good as you're going to get."

About the Authors

Herbert Burkholz is a frequent contributor to the *New York Times Magazine*, and the author of four previous novels, including SISTER BEAR, THE SPANISH SOLDIER, MULLIGAN'S SEED, and THE DEATH FREAK, written with Clifford Irving. He lives in Manhattan with his wife, editor Susan Burkholz.

Clifford Irving is the author of ten books, including THE HOAX. His most recent novel is the highly acclaimed TOM MIX AND PANCHO VILLA. He has traveled and lived throughout the world and currently makes his home in Mexico.

KEEPING YOU ON THE EDGE OF YOUR SEAT...

Spellbinding suspense from Ballantine Books